The Upper Hand

In the remote regions of the fixed stars or perhaps far beyond them, there may be some body absolutely at rest.

—NEWTON

The Upper Hand

John William Corrington

G. P. Putnam's Sons, New York

© 1967 BY JOHN WILLIAM CORRINGTON

Portions of this book have appeared in *Motive* and
The Southwest Review under the titles "Dr. Aorta"
and "To Carthage Then I Came" respectively.

*Library of Congress Catalog
Card Number: 66-20271*

A. M. D. G.
—*and for*
Shelley

CATABASIS

". . . crucified, died, and
was buried . . ."

> Does life's absurdity require one to escape
> it through hope or suicide—this is what must
> be clarified, hunted down and elucidated
> while brushing aside all the rest. Does the
> absurd dictate death?
>
> —ALBERT CAMUS
> *Le mythe de Sisyphe*

Chapter One

᭦ৡ

—God Almighty, the bus driver groans.

This is no ordinary summer rain. It has come up from the Gulf, hammering Baton Rouge, inundating Krotz Springs, following the line of Highway 20 all the way to Alexandria and north. It is July, and barring hurricanes from the Caribbean, no such weather is to be expected. It is an imposition.

The bus driver so conceives it. —M⋯⋯ ⋯⋯, he mutters at a particularly vicious sweep of wind as ⋯ twists the wheel in his hands. He blushes instantly and hopes the two forbidding ladies from Baton Rouge seated just behind (Louisiana State University, College of Education) have not heard him. The curtain of rain, thick as fog, has unnerved almost everyone in the coach. Most of the passengers wish they had stopped over in Alexandria. Better a night in Toonerville than an indeterminate period in hell. —Mother Mary, the bus driver snarls as an oncoming car, bright lights probing through the rain, lurches across the center line and back again. The LSU ladies glance at one another: it sounds like some kind of lunatic litany. They will be glad to get to Shreveport. Complaints will be lodged.

In the last seat before the Negro section of the bus, a thin youngish man with middle-brown hair and pale gray eyes is considering Shreveport, too, and his arrival there. He is not especially excited about it. It is not a destination—unless the second fall in the Via Dolorosa was one. It is simply a base he feels he must touch before running like a wasp-chased little leaguer clean through the right-field wall.

Because Christopher Nieman (thin, youngish, gray eyes now

snapped shut beneath a furrowed brow) has been, until a few hours before, a priest. Of the Roman Church. Ordained in Sussex, England, at the minimum canonical age of twenty-four. In 1941. And assistant pastor in various harried churches for the five intervening years.

Christopher Nieman (thin, youngish, gray eyes now tightly closed beneath a crosshatched forehead) is out of money, out of luck and, he suspects, hopelessly out of grace. As rain slashes at the bus, he opens his eyes to watch the storm pounding and surging against the window next to him. Jonah, he thinks. Probably could stop the rain by jumping off. And this is only the start. Riots, sudden heavings of the earth, great winds, young born of the union of swine and men, horses turning wild in nature, eating one another. Wherever I go, saxophone reeds breaking, drummers putting their sticks through the sheepskin, trembling cymbals and souring brass. Wombs drying up. The bottoms falling out of wells. Cows giving blood, donors' veins full of milk. This is going to be the shits. Christopher's little joke. He is cursed with the imagination of a Hieronymus Bosch.

The bus driver shakes his head like a balked bull and twists the wheel viciously. He has made this run a hundred times, but never in conditions so adverse. —Cocksucker, he says with outraged precision, on the border between whisper and speech. The LSU ladies nudge one another, and make an unspoken compact to report the driver when—and if—they arrive in Shreveport. They are not certain what he is saying, but the tone, the inflection, are clearly obscene.

The bus slues around a curve, and Christopher feels the road's surface change slightly for the better. It is the parish line. Now they are approaching Natchitoches. Next would be a left turn, a right, another left over the Cane River. At Christmas, they line the low riverbanks below with enormous displays of colored lights. Now it is late summer, and the river is hidden by sheets of rain. But Christopher keeps his eyes closed, still trying to sort out the tags and ends of an endless game of tag that had begun in Shreveport the same day in 1917 that President Wilson decided to make the world safe for democracy.

His last time through Natchitoches, Christopher remembers, he and another priest whose name he cannot recall had eaten rib-eyes together at Doug's Steak House and talked about Catholic education. Before lunch, a few beers.

—It's better than the Catholic press, Father So-and-so had said hopefully.

—So was *Der Sturmer*, Christopher had answered. —Anything is better than the Catholic press. *Pravda* is more realistic.

—But the schools, we have some colleges . . .

—All bad. Some better than others. The best only fit to turn out dago grocers and shanty-Irish republicans. The other kind of Republicans. The American kind.

—That's harsh, Father, and after all our Holy Father is an Ital—

—He's a good dago, Christopher said generously, and then studied his steak. —A little jest, Father, he said to the other's unbreathing silence. —We all have our tensions and releases. Better name-calling than girlie shows. An open mind, Father. And a closed fly.

He had finished his steak alone, drank long from the rose-colored plastic glass filled with water and what tasted like scented soap. The other priest was outside in the car, pale, stiff-lipped, unspeaking. They had driven back to Alexandria like that, and from then on the pastor had kept his eye on Christopher. As if there were a chance of his running amok or staggering into the quarters of the nuns who taught at St. Rose's School. Shrieking, —*I am undone.*

But of course he had done nothing, had celebrated his Masses and said his office, taught catechism to the children (who, he suspected, paid no mind to it, simply going along: the rite thing for the rote reason), met discussion groups of skittery Methodists and Episcopalians who were considering The Plunge, and visited the sick, the halt, and the aged. Until this morning.

It had been five-thirty A.M. In Alexandria's Church of St. Magnus Martyr (who was not only not a saint, but not a martyr either, since in fact he never lived. The whole corpus of acts attributed to him had been done, but by a couple of other saintly martyrs). There was Christopher in chasuble, alb *et al.* An altar boy who, bent double on the marble steps saying the *Confiteor,* had been caught by sleep, remained in that posture through the epistle. Rather than trouble him, Christopher had shifted the missal to the gospel side himself, had uttered, with some asperity, *Laus tibi Christe.* Now came the paean of affirmation:

—*Credo in unum Deum,* Christopher began, hearing his own voice, monotonous, unctuous with rubrical tone, hollow and graceless. The Latin flayed his tongue. He listened to it with fresh comprehension. It was committing him. Like a hastily written contract in an alien tongue. For a used car. Sign here:

In the nave of the church, crouched heavily in the first pew, two elderly woman fingered their beads, mumbled *Aves,* piously ignoring his Mass.

—No I don't, Christopher heard himself say aloud, in the vernacular. —No, hell no. I don't believe in one God begotten *or* made. I don't believe in His only divine son. I don't believe any of this . . .

He pulled up short. His voice had been low, barely audible. The server still slouched, weaving the cool morning air with fluttering eyelids, waiting in semicoma for time to procure water and wine. The ladies glanced up from their beads, having perhaps heard some unwonted word of English leaking out of the ancient humidor of the Latin service. —Crap, Christopher finished *secreto.* But it had gone too far. He felt unbearably hot. Hot as the hearthstone of hell. Not physically ill, but sick in a more inward way. Almost terrified. As if he had awakened suddenly to discover a tankard of bats' blood in one hand, the thigh of a child freshly roasted in the other.

This isn't going to get it, Christopher thought. This isn't going to work. I couldn't consecrate a slice of toast. I don't even . . . what's going on?

He had nudged aside the missal, reached for the covered chalice and pushed it behind an altar card. He stood, still facing the altar, his hands shaking, sweat pouring down his forehead, down his spine, the backs of his legs.

The altar boy had managed to straighten up. He had been half-recollecting, half-dreaming of his date the night before.

He was not used to conquest, not even dead certain how far is *all the way*. He had been considering whether or not to receive communion. Six of one, half dozen of the other. The matter was, he reckoned, grevious. But sufficient reflection? Full consent of the will? Wow.

Christopher, his eyes ruefully fixed on the crucifix (even as a child that image of superhumanity subhumanly suffering had unnerved him. Was it love or pity? Is pity grounds for marriage? Assuredly not. And for a priestly vocation? Ah, is not pity a mode of love? Is it not indeed?), was worming out of his chasuble. The pyx toppled and fell to the altar steps. —Father, the server faltered, stumbling uncertainly to his feet. —Father, are you . . . ?

—I believe so, Christopher said. —I bet I am.

By then he had dropped the chasuble, turned, and began unwinding the cords of his amice, tossing it aside as he descended from the altar in reverse introit, tugging almost desperately at the fastenings of his surplice.

The ladies had forsaken both beads and the joyful mysteries. One had half-risen, her ancient flaccid mouth open as if a cry of surprise and impending agony had once flown from it when Pompeii went down beneath the burden of its sins. The other was transfixed, only the dead gray wattle of used-up flesh beneath her chin quivering as she watched Christopher divest himself of his last ecclesiastical garment and move rapidly—but with dignity—in shirt sleeves, black slacks, and loafers toward the open doors of the church.

Staring after him, the altar boy almost lost his footing and clattered down the last marble step to be brought to a halt at the altar rail, his hands grasping it like a life raft, his eyes wide and almost intelligent in the half-light, his contorted face remarkably like that of St. Magnus Martyr whose statue in painted plaster (fabricated in New Jersey in the same mold from which St. Martin, St. Athanasius, St. Peter Suffering, and countless other worthies are spawned daily; only the paint and certain minor bits of paraphernalia are changed to protect the multiple copyright) loomed from the outer darkness of a side altar.

The old lady on her feet finally found voice. —Save the Host, she croaked. —The Most Blessed Sacrament. Don't let it fall. Don't let it . . .

But the altar boy was already down the long twilight aisle and out on the church steps. He had not yet managed to grasp even the bluntest implications of all this as he watched Christopher's figure, framed on either side by blinding summer green of trees and bushes, receding in the direction of the rising sun. The server squinted Christopher out of sight, pursed his lips and finally shrugged. He had been of two minds, anyway. Maybe he hadn't reflected sufficiently, but, he remembered, grinning with youthful coarseness, the will had consented. All the way. Which, if you started anything, Father Christopher always said, was the way to get it done.

Both old ladies passed him like groggy fragile Chicken Littles on the way to Turkey Lurkey's. Or more probably the rectory where the pastor, who, being a monsignor, was proof against all, even precipitate defection, and would beyond doubt provide counsel and spiritual balm—if not an explanation.

Back in his room, Christopher had poured himself a teacup full of Hennessy and downed it. He waited for the pastor, for the rhythmless clatter of heel taps and that sniffling in the hallway of the rectory that always preceded an actual thump on the door, a metaphorical box on the ear.

He stretched out on his bed and began reading the "at liberty" notices in a four-year-old *Variety*. His hands still shook; his eyes would not focus properly. It was necessary not to think just then. Not to grapple with the enormity of leaving a Mass half done, with broadcasting monstrous scandal to old ladies and a dozing altar boy. He concentrated instead upon the kind of lie he would tell Father Brophy.

It was easy enough. The heel taps, snuffling, and thump arrived in good time.

—A chest pain, Father, Christopher said weakly from his bed, agony and courage mixed in his sweating face.—I almost fell down. I . . . almost dropped the Host. Danger. Of sacrilege. Feared to consecrate.

The old man stood reaming his hairy ear. He was not in the

market for this kind of excuse. But he had no choice. He could buy it or call the chancery.

—Say? Christopher asked weakly. —What did I say? God knows, Father. In extremis, feeling yourself collapsing as if someone were folding you up in a pocket telescope, what do you say? Maybe it was *Eli, Eli, lama sabachthani?*

Then he was alone. Totally alone and empty. As if a movie in color had suddenly and imperceptibly changed into black and white without his realizing it. A few hours before, there had been reason for flowers and sweat, for pain and an early Mass. There had been, beneath the cheerless and ephemeral flesh of the universe the blood of God's infinite love, the sinew of His will, the bone of His promises. Now the world was void and without form. Like a ghastly rag doll. Purposeless, vacant—with a past that was one long shriek of bestial agony. With no future at all.

Christopher lay on his bed, impacted in his helplessness. God wills that the arm may move, that the tongue form words, that the heart reach out to touch another heart. But how, Christopher thought, if the day of grace should now be past and gone? What moves if God is dead?

Late in the afternoon he rose, moving to the dresser without volition, as if, an exhausted zombie, some inner mechanism had pulled him erect. There were confessions to be heard. He combed his hair with his fingers and pulled on a soutane.

The confessional was stifling. He leaned back against the unyielding wood and breathed deeply. He could not bring himself to kiss the purple stole that hung about his neck, half albatross, half noose. His hand moved upward to the sliding panel and pushed it slowly to one side.

—Bless me, Father, someone mumbled, —for I have sinned.

Christopher's eyes closed. He did not doubt it at all.

—Father, a croaking pimpled adolescent voice asked out of darkness, —if you were to do it with a girl, is it better to go all the way or pull it out before it . . . ?

Coitus interruptus, Christopher thought with a shiver. To pull or not to pull. Onan in an Olds.

—It's better to stay clear of any such situation. You're in mortal sin from the moment you . . .

And so on. An elderly lady whose cracked male voice is clearly recognizable even through the screen. It was Mrs. Blood.

—Father, I have dreams. Last night I dreamed I was in this huge building dressed all in silver. It was full of these savages —what looked like savages—and this huge black horse and it's . . . thing was down, and they held me and pulled down my and that horse reared and he and the savages, all those niggers they . . .

Christopher staring through the semidarkness at the small crucifix above the screened aperture through which the princess all in silver made her gasping report on the black horse and his accomplices. Christ's tiny alabaster face frozen in eternal agony, a hint of astonishment in the minute openness of his mouth. The eyes were too small to make out. Perhaps they were closed. Maybe they had fallen out during the years of enforced eavesdropping. Christopher suddenly got the jarring, almost overwhelming sensation that on the other side of the screen was hell. That this confessional was the portal, and the voice maundering on that of a charred and unspeakable fiend creating *ex tempore* from the treasury of his earthly and infernal observation. The sensation would not pass, and Christopher shivered in the Saturday-evening heat. Through a chink in the curtain covering his half of the confessional, he could see the altar light like a monstrous bloodshot eye winking occasionally as a vagrant breeze stirred through the sanctuary. Mrs. Blood was going on.

—That was Thursday night, Father. Friday night it was worse. I finished dishes, listened to "Amos and Andy," and "I Love a Mystery," and I dreamed I was in Berlin, Germany, when those Russians came in, and they took me out—I was a lot younger and as beautiful as I could be—and put me in one of their tanks. And they drove on shooting their cannon at people, people would stand up, and then just dissolve, and the other ones not shooting the cannon they held me and pulled down my . . .

—Excuse me, Christopher said, and stepped out of the confessional. There were perhaps a half-dozen people still in line next to the wall near the dark bulk of the pews. Christopher could not make out their faces. —Are all of you sorry, he asked softly. —Are you going to stop it or start it? Someone mumbled *yes* in an amazed voice. —*Ego te absolvo,* Christopher said, carving a brief cross in the thick candle-scented air. —And good luck.

He turned and walked out into the evening air where a small boy sat on the curb near the side door of the church trying to get his bicycle chain back on the sprocket. He did not see Christopher.

—Motherfucker, he snuffled, —dirty stinkin' motherfucker.

—That's right, Christopher said tiredly, shuffling toward the rectory like one of those walking wounded last in line when an angel troubles the water.

ᨦ ᨦ

The bus leans to Christopher's right, dumping him against the window. He can see the Natchitoches power-station road out there. Then they are in the curling turns outside town. Is it the oldest town west of the Mississippi? He can't remember. Was it the western terminus of the Natchez Trace? Or the eastern end of the Old Spanish Trail? He doesn't care. Ulysses Grant once stopped in Natchitoches. On his way to the Mexican War. If only the townspeople had known.

—Sonofabitch, the driver says just loudly enough for Christopher to hear. Outside, the road is in total darkness again. Wind is whipping at the coach. Rain has started to fall again like silver strings into a long tunnel dug through blackness by the headlights. The driver slows once more and begins fighting the wheel. —This wind is going to land us in hell, he grits.

ᨦ ᨦ

Two hours later the bus driver leans back in his seat and lights a cigarette, tossing the dead match down the doorwell. The rain has finally eased, and the road is bright with reflected light from filling stations and drive-in grocery stores. They are on the outskirts of Shreveport now, and Christopher rouses.

He takes a cigar from his pocket and lights it. He pulls on it till his eyes bulge and his neck tendons distend. Then he remembers to bite off the end. Great Christ, he thinks, losing faculties is one thing. I'm losing my functions. The red eye of the cigar is not comforting. It makes him think of that wild pyramid on the back of a dollar bill with a disembodied eye perched on top. *Novus Ordo Seclorum.* May it please your eyeship. A whole new Ordo. Not a jot or tittle, mote or beam from the old. This time I'm going to cut my own trail. All hits. Lots of runs. No errors.

They have come in Highway 20 which turns into Kingshighway just northwest of Dixie Gardens. They pass Ockley Drive, Archer Street. Levee on the right, Niggertown behind, vacant lots and a few houses on the left. He knows the name of the Broadmoor Drugstore manager. They pass the Stopmoor Restaurant and Mrs. Pat's grocery. There is Weber's Seabreeze where the root beer comes in prefrosted glasses. And the Mexican restaurant where the crosstown trolley turns and starts back toward Line Avenue. He knows all of it. He has grown up in it. A fantastic town. Indescribably mean people. Very proud. Last town to lower the Confederate flag. Confederate capital of Louisiana after the Yankees took New Orleans and Opelousas. Stratified. Negroes cowed past believing. Whites determined to keep it that way. Negroes not worth much in any case. Whites, either, for that matter. All locked in the same hamper like salt and pepper in a picnic lunch. Separate but equal shakers.

The bus station is downtown. Just beyond the main drag, which is Texas Street. Across from the bus station, up a few yards is Holy Trinity Church. It looks as if Julian the Apostate had done the decorations inside. Or the Metropolitan of Damascus. Christopher remembers it before the redecoration. It had been big and ugly and all right. Now it is big and ugly and all wrong. The bus hews in under its shed and passengers begin unfolding themselves, pulling down luggage from overhead. It feels late, and Christopher twists his neck and waits in his seat till the rest of the travelers push and fumble their way out. Then he follows them out into the night.

It is chilly, and the air, fresh and untainted by tobacco and
bodies and cheap hair oil, is sharp, almost painful to his nostrils.
Flat yellow lights set in the shed roof are not strong enough.
The edges of everything seem to melt and run. Christopher
cannot read the destination sign on the front of the bus next
to his. Fuzzy Negroes have unlatched the side panels of the bus
and are stacking vague luggage in dun-colored heaps. Christopher blinks and walks past into the station. As the door closes,
the stench of old cooking oil, cheap hamburger, restroom deo-
dorant falls around him like a rank blanket. He passes a bank
of lockers, each with its key projecting like a silver tongue from
its anonymous gray bulk. Farther in, there are dozens of seats
back to back, a wilderness of posters and drinking fountains,
vending machines and telephone booths. A low partition divides white seating from black seating. The chairs in both sec-
tions are separately frayed, dilapidated equally.

Christopher shakes his head and pushes into the coffee shop.
Nothing changes. Like the chairs. Only the occupants change.
Occupants. Falling into and through the bus-station chairs and
on into separate destinies and equal deaths. Fools dividing one
from another. And other fools caring whether they're separated or not. Whole generations dedicated to keeping that partition up—or pulling it down. They pulled down my. Up the.
Motherfuckers.

He orders coffee and feels numb. Still numb. Not bereaved
or frightened or sad or ashamed. Only numb as if someone has
kicked him solidly and unerringly in the spiritual nuts. The
metaphysical coccyx, he thinks. Where it hurts and you can't
turn it off.

He is not especially worried about walking out of St. Magnus
Martyr Church with the elements exposed on the altar. He is
not simply worried about Deity frowning and stoking up new
pits in the fiery ice, or ordering Satan to spit out Judas and prepare for a new mouthful. He is worried about twelve years
given away. He feels as if he were wearing a skin not his own, as
if the sacred chrism and the bishop's laying on of hands, and
the cool marble beneath his prostrate body had actually
changed him somehow. He notices things other people miss.

The catsup bottle looks like a candle holder. The folded napkin like a pyx. And phrases unrelated to anything around him keep tumbling through his head. Be not deceived. God is not mocked. Christopher is not deceived. The deception is over. He is still stunned at the size and shape of his wound. It is old. It will not heal. He will have to live with it. Like Philoctetes. A stinking mess. With the whole armor of God in a satchel, rusted and corroded. Would Jake's wrecking yard buy it? The buckler and the sword and the banner upon which is emblazoned in Southern Negroid, *Ah Willa Rise.*

He drinks his coffee thinking that things could be worse and thinking that such thinking is self-deception. Maybe a call to mother. But it is past ten o'clock, and mother will have turned off the phonograph, dusted Cab Calloway or Glen Gray, and called it a night. How I replaced my husband with Isham Jones, Christopher thinks. Or maybe she could call her autobiography *Benny Goodman in My Bed.* What a woman.

He lingers over his coffee remembering the gift she had sent him during his last year in major seminary in Sussex. The songs of Josh White. A decorous album. He had put it on the player in the seminary common-room the night before he was to sail home to celebrate his first solemn high Mass. Real folk music, the label said. What Josh White said, in part, was

> *You got bad blood, baby . . .*
> *Believe you need a shot.*
> *You got bad blood, baby . . .*
> *I believe you need a shot.*
>
> *Climb on this table, honey,*
> *Lemme see what else*
> *You got . . .*

Christopher had knocked the tone arm into another groove:

> *Some folks say a preacher*
> *Won't steal,*
> *But I caught one*
> *in my cornfield . . .*

Some folks say children would be better off if they came from eggs hatched in a communal nursery. Christopher remembers the verse he had picked up when he gave the tone arm another nudge.

As the coffee cools to drinking temperature, Christopher finds himself studying the people scattered about the coffee shop. It is a mixed lot: the kind of bag he used to get at early Mass on Sundays and holy days. There is an old man in some sort of cap, not a policeman's or busman's, not a baseball or a yachting cap. Just some kind of cap. He has, in addition, a terrifying protuberance, a gross and vilely colored excrescence growing out of the side of his head like a handle. It is growing just above his left ear, and has got to be five inches long. It is purple at the end and a sick, cold gray closer in to his head. Christopher's eyebrows come up. He catches himself repeating a pious ejaculation for the man before he can stop it.

Give him strength to bear it, Christopher whispers. God, how miserable to have a spare mounted just over your ear. Christopher sips his coffee and looks elsewhere. Through an eighteen-inch square slit in the wall behind the counter, a pair of anonymous sexless black arms reach for dirty dishes. Three or four feet farther down at an identical slit, identical—or similar—arms set out food as it is ordered. Christopher wonders momently whether the arms are the same. They appear separately, but seem to be equal. Maybe there is a machine back there with black arms. Maybe not, too, he thinks, depressed.

And the waitress. Another pathetic original. Harelipped. Upper lip nicked as if the busman had mistaken it for a round-trip ticket to Denver. Snip, ma'am. Yes, ma'am. Biff bam. Thank you, ma'am. And red frizzled hair in tight fantastic curls above. Below, the shape of a clothes rack. How can she, could she, escape damnation, Christopher wonders, fascinated. So terribly ugly, knowing it, reassured of it by every simple-minded fool like me who sits over cold coffee and stares at her. How can she, could she—if there were a God—keep from cursing Him up and down and then finding a gas jet? A miserable life better than no life at all? Complete with henna snakes for hair, and a rabbit's mouth. You call this living?

The coffee is gone, and Christopher reaches for his suitcase. But there is someone in a booth across from him. Another walking dossier against the notion of Deity? Not quite. Small, almost thin, except for beautifully terraced breasts, finely fleshed calves. Hips and thighs out of sight. Jet-black hair, falling around her shoulders, shining in the glare of a broken-shaded bulb above her. Next to an empty plate and cup, her hands rest on the table holding a papercovered book. Christopher can make out the title. *Two Guns on the Open Range.* By Billy Squawson.

Christopher signals for another cup of coffee. Rabbit sees, puckers, and obeys. The black machine takes dirty cup, presents clean full cup at other aperture. The old man with the odd part over his ear is scratching under his cap.

In seminary, Christopher had found continence a breeze. Women meant nothing to him. He had studied, and played exhausting games, bathed frequently, prayed long and deeply, and kept his hands off things. The few times lasciviousness had moved him, he had found a cold bottle of beer held between the legs and firm concentration on the decomposition of an imaginary corpse, stage by stage, a perfect cure. And when he had vanquished lust, there was the lukewarm beer for a victory toast. Of course, the seminary had helped in the struggle. There were no doors on closets or toilets. No keys or locks to rooms. And daily schedules so close-packed and exhausting that only the most enduring had strength left at the end of the day even to consider the sweets of sin.

But in the years of his parish work, it seemed women had changed. Or maybe he had changed. He was a late bloomer. There are such things, he thought. Young men who see a breast or a thigh outlined against a thin wet bathing suit. And nothing. They're not queer. Just nothing. It's like seeing a breast or thigh of chicken on the Sunday dinner table. The connotations haven't come clear yet. Biological or psychological. Jack the Ripper may not have started until he was fifty. Late puberty. Delayed responses. He was twenty-five before he saw what they were driving at in the movies, and almost thirty before he started wanting to drive on his own. By then the beer wasn't

doing much good on the outside, and it was for sure betraying
him on the inside. But he stood firm. Because he should. Because the man had committed suicide by leaping off his youth
into the priesthood. And even self-immolation has an implicit
code of honor. Once you jump, it is cowardly to grab for beams
or hanging cables on the way down. Hands by your sides. Eyes
on the altar light. Wake up below the iceberg. Dead. And cold,
Lord, cold.

Alongside his late-blooming venereal concerns, there had
come too a sudden and hilarious upheaval of imagination. For
better or worse, images came and shuffled through the ante-
room of his mind. In seminary, there had been no unregimented
time. In the parish, there had been too much. He blushed, remembering the hours in his office. He had a key to his office.
And he had walked all around Alexandria, that central city of
Louisiana, burned by sulky Union troops at the end of an embarrassing and useless campaign against old men and young
boys, and unwisely rebuilt thereafter to vex the Red River's
bilious waters as they passed full of offal from Shreveport and
north. He had wondered about things that, considering his
vows, should have been past wondering about. There was a
chemistry at work. It was a subterranean formula, and it
brewed slowly and its reaction was as unpredictable, as unstable
as the degradation of nitroglycerine.

Ah, Christopher thinks, watching the girl's bright fascinated
eyes as she turned a page of *Two Guns*. Ah, but when it goes, it
blows all to hell. The wind blew and the shit flew and I'll be
going in a minute, too. Dear Papa: It was all an error. My fault.
Hold no one accountable. Just a slow accumulation of things.
Cancel all I said. No more poverty or obedience. I wasn't myself
that day. I promised for a consideration. I thought I was going
to serve the Old Man, the Chief. It turns out the Grand Mogul
wasn't there to be served. Worse even than the Wizard of Oz.
Not even a wizened old sideshow barker or tent-show man behind a curtain running a wind machine. Nothing at all but a
red light, an empty cup, some wafers. And two thousand years
of incredible credibility. And a raft of saints, some of whom
must have known better, but decided to play it through. Code

of the self-castrated: play down the value of balls. And me. Flesh-and-blood end man in the longest-running minstrel show in the most rural of galaxies.

The girl reaches for her coffee, finds it empty, and glances up from the book. Her eyes meet Christopher's. Does he lower his decently? Not on your life. Does she frown and look away, a tincture of disdain disfiguring her full lovable mouth. Not very. She smiles and nods as if Christopher were an old lover whose reappearance is, if not a miracle, at least fortuitous. Then she gestures to the harelipped waitress. Who in turn calls to the black machine.

Christopher feels himself rising from his booth, going to the counter, picking up the fresh cup of coffee, paying for it. This is fantastic, he thinks, but he is too accustomed to the completion of gesture to cut it short. He does not know the rubrics, but he turns from the counter, cup on saucer raised in front of him.

—Here's your coffee, he tells the girl.

Who smiles and lays her *Two Guns* aside. Smiles, waiting, expectant.

Christopher has not lowered the cup. Not yet he hasn't. —You're beautiful, he says in an even casual voice.

Thinking, great God, I sound like a dago hairdresser at the sodality dance.

—Somebody up there likes you, he tries again. —You're lucky.

Mary Ann Downey's eyebrows raise a notch, but composure is her business. Part of it anyhow. —Thanks, she says in soft East Texas, a language as distinct and memorable as the brown of her forearms, the jet-black, almost lacquered quality of her eyes and hair. Christopher lowers the cup. —You're lucky, he says again, the tone of his voice revealing that, despite the matter of his conversation, he may not be a congenital idiot.

—Whatever you say, Mary Ann tells him. —I ain't gonna argue with you.

Christopher sits down. He has left his own coffee at the other table. But now he is paying no mind to bodily needs or comforts. He is in a position totally unlike anything he has ever experienced before. What's next? Why, in seminary, had he been called variously the Town Crier, the Great Pretender and the Moonlight Gambler? Not for nothing. Creation of sensation without contemplation was his long suite. He wishes, and is sorry instantly for wishing, that he had a moustache. He wants to offer her a cigarette, but he has none: he had smoked only three or four in his life before the seminary untimely cut off that debauchery, too. He is left with no resource but himself and a few cigars, and that is only a skinful of shudders and a pair of smokes better than nothing at all. But Mary Ann has the impulses of a St. Bernard:

—You see before you a girl with trouble, she says, as if Christopher were that old lover, and one whose entree had not expired since its last use.

—What? Christopher jumps into the lifeboat of a subject for discussion. This is a crucial moment. If Mary Ann asks for a hundred dollars, she is certain to get it. Just so the conversation does not lag.

—I can't figure out what this book means. I mean the fella who wrote it. This one cowboy . . . I mean the fella who wrote it keeps having one cowboy say this other cowboy gave him a bum steer.

—It means bad advice, Christopher said, thinking of Guido da Montefeltro.

—Okay, Mary Ann smiles blindingly, —I can see that. But I mean that way of saying it. That word. Bum steer.

Christopher is watching her teeth. He feels like he knows how seventeen-year-olds must feel confronted with a girl too beautiful to have been constructed in bathroom fantasy. Great God Almighty, Josh White sang in that third groove. Yea, Lord, Christopher thinks, hardly embarrassed any longer. Life impinges. No *ordo* for this. Semidouble. Feast of Saint Yummy: patron of beautiful white even teeth and lips that look smoother than Artie Shaw in *Chalumeau*.

—It's a metaphor, he tells her. —It means like steering a car, and somebody gives you wrong directions. You make a wrong turn.

—Lord, Mary Ann says, smile broader, giving Christopher a clear view of her perfect molars. —I thought it was a steer. I mean a bull with his balls gone. I couldn't figure what a bum one was. Seemed to me a steer wasn't much good by nature.

—Beef, Christopher says. —They're for beef. It keeps them docile.

—Seems like it'd drive 'em crazy. I guess you can't always know what something will do if you prod it a certain way. They jump all kinds of ways when the heat goes on, don't they?

Christopher has both arms folded, elbows on table.

—You never can tell, Christopher says, not sure of what she had last said, but bulling on as if he were.

—I reckon that solves half my problem, Mary Ann says, putting *Two Guns* into a long shabby leather purse. —Means I'm only fifty percent in trouble.

—Anything, Christopher offers solicitously. —Any little thing.

—I don't have a place to sleep, Mary Ann tells him, shrugging her shoulders so that he can see her breasts rise and fall, the velvet tendons alongside her neck flex and relax, the hollow of her throat fill and subside.

You have here a man in trouble, Christopher is thinking. Thinking also that there is a garage apartment behind his mother's house. To which he has no key, into which he has not planned to break until just now. But all bets are off. He remembers ruefully that there would have been no such small, decently kept apartment had his father not used it frequently for solo weekend retreats, fleeing wife and son to spend a few hours with Christ. And that it would have fallen into disrepair except for its rental value. But no one is there just now. His mother's last letter had said it was empty.

—You haven't got a problem in the world, Christopher tells Mary Ann. —You're one hundred percent out of the woods.

Yea, one believer can fire a hundred infidels. And though darkness cover the earth, where the spirit dwelleth, there is light.

—I feel better even before you tell me, Mary Ann says, the smile back double strength.

—That's the spirit, Christopher hears himself say, incredulous and cold around the thighs.

Christopher Nieman

I remember my uncle's face as he stood over the animal I had shot.

—Jesus Christ, he said disgustedly, —you've plugged a goddamned sheep.

And sure enough it was true. It lay there still twitching, its legs stiff and its eyes closed. But it was already dead. You could see most of its guts through the hole my buckshot had made.

By then my father had come up. His hat was off and the autumn air was whipping his thin hair about his ears.

—How much? he asked his brother, my uncle.

My uncle shrugged. —Nothing yet, he said. —We ain't got caught.

My father's face was always stiff. Somehow he looked like one of those thin-lipped proper bank tellers. The ones who end up running off with the money. But my uncle could make him stiffen up even more than usual. —I don't work like that, my father said. The wind whipped what was left of his reddish-brown hair forward over his forehead. Caligula holding to a point of honor.

The sheep shivered one last time and stopped. My uncle pulled out his knife. —I hate to work with mutton, he said as he bent and started cutting. —It smells like a witch's pussy. You can't get the stink off your knife. It stays on your hands.

He smiled up at me through the gloom and the mounting drizzle. —Why didn't you shoot a cow? Or even some other sonofabitch up here hunting?

—Where will I pay for this? my father asked querulously. He was looking at me as if he expected me to turn on him. I was too young for that. Besides it would have been wrong. The blood of a murdered father freezes in the son's veins.

My uncle looked as if he might start on my father when he was done with the sheep. —You see that sweetgum tree? he asked with exaggerated patience.

My father squinted in the twilight and reached for his glasses. He could not have told a gum tree from a Spanish bayonet.

—You just go over and knock on it, my uncle said, —and inside there's a little elf girl with a cash register. She collects for all the sheep and the wild flowers folks pick, and . . .

My father had already turned and started back toward the car parked a couple of miles away. I stayed near my uncle, who reared back laughing, his hands greasy with blood and rain, and tossed a handful of offal at my father's fading back. —Don't forget to get your tradin' stamps, he yelled into the darkness, and bent chuckling over his work again.

[*]

My mother paid no attention to my father. She had married him, attended to him for some years, and then let it drop. She never said so, but I think she had found him wanting. Wanting what exactly, I don't know. He wanted a lot. All he had, and that he had more than enough of, was religion. He was as Catholic as a converted Baptist minister, as zealous as if he had bought shares in the Holy Office and was bound to help them rise again. He managed the commandments, the laws of the church, as well as a man can. It was only that all his energy, all his spunk—and whatever small parcel of humanity he had— went to Rome. There was hardly anything left for Mother and me but money.

There was plenty of that. But I was too young to need it, and my mother, whose father had owned 53,000 acres in the middle of central Louisiana, surely didn't have any use for it. What we did need, we didn't get. Maybe to get something you have to know the name of it. This is true even in the best shops.

My mother was father's cross. She had grown up out of touch
with even the most basic of amenities. She rode like a dragoon,
roped like a cowboy. By the time she was eighteen, she had
been bitten twice by cottonmouths, and scratched from her
chin to her knees by a wildcat. When she was indoors, she listened to jazz records. Bix and Tram. Buddy Bolden, Chicago,
Kansas City. Even Isham Jones. She would set a stack of the
shellac platters on the phonograph and listen wordlessly till
the machine cut off.

My father did not ride. He could not tell a steer from a
heifer. Snakes terrified him, and music less solemn than a string
quartet made the palms of his hands sweat. Given a choice between horses, serpents, and a rhythm section, he would have
apologetically cursed God and died.

There was nothing between them but habit—and me. I
could have been gotten around, but habit held them together.
Habit, and possibly the fact that each of them was a kind of
hopeless human situation in different ways. Cowgirls and un-
ordained priests. It's a bad century for both.

My father had grown away from us. Away from the world. His
flesh hung on him like white clay badly shaped and poorly
glazed. I always drew away from his soft white puffy hands
(once, I was with a family when its eldest son was pulled out of
Caddo Lake two or three weeks after he had fallen drunk out
of his motorboat on a fishing trip. He was long past autopsy,
and I managed to hold my gorge only by concentrating on the
sorrowful mysteries or Lionel Hampton's discography or the
last hours of Maupassant or something. But his hands, thick and
pasty, the sodden flesh beginning to fall away from the bones,
white as Moby Dick's private parts; I thought of my father's
hands. That made me sicker than ever. Even the glorious mysteries and trying to reconstruct Paul Whiteman's 1928 reed section didn't hold it down. The family was very kind, and when
they were done heaving and crying, they ministered to me).
He hated his own flesh, and I think he hated my mother's tan,
beautiful, casual flesh, too. I think he did not hate me because
I was small and inoffensive and soon enough shipped off to

school where my poor freckled, runny-nosed, lonesome, future-less flesh was dealt with straitly and put to defining itself by the priests.

But he could not come to terms with life, with what he was made of—much less with what Mother was made of. He liked to eat by himself. Once when I was six or seven, he caught me picking my nose and eating the snot. He beat me fourteen or fifteen minutes without pausing, without apparent anger, his bloodless lips tight, his fat white face set and unalterable as Cromwell's deathmask. He did not like puppies or hamsters. Once I brought home a green snake. He shuddered violently and told me to get out with it before he killed it—and me. My mother laughed, took the snake from me as if it were a toy or a scarf, and let it coil around her arm. We went out and caught it flies and fed it before we set it free. Just before I went away to school, my mother promised me a puppy. I think she meant it. I think she wanted me to have it because I wanted one and because by then anything that shook my father, that put him off his desperately held balance, was a teetering step in the right direction.

I was at school only two or three months when my mother came to visit.

—Some dump, she said, looking around the parlor where the priests had us meet our parents. —This is supposed to be the good furniture, huh?

It was bad and worn and exuded a faint odor that may have been the heavenly sweat of Cardinal Newman or some other in-tricate Victorian. It was awful, with round; plush pillows con-nected to the tops of the big wing chairs and black wood ta-bles and chests that made you want to stage a break-out instead of pray or visit. There was a hand-colored photo of Pius XI on the wall, and another black-and-white print of some bishop or provincial or other with a suitable sentiment scrawled under his seated smirking excellence, and under that, Yours in Christ, † . . . . Bishop of Alexandria.

My mother swung her crossed leg. She wore silk hose, and even at that age I could tell she had gorgeous legs. The esthetic sense in children, some potty prelate said, is pure and unsullied. Hence it reflects knowledge of real beauty rather than that which is tainted and corrupt. But they still don't use kids for literary critics. Or to judge beauty contests. Anyhow, my mother lit a cigarette and regarded me for a long minute as if she had never seen me before. —Ummm, she said, as if she were thinking of buying me for the breakfast room. —You're the damndest kid I ever saw.

I hung my head and snuffled and fooled with the edge of my sweater and pulled on my front teeth, picked my nose unobtrusively and wiped it under the seat of the chair while my mother worked with her solid gold Zippo lighter which never lit as well as her plain old steel one.

Finally she came over and sat in the stiff chair next to me. —Arthur's pulled out, she said. There was no sign of anger or unhappiness in her voice or expression. She might have been talking about the milkman instead of my father.

—Oh, I said. —You think he'll be back?

—I don't know. Do you care?

—Do you?

She grinned and hugged me. —No, she said. —Having him gone is just like having him at home. Only even quieter. No more lonely. I'd just as soon he kept going.

—I don't care, I said. —I like to see Uncle Charlie, but Father doesn't show me much. All he ever does is get disgusted.

—When he's not disgusting, my mother said. —I don't like to burden a little kid, she went on, —but it's coming to that. If we're by ourselves we may as well see how we're going to manage.

She stood up. Then I didn't think of her exactly as beautiful. I know she was. Or at least I know she was vital and alive and not like other people, and that her brown body made me happy. But looking back at it, looking at pictures in an album that I found in the attic of the garage apartment, I wonder how I kept from choking a little every time I saw her. Even in the old and unflattering clothes of the late twenties, she looks wonderful. And there I am beside her, all teeth and knees and elbows, smiling with pastel enthusiasm and hunching over against her. Maybe I did realize. Maybe I've just forgotten the catch in my breath.

She stood up and walked around the room on tiptoe, flexing her calves, holding her arms over her head, drawing her blouse and suit-coat tight against her breasts, pulling in her flat stomach. —Free, she laughed ironically. —Free after ten years in the priory. I was a priest's mistress, she droned like a radio announcer describing a new movie coming to town. —Sunk in shame, driven by lust, would he ever free her? Oh hell yes. Ashamed of his own shit and lusting after a biscuit and a paper cup full of grape juice at midnight and a couple of hours of prayer in the morning.

I just sat there and was nervous. My mother had never gone on about her life in front of me. I guess freedom is like strong drink. It gets the better of you and you start telling the truth.

Finally she came back and sat beside me again. —Look, she said, —you really do like Charlie, don't you?

—Sure, I said. —I always have.

—That's good. He may come and stay with us for a while.

I felt funny. As if something were about to happen. Not necessarily bad. Just something. I smiled like an idiot. That seemed to satisfy her.

—You want to come on back home?

—Yes, I said. —Sure. Can I have that puppy?

My mother's eyebrows went up. —Puppy? Good God, you never forget anything. Sure, you can have it. Do you learn anything around this dump?

—No, I said.

—That's right, my mother said, getting ready to leave. —We'll come for you next Saturday.

—Okay.

She leaned down to kiss me. Her perfume was only part of the smell. The rest was her, and it was too good to be true.

—By the way.

—Yes?

—Don't wipe it under chairs, she said without smiling.

—So was that sheep Chris killed. Just as long for him. I let you alone about that mule because it was the only time anybody ever killed anything over me even if it wasn't but a mule when you shot at a nigger wanting to kill Arthur. It was a laugh. But you keep the needle out for Chris who hadn't ever pulled a trigger before.

My uncle said nothing for the space of Bix Beiderbecke's chorus. An unintended kindness.

—That boy needs to go away for some good schooling.

—You mean you need that boy to go away. For whatever, my mother said.

—Listen, Uncle Charlie said, —I'm tired of feeling like a goddamned cornered rat in my own house.

—My house, Mother said gently, as if she were recalling to herself the fact of possession rather than correcting Uncle Charlie's presumption.

—Your house. Anybody's house. I can't live in it with that spook looking over my shoulder.

I unraveled myself from the balustrade and crawled back to my room. To get ready for a trip. I heard another beer bottle open. My mother's voice, soft, insinuating. Uncle Charlie's, lower, charged with something warmer than anger. The phonograph clucked, and as I climbed into bed in darkness, far, immeasurably far away, Isham Jones was playing "If You Were Only Mine."

But it was a longer trip than I had thought. Uncle Charlie had the knife out, and he was sawing on the umbilical cord. It was all the way to England, to a Benedictine school in East Sussex just outside Eastbourne. Not because she wanted me to go (though she must have thought it was better for us both—distance instead of either routine or growing coldness as the bar between our bodies) nor because my uncle overawed her. But because she had probably intended to send me even before, but could think of no reason sufficient to override the meaning of our nearness.

The trip, the school, the cold fabulous unreal quality of my life at the edge of the English Sea. One long indescribable panorama that I could not believe even as I moved within it, and

can no more believe now than I could then. It seems, in retrospect, to have been some imprecise continuum, ragged, cold,
healthy—like that ritualized tapestry that describes in two-
dimensional figures the history of those days that brought the
conquerer to England's shores only a mile or so from where I
used to walk, that brought King Harold down like a felled oak
to sleep forever in that chill soil as a possibility impossibilized.

I was lonely. Not simply for my mother, not for the handful of
friends whose faces faded and faded in the long evenings full
of study and prayer and English rain. But mostly for the soil,
the peculiar light, the unendurable summer heat of Louisiana.
I would fall asleep trying to recall not simply with my mind
but with all my senses the quality, the character of a summer
morning standing barefoot in the dew-drenched grass, gardenias and mimosa blooming, and the thick, almost feminine
smell of the early breeze as the sun began its insane struggle up
the sky's wide road. I missed the dust standing like water in
rutted roads beyond Kingshighway and the levee; the wine-
dark water of Bayou Pierre motionless, weed-choked, big with
moss on the slick red clay banks, reflecting endlessly like the
serene face of one beloved in the eyes of the other, the dark blue
of the sky above, and its thick tufted clouds white and dense as
fresh-picked cotton.

I loved England the way it is possible to love a pretty cousin
who lives in a distant town, and whose home, life and ways are
so different from your own that you find them flawless for lack
of comparison's ground. I was whipped by the Benedictines
(who believed not so much that knowledge's entrance is inevitably bloody, as that a good warm belting opens the pores, con-
centrates the attention, and lays whole leagues of minor devils
who otherwise cavort through the adolescent mind), pum-
meled by my classmates, smashed in Rugby matches, sent into
chattering near-hysteria by the Channel gales which blew
sometimes for two or three weeks on end. But it was good, and
if I had a son—if it should be that I ever had a son—I would
send him to Bearcombe College.

In my fourth year at the school—two more and I would be
ready for the university—Father Madden sent for me. I knew

what he wanted. Almost all the boys were called in sooner or later. It was the regula, part of the normal procedure. Only a few of us so hardened in sin, so notorious in temperament, so undistinguished in scholarship and spiritual growth that we bordered on hourly expulsion failed to make our hegira to Father Madden's office. He was the prefect of spiritual activities.

Most—at least many—of the visits were perfunctory; the question was asked, the answer given (or the gambit declined, if you like), and the interview terminated. But I was not on the *pro forma* list. I was quiet, withdrawn, given to daydreaming. My work was good enough, and above all I did not take part in the endless and occasionally spectacular nonsense that keeps any collection of young males from being stale or even stable. I did not because I was not asked; I was not asked because courage was, it appeared, judged to be in some proportional relationship to playing-field lung power. Had I howled, roared, keened and shrieked, for all my Rugby ineptitude, I would probably have become one of the chief monsters of minor vice who were frequently beaten, nearly sent down, but unsummoned by Father Madden.

Father Madden was a birddog of a priest. Long. Immeasurably long. Arms, legs, nose, ears—everything was lengthy and strait. His eyebrows, shaggy and unkempt, hung like vague gray clouds over eyes that bore within them the chill sheen of the self-made zealot. His fingers were thin as wire, and twined and twisted as if he were weaving a basket while he talked. He spoke in a low excited fanatic's voice as if even the most casual matter was somehow at least as significant as the burning of Savonarola, or the bringing down of the Medici. Like every birddog, Father Madden had a speciality: not quail or doves. Father Madden hunted priests. Not priests in fact, but priests *in potentia*. Each year he made inroads on our sixth form, pointing the boys who had what he considered the Qualifications. He could flush the single child out of a whole covey (we were still children: caught in the glandular, emotional and intellectual upheaval of adolescence, unable to conceive, really, of anything so hard, so cruel, so terrible as an immutable decision) whose rearing (or lack of it) made him lean in the di-

rection of the most exalted and awesome of man's tasks on earth.
Father Madden rarely missed. There were those who, after a
few minutes' talk, were dismissed (and who, if they were sensitive, must have felt forever afterward that the base metal of
their character had somehow showed through the gilt. I wonder if any of them, after their banishment by Father Madden,
chose the priesthood anyhow. And, if so, whether they survived with that hint of preordained failure simmering away in
some almost forgotten pot on the hindmost burner), but those
who stayed with Father Madden for an hour remained with
Mother Church forever. With one exception.

So when my turn came, I was as skittery as a dove over Baton
Rouge in the fall who has been shot at all the way down from
St. Louis.

Father Madden cleared his throat. Not then, but much later,
when I began feeling the full extent of my sentence, I thought
Judge Jeffreys must have cleared his throat that way: length-
ily and rich with phlegm, the tongue shaping and projecting
its sound.

—You have a duty, he said finally, his voice still laced with
the liquor of his throat's clearing. —We are all soldiers bound
to serve.

I did not meet his eyes. I knew that he was staring intensely
at me. Instead I cast about for something to fix my attention on.
There was a tall bookcase to one side of his austere unclut-
tered desk. In it were piles of anonymous papers, all, so far as I
could tell, handwritten. Reports, I thought, on each of us. Not
only of our deportment, our conversation and our character.
But of our vices, our weaknesses, our most private thoughts, our
most bizarre and degenerate fantasies. This line of thought was
as bad as looking Father Madden dead in the eye. Because I was
convincing myself that he knew Jack Munston liked to exhibit
himself, that Charles Parker, besides bringing forbidden playing cards into the school, drank distilled spirits purchased from
a publican at the Three Bells in the Halisham Road. That
Percy Ridgemouth masturbated to jazz music, and worst of all,
that I had, on three separate occasions, taken Christ's name in

vain, and once had used that Holy Name to endorse a gross and contemptible lie.

—What is the duty of a soldier of Christ? Father Madden asked me.

—To do right, I gasped. I was not prepared to volunteer.

Father Madden snorted. —Right? What is right?

Pilate, asking a similar question of a more competent authority, drew a blank. I wonder if Father Madden expected an answer.

But, perhaps like Pilate, he did not pause.

—Your duty, your plain duty, is to begin this day examining your conscience to discover if you may have a vocation.

There were books on the shelf, too. Old books with faded backs, some of leather with quietly collapsing gilt patterns baroque and once splendid. But I could not make out titles. Father Madden pressed in again.

—Have you considered elevating yourself from the rank of common soldier to the estate of an officer, perhaps, someday, even to that of a prince?

I had considered almost nothing. I wanted my mother. I had thought of stowing away on a ship bound for New Orleans or Houston. I had the mentality of an enlisted man. Perhaps in the medical corps. Maybe a stretcher bearer. For others wounded even more severely.

—Look, Father Madden was saying. He pointed with his thumb at a large dark canvas of the Crucifixion behind his desk. I had not noticed it before. It was unspeakable. It was not the lovely set-piece of El Greco or even the pseudorealism of one of the early Renaissance painters. It was after Matthias Grünewald.

My eyes widened. I could hardly believe what I saw. Instead of bright gentle eyes, a clean loincloth, and all the usual baubles associated with the planned demise of God's favorite son, there on a ragged unfinished cross, Christ sprawled like a broken mindless animal skewered to a board.

—Look. No, don't turn your eyes from Him. You put Him there. Have the courage to look upon your own doing.

I could not look away. I couldn't even manage to unfocus my eyes. They moved up from the twisted unsprung feet wet with muddy blood, up the spare shanks unnatural in atrocious tension, past an anonymous patch of cheap cloth that concealed the unused heart of his manhood. No portion of his legs and thighs was left unscarred, unbroken by the lash, by the fists and boots of soldiers (like myself) who did what they were told.

—Notice the hands, Father Madden said softly, like some kind of ghastly connoiseur. —The hands twist like spiders on pins. He has lost control of the fingers; they curl and straighten on their own like independent creatures. Which of those nails did you drive into his flesh?

None, I wanted to cry, to scream. This is an atrocity.

—I wasn't there, I squeaked. —I wasn't even born for thousands of years.

I had not become suddenly brave. I just couldn't stand it. It was worse than the time my father had caught me with a roll I had stolen from a bread truck. Worst of all, with no memory of hammer and nails, no recollection of casting lots for a cloak, still the symbol of that cross was burned into my mind as indelibly as Cain's mark was branded into his forehead. I could see, taking the place of Grünewald's picture, Father Madden's books, great shadows looming. Not outside my mind, or yet within it. Shadows tall and terrible doing things I could not quite make out. *And it was about the sixth hour, and there was a darkness over all the earth.*

Father Madden's eyebrows shot up as if he had been confronted suddenly with something red hot and dripping straight out of hell.

—You weren't there? he gasped uncomprehendingly. —You took no part in it?

Father Madden fumbled madly amongst the papers and debris on his desk, his face still white and caught in that simulacrum of confusion. At last he drew back from the pile a small dog-eared Testament. He thumbed through it, found a place, and began to read.

—*But a certain maid beheld him as he sat by the fire and*

earnestly looked upon him, and said, This man was also with
him. And he denied him, saying, Woman, I know him not.

The shadows went mad, and I looked upward past Father
Madden's mottled, accusing face, toward Grünewald's transfixed monster. But it was the wrong choice. Because that brutal
face, that lax jaw, the dull forsaken defeated eyes told me more
fully that of course I had been out there, of course I had laughed
and drunk cheap wine to strengthen my belly against the
unique stench of innocent blood, to dull my ears against God's
dying cries, to steady my hand for the task of nailing the universe to a stripped and splintered tree.

I felt for a moment as if I were going out of myself, as if that
portion of me which was still a child, still innocent and had no
part of all this, were fleeing into the darkness of space to escape
an indictment too awful even to consider.

Then Father Madden was speaking again. His voice was soft,
muted, as if he felt a pain all his own. —Were you there? he
asked me. —Were you out there?

At first I did not speak. It was as if the apparatus of speech
had been broken, crippled. As if a Roman boot had been set
against my throat. —Yes, I said at last. —Yes, I was there.

I heard Father Madden's voice going on: —O Christ Jesus,
whose most precious blood purchased salvation's key, give unto
this boy . . .

But I did not hear the rest because I was lost somewhere in
the depths of shadowy uncertain things I could not understand,
clotted with guilt, broken with shame, thrilled by the awful
memory of the crime I had denied, and which had yet come to
claim me. I was aware somehow of doors inside me shutting, of
rising scaffolds of lust and ambition beginning to crack and
tumble in the hurricane wind of this repentance.

—Now, Father Madden was saying, his prayer at an end.
—Now will you help us take Him down? Will you help us take
Him down from the cross?

—Yes, I said. —Yes, Father, I will. Yes.

And moved in tranced silence to the door, down the dark
hallway, and into the priest's garden, where, before a weath-

ered and unpainted cross, I fell on my knees and wept bitterly, the strong English wind chilling my tears as fast as they fell.

&»

A few months after I began minor seminary, I received a letter from Mother. She and Uncle Charlie were married. And there was a child. She did not mention in which order the events had take place. She did not say anything about what I had decided. Only about the baby, who for some insane reason my uncle had demanded be baptized Christopher, who had died almost before the baptismal water and oil were dry.

> I hope it doesn't upset you. It doesn't mean anything. Except that Charlie is kind of crazy. Maybe he misses you more than he lets on. Will they let you come home any time soon? I want to see you. . . .

Or maybe Charlie didn't miss me at all. Or maybe nothing. Along with the letter, I received a bedraggled package. Inside was a package of Nabisco wafers and a cracked copy of Benny Goodman's orchestra playing "When Buddha Smiles." I never did get that puppy.

Chapter Two

Archer Street is dark and quiet except for a patrol of neighborhood dogs who gather nightly when their masters turn them out of doors. They attack slyly and in force those garbage cans unprotected by wire netting or unweighted with concrete blocks. They cause sometimes great commotion and those who own no dog—even those who do—curse and make note to clean up the debris next day. Once in a while, pushed far enough by other matters, a resident takes his stolen Army .45 or his souvenir Walther P.38 and blasts one of the raiders into garbage itself. Next morning an unamazed trash collector (who, for some reason beyond reason, is always and invariably a white man though no other such menial task above, up to that of waitress in a cafe, is handled by anyone lighter than Spanish tan) drops the carcass amongst empty tomato-juice cans, old bones, whisky bottles, bits of orange peel and a flyblown broken light fixture and heads for the next house still incurious and proof against such minor anomalies as a half-boxer, half-collie with a slug between its mild glazed eyes.

Archer Street is part of a Shreveport suburb on the edge of town pointing down the long flat dusty cotton plain toward Natchitoches. If the houses, built in the early and middle thirties, seem a bit older, a little draggled for lack of care during the late war, the lawns are wide, the grass secure, the trees less a welter of stunted branchless parvenus than those in newer additions.

The rain is done, or at least paused, and above a scattering of

stars leak unromantic shards of light through the almost perpetual haze that cuts off Louisiana (indeed, the whole Deep
South) from a clear view of heaven. There is a smell in the air.
Stronger than smell: a stench, except that it is not unpleasant.
It is the frank unsubtle odor of vegetation burgeoning and rotting, the blunt reek of semitropical plant life sweating and mul-
tiplying, passing off oxygen, gulping carbon dioxide, screwing
itself up for the coming light when photosynthesis and the
shedding of tons of moisture will begin again. This odor, this
reek permeates everything. It is especially strong in the early
morning. It is the olfactory signification of which damp rot,
mildew, rust, mold and ubiquitous moss is the visual. This eu-
phoric fecundity of plant life is matched by the teeming of
frogs, toads, snakes, spiders, moths, mosquitoes, centipedes,
flies of every sort and size, crickets, and a whole range of vermin
too small to be handled with a .38, too numerous to be put
down. The thick damp air is alive with croaks, barks, squeaks,
hums, thumps, scratches, buzzes, chirps and snufflings. The effect is somewhat as if one were to provide Latin-American
rhythm instruments to a home for the feeble-minded. It is not
especially loud, but what lacks in volume is made up in monotonous and unbroken intensity. Only daylight ends it, and then
only for so long as daylight lasts.

This is where Christopher spent his last summer at home before his ordination. Not where he was born (that was farther
into town, on Prospect Street, in a dilapidated house next door
to the Turners, and only a door or two from old Iambiah Tag-
gert, reputed to be the last living remnant of General Nathan
Bedford Forrest's cavalry, and who died, within Christopher's
hearing, renewing the curse of Ham on Negroes, the curse of
the Cross on Jews, and the curse of Babylon's whore on the
whole of Popery) but where, during the long vacation at his
English seminary, he had returned to spend one loving uncomfortable summer with his mother (during which time his uncle,
once more beloved than his father but by then as distant and
formally anathema as the stone demons who stalk the upper
walls of Notre Dame or Sacré Coeur, had found a sullen trip to
Oklahoma, at breakneck speed, in order). After his ordina-

tion and assignment to the diocese of Alexandria, he would return here for his two-week August leave from St. Magnus Martyr. He would return in a black suit with the high reversed collar which had never accommodated itself to his throat but had gone on feeling like the lower half of a stock or the dull but still lethal edge of a guillotine blade coming at him not down from the obscure heavens but up from simple hell. He would get rid of the suit and wear jeans and a T-shirt and not cut his hair or shave, would ride or fish or cut the lawn or simply sit in the paneled den where his mother spent much of her time writing innumerable letters having to do with her Alcoa or A.T.&T. stock or the cattle ranch near Ft. Worth or the mineral leases down near Anahuac and Lake Charles. As she wrote, she would talk to him, he would answer, though not at length, because even then, even the first summer after his ordination on February 6 (the feast of St. Dorothy who, in the second century, according to custom, was questioned concerning her religious beliefs as she relaxed on a *catasta*, an iron bed over a slow fire. The feast, too, of St. Vedast of the Franks who, in art, is depicted dragging a goose from the mouth of a wolf), he was bemused, wondering or nearly wondering if he had submitted himself for consecration or had submitted merely a young and undirected skin in which the multitudinous elements of a boy-man were still reacting and interreacting, without having yet reached any sort of balance at all, and surely not the kind of balance properly required if the skin and its mulling contents are to set themselves an irreversible course.

And while she wrote and talked, and he answered and considered, there would be playing, over the harsh hollow rumble of the attic fan, some jazz or swing recording so well known to them both that it could be heard, listened to, comprehended without interrupting the other one or two or more things they were doing simultaneously.

It would be Tommy Dorsey's orchestra, and Christopher could distinguish, without effort or even the consciousness of distinguishing, between the trumpets of Chuck Peterson and Ziggy Elman, and toward the end of the record he would—might—catch himself listening for the tiny error, the partially misplayed high trumpet note which was not only not apparent to ninety-nine people out of a hundred, but which, when pointed out to them, so tiny, so lost in the pulsating din of the orchestra's mounting dramatic and flawless roar, would make them frown and wonder first how Christopher had managed to discover it, and then, having hit upon it with microscopic hearing, why he had considered it worth pointing out. It was the second question that perplexed them most.

Or it might be Jerry Gray's orchestra, a bland and exact shadow-image not of what Glenn Miller's orchestra would have been had he survived the war, but what it had been in 1940, and which Miller had already surpassed before stepping into that Grumman Norseman which took off toward Paris to vanish forever like the clipped and final release of a staccato note. Christopher would hear, without trying, without even wanting to hear, a single trumpet (the third trumpet, he thought), in a harmon mute, hang over at the end of a phrase in "All the Things You Are."

His mother would notice none of this. Made of happier, or at least less exacting stuff, she would pay no attention to details, hardly even knowing one instrument from another, much less who played what instrument in which orchestra, but would smile and turn toward the expensive phonograph when the orchestra, playing ensemble, would reach a hard-driving, rhythm-forcing passage in which the blood pressure of the musicians could almost be measured, or when, from the heavy glue of a poor arrangement, a soloist would climb like one of Jacob's angels headed for home, and sign his anonymous character across the fragile shellac surface of the record in a ribbon of total and unmarred egotism like the shriek of a siren or the bubbling moan of a diving fighter plane. It was the *élan*, the thrust of music, by which she judged it. Not by volume or approach to hysteria in it, but by the pile-driving, overpowering brutality through which it made its point or captured its quivering objective. Of late, she had begun to buy Stan Kenton. "Intermission Riff" was her favorite. She was big, too, for "Thermopolae."

Behind the square two-story frame house with brick pillars

(almost an ironic reversal of the plantation house in Jefferson Parish where Christopher's remote maternal ancestor had not lived but worked as sharecropper in the years after the other war), an apartment perches over the garage. It has three rooms and a toilet-showerstall, and Christopher knows every inch of it. It was at first his playhouse, later his refuge, and at last, with the priesthood creeping over him, his cell, refectory and chapel. In those latter days, an icon of the Virgin and Child was propped up in the bookcase opposite his bed between *The Ordeal of Richard Feverel* and Freeman's *R. E. Lee.* In the long summer twilight, as he considered the acts and responsibilities of the priesthood, saw himself robed for the altar, hungering mutely to adore, he would fall asleep, and so falling, the last image before his eyes would be that of the distant dreamless indifferent eyes of a blue, brown, and gold Madonna, her delicate and impossible raised hand, and the small unchildlike infant, crowned and gauded, seated in the crook of her other arm, his large wise eyes staring out in static vacuity past a gold orb toward Christopher, his servant-to-be, who asked so often then and with much trepidation, —Is it I, Lord?

⋙ ⋘

That question, among others, has been answered in its own time. Now Christopher, again without collar or vest, with a quizzically smiling young woman he has accosted in the Southern Trailways bus terminal, creeps slowly down the driveway past the house toward the garage apartment. In the coolness of late evening, the lightless neutral darkness, Christopher has about him the air of a thief or an assassin—perhaps a betrayer. He waves the girl to silence even as the noisy cab pulls away. She giggles, hand to mouth, tanned shoulders heaving.

—What's the matter, sugar? Ain't you ever took a girl home before?

—No, listen, Christopher says, —you don't understand. I haven't been home . . . I'm not even supposed to be home.

—You just come from the war?

—No, Christopher whispers. —I wasn't in it. I was at this church . . .

—You ain't a preacher, are you? Mary Ann asks suspiciously.
—If you're a Baptist preacher I'd just as soon go on back to
that bus . . .

—No, Christopher laughs in echo of her. —No, I'm not a
preacher. I'm not a Baptist.

They are moving down the concrete driveway. Christopher
is thankful that his mother's room is on the far side of the
house. And that she sleeps, when she does sleep, like a cowboy at the end of roundup. Not that she would be scandalized,
much less interfere. She would most likely be edified by all this.
But she would laugh. Christopher is certain of that. Which, as
a matter of fact, is what he would do himself except that the
joke is ruined by being attentuated (long-drawed-out, you could
say), by taking its substance and its form from the fact that he
has spent almost fifteen years of his life marching doggedly up
a blind alley assuming the plaster figures in the Christmas
scene at the far end are really flesh and blood, and that at least
one of them (the tiny squalling one in the manger) was soul
and divinity of the world's maker. It is funny as hell, but hard
to laugh. Harder to listen to her, his mother, who is not cruel
but who has never cultivated restraint and cannot be expected
suddenly to acquire it when faced with the most implausible
and totally uproarious thing that has ever come her way.

So in silence, barring continued small giggles from both him
and her (hers over the conspiritorial manner of it all; his over
the idea that he is a Baptist preacher), they reach the garage
and stare up at the lightless windows of the apartment.

Christopher mounts the wooden steps first. He has forgotten
the feel of them. He is fumbling with the locked door.

—What's Bossier City like? she asks him in a stage whisper.

—You don't want to fool with Bossier just now, he says.

—Huh?

—They're having an election for sheriff. You don't want to
fool around over there when there's an election.

Mary Ann is not outraged. —You got me wrong, she says
simply, sweetly. —I was thinking about being a waitress.

Christopher blushes as he recalls that the door yields to a

certain peculiar pressure of the shoulder. —Bad hours, he tells her. —Low pay.

—I got to do something.

—Sure. We all got to do something.

—To eat.

He finds the proper posture and leans against the door. It opens smoothly, silently. The air inside is hot, but there is none of the odor of mildew, old newspapers and mothballs that usually comes pouring out when he opens the door for the first time in a year. Maybe his mother has had it aired out.

The light switch is a cinch. Christopher pulls the window shade down, and turns on the window fan at the other end of the room. The place is clean and looks lived in. He is surprised that his mother has bothered. Usually she leaves the dust and mildew alone. In order to give Christopher more and better chances for humility. What good is a mother, she asks with sweet irony, if she can't help her son's spiritual growth? This is fairly representative of her feeling about Christopher's priesthood. She believes nothing, and feels that he is serving a nonentity. Her view is that when your kid decides to commit emotional and spiritual hara-kiri, you either laugh or flip. Being essentially unflippable, she laughs ruefully. Christopher expects there may be something more: she has not forgotten his attitude when her brother-in-law, his uncle, had come to live with them. She may even believe that this pushed him toward the priesthood. Which is not so (he thinks) but no one nourishes a grudge so long, so avidly as one who has done you harm and knows you know it. So it had been with Uncle Charlie. And, Christopher recalls, civil wars are always the worst kind. They also call them intestine wars.

Mary Ann tosses her shopping bag over beside a broken-down mauve sofa. —This is okay, she says in apparent relief. —This ain't bad. We had a couch like this in Mama and Daddy's trailer. Took three years to pay it out. They paid four dollars and sixty-seven cents a month. Daddy used to flop down on it. He'd lay back in the evening with a beer—just that one beer— and tell Gene Autry and me how it was upstairs.

—Gene . . . upstairs . . . ?

—My little brother. Gene Autry. Upstairs. In the air. My daddy dusted.

—Crops?

—Till the niggers and the rich farmers killed him. If you're poor and white you ain't got a chance. This earth is hell if you ain't got anything. Did you ever think we could all maybe be in hell?

—Yes, Christopher says, almost eagerly. Not because he has given much thought to the morphology of hell in the world's body, but because he is apprehensive of the coming moments, and this looks like a subject within what might be called his field of interest. The whole situation is beginning to close in on him like the walls of a Spanish torture chamber. He has picked up a girl, brought her to his mother's home. Now what to do? He knows what he wants to do and knows pretty much how to do it. But to begin. A good beginning is most of the game. Of most games. There are games that begin well enough and then go sour. It is not enough just to be gamey.

He could sit down beside her and ask about her family. Or kiss her neck, or ask her if she's ready for bed. There are gambits enough to fill all the books St. John the Divine said he could write, thus filling the earth itself. But Christopher has been dissembling too long. He would as soon not begin his new life with an act of hypocrisy. He is born again, coming out of the church and out of her vestments. He is still within the pall of the birth trauma. Now is the time to stand up straight. Life, he considers, is real. What about that?

—Do you like to dance? Christopher asks, fingering some records on a small table next to an old phonograph. He puts on Vaughn Monroe. Who sings, the tune slipping with difficulty between his adenoids: "There, I've Said It Again." Then "My Devotion." Christopher wonders if the alto sax is Andy Bagni. It is too smooth to be real. It almost takes his mind off Mary Ann, who has waggled her head in affirmation, and is already removing her abbreviated jacket to dance. When Christopher turns it is like getting hit in the face with a pot of paradise soup. For just a fraction of a second he thinks she has begun to strip.

He is hot, cold, and beyond temperature all at once. Then he
sees she is wearing a strapless dress. It is old gold, the fabric
almost like that of a croker sack. It is unsupported except by
the indescribable thrust of her breasts. Her shoulders are like
those of a healthy young boy, her neck smoothly muscled, firm
and tanned like her long arms. Her color is almost light walnut,
and Christopher, already her victim, wonders why the darkness
of her flesh entices him. Or does it? He has nothing with which
to compare this response. He has, by plan and command, been
for years like a camera with a broken shutter. Beauty makes
him cringe like a physical assault. Once before he had been
moved by the softness, the impenetrable depths of dark hair
like Mary Ann's. A girl of the parish while he knelt in the back
pew of St. Magnus Martyr waiting to preach. But, with the
stealth of one who knows nothing, suspects all, he had coerced
himself. He had not looked down. He had closed his eyes and
pictured, one after another, the ninety-eight wounds of our
Blessed Lord. He imagined them breaking open again, each
tiny agonized mouth beginning to chirp again in the ancient
language of blood and suffering. He had felt his crotch melt,
felt tears well up in his eyes, and the cool crystalline power of
grace fill him again. As he stood passing time with people on the
church steps afterward, he had seen that hair, that girl again.
Final blessing, or confirmation of grace: the girl's face had
been as plain as the palm side of a catcher's mitt. She had been
dumpy in the bargain.

    —Hell is neither here nor there, Christopher quotes without
recalling from whom. —Hell is everywhere.

    —You reckon God tries people in this hell, and if they like
it here, He sends 'em on to the other hell?

    Christopher's eyebrows come up. He forgets Vaughn Mon-
roe's alto saxophonist. This is one strange girl.

    —And if they don't like it here, if they just don't fit, if they
keep wanting something else, why then He takes 'em to
heaven?

    —I don't know, Christopher says seriously. It is not that his
crotch has reordered itself, but Mary Ann is moving toward
troublesome ground. She is rendering herself human, indi-

vidual, conscious. Priest or not, Christopher is not much for using people. There are too many nonpeople around.

The phonograph chokes off, cackles as if it were laying records instead of merely changing them. There is a pause, a snarl,
and out comes Artie Shaw. "Moonglow." Many violins, and the
thick sexual intimations of Shaw's clarinet. Music for coupling,
Christopher thinks. He fumbles in the cabinet for more of the
same.

—I think probably my daddy is in heaven. He always wanted
off this earth. He couldn't live with things the way they are.

Christopher cannot recall that escapist tendencies are among
the qualities required for beatification or canonization. But
other folds, other sheep. Maybe other shepherds. Maybe no
sheep folds at all. Outside the yammering of insects and small
animals continues like the scrapings of a mad country fiddler.
Christopher breathes deeply of the cool moist air pulled across
him by the grumbling fan. The opposite window shade flaps
absently in the uneven breeze.

Mary Ann is up and moving with the music. Time shifts from
one foot to the other like a clumsy adolescent. Motion without
direction. Falls the shadow, Christopher thinks, watching her,
wishing she was young and knew nothing; that he was young
and knew more. That they were sweethearts and tonight was
the night. It *is* the night, but the rest is absurd. And Christopher
feels a thread of resentment stitch itself through his mind. The
priesthood has left him an emotional steer. Something out of
Billy Squawson. He is not supposed to respond to all this like a
balky child. He is supposed to have the reflexes of a man. But
then, he recalls wryly, the making of a priest does not take
nights like this into account.

—Come on, honey, Mary Ann smiles. —You're lettin' all the
records play out.

As Christopher moves to meet her in the middle of the room,
everything seems to jump into extraordinary clarity. Tufts
on the sofa stand out like the eyes of a praying mantis. His skin
is exquisitely tender; the breeze mauls it. Mary Ann kicks off
her shoes. She wears no stockings. Christopher sees the small
bones of her ankles moving beneath the flesh, a tiny white scar

on her tan calf. She hums the melody line of Butterfield's trumpet. It is "Stardust," and Christopher may not be able to stand
it. He has never been so aware of his body. The softness of his
belly sickens him. He can feel the hair in his armpits. Mary
Ann smiles and beckons, her arms, both of them, slipping
around his neck. His face passes hers, his hands rest on her hips.
She must feel the throbbing in his trousers. It is probably shaking the apartment. They move, sway, their bodies touch and
cling. Christopher is fairly sure he is dying or dead. The girl is
right; this has got to be hell. Nothing on earth ever had such
total clarity, such absolute substance. His hips move into hers,
the slight swell of her stomach filling just below his own. She
giggles like the girl he has wished she was. Hell is everywhere,
and it whirls him like a miniature tornado. It fills his nose with
the keen odor of her body, the sweetness of her hair. He buries
his lips in her neck and feels her arms close about him like a
collar of damnation. From here on, it is downhill all the way.
His knees quiver and he misses a step. He cannot feel his legs
any longer. Only a drink of high-octane gasoline or something
like it can keep him going. He kisses Mary Ann's nude shoulders
and wonders if it is in the cards to kill her and commit suicide.
What else could follow this?

—Sorry, Christopher mutters, —I never . . .

—I bet you ain't, Mary Ann says cheerfully. There is something ambiguous in her eyes. For some reason this slim clumsy
cross between a boy and a man gets to her. She likes the way his
body seeks hers without pretense, without sophistication. She
grinds her hips slightly, feels him shiver. There is something
goofy in this guy. Even though he has said he is not a preacher,
she wonders what he has in mind. She remembers the man who,
dressed in black, carrying a Bible, had come into a little spot
she had worked in Wichita Falls. He had taken a girl named
Agnes (called, inevitably, Texas Aggie) upstairs. It was two
hours before he came down, still all in black despite the ninety-
seven degrees of temperature. The girl had not come down at
all. When Mary Ann went up, she found Aggie lying in the
shower, crying, shouting, scrubbing herself compulsively with
an outsized bar of laundry soap. She told Mary Ann she had

started by giving him a mouth job as he read aloud from the *Psalm of Psalms*. The rest she would not—or could not—describe, and when the other girls pressed her, sailed off into another bout with hysteria. Which was unusual for a girl who was about ready for her ten-year service pin.

Mary Ann is warming up. Her idea of fun is, as it were, a busman's holiday. She can feel the sweet telltale warmth flooding her thighs, running down her long legs, up her back. This dancing is all right, but, like peeling an orange, when you are done peeling, it is time to eat.

—You want to catch my zipper, honey, she says into Christopher's ear, in a conversational tone.

—Do I . . . ?

—It's kinda warm, Mary Ann says for no reason she can imagine. When she hears her words, she almost falls over backward laughing. She is not much used to needing excuses for undressing.

Christopher is, as it were, getting hold of himself. The enemy of love is thought, and Mary Ann has driven him past thinking. Without even pausing in the dance, he finds the zipper and pulls it down slowly. It is Mary Ann's turn to shiver as the breeze touches her back. Christopher kisses her shoulders again, and as the record changes, he dances them both toward the wall and switches off the light.

It is pitch dark now, and they almost trip over the small coffee table in front of the sofa. Christopher giggles, moves back from Mary Ann for a moment and then, breaking the rhythm he has never had much control over, kisses her on the mouth. It is a long leisurely kiss, lips parted; each of them seeking the other as if afraid of the dark. Mary Ann begins it, by reflex, professionally. But again, something reaches her. If Christopher, who is on the verge of losing his seed, could see in the dark, he would notice that Mary Ann's eyes, at first open and mildly curious, begin to close. Her hands knead his wilted shirt, his unschooled flesh. The movement is standard enough, but she does it with feeling, wondering what this guy has that is better than proficiency.

They are past the coffee table now, and Mary Ann, taking a

chance, figuring by dead reckoning, falls backward onto the sofa. Christopher falls beside her, the kiss unbroken, his hands moving up her legs, caressing her breasts, wondering, exploring, discovering.

At first neither of them hears the footfalls on the wooden steps outside. Mary Ann is loosening Christopher's belt, Christopher is lost in the impenetrable mystery of her bra snaps. Then both of them hear simultaneously. Christopher snaps erect like a soldier shooting craps—or, as the old irreverent comparison goes, like a priest in a cat-house.

Mary Ann sits up slowly. She is disgusted. It was looking like a good evening. Now it could be some silly scene, and maybe end without even a place to stay. Carthage was never like this.

But she and Christopher are both more or less back together by the time they hear a key reproducing Christopher's earlier fumbling.

—You reckon it's your wife? she asks Christopher.

—Wife? Good Jesus, no. I'm not married. I never had a wife. My mother . . .

—Oh, Mary Ann says. —Your mother. Maybe I ought to put my jacket on.

Christopher shrugs with something between despair and resignation. —Just for a minute, he tells her. —Maybe you could leave some of the buttons loose.

Mary Ann Downey

ᦁ

What I remember is the dark wet plowed fields under a gray spring sky full of rain. And how I hated the cotton going in and the earth nurturing it, and the cotton coming up and the niggers seeing to it and the stalks sprouting leaves. And I remember every morning coming out of the trailer in a new town in Florida or Georgia or Alabama or Mississippi or Louisiana and how the cotton would have followed us, and I would hate it and wish to God they had never invented it.

But he would start to getting sober as the summer came on, and my mother would heal up and there would be no new bruises after April. So that by July or August he would look twenty-five again instead of the forty-three he was or the seventy he looked in mid-December or January when the winter was full on him and whisky had to tide him over till the following summer.

But outside the trailer there was always cotton, and in the midst of it, a dusty or grassy plot long and narrow with a dilapidated doorless shed twenty feet high and thirty feet long and forty feet across as if they were parking airliners instead of Stearmans and Old Fairchild trainers and even Curtiss Jennies and Aeroncas and bastard hulks thrown together out of pieces salvaged from wrecks and junkyards all over the South.

When he was flying, he would buy me and Gene Autry candy and sometimes fireworks near the Fourth of July.

—You want some of them cherry bombs, Gene Autry?

—And some of them Roman candles too, my little brother told him. —You can shoot them Roman candles at people.

—You can get your ass kicked loose from your tailbone, too, my father said, not cross but only casual. Not like in the winter.

—Them cherry bombs can blow a crapper right apart, my father told my mother.

—Who'd want to blow a toilet up?

My father shrugged. —Christ, it ain't that anybody wants to. We just used to do it. There was one behind this diner, and Joe Alexander went in and dropped a long-fused cherry bomb in. And we went in and got to eating hamburgers and hash-browns. When that thing went off, it knocked a piece of the commode into the kitchen. There was so much commotion we couldn't even pay for the food.

So he bought us the fireworks and sat on the steps of the trailer and watched us shoot them off.

—Whree, Gene Autry yelled. —Look at that sonofabitch of a Roman candle.

—Gene, Mother called out automatically. —Watch your talk.

—Look at . . .

He turned the Roman candle on me. Papa threw his half-empty beer bottle and caught him between the shoulder blades.

—Watch where you point that goddamned thing, he said mildly.

When Gene stopped crying we all had some ice cream and cupcakes with chocolate icing and marshmallow in the middles.

Mama was talking. —They need machinists in Dallas, she said without much hope. —I heard in at the store.

—Machinists are dime a dozen, my father said, finishing his ice cream and opening another beer. —By the time you get where they need 'em, they already got 'em.

—It's good work, Mama went on doggedly. —You can save and buy a house.

—Any work's good if you like it.

—Not if it kills you.

—You got to die, my father said. —That's pretty sure.

—Not young.

My father rolled beer in his mouth and swallowed it slowly, staring out into the sunset. —I don't want to go over all that ground again. I make good money. You ain't got any complaint.

—Oh, I got one. But by the time it gets registered, it'll be too late.

In the winter, about then my father would get ugly. But not in the summer. He didn't care about much of anything in the summer. He would smile and ignore her and watch the sunset for signs of cloud, and if it was clear she could talk till hell had an iron floor. Because he was thinking—no, not thinking, already living—tomorrow when he would be shut of the earth and everything on it, including us, and feel boiling back across that unscreened cockpit a wind like the breath of God or whatever breathed life for him. He would even be shut of the thought of whisky and age and the winter coming up in four or five months when the thought of age and the fact of whisky would be all that would occupy him.

So he ignored my mother the way a mule pays no heed to flies, snapping his hide and spinning off the pests with unconcern that must even get to flies if they have any temperament at all.

But it didn't get to my mother. She had dulled her blade on the timber of my father's ways for too long. Even if you stayed patient with him you would probably get nowhere. If you lost your temper, he would knock you down. So she talked on quietly that Fourth of July evening as if every word were a drop of water and she had faith in what enough drops could do even to a slab of solid granite.

But there wasn't that much time. She didn't have time to wear much off him. She had less than eighteen hours in fact.

Because the next morning he was up early and putting on a white T-shirt when I woke, and I watched the softness of his belly where it was beginning to sag, and how the hot indecent sun caught and set fire to the thick hair of his chest. And Gene Autry was nursing his thumb where he had scorched it with a nigger-chaser the night before.

My mother had been up. She had coffee and pancakes and

two little pork chops ready for him. He took them outside under the canvas leanto we used for a porch and set them down on an old card table we had. He was smiling and kidding with us. He always smiled and made fun when he was working and it was almost time to fly. He tousled Gene Autry's hair.

—You gonna be big enough to go up pretty soon, he said, draining his coffee and passing the cup for me to fill. —In a couple of years we'll buy us a two-seater and go to taking aerial photographs. I hear you can make a pile.

—I don't want to fly, Gene Autry told him. —I want to ride.

—All right, Papa said. —I'll buy you a horse with wings.

But then Mr. Murray, the man who owned the plantation, drove up in his truck. He was going to carry my father over to the strip. It was only a walk over there, but the planters liked to talk to the men who dusted for them. It made them feel like they were flying too.

—You want to watch them high-tension wires over the edge of the lake, Mr. Murray told my father. —And that steeple on the nigger church. Those niggers claim it's the highest steeple in East Texas.

—Don't worry, my father said, finishing his second cup of coffee. —It ain't so high I can't get over it.

—Too low, you can't go under it, Gene Autry sang.

—Anyhow, Mr. Murray went on, —you want to watch that Stinson, too. I had it gone over like it was the *Queen Mary*, but it's had some kind of electrical trouble. They said it's fixed. But I lost two days last week because the fella come through ahead of you and flew some said it was missin' when he climbed. But they couldn't find nothin'.

Mr. Murray was heavyset, red-faced and earnest. My father smiled at him. He even liked employers when he was fixing to fly.

—Did you pay him? The one who wouldn't fly on account of the missing?

Murray waggled his head. My father smiled. —I reckon it'll be all right now. I guess he just wanted a vacation.

Mr. Murray went on, and my father ate the last of his pancakes and threw down the rest of his coffee. The sun was full

up then, though still low in the east, and the trees and grass—
even the cotton plants—still covered with dew glittered like
fields full of diamonds. My father stretched and scratched himself through his T-shirt.

—Not a cloud, he said. —Not so much as a string of sheeps'
wool. It'll be cool and smooth till noon.

He looked over at me where I was sitting on the bottom step
of the trailer.

—You got to go up with me sometime, sis, he said. —Gene
Autry's got horses where his brain ought to be, but you'd love
it. You'd like that wind in your face so fierce you can hardly
breathe.

—I don't know, I said. —I guess if you like it . . .

—Sure, you'd like it. It's good to be up there. You look down
and all this is like a Monopoly board. Cars look like ants. You
can't even make people out.

—How about when you come down on the cotton? I asked
him.

—That's different. That's work. It ain't much fun, but it's not
bad.

I walked across the road with him. Gene Autry waved carelessly as we went, and my mother stayed inside the trailer. As
we got to the hangar, I looked back and saw her leaning out
the window over the sink staring after us. It was too far away to
tell her expression. Maybe she didn't have one.

When we got to the hangar, Mr. Murray and some other men
were near the plane. It was an old two-winger with a metal container slung underneath for the poison. The men were watching a pair of niggers starting it, turning over the engine. There
was no cowling, and you could see where the motor mounts
joined the fuselage. I hated that kind because they always
looked like the engines were ready to fall out.

The nigger in the cockpit signaled, grinning, and the one outside leaned against the propeller, turning it slowly. After a few
turns, the engine caught, sputtered, and died. Trails of white
smoke came boiling out of the exhaust.

One of the white men had a sack of Old North State and some
Ritz-La papers, rolling a cigarette. He put it in his mouth and

turned it with his tongue, smiling as he watched the nigger pushing the propeller again.

—That nigger got clouted on the head with a prop the last time he started one. Fell as he turned her, and it knocked him back thirty feet.

—Woulda killed you or me outright, Mr. Murray said seriously.

—Aw, I don't know, Bill, the other man said, lighting his thin cigarette. —I don't reckon it would have hurt you.

My father laughed with the others and went on pulling his worn leather gloves over his scarred hands. He had an old aviator's cap, too, with goggles and all, but he never put that on till he was up. Then, as he finished, the engine caught.

My father's eyes lighted up as the nigger inside revved the engine till it hurt our ears. Over and over, the engine slowed and built up again, whining, howling, roaring, until the man with Mr. Murray waved his hand and the nigger in the cockpit, still grinning, slipped the throttle back and climbed out. Then the man turned to my father.

—It's all yours, he said. —Stay low. That dust costs money.

My father nodded and turned back to me. I could see how anxious he was to go to the plane, but he leaned down and kissed me.

—You tell your mamma not to worry, he shouted into my ear. —You tell her it's no good being a low-down machinist.

And I nodded, holding down my skirt and squinting against the sound. And I kissed his cheek where he had missed with the razor that morning.

—Listen, he said as he started away, —maybe I'll find something up there and bring it back to you.

He always told me that. Once it had been a sparrow that had been stunned against the leading edge of the upper wing and fell into the cockpit. Another time it had been some long feathers that must have come from a goose. But he always said that, no matter what.

—You never know what you'll find, he called, and then shouted something more, his lips and eyes smiling, his gloved hand waving, but I could not make it out, unless, I remember thinking then, it was, —I love you, but he hardly ever said that unless I was going off to grandmaw's or at least overnight to one of my aunt's, and then he had turned and was running toward the old canvas-covered biplane. And a minute later he was in the air.

                                  ৎও ৪৯

We were washing the morning dishes, at least I was. My mother was already picking the rind off some bologna and getting ready to fry it for his lunch. She sliced into the edges of each piece so it wouldn't baloon up in the middle and not cook through.

—Well, she said, answering a question I had not asked. —If he was to hang himself with a length of cable, I'd cut him down till the knife went dull. Then I'd pick at it with my teeth and fingernails. You don't accept him hanging hisself and you don't accept him up in that damned boxkite he makes believe is a plane. All right, you accept it: you don't blind him while he's asleep. You don't leave him and drive the whole rig away while he's up. But what you do do is keep at him. You talk and whine and push him right up to hitting and maybe past. You keep it up over his dinner, over the top of his paper. If you're out fishing, you say something about it. Maybe even at night in bed. And you know just about how far all of it will get you, since you're dealing with a fanatic and had just as well try to get Billy Sunday off the Bible and on to the bottle. But you don't deal in anything as simple-minded as what will probably happen because . . .

I was finished with the dishes and wanted some air when we heard it. I looked at mother, but she went on with the bologna and if I had not seen her lips compress and her teeth tight against them I would have thought the sound came from my mind. But Gene Autry was playing cowboy by himself outside. When the distant edgeless deep roar of it rattled the dishes I was just done with, he put his head in the door, eyes wide and excited.

—Jeezus, he squeaked. —You oughta see. Smoke. It must

go up a mile in the air. Like somebody blew a well. You reckon
somebody blew a well?

—Hush, I said.

—Go on, my mother told me. —Go on across there.

—Do you think . . . ?

—I wanta go, Gene Autry started. —I wanta go see. How
come she always . . . ?

Then he saw mother's face and stopped complaining. As I
stepped down past him, he began to whimper, and walking
away from the trailer, my eyes fixed on the column of dark oily
smoke as if the stalks were frozen, I knew what mother knew,
and what even a little snotty-nosed kid knew. I tried to puke,
and then I tried not to puke and the men who always stood
around the hangar were running toward a patch of trees on the
far side of a wide cotton field, with the two niggers in the lead.
I was running too by then—all of us running toward the smoke
like it says the Hebrews followed a pillar of cloud by day. And
I was stumbling and tripped up short and fell on my face into
the cotton plants, and then, sure enough, I puked.

⋖⋗

It had been the nigger Baptist church, of course. And it had
been electrical trouble, too. So that he stalled (Mr. Murray
told me this, in a sober voice at first, but soon kind of lively and
almost as if he were announcing a baseball game or one of those
secret cockfights they still had in the fall) and slewed off on
one wing and into that damned nigger steeple that was higher
than any other nigger steeple in East Texas. I remember wanting to brand every nigger who went to that church with
"Blessed are the meek" and "Thou shalt not kill." But I wished
later I hadn't gotten to thinking like that. Because I couldn't
get "Blessed are those who mourn" out of my mind, and there
wasn't any way I could be comforted.

But Mr. Murray was still telling me about it. Telling me more
than I had asked. More than I wanted or needed to know.

—It went up like a pine knot soaked in coal oil. He had just
gone up again to get that last strip done before lunch. It was

full of gas. When he tilted into that steeple, it went off like a bomb.

I didn't want to ask what had happened to him, whether they had found him. But Mr. Murray was still talking.

—So we managed to get through the weeds and into the scrub pine and back where the gum and the oak and the rest was. The plane was back in there, burning, and it wasn't no use to go much farther. But then one of the boys—that little nigger who was in the cockpit this morning—found him, found your papa.

—He was just lying in the brush with his arms across his chest and looking back up at the sky like he couldn't figure how he come down out of it so fast. But he wasn't burned. Only scorched a little. It didn't bust him up too much, either.

Sure enough, it hadn't. They took him into Carthage and laid him out. Mr. Murray paid for a new suit and the undertaker out of his own pocket till the compensation insurance paid off. That night, Mr. Murray sat up with us in the undertaker's parlor. Mother and Gene Autry and I had soft chairs. Mr. Murray had a straight-backed cane-bottom. The two niggers had come, too. They were sitting on a bench at the back of the room. One of them, the one who had got hit in the head by the propeller, had fallen asleep. I thought, couldst thou not watch with me one hour, but it was nice of them to come.

My father was up at the front of the room with a couple of flower sprays around him. His face was that pale yellow like old paper, and his mouth was only a crooked gray line across his face, with the lips all wrong. There was a lot of powder or putty or something on his left temple where the crash had hurt him. His hands were folded across his belly, and that was where it fell apart. They weren't his hands: they looked like a couple of dummy hands carved out of yellow pine, and carved badly with no harmony between the parts, so that one finger stood out while another curved in naturally. The hands looked like they had been broken off a cigar-store Indian, and when I saw them, I wanted to start crying all over again. But you can't mend nothing with tears. So I sat down on one of the soft chairs next to Gene Autry who had almost stopped sniffling by then, and only once in a while gasped and shook with the tail end of his crying. Mr. Murray wanted to comfort my mother, but he didn't know how. So he talked. I reckon he couldn't stand the silence rushing out of that coffin up at the head of the room like a cataract through a mountain pass. Maybe he felt like the crash was his fault some. Maybe he was right.

—I always wanted to fly, he said. —I mean I wanted something besides planting and picking. My daddy had the first tractor in Harrison County. He was always ready for something new. I wanted to go to sea, but somebody had to take care of my daddy's place after he fell off his tractor and lost his leg. So then I thought maybe I could learn to fly. But there never was time.

—You're better off, my mother said. She was mostly ignoring Mr. Murray, but she had to stay courteous till we got my father buried. She hadn't told me that but I knew how she thought. I had listened to her thinking out loud often enough.

—You got to expect accidents, Mr. Murray went on, his flat red face almost expressionless, but his heavy mouth still set to show something like sympathy, like it had been since that afternoon when I came running through the cotton with the front of my dress ruined, covered already with puke and covering then with tears. I wanted to clean that expression off his face with a twelve-gauge or a hatchet or even a two-by-four. But I just sat and looked at the coffin like I expected something to happen there.

—It could have been me, and it could have happened crossing the road. They kill twenty thousand people a year on the highway. I heard that on the radio.

—Except it wasn't you and it wasn't a road, and I don't give a goddamn if they kill every sonofabitch in Texas with a cotton plant even growing in his back yard by accident, my mother said, not raising her voice, but looking square at Mr. Murray.

—Ma'am, there ain't no sense . . .

—You got that right, my mother said. —There ain't a pinch of sense in the whole shooting match. If it was legal, I'd crawl

in that box with L. J. and you could put us both away together.
If it wasn't for these two children, I'd see to it tonight.

—Ma'am . . .

—Go on, my mother said, loud enough to wake the nigger.
—Go on and leave us with him. I ain't got time for any more
jawing.

It went from twilight into pitch black, and Gene dozed
against my mother's arm. She never paid any attention, only sitting dry-eyed and slumped a little, watching that coffin where
you could just see my father's profile (but not his hands) outlined against the frilly silk or whatever it was they used in that
coffin. They had a soft yellow light up over him, almost the
color of one of those lamps that don't draw bugs. It kind of
took the edges off things, and after a couple of hours just sitting
there I got to seeing things. It looked like his eyelids fluttered.
Then it looked like he moved his head a little, and I almost
reached over and touched my mother. But her eyes were still
wide open and fixed right where mine were, so I knew I was seeing things.

And inside my mind I kept hearing things. I heard wind, the
sound of a plane passing far off, and I bet there wasn't wind,
and no plane above at all. I got the name of some old song in
my mind, and no matter how I tried to think of God or tomorrow or hard times or even of him, I kept hearing that song and
the name of it:

. . . you and the night and the music . . .

until I almost laughed out loud, or went to humming it.

Once in a while I looked out the window next to me, through
the torn shade. I could see a run-down diner across the way. It
had started to rain a little, and the streetlight above the diner
had a halo of diffused light around it. There was a girl standing
just outside with a magazine or newspaper over her head,
looking up and down the street. When I looked again, a man
had stopped and was talking to her. After they stood there in
the rain talking a while, he took her arm and they went into the
diner.

It was crazy, but I wanted to call out to them and say, Hey, my papa's dead. Why don't you come over and see him? But I just turned my head away, and my eyes stopped short, flush on that coffin again.

∴ ∵

It wasn't much of a place, but it did for us, and they didn't charge rent. So we left the trailer right where it had been, and my mother got a man to come out and look at the truck and buy it. Because she didn't know how to drive and I was too young and we needed money then while she was looking for a job. But looking for a job was like trying to sex a chick. There was jobs around, but she couldn't find anything—at least nothing she could do. Or would do. The compensation money was going, and it looked like root hog or die.

But Mama was past rooting. I don't know if it was Papa getting killed or just the general wear and tear, but she started having a drink out of his bottle when she came home from job hunting. And when that bottle was gone, one evening she came home carrying a pair. Not I.W. Harper like Papa drank, but Old Charter, which was cheaper and got to her quicker. From then on, she was gone by an hour after supper.

—I ain't made out of iron, she said. —I'm just flesh and blood. The edge is gone off of it. I wish to God I was under ground.

—If you keep that up, you're going to get your wish, I told her. —Papa could handle that stuff. You can't do it. It'll break you for sure.

—Shit, she said, lolling on the built-in bed. —Shit, we're all going down the drain. All we got ahead of us is six feet. Like your daddy.

I never heard her say shit out in front of Gene Autry or me before. It hit me that she was right. At least for her. She was over the side, and there wasn't any life preserver to haul her back. But I wasn't even on the rail yet. I remembered, for some crazy reason, that girl outside the diner in Carthage, and how the man came along. Sometimes I play-imagined what happened after they went inside: chopped sirloin and hash-browns, maybe a Roy Acuff record or the new one by Tex Williams about smoking that cigarette. And he was holding her hand across the table and smiling and saying, Little girl . . .

So it came finally that I had to go looking. I hated to leave her, but the way it worked out, she didn't even know when I left. I didn't want Gene Autry to stay behind, either. But he was five years younger than me, and not too smart even for that age. And even then, before I had set foot in the world, I knew how it was, that living in the world was like swimming in a river: you traveled light or got pulled under.

It was a cold night coming and a long road, and I guess I couldn't help looking back at the trailer where there was one light you could see through the rear window. It was over my mother's bed, and she was lying under it with her mouth open and a bottle with two or three fingers of whisky on the night table, and a lot more bed than one woman alone could use. Gene would be home from the consolidated school soon, go in and turn out the light over Mama, and finally find my note on the table propped against what was left of the bread.

I looked up into the evening sky, but it was dark and solid with clouds. There was one of those long moaning winds blowing from the northwest, and four miles of highway to the bus stop and God knows how far to something worth having. And first a mile-and-a-half side trip by Shady Grove Cemetery to see to my inheritance.

Chapter Three

Billy Bob Stoker is three ways afflicted. First there is loneliness. He is far from home, amidst alien cotton, here on Archer Street in the depth of night. And cold, Lord, cold. Inside his apartment there is some man with a girl. Beautiful. Mexican, maybe a nigger even. But beautiful and warm. And inside too is his Catahoula hound, Jeremiah. It seems like next to Mississippi everything he needs is there inside. That is the first kind of affliction.

Never mind the second kind. That is metaphysical and has to do with Jesus. But Jesus is a long way off, farther than Mississippi.

The third affliction, that which brings tears to his eyes, is he has to pee something awful. Despite all of it he still hates to trouble them. Somehow it seems wrong to trouble people having pleasure in a world where there is little pleasure. No goodness at all and little pleasure. But Billy Bob's condition is desperate, and he feels, after all, one can share the misery, make the misery less by spreading it around, or if not less at least, divided up into equal portions, everyone can handle his own piece.

He makes a production of fumbling with the lock. He could get in without a sound, but that would be pushing things too far. So he pokes at the keyhole and misses it several times. He elbows the door, lets the screen slam against his back, and finally manages to unlock the door and step inside.

It is warm in here. The cool night air drifts past him and

causes that special warmth to dissipate. Even across the length of the room he can smell her. Not perfume, not perspiration, but some strange heady combination of both which makes him think back, think forward, think sideways, think of women, of the toils of lust, of adamantine chains and penal farms.

As he steps in, the man and the girl move apart.

—You got to excuse me, Billy Bob Stoker says. —I didn't mean to cause youall no inconvenience. I mean I would have just walked around outside awhile or something but my hound is out on the back porch and he's got to be fed and run. He always gets out at night. I always leave him loose at night to run around. If he don't run he's no good the next day. He gets off his feed.

Billy Bob is speaking more and more rapidly, as if making excuses for invading his own apartment. He senses the stupidity of defending the right to come into a place where he pays rent money every week, but still it seems necessary. The man looks heartbroken, as if something has just escaped him, as if he had been on the verge of some spiritual discovery.

The girl looks up lazily and studies Billy Bob. Not with distaste, but with the kind of honest, straightforward regard that she might have brought to bear on a polo pony had she been in the horsey set; an Olympic athlete if she had had time and money to spend in Rome. Or perhaps, Billy Bob does not quite articulate it in his mind, the way a girl might look at a man who is coming in to pay $25 for a trick.

—Come on in, Mary Ann says finally. —There's plenty of room. Ain't nothing happening.

Christopher stares at her in desperation, then looks back at Billy Bob. —Are you staying here? he asks. —I mean are you renting this place?

Billy Bob wags his head. —Yeah, I'm renting this place. I've been here about two weeks. Does your ma know you're home?

Desperation turns to demolition of character. Christoper studies Billy Bob for a moment. —You know me, he says. —Have I met you?

—Naw, Billy Bob says. —I ain't never met you. I just saw a picture of you on top of your mamma's desk. She got a picture

of you when you was a little boy, and another picture of you
when you was middle-sized wearing some of them funny short
pants like they wear over wherever it was you went to school.
And then she's got a picture of you in there with one of them
backwards collars on and a black suit. She told me you was a
priest. Is that a fact?

Christopher shrugs and stares out the window. The night
air that had been cool and pleasant, just the right touch to bank
the blast of his own passion and the mounting heat of Mary
Ann's body in his arms, now suddenly feels cold. For the first
time since he boarded the bus at Alexandria he begins to realize what he has done. He begins to realize how far things have
gone; how far things are likely yet to go.

—I tried it, he says. —It didn't work out the way I figured
it would.

—Preaching's a hard row, Billy Bob says without emphasis.
—Many are called but few are chosen.

Many are cold but few are frozen, Christopher thinks. He
must reckon I'm some kind of animal crawled out from under a
rock.

—Anyhow, Billy Bob says —your ma was telling me she
hoped you'd come up this summer, at least for a week or so. She
said youall got time off once in a while.

Maybe time off for good behavior, Christopher thinks. Going
into the priesthood is like breaking the sound barrier. All
the controls get reversed. Nothing works the way it should.
Some men have all they can do to make a woman. And just this
morning I made God on the altar, or so they tell me. But that
was just a fiction. Maybe making women is a fiction too. Maybe
no one ever has. Maybe sexual intercourse is an hallucination.
Maybe nothing happens the way the legends tell us. Maybe the
whole thing is a nightmare built out of the constituents of a
chemistry set in the hands of a fourteen-year-old God who is
trying to sweep up the mess He's made before His folks come
home.

—I guess I'll go in and see my mother tomorrow, Christopher
says. —She didn't know I was coming home.

Mary Ann has been sitting quietly. She looks from Billy Bob

to Christopher then back at Billy Bob. At first she does not understand what passes between them. She knows what a priest is, but only vaguely. She cannot quite make the connection between Christopher and priest.

—You're a priest, she says. —A Catholic priest.

—No, not any more, Christopher says. —I'm retired, at half pay. If they can catch up with me to give me my check.

—Well, Billy Bob says, passing through the room, —if youall will excuse me just a minute I'll go let out my hound. He walks first to the bathroom and closes the door. He stares in the mirror as he relieves himself. Lord, Lord, he thinks, how far flesh can slip. I thought I was in a bad way, but that fellow in there makes me look like a lily-white angel. He done took on the burden and throwed it over. I made a few mistakes in the sheriff's office, but leastwise I didn't get myself into the ministry and make my mistakes there. Lord, it was bad enough back there in the jail. What if it had been in the rear end of a Baptist church? Merciful God. I reckon some nights Jesus Christ must cry himself to sleep over what He's got down here serving Him.

Billy Bob walks out onto the porch and turns loose a particolored hound whose colorless eyes stare up at him with brute love and exquisite pleasure. Jeremiah switches around the room, first of all leaping at Christopher, licking his hands, trying to climb into his lap. Then, spying Mary Ann, he runs over and tries to nuzzle under her dress. She laughs and pushes him away gently, not so much as if he were a dog but as if he were one more male in heat pressing close, trying to discover the secret she carries with her.

Billy Bob turns him loose through the front door, then comes in and sits down. —I'd like to offer you something to drink, he says, —but I don't have anything in the house. I don't drink much myself.

—You don't reckon we could come up with a few beers? Mary Ann asks.

—Well, the pak-a-sak is closed, and the ice house is closed. But there's a place up there on Centenary Boulevard where you come toward the overpass. We can probably get some beer there.

—You mean the Smile-a-While, Christopher says.

—That's right, Billy Bob says. —Old man with a blue nose stays there all the night long. I understand he sells more beer at night than he does in the daytime.

—He sells more to kids under fifteen than he does to men over twenty-one, Christopher says. —That's the worst old son-ofabitch in the parish. He sold me my first can of beer when I was eleven. I bought it the day before I left for England.

—Figuring, Billy Bob cuts in on him, —that if you was old enough to make a trip all the way to England then you was surely old enough to have yourself a beer. Is that right?

Christopher smiles. He likes Billy Bob Stoker. He knows men like Stoker. He has known them all his life. They are the kind of people he can talk to. There is not much play about them, and what they think they say. There is something to be said for crudity.

—I reckon I've got enough money to buy a case of beer, Billy Bob says. —I don't have to be on the job tomorrow till ten o'clock. I done told 'em ahead of time I wasn't going to be in, that I had something I was going to do.

—I got a couple of dollars, Mary Ann says.

—No, Christopher stops them. —No, let me buy it. The only question is how to get it. That place is six miles away from here.

—Well, Billy Bob says, —it would be a dry walk in. Course, we could drink the beer walking back.

Christopher frowns for a minute. —Wait, he says, —I've got a key to my mother's car.

In the garage directly under the apartment is parked a 1941 two-door Ford sedan. Charlie had given it to Christopher's mother. It still runs like clockwork. All during the war she had managed to get parts for it by buying old wrecked '41 Fords and cannibalizing them, placing the parts she needed on her car. This for tires, seats, carburetors, finally an engine block. The far end of the back yard is scattered with hulks of old '41 Fords, junked, their stark metal bones rusting, falling apart in the deep grass of the back yard.

—Tell you what, Billy Bob says. —I could get the garage open and we could push that car all the way out to the street. Then we could push it down maybe fifteen or twenty yards and get in and start it, real quiet. Then maybe your mamma won't even wake up. What do you think about that?

—What if mamma does wake up? Mary Ann says. —Is mama gonna raise a stink?

—I don't see why she should, Christopher says.

—Well, Mary Ann says, —I suppose if someone was a priest's mama and the priest came home and he had a girl up in the apartment and he was fixin' to make off with the car and go buy beer . . . I mean if she was a real Catholic mama that might sorta shake her up.

—I got problems, Christopher says, —but that's not one of them.

—Might as well get on with it, Billy Bob says, standing up. —The night's far enough gone, we might as well grease up the rest of it.

—There you go, chief, Mary Ann tells him. —Give me six or eight beers, and I'll dance with both of you all the way over to Clarksdale.

—Would God you could, Billy Bob sighs deeply and starts down the stairs.

❧ ❧

They come back with two cases of beer and push the car quietly back into the garage. The Catahoula yips and snorts and wags its whole hindquarters all the way upstairs. He almost knocks Christopher off the top landing as Billy Bob unlocks the door.

—Come on, goddamnit, Billy Bob growls at the dog. —Quit acting like a damned fool. Ain't you ever been to a party before?

They drink and laugh and manage to avoid asking all the natural questions. It is like a reunion of Angola exconvicts, each aware of his own peccadilloes, touchy about them, and hence deferential to the others. Except Mary Ann. There is no deference in her. She is simply not very curious. This is a one-night stand, a place to pause and have a drink and a laugh. You don't ask the bartender or the carhop for a life story. Why get things mixed up?

Meanwhile Mary Ann is trying to keep her promise. Billy Bob turns on an old Philco radio and she dances with them in turn, first with Christopher, then Billy Bob. The Catahoula, his dignity recovered, sits on the worn sofa, tongue out, slobbering quietly. The night wind dies, and as they dance, the room grows hotter, more humid. Billy Bob's face, always red, looks as if he were on the verge of apoplexy. Christopher, with unconscious perversity, becomes even more pale than usual. His brown hair, a month or more uncut, falls over his eyes like a spaniel's mane. Mary Ann, a beer in one hand, is smiling more and more broadly as if some hilarious joke were in the offing. Her tan flesh is covered with a light oil of perspiration, her hair damp, falling naturally over her shoulders. Each time she tosses her head back and leans over for another beer, the loose top of her dress shifts forward, revealing for just a second or two the rich fullness of her breasts. Christopher's eyebrows do gymnastics. Billy Bob licks his lips and feels the devil stir in his guts. The Catahoula grins and drools. The temperature rises. There is an empty moment on the radio; then Gordon Jenkins' violins fill it:

> *I go out walking after midnight*
> *Along a lonely thoroughfare,*
> *It's not the time or place*
> *To look for you,*
> *But maybe you'll be there . . .*

—Listen, Mary Ann says as she eyes the diminished beer supply. —I got to get some rest. It's a long way to anywhere from here and I got to get moving tomorrow. I need to sleep some.

—Sure, Billy Bob says solicitously. —Sure. That makes sense.

—Yes, Christopher echoes, amazed at the strength of his own voice. —Time for bed.

—Well? Mary Ann says interrogatively.

—Sure, Billy Bob repeats numbly, the beer finally beginning to operate.

—Yes, Christopher says again, shivering in the blast-furnace heat.

Mary Ann pauses for a moment. —Well, what about the sleeping arrangements? Youall got that figured out?

—Why, Billy Bob stutters, —you got to use my bed. It's . . . a double bed.

—Sure, Christopher puts in. —And somebody can use this sofa.

The Catahoula looks up inquisitively, licks his paw, and collapses on his belly, eyes walled, tongue lolling. Christopher and Billy Bob stare at each other. Not in anger, not in mutual challenge so much as in kindred bewilderment.

—No use anybody sleeping on the floor in his own place, Mary Ann says, solving nothing. Christopher owns; Billy Bob rents. If you find a bucketful of doubloons under a house so encumbered, who has claim, owner or renter?

—Jesus, Billy Bob says, shaking his head. —No, it ain't no sense on earth in anybody spending a night on this floor.

—That's right, Christopher puts in. —We need some kind of arrangement.

Mary Ann stands on tiptoe, raising her slender arms high above her head, yawning prettily. —Youall work it out, she smiles. —However you've got a mind to.

She walks into the bedroom, already lifting her skirt, shucking off the damp dress.

Billy Bob sits down heavily on the sofa next to the Catahoula, Jeremiah. —Reckon you want to play a hand or two of showdown poker before bed? he asks Christopher in a forced, unhappy voice.

—Shit, Christopher says, feeling suddenly, incomprehensibly at home. As if he had never left. —I'll play you a game of Russian roulette. With an automatic. And go first.

Billy Bob does not move. He shakes his head slowly, his lips pursed, eyes lowered.

—Naw, he says, —we can't do it. I ain't got no cards. I give

up playing-cards when I was saved over to the Mount Hebron
Baptist Church in Mississippi.

Christopher squats and fidgets. He is like a starved man who
knows with awful and consuming certainty the location of a
nine-coarse meal. His imagination has never functioned so
well before. At first he was too young to imagine such things,
and then pledged to avoid what he did not know how to imagine. He is amazed at the clarity, the precision, the force of his
lust. It seems he has been some sort of degenerate all
along without even knowing it.

But if necessity is the mother of invention, the mother of
makeshift is surely the rutting instinct. Christopher's mind
works like some kind of supercalculating machine, raising, esti-
mating, rejecting plans for disposing of or rendering tempo-
rarily inoperative his drunken rival. Murder passes through
the machine, hangs in the gears for a moment, and then falls
into the discard heap. Immoral. Stoker is pleasant and unobjec-
tionable, having only the bad fortune to be in the way. Besides, the calculator purrs cannily, it would take a good hour to
drag the body over to Bayou Pierre and get back. If a solu-
tion is not forthcoming sooner than that, the machine avers,
Christopher Nieman is as likely to do away with himself as
with Billy Bob.

—Wait, Christopher yells hoarsely, sweat rolling in even
greater profusion down his face. —Wait. I've got it.

Billy Bob, barely navigating under the cargo of beer he has
taken on, waits. Christopher is too desperate to notice, but
Billy Bob stands no better than a sixty-forty chance of making
it to the bedroom even if Christopher helps him.

—Dice, Christopher says excitedly.

—Bones? Craps?

—Sure. I can get some. Didn't you see them?

Billy Bob shakes his fuddled head slowly. —Them things is
an abomination. *Every toss is a nail in the cross,* he croaks mechanically, like an old Ediphone recording of Billy Sunday.
—*He who stops to game or gamble, forever in hell's fire will
ramble.*

Christopher pauses to blink in reflex. He has been too long a professional not to gape for a fraction of a second at the idea of the damned rambling. But the impropriety passes and Christopher is already on his feet moving toward the door. His fingers fumble unconsciously with his shirt buttons. Jeremiah lies on his back, an amazing length of tongue obscuring one eye. He is gently scratching his parts, one leg thrashing mechanically, rhythmically in the air.

Christopher is back almost before the screen door can slam. In his hands are an enormous pair of dice. They come after long residence pendant from the rear-view mirror of his mother's car. Uncle Charlie had bought them one evening at the Louisana State Fair, when, in a condition approximating Billy Bob's, he had taken to reaching for Mrs. Nieman's breasts as they stood before the poultry and swine exhibit building, and would not stop. —Boxcars, he had laughed. And so on, in moderate staggering chase all over the fairgrounds. —Boxcars, goddamnit to hell. Lemme hook onto those . . . boxcars.

They are at least four and a half inches square, made of felt or some other light substance, and liberally spotted. Probably their most remarkable characteristic is that they are covered with synthetic fur. The spots peek out from under it with surrealistic coyness. Billy Bob studies each one carefully. They look all right to him.

—Roll 'em, Billy Bob mumbles, falling against the low coffee table, displacing a shower of empty beer cans. Billy Bob stares at them and swallows hard. —Go on, he groans. —Let's see what you got.

Christopher hesitates for a moment. He sees that Billy Bob has between eight and ten sheets in a rising wind. But even against an egregious drunk it is a risk. Because Christopher knows exactly what he's got. Then his eyes fall on the skimpy jacket of Mary Ann's dress. It lies a few inches from Jeremiah's nose, draped artlessly over the arm of the ramshackle sofa. The Catahoula paws at it tenderly, grinning and grinning, his fangs catching the weak lamplight, seeming to shine with a luminosity of their own.

—Come on, Billy Bob grunts almost on the far side of intelligibility. —Lesse whatcha got.

Christopher rolls the fur-bearing dice across the floor, knowing without following their frenetic course exactly what will turn up. His eyes are glued to that cheap cotton jacket. He reaches for it before the dice cease their wandering and blink their message. He presses his face into its fragrance and is already rising as Billy Bob croaks:

—Seven. Goddamned seven. You done passed on me, he finishes, losing the last of his precarious hold on consciousness and sprawling full length on the floor just short of the dice. —A pass, he whispers, passing out.

While Christopher, suddenly and enormously sober, blessing somewhere in the recesses of his mind Uncle Charlie and his con-man soul, steps across him to grasp the knob of the closed door, opening passage into a new life. Leaving behind a scratching, grinning hound, a stymied dreaming rival, and two fuzzy dice—one bearing nothing but threes, the other covered with fours.

Billy Bob Stoker

᭰ᔒ

I remember outside town where they had the graveyard right next to this old clapboard Baptist church, and in it mostly little white stones or crosses, some from before the Confederate War, and this great big piece of black marble right on the edge of the plots, and even turned different from the other markers so that it faced out toward the highway that cut north through the Delta country to Memphis and south through Vicksburg and Natchez and Woodville and on down to Louisiana.

There was nothing like that piece of marble. It was four feet high and four and a half wide and almost three thick. And on the side facing the road, chiseled real deep, so deep that there was always shadow standing in each letter, was one word.

BIRDSONG

it said. Even when I was a little boy walking into town to a movie-show or to fetch some coal oil or to ask after Mrs. Noddy for my mama, I always stopped by that stone. —Mornin', Mr. Birdsong, I'd say. I thought it was nice about that stone, because a burying ground is usually a sad heart-squeezer of a place with crowds of little poems on the stones, and the graves full of people who died young or of some awful disease, or drunk in an automobile. Even graves with little children who died of croup or fever when they weren't but maybe a year or so old.

But old BIRDSONG helped out. You passed by the graveyard,

and when you had got to thinking about worms and rot and darkness unending and were about to pass over into thinking about damnation, you'd see that big happy expensive piece of black marble: BIRDSONG. And you'd turn your head, and sure enough, there was a mockingbird or a robin or a finch. Something anyhow with feathers, and burbling away in the dry summer grass. And your spirit lifted up. It had to. You heard life all around you, and the hot road under your feet and the sun gouging a hole between your shoulders and all the rest of it just passed off. That's what that big gravestone meant to me when I was little. I don't recall as I ever even asked about the man under it. He could've been a double-dyed sonofabitch so far as I know. But that stone of his made all the difference.

Even when I got older it was something. Because out in the country where I grew up everything was mostly coarse and homemade and as cheap as it could be. You didn't hardly see anything expensive from town out there. But that silly-assed tombstone made me remember the world was full of beautiful expensive smooth big things that you could get if you had a little money. You could even have them put up over you when you died.

And that wasn't all. There was another thing about the BIRD- SONG stone. It seems silly when I remember about it, and it was an accident, something that was bound to happen one way or another right about that time, but even so I remember. What it was was when I had got to be about ten or eleven. I went up past the graveyard almost every day summer and winter on account of it being the way to school, to town, and to almost anywhere I went except fishing or 'coon hunting. And most often when I went by, I'd stop a spell and walk around the graveyard reading the stones. I can still see some of them: a thin worn old stone with ivy leaves cut in the top, and SAML. WHICHER carved on it. And the dates 1791–1843. And one with a cross. It said JOS. G. TALLEY, 14TH MISSISSIPPI REGT., CONFEDERATE STATES ARMY, MADE SACRIFICE FOR GOD AND COUNTRY IN VA. MAY 1864.

But I always got around to old BIRDSONG. I'd come at it from one end or the other, but I always ended up leaning across it staring over the side toward the road, looking down at the carved letters upside down:

CNOSDRIB

Or out at the cars passing in the summer evening, throwing pebbles up on the grass, cigarettes burning in the dark. Just laying over that old stone and kind of rubbing it and feeling its big smooth side against my belly. And one evening my old pecker come up like it had got infected by the contact and had turned to stone itself. It scared me some, but the feeling was more than the scare, so I just kept on sliding my cock back and forth and staring out at the cars going by with my mouth open like a slit boar, and pretty soon you know what happened. But it never had before, and it soaked my trousers and felt like somebody had stuffed a dead catfish in through my fly. It was awful, but it felt fine. At first I thought, Jesus Christ, I've sinned against this here stone, and now I'm sure to bleed my guts out for it. But right then I didn't care. I just laid on that stone, tired and sweaty, and grinned at the passing cars.

Sad to say, that wasn't the end of it. I mean it didn't get any worse, but I kept at that stone night in and night out. Sometimes it would be raining anvils and muleshoes, or cold as an Eskimo's gadget, but there I was out in the graveyard whomping old BIRDSONG of an evening. For four years. While I was growing up. God's wonder it didn't warp me or make me morbid or get me caught and shipped off to the funny-farm where they send kids who geek chickens or poke sheep. But I was sneaky and resourceful, and anyhow, what do you make of a kid leaning up against a tombstone? Even if his tail does move back and forth a little. Even if he does grin like a goddamned fool.

I don't know. I reckon I might still be out there shaming the dead and ruining my health and compromising my moral life. But when I was fourteen, I got religion. Not some of this canned horseshit they fling at you over the radio or sell like fatback in those supermarket city churches. But the real old-time stuff that sets your soul to quivering inside you like a leaf in a high wind. The kind that burns and chills and makes you want Jesus so bad your mouth goes dry and you can smell something like electric wiring all shorted out.

But I got to be honest. If it hadn't been for old BIRDSONG I might not ever have come across Jesus. Because it was grace and that damned stone that had me out in the graveyard one night when they were having a revival over in the church. It was cold, Lord, cold, with the ground froze like it knew the crops was all in. And when I finished my business with BIRDSONG I was pretty near froze solid myself. And on top of that I had to pee like a crazy man. I could pee out there. I could. But even then, lost in some kind of off-color living, I drew the line at pissing all over dead people. My folks for five generations were buried in that yard, and since we hadn't had a sackful of shit to call our own for five generations, none of them had a stone. I didn't even know where my great-grandaddy was. So I headed for the church. It wasn't much, but they had a crapper out back where there wasn't anybody buried.

So there I was, staring at the plank wall and listening to the hollow splash down below, and thinking about a Ford V-8 automobile with a greyhound on the hood that I had seen run by a while before. It was awful cold, and I peed for what seemed a long time, so I put my hands out against the jakes' walls and stopped thinking about anything.

Until, not sudden but slow like sometimes they bring up light in a movie house after the picture's done, I come to realizing that I was hearing somebody inside the church, and I was listening to what he was saying.

—Lord Jesus, spare these people. Lord Jesus, spare 'em. Don't mind their meanness nor their ugly twisted souls nor their dumb hard heads. Ignore their foul mouths and their hands that itch after every two-bit piece they see. Pay no heed to their eyes seeking out sin and their private parts welcoming it. Spare these people. Turn thy sight, O Lord, from the strutting and stumbling, growling and groaning, backsliding and backbiting that shames their days and desecrates their nights. Lord, send 'em repentance. Lord, melt their stony hearts, thaw the ice that binds their spirits. Lord, show 'em your power. Lord,

send down thy power. Lord, make 'em know you, come to
know you. Lord, be not merciful when mercy will not serve.
Lord, be not loving when love is a scandal. Lord, be not forgiv-
ing when thy forgiveness puffs 'em up and plants new outrage
in their ugly clotted minds.

—Lord, make it to thunder, Lord, let the proud stumble in
the storm of thy wrath. Lord, make the rain to fall. Lord, let
the harlots and makers of harlots drown in the downpouring of
thy justice. Hear me, Lord, Jesus hear me, God hear me. Turn
not thy judgment from us, Lord, let the rain fall . . .

I was still hanging over the jakes while the preacher went on.
At first I thought I was still leaking a little. Then it got louder,
the sound I heard. Then, before I could get my jeans buttoned
and out of that jakes, it hit full tilt.

You may have seen rain, but you never saw the beat of this.
It rained like somebody had found heaven's plug and given it
one good pull. It rained so goddamned hard I couldn't even see
the Baptist church, much less the road. There was thunder and
lightning and everything that preacher ordered. A wind come
with it and damned near pulled the outhouse over on top of
me. It broke out windows in the church and pushed a sapling
through the windshield of a Pierce-Arrow parked next to the
church. And when I squinted out toward the road, a bolt of
lightning hit BIRDSONG and raised chips of marble like a rifle
bullet. And it was right then I got converted. You don't have to
jam a red-hot poker up my fanny for me to see the light.

So two nights later I walked down the aisle of that self-same
church with that identical preacher holding out his hands and
beckoning, trying to look like a good shepherd gathering in a
stray. When I got there, he asked me real loud about Jesus as a
personal savior, and I said, yes, Lord, I need Him. I want Him,
I got to have Him. And he asked if I meant to give over idols
of the flesh and the world and cleave only to religion, to the
love of God and man, and I said, sure enough, there's no other
way. That's for me. And I meant it. So they took me and baptized me in a big tank they had, and when I come up out of
there I was as clean and pure as a lamb new cast. My soul was
a joy to the angels and a caution to dark powers. There wasn't

anything in the universe as pleasing to God just then as my new soul. And I meant to keep it that way.

But the world is a hard place and a snare is set at every turning. There's a halter by your breakfast plate, and pieces of silver set out where you do your work. A fierce terrible wind blows out of hell and it carries the genius of pestilence to sear the soul and bring it down like a dove under the gun.

There's no use going into it. The dirt on a man's soul is his own business. I never meant wrong, only that the world twists everything and the flesh pulls us down. Even giving of ourselves blackens us, and the love of man turns to our condemnation. If you don't think so, give it a try. See if you can live straight in this world.

Chapter Four

The night's long rain has washed out the sky, and only a fringe of cloud lies across the eastern horizon as the sun rises. It climbs gently, leaving the grass and shrubs bright with mingled dew and rain, the pavement sprinkled with slivers of moisture, and the ropy glistening paths of retreating snails. Bits of orange peel and milk-bottle caps litter the lawns. One small dog of uncertain breed slinks around the side of a garage, hamhock drooping from his jaws.

The houses are still dark under their eaves, the trees still deep olive below the sun's level. A newsboy, heaving copies of *The Shreveport Times* onto shadowed porches, whistled a tune he has heard on "The Camel Caravan." Something about a dancer. The middle part especially moves him, and as he passes down Archer Street, he sings it in uncertain contralto to astonished mockingbirds:

> *Once you said*
> *His love must wait its turn.*
> *You wanted fame instead,*
> *I guess that's your concern . . .*
> *We live and learn . . .*

We do indeed, Mary Ann Downey is thinking as she rises from the tousled bed and slips into her dress that looks even more like sackcloth in the early light. She cocks her head to hear the newsboy's song as he moves on. As she does so, twisting her dress until it suits her, she studies Christopher Nieman's pale body stretched out on the bed, one arm across his face, the other curled around the pillow she has just vacated. It is a boy's body, almost without hair, muscles firm and smooth, but without definition. In the half-shadow, he looks like a young athlete fallen asleep after some gruelling contest. The metaphor is not satisfactory, but it will do: he has traveled far in the brief hours between dice and sleep.

He has overleaped in a single bound the cavorting and shilly-shallying of adolescence, those numberless acned Arabian Nights. He has tasted woman and love and tenderness, its riches and its tricks. If he were never to awaken, his life would still be complete. He dreams of her pink tongue seeking his, her arms, silky and firm, strong and yielding; of her legs tight around his hips as if she were drawing his soul from him. He turns ever so slightly and smiles. There will be time.

But not enough to toss away the dawn, Mary Ann is thinking. She steps quietly into the parlor, only to bring down a final dismal cascade of empty beer cans as she brushes against the low table and almost steps into Billy Bob Stoker's face. He lies as if paralyzed, his large hands opening and closing upon nothing. He is not at peace. Mississippi floods his dreams. An old graveyard on the highway, and the deep scarlet ribbon of a sin without a name. His face twists as Mary Ann pauses above him. Jeremiah, still caught in sleep on the sofa, eyes half open, paws spread as if to embrace the universe, *urbi et orbi*, moans like a frightened puppy, a canine Cassandra who shares his master's dream.

For no reason she can then supply, Mary Ann drops to one knee and brushes her lips across Billy Bob's frowning forehead. Perhaps it is a consolation prize. Possibly she thinks of a distant brother. Or maybe she knows the stuff of evil dreams, the kind in which you are falling suddenly out of the sky past a broken steeple, into a dusty field, the kind which murders sleep.

Down the unsteady stairs, up the long driveway where unclipped strands of wet hedge gently touch her face. She walks slowly at first, purse under her arm, comb moving effortlessly through her long black hair. Far down the street toward Youree Drive, she can hear the newsboy whistling again, having given up his imitation of Vaughn Monroe.

She moves toward the sun, past a vacant lot, past a white frame house where a bald man in his undershirt and overalls is looking for his paper which invariably lands in the flowerbed. And reaches Kingshighway in time to see the sun clear the long leaves and transform shadows into surprises. The trolley stop is a quarter-mile away, and there is no sidewalk, but she sees only the summer flowers and the cloudless sky. She wonders if New Orleans is like they say. Then, she finds herself singing, too.

Dance on and on and on,
A thousand people here
Have come to see the show
As round and round you go . . .

LA BAS

". . . descended into hell . . ."

*If man had the singular fancy of
making himself absurd—a taste con-
fined to himself but attested by evidence exceedingly strong—he could
be as absurd as he liked; but God
could not be absurd.*

—Henry Adams

Mont St. Michel & Chartres

Chapter One

We are speaking now of New Orleans, a city joined by geography, by custom, by law to a state called Louisiana, which itself was once no more than the territory contiguous to New Orleans, a wilderness untracked and unmapped except by the moccasins of Indians and trappers and the uncertain cartography of Louis's (later Napoleon's) functionaries who would not know with any precision what they had dominion over until long after it had passed from their hands.

And we are standing now at the corner of Canal and Royal streets in the heart of that city where names like Canal and Royal are the exceptions, and where streets and avenues and circuses named Basin and Perdido, Jeff Davis and Lee and Burgundy and Ursulines and Ptchopatoulas are the rule.

This particular corner is not romantic. It is not possible to smell magnolia or cape jasmine here even in May and June; only diesel and cigar smoke, a stirring of stale cooking oil, a hint of rotting garden produce. There are shops here where tourists buy cheap radios and fifty-cent pipes and three-for-a-dime cigars and records by various small musical groups specializing in Afro-Cuban rhythms and repetitious lyrics. There is a pathetic imitation of the New York penny arcade with five-minute photo booths, pinball machines, a shooting gallery and a gadget that prints phony newspaper headlines. You too can see your name in headlines. Across the street you can buy shirts for $1.75 and whole suits (though no longer with two pairs of pants) for $29.95, though the shirts are cut badly, and collars frequently part company with bodies; though the suits are not well tailored or finished and frequently make their wearers look as if they had been deformed by some tragic and mysterious illness.

It is here, at this corner, that Mrs. Mailer gets off her streetcar and begins walking into the French Quarter. She is wearing a shawl and a small hat with a crumpled, defeated paper daisy on it. In her worn, delicately veined hands, Mrs. Mailer holds a large wicker basket suitable for bearing wet wash to the clothesline, or for carrying unwanted kittens to the Mississippi River bridge. This basket is outsized and its wicker frame is beginning to disintegrate. Thus it offers a multitude of sharp points and broken slivers to passersby and streetcar riders who find themselves sitting or standing near Mrs. Mailer. The basket is a source of irritation to streetcar conductors and passengers, to tourists and workmen and shop girls and businessmen who happen to be passing this busy corner.

Then there is Mrs. Mailer herself to consider. She is small, very small. So small, in fact, that while kindness denominates her *petite*, honesty cries *large dwarf*. But it is her face, her small round face beneath the archaic and tacky hat with ruined daisy that claims every glance. It is the face of the archetypal American mother: there is warmth, kindness in that face. The lines and creases lacing in and out around her snub nose and sweetly pouting lips could as well have been etched by humor as age. Perhaps both have played their part, for surely those eyes, twinkling and wise and blue, hold within them reels of memorable scenes, tragedy and laughter in equal parts, love and despair merged in the slow inexorable cycle of passing years. There are things this old lady must know; there are things she represents, things that seem to gather about her as if she were a kind of epicenter from which the whole French Quarter is filled with something it might otherwise lack.

But that basket. She passes down Royal Street, and as she comes abreast of Brennen's Restaurant, a workman kneeling, repairing the rich gold-script sign that is a signature of the place, turns his head to ask for a tool from his helper. He catches a broken wicker rod right in the eye. The pain is fantastic. Mrs.

Mailer, who has been walking and smiling and dreaming, pulls back her basket (which is filled on top, innocently enough, with gardenia and cape jasmine blossoms), and frowns at the howl of agony erupting from the workman who, kneeling, is perhaps five inches shorter than Mrs. Mailer.

—Goddamnit to hell, lady, watch what you do with that hamper, will you?

This, for a New Orleans workman, represents self-control equivalent to Sacher-Masoch passing up a free flagellation. But Mrs. Mailer is still frowning; she is inspecting her posies and backing away from the workman, whose face is covered with tears, whose hands are pressed over his eye.

—Kiss my ass, Mrs. Mailer says evenly, as if making a suggestion to an erring daughter-in-law. —Take it to the fucking mayor, you brokenballed chickenshit.

The workman lunges for Mrs. Mailer. Sure he knows it is a woman, and an uncommonly small woman at that. But pain knows no reason, and pain surcharged with such massive insult is a mad mad thing. Anyhow, he misses her and sprawls face downward across the pavement, his hands perhaps six inches from Mrs. Mailer's high-sided sober shoes. Close enough. Mrs. Mailer, frowning still, lifts her tiny foot and buries her heel half an inch in the workman's hand. So hard that when she lifts her foot to free it, the hand comes, too. She shakes her foot several times.

This time the shriek can be heard clearly (though not precisely identified) in front of Kolb's German Restaurant on St. Charles Street, and almost down to Nick's Hellenic Bar near North Peters on Canal. Passersby stare suddenly, attention drawn to the preposterous sight of a swarthy overweight Sicilian workman sprawled at the feet of a tiny little old lady. A masher? Surely not. Not even here in the French Quarter where exotics of every sort are common as red snapper turds on the bottom of the Gulf. But what else? An old flower lady attacking a sign-repair man? God forbid. Neither is plausible, but someone has to choose. And quick as cowboy justice, a young advertising man chooses and acts. He pushes Mrs. Mailer aside gently but firmly and steps on the workman's arm.

This time the sound is very small, very faint. A kind of gargling as if someone reaching for his accustomed Listerine had taken a swig and then glanced at the label to read there: HCl. The workman is on his back. His mouth is open like that of a coronary victim, which indeed by now he may be. The young ad man still has his heel and toe hard down on the curb. In between is a wrist. The young ad man smiles deprecatingly, a little embarrassed, perhaps. A lounging waiter out of Brennen's is holding his attaché case now, and someone else is just inside ringing up the police. The workman's helper has disappeared with the tool kit. The workman is no longer gargling. He is blue turning gray in the face, and there seems to be no end to this mess.

Meanwhile Mrs. Mailer is walking, walking with little uncertain steps past the Court of Four Brothers, crossing over to take a look down Pirate's Alley. She is smiling and nodding. A passing priest in a panama hat with a camera (Exacta) hanging around his neck like a small mechanical albatross drops a dollar in her basket and plucks out a cape jasmine blossom. Mrs. Mailer stares at him quizzically, still smiling, and hastens to cover the vacant spot in the tray by spreading her flowers about. A Negro starts toward her out of a dilapidated doorway near the Sunshine Boarding House. She shakes her head, not smiling at all, and balls her fist. The Negro retreats, shaking his head in perfect mimicry, snapping his fingers and singing:

> You say you gonna leave me,
> Fact is I wisht you would.
> Say you gonna leave me,
> I wisht I wisht you would.
> You tears up my well-bein',
> Baby, why ain't you no goddamn good.

From the balcony of 808 Royal Street, a heavy personage with sunglasses and thinning hair stares down on Mrs. Mailer as she approaches past the corner A&P, past the import store and the Bruise & Son antique shop. The sunglasses are prescription and very thick. Behind them are vague uncentered eyes almost colorless, irises edgeless and confused with the tiny pupils. He is fat, with excess flesh drooping downward from his shoulders and gathered in around the hips like a smock of lifeless plush. He wears only an undershirt. There is no hair on his chest or arms. He lifts his left arm to push back a plaque of hair away from his round face. On the side of the biceps, just below the armpit, there is a shiny scar that stands out against the bloodless dead-white skin around it.

Mrs. Mailer glances upward and sees a blurred motion of scratching as the personage vanishes backward off the balcony into shadow. She nods twice and turns back to walk down St. Ann Street toward Decatur Street, past Jackson Square. She stops in front of the Café du Monde, and hangs her wicker basket on the iron rail that separates the open sidewalk from the tables where steaming coffee and hot square donuts are being served to tourists just up and locals about to go to bed somewhere or other.

Mrs. Mailer leans over and hitches up her stockings (genuine linsey-woolsey: her single clear-cut affectation. All the rest is genuine, depending upon how you understand it) and retrieves her basket. She inches through the early French Market crowd toward an empty table in the covered outdoor café. A teacher of college English from Baton Rouge catches a sliver of wicker in the ear. His singularly beautiful wife glares at Mrs. Mailer, who smiles widely. The teacher shrugs and begins talking expansively and at length again.

It is a beauteous morning, calm and free. There is the faintest of river breezes, and the stench of cabbages, tomatoes, fresh fish and street-leavings is leavened by a tincture of early-morning rain just fading from the street, still rising from concrete and grass as the sun climbs. In another hour it will be hot; in another two, unbearable. But this is an excellent hour, and Mrs. Mailer has long since mastered the art of seizing the hour, knowing that whole days are hard to come by and scarcely ever seizable. She breathes deeply, catching the thick Byzantine odor of her flowers in arcane admixture with the morning's other scents.

It is rumored in the Quarter that Mrs. Mailer was once a

beautiful woman. It is the kind of rumor that draws sighs from
the old wreck who hawks the *States-Item* outside a cigar store
on the corner of Canal and Royal, and snickers from the
young punk in a surplus Eisenhower jacket who delivers for
Silvio's grocery. It is said too that Mrs. Mailer had once been a
veritable belle. That all Boston high life knew her face, was
captivated by the grace of her carriage as she waltzed away the
evenings, rode past mornings and strolled through afternoons
in that famous derelict old town.

But providence had dealt harshly with her. A man from New
Orleans had won her, wed her and brought her to the South.
To preside, she had thought, over another society as hopelessly
decadent and purposeless as her own—hence one of proper de-
meanor, one of meet character. She had come imperious, had
arranged a party meant to establish her credentials, her indis-
putable claim to social authority in the town.

But things had gone, to say the least, badly. The party was
well attended, but by most peculiar people, and only a few
women turned up at all. There was loud uncultivated talk, and
a band of darkies playing crude jazz. Jelly Roll somebody and
his Red Hot Peppers. Worse than no music at all. And it got
worse still. An indecent story told loudly, a story not only in-
delicate but strange. Followed by loud laughter—including
deep throaty laughter from one tall muscular woman whose evening gown kept slipping lower and lower, revealing, paradoxi-
cally, less and less. And more drinking. Until one man minced
into a corner and vomited, and the band played raw sensual
music, and Mrs. Mailer began to believe that she had somehow died without knowing it and been translated directly into
hell, and not only hell, but that particular province of perdition wherein dwelled the sons of Belial whose offenses and
the character of them were well recorded in the racial memory of Mrs. Mailer's glacial ancestry.

She could not find her husband. She wanted it to end. Someone came running into the room calling in loud falsetto, —Lusitania's gone down.

—Who's she? someone howled.

—Who's he? another guffawed.

—Lusitania's missed the party.

—Let's everybody go down.

And as Mrs. Mailer watched, the tall muscular woman began dancing with the man who had minced back from his untidy corner. After a dozen faltering drunken steps, the woman's dress fell down entirely as they played the "Jelly-Roll Blues," and Mrs. Mailer saw that the woman had no breasts at all, but a quantity of hair below the shaved line of décolleté, and as her head twisted away in horror, she saw coming down the spiral staircase her husband, laughing, smiling, waving to everyone, and wearing a lovely dark blue gown.

It was not a long trip from the St. Charles Street house Mrs. Mailer left that evening to the boarding house on Decatur that locals called Shank of the Night, in honor of the glad and frenetic times to be had in the parlor and certain upper rooms (and, some said, named too for the various soft and hard sores that sometimes informed a roisterer that there might be a venereal surtax on the flat rate he had paid in coin for his merriment).

It was not much farther into Storyville itself where Mahogany Hall and Tillie's, the Round House and Hotel de Ville were swinging from six to six, seven days a week. Mrs. Mailer did not fit at first, but when, once in a while, she considered poisoning or strangling her next woozy trick, she would remember that party, that staircase, and what she had seen descending it —and the next mark, crude or full of finesse, half drunk or somberly sober, would get a splendid turn. Not for his own sake, but in honor of masculinity which, with all its defects, served to cleanse Mrs. Mailer's memory for at least the duration of her frivolous labors.

⋅⋅§ §⋅⋅

Whatever she may have lost in transit from Boston to bordello, Mrs. Mailer learned considerable. For example, she found that Jelly Roll somebody's name was Morton, and that the Red Hot Peppers were better known between Rampart Street and the river than was President Wilson—and far more seriously appreciated. She found too that Mr. Jelly owned part of the

house in which she now earned her bread. Life, somebody had
said, reminds me of leapfrog.

Whether a hooker's working life is gray or gold is a question
up for grabs. But it tends to be short. Like other athletes, the
whore begins to fade, to fall from major to minor league, until
finally only manager status is left. But there are more worn-out
old pros in this circuit, too, than there are clubs to run. Which
means some of the girls are going to end out on the street. Mrs.
Mailer had stayed in the bullpen (or batter's box: tailor the
metaphor to suit yourself) from 1915 to 1934. Twenty years on
the ball is pretty good what with changing fashions and that
loathsome masculine characteristic of preferring a pretty face
and a slim waist to almost any amount of style, drive and experience. So Mrs. Mailer had survived Storyville, Jelly Roll, the
heyday of St. Charles Street society (which she had never en-
countered in an upright position anyhow) and the prewar Indian summer of distant Boston's long influencial reign. The
wind spares what is under the rock. Only top water makes
waves. Under rocks or in deep water it is darker, and the pressure is constant. But there are consolations.

By the time Mrs. Mailer is past her working life in the now
more or less orderly houses remaining after the Navy, full of
jazz haters, has run all the Adams and Eves out of the Quarter
and posted cops with flaming swords at the gate, a number of
new enterprises have, as it were, popped up. An Oriental habit
has caught on. Even in New Orleans there are any number of
what Mrs. Mailer had been raised to call dope fiends. From pot
to hash, the whole spectrum of personality disintegrators is
worth a good hard push. Her last madam had put Mrs. Mailer
in the way of an ancient Sicilian type who got his bags buried
in shipments of imported garlic, in the numberless crates of
antipasto and anchovies (which tin has the pony?) he regularly
received.

As it turns out, Mrs. Mailer outlasts the Sicilian, too, and
becomes chief hash-slinger for the Quarter. As the market
widens and the take increases, she does very well indeed. She
could retire. She could buy a half-block of St. Charles Street
and go see what, if anything, she had missed. But blood tells.

Mrs. Mailer comes from a long line of hard bargainers and daring merchant adventurers. Her great-grandfather had sold slaves to William Byrd at Berkeley's Hundred (her grandfather, as a matter of fact, had fought in the same vicinity to free those slaves, but then, as some New England contemporary had said, a foolish consistency is the hobgoblin of tiny minds) and she could not turn the trade over to bunglers. One continues. One keeps on keeping on.

And so now, in 1946, a little pinched of face, a little gaunt, perhaps a trifle more cynical than when she had first come South, Mrs. Mailer still roams the Quarter with a basket of flowers, magnolia blooms, camellias, cape jasmine, gardenias. And under the blossoms are tiny packets of what looks like sugar or plaster of paris. Each is worth twenty times the price of all the flowers, and the value of all those bags is considerable indeed. Back in her apartment on Royal Street, in the false bottom of an old icebox, Mrs. Mailer has almost a kilo of this same white powder. It is enough to keep every mainliner on the North American continent jumping like a flea in heat for two or three months. It is also worth something over $300,000, and federal narcotics agents would give its weight in blood to know the name of the smart vicious supercriminal who controls dope in New Orleans. Once they got close. They had their eyes on a Negro garage mechanic, a grocery delivery boy, an old lady who sells flowers. But when they were brought in, all of them were clean, and none of them would talk of that shadowy *éminence grise* somewhere above who ran the ugly show.

Mrs. Mailer was clean that day because she was handling one of her sidelines. She was scouting the bars and nightspots, prowling the hamburger joints and ten-cent stores looking for young talent. Benny Boundoch, Brigadier of the Bordellos, needs new troops constantly. The war against virtue is not without attrition. Nature, like law, is against him. Girls, however careful, will get knocked up. Then new girls must, to turn a phrase, fill the gap while the wounded are sent over to the medical corps where Dr. Aorta, a new resident of the Quarter, is rapidly building the reputation of a great exterminator. What girl who comes to him leaves unemptied? He is an expert in purge. His spe-

cialty is thwarting invasion of privacy. Embryonic sallies re-
pulsed fill him with some indefinable pleasure.

It is a full life, then: narcotics, prostitution, abortion. Only a
professional assassin is needed to round out the scheme. But in
that particular racket, a good man is hard to find. A whore on
hash is a girl you can trust. She will not leave her supply; she
will not even argue much over the price. Dr. Aorta is dependable because he loves his work. Neither the whoremaster nor
the abortionist sweats Mrs. Mailer. She is, as in another place
all her ancestors were, a pillar of this subterranean commun-
ity. Custom and tradition link her with such dim and legendary
figures as King Oliver and May Twiggs, Sally Suckup and
Buddy Bolden. Some of the newer residents can see, in their
mind's eye, Mrs. Mailer as toast of the main deck when the
great steamers roved the Mississippi. If the dream is fraudulent, Mrs. Mailer has the qualities to sustain it. She is, with
marvelous *esprit,* an embodiment of that old South which
was marked by red lights instead of white pillars, and unlike
that even older South, she has survived her Appomattox,
brought on by Wilson's navy standing in for Lincoln's army,
and has endured.

Now she stares out at the excursion busses gathered on the
corner of Jackson Square. Drivers are hustling early-rising tourists, but most of the *ausländers* are attracted to horse-drawn
hackneys piloted by smiling Uncle Toms who carry the weight
of legend on their stooped shoulders and its cold reality in their
hearts. Inside the wrought-iron fence surrounding the square
Mrs. Mailer can barely make out the upheld cocked hat of Andrew Jackson, but she is familiar with the inscription on the
statue's base: *The Union Must and Shall Be Preserved.* Carved
there by Yankees during the city's occupation, the words are lost
on Mrs. Mailer. She believes they have to do with Jackson's
fierce defense of his own marriage and the questioned integrity
of his wife—which integrity, whether or not it was, was, being
preserved, whether it was or not. She admires the general and
thinks more men should duel on behalf of women. It would
keep them away from home, off the bottle, and out of vicious
moods. She likes a man who looks out for his cunt.

Directly across from her table is a red brick building containing, on the ground floor, a wine merchant's, and a grocer
specializing in foreign delicacies. But high above the signs of
commerce there is something amazing attached to the bricks.
It is a white representation of a seahorse, perhaps two and a
half feet high, and staring in profile out at the endless traffic
that comes toward the French Market from Canal past the Jax
Brewery.

A waiter elbows Mrs. Mailer and makes as if to snatch one
of her blossoms. She fixes him with a hard stare.

—You wanna die, cocksucker?

He grins lamely. —One with, two without, and a double
plate of those sponges, Mrs. Mailer tells him.

The waiter, a buck-toothed Frenchie with curly, waxed hair
and a moustache that looks like dried blood on his upper
lip, tries for humor again.

—How much for a sky-ride?

—You better blast off under your own power, turkey-geek. I
got a nigger who owes me one murder and a pair of castrations.

The waiter, overawed or outlipped, blasts off just as the fat
man from Royal Street slumps down in a chair opposite Mrs.
Mailer. He lifts his glasses for a moment and stares at her as if
to verify her identity. Mrs. Mailer shivers despite herself. As
if a cloud had suddenly dumped snow into the summer air.
She has been around, Mrs. Mailer has, and she has come up
against every kind of human granite quarried. She has worked
out of a trailer-house handling three or four dozen tricks a
night. She has had a Swedish sailor, in the very vortex of orgasm, suffer a massive coronary and fall forward like a ton of
fish, his dead forehead striking hers and knocking her cold so
that she awoke still under the load two hours later with other
customers pounding on the trailer's thin door and screaming,
asking if she were still alive and working. She has even lived
for a year with a Methodist minister whose wife, so he claimed,
did not understand him. Which was probably so. In the year
that passed before Mrs. Mailer decided that there is more to living than religion, the minister never so much as removed his
shirt. He rather unbuttoned his fly and ordered Mrs. Mailer to

place her bare foot inside and wiggle her toes. All of that is past, however, and even provides laughs in retrospect. But Mrs. Mailer finds nothing to laugh about in the fat man opposite who has lowered his glasses and lit a cigarette with a small silver lighter inscribed in some foreign tongue, and with a blank spot above, as if a plaque or crest had been lost from it. She wishes frequently that she had never hooked up with him, but what can a girl say to money? Yes I will yes, is what she will likely say, even if the deal is with a real wild card who looks like he is mainlining Formalin or sniffing airplane glue.

The waiter, subdued now and smirking at the fat man, sets a cup of coffee, chicory and milk in front of him, two cups black before Mrs. Mailer, and a plate of *bagnets* between them.

—Any other little thing for youall this morning?

—Go off, Dr. Aorta says, before Mrs. Mailer can say haul ass. The waiter gets the message. He picks up the half-dollar Dr. Aorta has set on the tabletop and moves away quickly. Mrs. Mailer sips her coffee even though it is too hot. She cannot stand to be around Dr. Aorta without doing something, without being occupied. It is not the Protestant ethic; it is simply that the doctor gives her the horribles, and glands will not be reasonable.

Dr. Aorta whistles tunelessly a stately slow-paced march, holds his cigarette between thumb and first finger as if it were potentially dangerous. He nigger-lips, Mrs. Mailer thinks, seeing the cigarette's butt wet half an inch up its length. The doctor's hands are remarkably pale and their shape is enough to give an art historian palpitations. The fingers are like sausages with little definition between knuckle and joint, and the palms are as thick as those seen almost universally in the work of Flemish masters. They appear to have little strength, but Mrs. Mailer is not so sure. She has an excellent intuition, and it rings like a burglar alarm every time Dr. Aorta shambles into view.

—A miserable morning, Dr. Aorta says, dropping his cigarette to the floor unsnuffed and lifting his coffee cup in both hands. —Miserable night. I don't sleep anymore. Only some in the afternoon.

—You ought to see a doctor, Mrs. Mailer says placatingly,

inanely. She is anyone's match ninety-nine percent of the time, but the doctor puts her off.

—Quacks, he says, as if she had said nothing, as if he had thought of going to a doctor himself. —Filthy quacks with pedestrian experience and no insight. I know what is wrong. I need a change.

—Whyn't you take a vacation? Mrs. Mailer asks. —You can afford it, she laughs.

—I don't travel. This is as far as I go. I think this is too far. One of these days . . .

Mrs. Mailer has no idea what Dr. Aorta fears, but she suspects that it would dwarf anything she has ever had reason to fear. If she were inclined to theology, she might imagine that Aorta had made compact with the devil. But she is early twentieth-century urban. She knows that mares are not inseminated by an east wind, and she has not lately heard of the devil in any context more profound than that of archaic slang.

—I got a mark, she says after a respectful pause, dedicated, she supposes, to the unnamed agents that stalk Aorta's destiny denying him rest and a vacation. If he were to tell her his secret agony is hemorrhoids, she would not believe him.

—How much?

—Two-fifty. Cut and collect. Nice girl. Worked out of the Black Hole till last April. She went for love. Some spic. He bumped her and went native again. Mexico or Puerto Rico. Bad asses.

—Two-fifty is okay. You don't get a lot of two-fifties any more. Last April? A long time.

—Too many operators operating. Competition pulls the price down. Only this girl says she wants to see another April, so she wants you. Maybe she wants to go after that greaser.

—I should let my hand slip and do her a favor. Last April is a long time.

—None of that. Then you got to get in Marshall Fields and out goes fifty. And somebody is bound to catch up with that nigger yet. He's been playing garbage man for every cutter in town since 1940. He dumps everything. Once he got one into the tank at Tulane Medical School. It was six weeks before that one came up and they found four bullets in it. My God, the cops were squirting all over the Quarter. They tried to grill everything but the priests over at the cathedral. And Marshall Fields. He just pulled his cart up and sorted out the garbage while the bulls were leaning on me. If I had crapped out and told 'em it was that jig, they'd have pulled me in for a psycho check.

Dr. Aorta is paying no attention. He lights another cigarette and dusts powdered sugar off his hands.

Mrs. Mailer sniffs. —Jesus Christ, she chokes. —Not out on the street. What are you smoking?

Dr. Aorta's eyebrows come together. —Shut up, he says. —Without a public announcement, shut up.

Mrs. Mailer shrugs. —It's your seven years. Just don't louse up the supply. You ought to tell me where you get it. What if something happened to you? What would I do?

—What did you do before I got here?

Mrs. Mailer shudders. —It was awful, she says. —I wasn't meant for that. I was raised better.

—It will be awful again, Dr. Aorta says, finishing his cigarette and dropping the butt into his coffee cup. —It always becomes awful again. Don't get used to this good living. You will be back in the trailer before it is over.

—Where will you be?

Aorta smiles and squints up at the seahorse rampant and enraged against the red bourgeois bricks. He wonders as often as he sees the figure what kind of mind has ordered it placed there. —When it's over? Scattered all over the world. I have it in my will. They must burn me and scatter my ashes from planes over America, Europe, and Asia. I don't give a damn for the rest. I want to be cremated.

—How come? Mrs. Mailer asks, recollecting, without knowing why, the Methodist preacher and the strength of her past premonitions.

—I am eccentric, Dr. Aorta tells her. —I want to cover the earth. His soul goes marching on. What about your soul, Mrs. Mailer?

—My what?

—You believe in God?

—I don't care. If He ain't up there He can't hurt me. If He is, why don't He send me a five-dollar bill?

Aorta is still studying the seahorse. From twenty fathoms. Down where nothing burns. But rust is the same as burning. Under the sea. And they say God is down there as He is everywhere with His flail, His punishing instrument which men call time. Striking away youth, flesh, life, monuments, pretensions, blow after blow.

In Mexico, Dr. Aorta had studied theology. In the lean year before he had come across, there had been only a set of the Church fathers in English. He had read the Greek and Latin fathers, the doctors, the medieval theoreticians who had closed the universe within their dialectic.

—He may send you ten pounds pure.

—You're crazy, Mrs. Mailer squeaks. She does not usually speak so to Dr. Aorta. But ten pounds. Pure. Could even the Lord so provide?

—Drink your coffee.

Mrs. Mailer is trembling. She thinks at first he is joking. But he never jokes. He always means it. But where could you stash ten pounds? Where could you get ten pounds? He has to be kidding. But he never . . . this time he is.

Dr. Aorta shifts his sunglasses and flicks ashes into his pale coffee, pale saucer. —Some Turk, he says. —In Vera Cruz. He wanted to go home. He sold his patrimony to my Mexican friend. The friend sent a small part on.

—A small part . . .

—Infinitesimally small. The Turk had two hundred and ten kilos in his yacht . . .

—What's kilos? Mrs. Mailer quavers. She pushes her flower basket under the table. There are four ounces in it. Once she would have thought that was big time. He . . . it *was* big time. It would stoke every crazy fire in New Orleans for two days. But ten pounds. Even her cut, her measly cut, would be enough to quit.

Dr. Aorta is shaking his head slowly. —No vacation this year either. A woman's work is never done.

The cliché brings Mrs. Mailer back to life. —But you sure cut into their business, she leers.

Aorta frowns almost sadly.

—Did you ever think that this is all delusion? This stuff. For a few hours it pushes away the world, but the world comes back, like . . . the wooden wheel on a string. What is it?

—Yo-yo, Mrs. Mailer says hesitantly.

—Yo-yo. And the job. You come to the apartment with something in your belly and you go to sleep. And I come in. And later you wake up and walk out without anything in your belly. Maybe you come to believe nothing was ever in your belly. But there was. There was something. And you and I know about the yo-yo, how it comes back. We know about what this girl had in her belly. You have seen me wash it off my hands.

All this makes Mrs. Mailer uncomfortable. She has not heard anything like it in thirty years. Not since Boston. What is worse, Dr. Aorta, beginning gravely, is starting to grin. At least it is something like a grin. What do you make of such talk when the speaker is grinning?

—And Boundoch's whorehouse, Dr. Aorta goes on, his wide tight-lipped smile malicious beneath vague swimming spectacled eyes which take no part in the mouth's twisting. —More illusion. You go there for love. The one place in town where for certain there is no love. Did you love, Mrs. Mailer? When they came to the trailer. Did you love?

Mrs. Mailer feels somehow that she should resent this, that Dr. Aorta is insulting her profoundly. But it is only a feeling, some inchoate long-dormant chord of sensibility faintly strumming in response to his words. He is talking to her as if she were a sentient being. She suspects that at least she should be bored. But it is fascinating. Like a crone in the balcony of a seedy theater watching in an ancient silent movie the brutal rape of a young virgin.

—No, Mrs. Mailer, Dr. Aorta says, tapping a Picayune cigarette with his carefully manicured thumbnail. —No one has loved you. Have they?

—My husband, Mrs. Mailer begins automatically. For years she has told the story of how her husband went down with *Lusi-*

tania. A splendid hairy man he had been. Ladies and children first. Has told the story so often, added so many likely touches at each telling that, except for the ineradicable memory of that bright blue gown, she might by now have begun to believe it herself. But it is no good. Belief or the lack of it—neither matters with this man. It is as if Dr. Aorta could see into her, as if he knows in consummate detail every lie and self-deception that she has fabricated in those thirty years. As if he knows that Mr. Jelly Roll refused her offered body one night in 1916, that she has lost track of the number of abortions she has had, and similarly lost track of the fruit of a drunken night that developed too far for the curette before she could gather the price of its handler. Dr. Aorta knows good and evil, Mrs. Mailer suspects. To lie to him is to waste breath.

—No, Dr. Aorta is saying with humorous indifference, —no one. Life is very long. What do you do with so much life?

—Live it, Mrs. Mailer shoots back, feeling at last the firm ground of positivist cliché beneath her.

—Just so, Dr. Aorta returns, rising and moving past the moustached waiter who steps a pace or two out of his path. —Just so. You live it, which is to say you purchase or manufacture one kind of illusion or another. Which is to say you butcher reality. Which means we kill everything but ourselves in order to pretend to live. Which is to say . . .

Mrs. Mailer is walking behind him now, astounded that he is talking out loud, his voice carrying across, above the dull thunder of conversation from the tables all around them. The LSU instructor of English looks up with a puzzled frown just in time to catch Mrs. Mailer's untidy basket in the back of his head. His lovely wife shies her purse at Mrs. Mailer, who pays no mind, following in Dr. Aorta's wake like a tranced seahorse. Rapture of the deep, perhaps. Breathing in an alien element.

—. . . that Schopenhauer has something to recommend him.

Doctor Aorta

⚜

What I remember is of little consequence because I have mastered the art of remembering almost nothing but what is of no importance. I can remember the number of steel crosspieces in the railway bridge across the Rhine at Strasbourg. I remember very clearly the countryside in Surrey one sees headed southwest from London. I recall the number of stairs going down to the Underground platform at the Russell Square Station, and a peculiar bulbous growth on the side of a tree in the Champs Elysées.

I remember a woman in Barcelona who, they say, had mastered the art of removing a five-month fetus with the crudest of instruments and a drug, the name of which I was unable to discover; I have not forgotten three blind men in Lyons who received certain medical attentions from me in 1943.

I cannot forget the names of the first four Roman popes, the bishop who saw Joan of Lorraine to the stake, the year of Alexander the Great's death, or the fate of Caligula's son.

But what I recall best is that life is a bore. There is nothing in it but one banality after another, and the aspects of it which most stir our hopes and expectations are precisely those which we find at last most tedious and meaningless.

Neither family nor religion nor nationality had, in my youth, nets fine enough to snare me. I was, in the Italian phrase, born with my eyes open. I suspect my mouth was open, too. In a broad and heartfelt yawn.

As a child I was cross, pettish and almost without curiosity.

I could sit for hours staring into open fires, examining my fingers, counting the tassels on a lampshade beside my mother's bed. I cared for nothing and remembered everything.

I remember the wistful Jewishness of my father and the arrogant Germanity of my mother. There was nothing in it, of course. They were both Germans, both Jews, and both bored me dreadfully with their proffered heroes: Judas Maccabeus or Tristan, Josephus or Nietzsche. My father kept the kosher; my mother flaunted pork and the entrails of fowls. Butter and beef at the same meal, chops of lamb with a cheese sauce.

My father practiced law. My mother, in the early days, be-tween the wars, interested herself in politics, supporting one party and then another, seeking always to find a scapegoat upon whom to fix our loss in 1918.

Had the workers worked? It seemed so. Had the businessmen sacrificed? To some degree. Had the politicians promoted wise policies? As wise as—or at least no more foolish than—usual. Had the soldiers fought? The lists of dead and maimed surely indicated it.

And so on. Until she came upon the Catholics. Bavaria was Catholic. Austria was Catholic. Italy was Catholic. And all had in some way participated in the defeat. Bavarian troops in the southern sector had, on occasion, fought badly. The Austrians had never managed to get down into Italy's heart. And the Italians had betrayed ancient friendships and sided with the allies. It had been, my mother decided, the Catholics. So my mother told me, so she told my father. So she informed her friends.

Unfortunately, even as she did so, in fact, as if in answer to her, there was an Austrian of Catholic rearing in Bavaria (with considerable admiration for the current Italian dictator), who had struck upon another villain for the same show. I have often wondered incuriously if my mother's harping created him like a genie in a bottle. There seems to be a universal economy in nature; perhaps there is a universal balance, too.

My father was a nonentity. I do not mean to insult him, or even to suggest that he was not a good man. If one finds plea-sure in moral assessment, my father might be termed an hon-orable and decent man, full of justice and respect for his fellows and contempt for those who ride the earth as if they had been born jack-booted and sharp-spurred, above the common lot of men. In fact, I suspect it may have been these very qualities that made father a nonentity philosophically during the days of the Weimar Republic, and a nonentity physically as well during what followed the republic's collapse.

I was twenty-one in 1926. Times were bad then, though less bad than a few years before. We lived in Karlsruhe in those days, a quiet town built almost in a circle, and full of people who had, or so it seemed, nothing but their own private interests at heart. My mother's anti-Catholicism was a curiosity among them, but my father's kindness and generosity made most people there simply shrug off mother's lunatic sentiments. There was no talk of war or army in the Rhineland, and even nationality seemed muted.

So it seemed. In 1926. When I was about to leave for medical training in Edinburgh. Not because I wished to practice medicine, but because it was necessary that I learn a profession and the law was then, so my father said, a dead end. Not because Edinburgh was more advanced in medical skills than German universities, but because my father wished that I should become cosmopolitan, one who knew many cities and the ways of men. And, though I may do his memory an injustice, because my going to Scotland scandalized and outraged my mother past ranting, past tears. Almost to the point of violence. But actual violence was beyond her. Only her tongue knew violence, and both I and my father died a thousand little deaths from its woundings.

Before I left, there was a ritual to be undergone. I had avoided rites and ceremonies of all sorts since the gloomy misery of bar mitzvah. But there was no escaping a final talk with my father before I left home for Great Britain. I was surprised to find he had no more taste for it than I. He was no rhetorician and no debater, either. He did not relish talking into the air, and in those days I was no more audience than a pillar of salt or a bag of stones.

—You have no faith, he told me. —Your Jewishness is dead in you. Nothing quickens your spirit.

—Yes, I said, trying, unconsciously perhaps, to speed him along, to make the thing easier for both of us.

—What do you know that makes you the way you are? my father asked.

I could feel my breath short and quick. It was as if my gentle father had become an inquisitor. —I know I have four thousand marks and a ticket to London in my pocket, I said. —What else am I supposed to know?

—What do you feel? What of God?

I did not mean to sound supercilious, but where could all this lead? —I feel fine. I cannot say how God feels. There is no commerce between us. I await His pleasure.

My father shook his head, his small Trotskyish beard waggling slowly. —Nor is there commerce between my son and me. Where is the world going when father and son part as strangers?

I wanted to tell him that parents and children always part as strangers, and that when we met again it would be as two who have known one another casually in another time, but have found little to bind, and hardly anything to enlarge, the relationship between them. But I told him nothing, for in those days there was still a kind of customary positioning of persons: fathers told; sons listened. For twenty years of decent food and housing, for the four thousand marks and the London ticket, I owed him that much. As he turned from me toward the study window looking out upon our garden filled with autumn flowers and evergreen trees, I backed toward the door. Something within me—not love or reverence or even sentiment, but rather something without a name, some odd impulse, some prophetic instinct—made me pause and fix him, his stooped shoulders and balding head, his long, slim, almost womanish hands in the tissue of my memory. I remember that he had taken off his gold-rimmed pince-nez and was wiping it slowly, mechanically, as I hesitated there.

—Good-bye, Frederick, he said with unaccustomed softness and precision. —Good-bye and good fortune.

But I said nothing, moving out of the room like one who has invaded the past with the help of a machine and who must nei-

ther speak nor act in that already determined, already consummated time. I remember, as I left the house and hailed a
cab, wishing that I might have seen his face as he stared out into
the garden searching the neat lawn, the swaying dahlias for the
thumbprint of his God, or a butterfly bearing word of his destiny. I was sorry to be taking his son from him, but sorrow is an
unclinical emotion, and the fires it kindles wink out in the light
of stars.

I did not see him again. Not alive. Not in the flesh. I saw only,
in 1942, in the Munich Gestapo Records Room some photographs of him following his final interrogation. The change was
astounding, the damage beyond description. An autopsy would
have been out of the question.

&§ §&

I remember Britain. A museum full of various pasts stuffed
and cared for as if history were truth rather than hallucination,
as if men and events of one century mattered to those of another. As if it were more than a secular monstrance holding ancient and crumbling wafers from which the spirit had flown
ages before. I remember thinking that Trafalgar Square had
about it the same sort of fantasy as Red Square in Moscow, but
lacked even a corpse. I was glad to be back in Germany in 1932.
It was a strange time, but despite the strangeness, it was a time
in which realities were faced and dealt with; a time in which
ultimate issues were resolved by ultimate means.

There was, soon after I returned, a change of government.
The German corpse, Old Hindenburg, a monument and parody
of himself, still lumbered and coughed on for a little while as
chief of state. But realism had caught all of us by the throat.
When the new chancellor was called on to form a government,
I thought of the violent days in Texas of the United States. Gun-
fighters. The trappings of civilization: some indeed could read
and write. But blood and iron was the currency and purchase
then. So with Germany. Surrealism had succeeded no better
than starvation. Dignity had worn its shoes through. The time
had come for reality to take charge.

I remember the rallies at Nuremburg. Utter honesty. As if

wolves or hydrogen atoms or volcanoes could talk and assume
political roles. Destruction, violence, greatness, eternity. The
Reich will last a thousand years. Of course it wouldn't. Not a
century. Probably not a decade. But there is, as my father
might have said, a time to build and a time to tear down. What
of the time to do both and neither simultaneously? So all of
them (not "us": I was not that kind of German. I was of no na-
tion. But had I not been in Germany, you understand, I would
have crossed seven oceans to be there where boredom was, for
twelve years, somewhat abated) became one, and the dedica-
tion, like any similar pact, was final and irreversible. We (by
then it was "we." I had a party card and the good opinion of
certain officials in the SS. Medical units were already formed to
handle those wounded in street brawls with Communists at
first; in house-to-house searches for Jews later on) had begun a
social experiment. What I thought of it is of no consequence:
it was active, like the lashing of a caged panther's tail, like an
angry squirming serpent. And Aristotle himself admitted that
the end of life is an action—not a quality. So there was nothing
moral to consider. I neither approved nor disapproved of the
party and its ends and means. I was not a priest or a logician,
though I had the cunning of one and the subtlety of the other.
I had come to despise both functions. I thought then, and I
think now, that my mind and spirit were meant to animate an
athlete, but the body was no good: bad eyes, a slight tendency
toward bronchial complications, and corpulence. Not really fat
until much later, but always too bulky for the playing field.
And not that sort of athlete anyhow: rather a gladiator in the
arena of the late emperors—those whose thumbs were always
down, whose own blood was shed like water, Galba, Otho? And
so in this more degenerate time, a career of imposing my will
on material like an artist. But not stone or paint or language.
Rather flesh. Not the playing field for me, but the surgeon's
auditorium. Finally, at Ravensbrück, at Belsen, at Dachau, the
inestimable privilege of free experiment untrammeled by any
subsidiary consideration, any irrelevancy.

I remember that world, the dark universe that Germany became after 1934, as if it had been a dream. Those of us who had

position were absolute. We were given ranks and duties, and it was not asked of us how or at what cost in relevancies we accomplished our duties or made use of our ranks. There was, you see, a philosophy at work here: a conception as plain and hardy as the fabric of creation itself, stripped of the myriad absurdities and suppositions of our enemies. That which deserves to live, lives. That which can exert its power on another proves its right to do so by the very act of so doing. While I worked with muscular transplants at Ravensbrück, making use of Polish women, political prisoners, there was no need to consider anything beyond the medical proprieties. In a sense, these women had no purpose or existence outside the experiments. By the fact of their being unable to determine their own destinies, they had no destinies of their own. One suffers because one cannot, for one reason or another, avoid it. One rules because he is placed in a position where there is no real alternative to ruling. One becomes, in a more complex sense, a guinea pig because he is not a surgeon.

I recall an evening in the officer's club in Munich. We had driven in from Dachau, the camp commandant and I, to meet the commandant's brother, a colonel in the Seventh Panzer Grenadiers. It was late 1943, and the colonel's division was on its way to the eastern front.

The club was filled with uproarious laughter, lovely women, plenty of wine, relatively little food, but many delicacies from France and the Balkans. There were candles in place of the electric lights disrupted by an earlier air attack, velvet curtains, rich crystal, and even a small string orchestra composed of wounded soldiers recuperating at the hospital just outside the city.

We were at bay in those days. Nothing was yet settled, and the euphoria of all-out war flooded the veins, affecting all of us like raw alcohol. The colonel had lost fingers under American strafing in North Africa.

—Three of them abreast like circus performers, he told us. —Machine guns and cannons going, chewing up the column, killing scores of men. My hand was on the door. A twenty-millimeter shell hit it.

—The pigs, his brother, the commandant, snorted. —Stinking carrion. Dredged from every gutter in Europe. We could handle them at the camp. The commandant nudged me. —Couldn't we handle them?

—Certainly, I said, reaching for some cheese expropriated from Yugoslavia. —I could use them.

The colonel paid no attention. —They flew past, and I held my hand out before my face and I couldn't believe it. Not my hand. Christ, you can't get a new hand.

—You can't requisition a new hand, the commandant said, frowning. —Can you? his elbow in my ribs as I sliced a piece of Circassian salmon.

—Not yet, I said. —Give us time.

—My men were firing, the colonel went on. —Even with rifles. My driver used his pistol.

—Any good? the commadant asked. —Any good?

—They flew past still in formation, the colonel said, leaning back, his head raised, eyes on the distant wall. —Right past and into the sand a quarter of a mile up the road. Still in formation. It killed two of them and they brought the third one back to me. All of them had been hit with the small-arms fire. A Panzer column had brought down three *Ami* fighters. The men were delirious. It was a good omen.

—No need to ask what disposition you made of the pilot, his brother, the commandant, said with heavy slyness.

—No need whatever, the colonel answered, his eyes snapping back to us. —I don't turn cheeks.

—Ah, the commandant said. —You're a bad Christian. I may be the greatest Christian in history.

—Our mother, rest her, would wonder at that, the colonel said.

—No, the commandant beamed, pleased at the riposte he was so laboriously preparing. —Think how much good came into the world with the death of one Jew.

Neither the colonel nor I replied.

—This week alone, the commandant bawled, his sides heaving. —I've done three thousand times as well.

The colonel grinned despite himself. I thought it wise to

laugh. Even a surgeon does well to keep his patients cheerful. Everyone is potentially someone's guinea pig.

But for all his stupidity, the commandant had made a point: if there is a class of mankind who value self-sacrifice, by all means those who value survival should give them a surfeit of opportunity to be victims. If there is a kind of mentality that sees merit in the failure to overwhelm, then satisfy it by crushing it out of existence. The commandant observed once, as we passed by the ovens on the way to inspect a new shipment, that the sufferer possesses at least one advantage over the survivor. He leaves the victor to clean up the mess.

᭞ ᭞

There is no use in remembering those latter days. The philosophy that had begun us sustained those of us still able to function when the vast hordes of *Sklavenvolk* rolled across Germany like a wave of filth. What deserved to survive survived. One way or another. In those last weeks, in February of 1945, a prisoner tried to betray me to the commandant as a Jew. By then I had nearly forgotten that I was a Jew. I did not think of myself as a Jew but as a kind of device. My Jewishness meant nothing by then, of course, but the commandant would have his joke. He called me in to face my accuser.

—This is Herr Krankowytz, Major, the commandant said smoothly. —He claims to have known you in better days. He even has information concerning your family.

Herr Krankowytz was a shambles. His body was hardly larger in height or thickness than a ten-year-old boy's. He had no hair. Only one eye, and that eye damaged—apparently either cataract or serious searing of the cornea—so badly that he had to face the commandant in order to focus on me out of one sound corner of that eye. His hands moved incessantly in the sacking which covered his bones. He seemed poorly nourished, depressed. Prognosis was unfavorable.

Herr Krankowytz leered at me. His gums were black as if he chewed betel. He had no teeth. —Arugh, he snuffled and wiped his nose with the palm of his hand. —That's him. I knew his father. I knew your father. They took your father. In uniforms just like that. They came for him.

I stared at the commandant. Herr Krankowytz did not interest me. —Do you want to take this up with Berlin?

—Why, no, the commandant grinned. —What do I gain? This campaign is over anyhow. It's a good thing to find a Jew on my staff. It might make all the difference. I could claim I was a defender of the Hebrews. You can be my exhibit.

—The war is still on, I said. —I have work to do. I'm no good as an exhibit. This lunatic is lying. My family died in South Africa. Look at my service record. Look in my party record.

They were perfect forgeries, my records, blending truth and fiction so skillfully that even the Gestapo could not discern the end of one and the start of the other. Proof of that was my being still a surgeon instead of sharing a pest-ridden shed outside with Krankowytz and the rest of the guinea swine.

—So it is, so you do, the commandant grinned widely. —You can take Herr Krankowytz with you. No need to ask if you have use for him?

—No need whatever, I said.

⟨§ §⟩

As his complaints gained upon him, Herr Krankowytz swore that he had invaluable information for me. He had an orderly bring me to him. He was in a special ward where we kept donors of vital organs until we had a need for their services. Krankowytz was in restraint. His bald head gleamed with perspiration. He could not see me.

—You, he whispered. —Do you know what God has in store for you? Do you?

I shrugged and stared at his naked fleshless body. —Do you know? I asked him. —Has your God been down with manna and prophecies? Tell Him to step up the calorie content of the first. And to spare you the second.

—*Cave, cave, Deus videt,* Krankowytz choked.

—Latin from you? Does the priesthood attract you?

—God is not mocked, he rattled through gathering phlegm. —Beware.

—God is mocked. And blocked and shocked, I said. —God is one more entity to manipulate. If He comes down into the ward here for you, I'll have guards strap Him in this cot next to yours. If He resists, they'll use a machine pistol on Him. If that won't work, we'll ignore Him.

—God sees . . .

—God is dead. Autopsy in the late nineteenth century revealed substantiosclerosis, softening of the essence, deafness, blindness, and general debility. He was buried at Jena and mourned nowhere at all. So far as you're concerned, I am God.

—Arugh, Krankowytz cleared his throat. —All right, God. I can tell you about your mother.

—My parents are dead.

—Not yet. Not yet she isn't. She's in the camp. Just a number like the rest of us, and no idea her own son is helping to murder her.

—My mother is dead.

—No, God, no. You're fuzzy on the omniscience today, Krankowytz muttered. He seemed to be cheered by my visit. —When she first came, he went on, —she said it was all a mistake. That no loyal German, no one who stood four-square for the Fatherland could be brought to this. That one fine day the Führer himself would come driving into the compound in his Mercedes-Benz and announce to everyone that she was innocent, had been brought here by mistake. That no amount of Jewish blood could obscure true Germany. He would carry her to München to the Sportsplatz and show her to the people, a Nordic heroine.

I said nothing, but a chill went from my buttocks to my neck. I had never seen this man in my childhood so far as I could remember, but he was talking of my mother in such a way as to preclude his lying. He had to know her.

Krankowytz paused, licked his lips, shifted his immobilized shoulders and arms. —These straps make it hard to wipe one's eye, he said apologetically.

—Be glad you still have an eye, I told him.

He shrugged and licked his lips again. —At first they despised her. My God, how they mistreated her, cursed her, poured filth onto the rags she had to sleep on. One woman whose son had already gone to the ovens tried to kill her with a piece of kindling sharpened at one end. But finally people grew ashamed. They saw at last that she was no different from them —only a Jew doomed to the gas and the ovens. Or to your little hospital here. They came to see that she was only responding in her own way to what all of us had to grasp and struggle with. She had loved Germany like the rest of us—wanted to go on loving it, fighting for it—but Germany was killing her. Not just Hitler. Germany.

—What happened? I asked, leaning down over him, fascinated despite myself, caught between belief and refusal. —What more?

Krankowytz smiled; perspiration poured off his naked skull and down into his eyes. He no longer winced at the salty drainage, and sweat stood in the deep sockets like runoff in stagnant pools. His single sighted eye burned from under it like that of a drowned sailor who mourns the life above, drifting downward into another world.

—Not so fast, God, Krankowytz sighed, his mouth tightening in pain. —Even the gods have to pay. The god searching out his parentage. It costs.

I shrugged. —You want a month of life. Perhaps an orange. Or a pack of cigarettes and time enough to smoke them.

—You're a cheap god, he said, his voice no longer strong. —A god's mother is worth a glass of wine.

—You want wine?

—No, Krankowytz shook his head slowly, sweat spilling out of his eyes like enormous and grotesque tears. —No, I don't want a drink. I couldn't even taste it. None of my senses is any good now. You've seen to that. I'm talking to three of you now. As if one weren't bad enough.

—What do you want?

Krankowytz tried to smile. The dark empty cavern of his mouth gaped. I moved back reflexively. Krankowytz smiled wider. —I know, he said. —My looks are gone. In the compound the girls ignore me. But then they don't look good either.

—What do you want?

—I thought about that a long time before I had them send

for you. I thought about it while they were examining me. I thought about it while they kept me in the ice. I didn't think about it while they opened me up to see if my organs were satisfactory. They only gave me a little anesthetic, and I was thinking about the operation.

—All right. What?

Krankowytz shifted as much as he could in the confines of his restraint. —I thought of freedom which you cannot give and life in here while my friends die. Which I could not stand. And of food and tobacco. Even of women, which I do not want. There is so little I can still bring myself to care about. So little you can offer me. Still I must have something. I've got to get something.

—I'm tired of this, I said. —Let's get it over with.

—Yes, Krankowytz breathed. —You've hit on it. That's what I want.

—What?

—To end it. To get on with it. I want to die.

—That, I said, —can be arranged. Have you any preference as to how and when?

—Oh yes, Krankowytz said excitedly. —Certainly. As soon as possible. And in the ovens.

I thought I had misunderstood. You'll end in the ovens. All of them do.

—No, I want to die in them. I want to be put in them alive.

I almost fell backward. —You've gone mad. You've lost your reason.

—No, he said. —I know what I'm about. If I go into the ovens you can't use me. They won't put my nerves in a Nazi pilot or my bone in the arm of a Gestapo man. Parts of me won't be turned to my own condemnation. You'll get no good out of me if I go into the ovens.

—It's absurd, I told him. —I can't do it.

Krankowytz frowned and shook his head in mock sadness. —What kind of god are you? he asked. —A maimed god?

—What if I could arrange it? You don't mean it. You couldn't go through with it. You couldn't stand it.

—Great God, Krankowytz muttered. —A little more pain

after all this? It's the coward's way out. The ovens are the least of it. You make the arrangements, deity, and we'll see you find your mother.

—I have to go. I'll think about this.

—Wait, Krankowytz called as I turned to leave. He raised himself on the bed, straining against the straps holding his wrists. His head, against the room's faint light, seemed enormous; his neck no larger in diameter than an eel. —There's one more thing, he said. —One more thing.

—What?

—At the oven. When I am put into the oven . . .

—Yes?

—I want you to read a Psalm. I want at the end to hear the words of David. Even in your voice. You'll have to do that. You have to be a Jew for a few minutes.

—Read you a Psalm? This is ludicrous.

Krankowytz tried to shrug. He fell backward on his cot. —It's all ludicrous, God. There's no humanity, no sense in all this. And the end when I'm dead and you're dead and they've butchered that filth in Berlin, nothing will have changed. They'll make great resolves that none of us shall have died in vain, that none of your kind will ever hold power again. And in twenty years we'll all be squeaking and strutting and stumbling through the history books. It will go down as a terrible mistake. We're all dying in vain and your kind . . .

I stopped him. No use hearing the rest. —My kind will always hold power. Always.

—Yes, Krankowytz said. —Till the earth falls asunder and gives up its dead. Till the seas boil away and the . . .

—Bones of ancient ships show themselves again.

—Yes, Krankowytz said. —Till then. But not forever.

—There is no forever, I said. There is only a collection of nows. For the rest you're welcome to it. Whatever you find beyond the ovens, I make you a gift of it.

—Thank you, God. I'll use it to send you justice.

I shook my head. —Not here you won't. This world belongs to us, remember.

Krankowytz squinted and seemed to collapse within himself.

—I can hardly remember my name. What's my name, God? he said weakly, the last vestiges of humor leaking from his reed-thin body. —What's my name?

—Legion, I said, and turned from the bed into the cool clear air of the hall beyond.

• •

It was not, in fact, very hard to arrange. I knew men who worked in the crematorium, and any of them was ready to earn himself cigarettes, alcohol, or even a day or so of relaxation in the infirmary. None of them had any objection to accommodating a corpse prematurely. They had seen too much even to recall that some people do not burn others alive. A corporal I knew, had known since the early days of the Rhineland adventure, was in charge of a late duty shift at the ovens. He laughed when I told him of Krankowytz.

—You've got a real original there, he said. —Wants out, does he? Wants out by way of the furnace, does he? My God, you must run some fine little hospital over there, doctor. He'd rather visit me, would he?

—He's mad, but I thought it might amuse you to humor him.

—It's all one with me, sir. You bring it in here, sign an order, and I burn it. Old paper, clothes, files, garbage, people, snooker tables, pigs, furniture—I'll even try burning water if you say so. I don't care. I have a job to do, orders to obey. No one asks me how I feel about burning the regimental rubbish at six-thirty in the morning. They don't ask me how I like burning rabbis at seven-thirty, either. We all have our jobs to do, don't we? You bring your friend—I mean that fellow who wants to die—over here any night late and we'll see what's he made of, if you take my meaning, ha, ha.

• •

Herr Krankowytz was naked. A light bulb just above him was in similar condition, and it cast long wild shadows against the concrete walls of the crematorium. Krankowytz was strapped to a metal stretcher the corporal had supplied. His eyes were shut tight.

—No hard feelings, the corporal said. —It's just that we can't have you thrashing around in there, can we? These ovens weren't made for that. You could jam one of the gas jets.

The corporal was in his shirt sleeves. His tunic hung on a wall peg. Behind him were the two furnaces, from one of which came an odd breathy roar. Like that of a mechanical animal, perhaps. The corporal turned valves and the hissing receded.

—So this is the oblation, eh, the corporal grinned kindly. —Well, old fellow, you'll be out of it. Only a little flash and you're gathered to your fathers. Like lightning.

But Krankowytz was not amused. —Where are . . . he began.

—The others? Come now, it's past midnight. We have to clean up sometimes. You'll be the only business between now and six-thirty.

Krankowytz opened his eyes and looked around. His single good eye widened, and he reared up on the stretcher as far as the metal straps permitted. —This place . . . is clean, he finished in confusion.

The corporal laughed warmly. —What did you expect? A charnelhouse? Skulls, and the floor running with Jewish blood? Listen, this is a military establishment. A government undertaking. You people must be raised on melodrama. If this place gets littered, I might follow you into the ovens when my captain discovers it.

—Let's get on with it, I said. —Someone could turn up.

—Not a chance, the corporal said. —Nobody comes here unless he has to.

But the corporal opened one of the metal doors and fitted the end of Krankowytz's metal stretcher into grooves that ran down into the furnace. Down inside, we could see dark red flickering against total blackness. —Down as low as they go. Makes for an easy entry, the corporal said deferentially.

—All right, I said to Krankowytz, —What can you tell me?

He was no longer self-assured, no longer playing a bald bony Prometheus to my uncertain eagle. He licked his lips and stared down past his thin gray feet into the muttering furnace.

—Where, he began, and lost his voice. —Where, he tried again, —are the Psalms? You've forgotten the Psalms.

—No, I said, taking a small Old Testament from my tunic pocket. It was the version read in Protestant Evangelical Churches. What difference did it make? The same nonexistent God is celebrated in all versions.

—All right, he said. —The Ninety-third Psalm. Read it to me slowly.

—First. What you have to tell me.

—Number 71633. Compound seven. Block fourteen. When you see her tell her Krankowytz sends her a son and prays she survives him.

He fell back on the stretcher, his bald head bright with sweat, his eyes closed tightly again, his hands, blue with chill and terror, clenched like bony misshapen stumps where hands had been.

I licked my lips and adjusted my spectacles. The oven made it quite warm, and my lenses were fogging. The corporal was fidgeting, whistling soundlessly, or at least puckering his lips and staring disinterestedly out the window into total darkness. It was not only his lack of sentiment (which made good sense) but his inability to discern history-in-little being punched and cramped into the blasé confines of his tedious and torpid life.

—Any time you're ready, gentlemen, he said with exaggerated patience. —Any time at all.

—Read, Krankowytz murmured. —For God's sake, read.

—The Lord reigneth, he is clothed with majesty, I began. Krankowytz closed his eyes. His thin colorless lips parted. For a moment I thought that he was going to whistle too. But he began to follow my words in Hebrew.

—Thy throne is established of old. Thou art from everlasting.

—Ah God, Krankowytz moaned in German. The corporal, no longer whistling, his face composed and solemn as that of a hired mute or casket merchant, was beginning to lower Krankowytz into the sullen flickering crimson darkness of the furnace.

—The floods have lifted up, O Lord, the floods have lifted up their voice. The floods lift up their waves.

Krankowytz pulled his bare feet upward as the end of the stretcher dipped down. His knees, unhindered, rose almost to his chin as if he were some gross parody of a sharp-shinned hysterical embryo. He did not shriek, but rather went on reciting the Psalm in Hebrew, only louder. And as his legs disappeared, louder still, until it was almost impossible to distinguish words, and the difference between Krankowytz's prayer and the howl of a doomed animal was in fact no difference at all.

—Thy testimonies are very sure, I read.

—Ah God, Krankowytz screamed, his face turned toward me now, his eye wide, his nostrils distended. —Ah, God.

He meant not the Hebrew deity then—not the creature who haunted burning bushes, who demanded sacrifice, burnt offering, holocaust. He meant me. It was in his face, in the stiff horrified, almost wooden set of his jaw, his wide-open mouth. —Ah God, he shrieked as the flames reached his feet, as the corporal let the stretcher slide still more rapidly with one hand, turning up the gas with his other.

—Holiness becometh thine house, O Lord, forever, I shouted above Krankowytz' rising shriek. Then the oven door slammed shut, and the furnace burner went on full. —Forever, I said again, my voice low, my eyes still on the featureless iron door of the oven.

—Selah, the corporal said, and spoke no more.

Chapter Two

᭐

—There goes one ugly sonofabitch, Billy Bob Stoker tells Christopher and Mrs. Nieman as he watches Dr. Aorta stalk between the tables muttering, and out into the morning sun.

Christopher is wilted, his face shaded up with two days' growth of beard. He holds his coffee cup with both hands and pays no attention to Billy Bob's observation. Mrs. Nieman smiles. She is glad to be out of Shreveport. Glad especially to be with her son and his new friend.

—I knew you two would get along, she drawls. Under the table Jeremiah scratches at her ankle begging a *bagnet,* for which he has gained an instant and insatiable lust.

—Same mold, Billy Bob says, still watching Dr. Aorta's progress, and that of the dainty little old lady who moves in his wake. —Couple of bad pennies.

—Not so bad, Mrs. Nieman smiles. —Boys get confused. They make mistakes.

Christopher's eyebrows lift. His eyes are on Dr. Aorta's back. In his black suit, with his slouching walk, he looks like Father Brophy. —Mistakes, Christopher mumbles, shivering.

—Some boys make worse mistakes than others, his mother says comfortingly. —You can't win 'em all.

—I knew this feller, Billy Bob says thoughtfully, —who woke up one night still drunk from foolin' around all evening. He heard all this racket, people movin' all around him. He took and loaded his thirty-eight and went to shootin'. He thought it was some fellers from Hattiesburg come to kill him on account of money he owed for cards. When he come to hisself, it turned out he'd killed his wife and three of his kids. Only his mother-in-law got away to tell about it. Ain't that the goddamnedest thing you ever heard?

Christopher's shakes are not lessened by Billy Bob's story.

—Doesn't Billy Bob kind of remind you of Charlie? his mother asks him. —I mean the old Charlie. Before all the dustup.

Christopher stares at Billy Bob sullenly. —I hadn't thought of that, he says. —Maybe he does.

—It's the goddamnedest thing I ever heard, Billy Bob says.

—Charlie was all right, Mrs. Nieman tells Christopher. —Sometimes he was all right. He made a few mistakes.

Christopher squints his eyes against the sun and fumbles for his coffee. Jeremiah moans softly beneath the table, his colorless eyes glued to Andrew Jackson's distant statue. Christopher has never thought of himself as like Charlie. But mistakes are mistakes. Besides, it is doubtful that Charlie's record of errors includes the betrayal of God. On one ground anyway, Christopher is miles ahead. Charlie, wherever he is beyond the Arbuckles, will have to tempt the devil to catch up.

—I reckon we ought to hunt us a place, Billy Bob says, still thinking of man's propensity for error.

—No, Mrs. Nieman says, stretching her marvelous legs, running her fingers through loam-colored hair tied back with an off-white headband. She is aware that Billy Bob watches her. Not brazenly; perhaps even shyly. But he watches and his coffee cup rattles in its saucer. It is a kind of salute. —No, she says again, a little more warmly. —Youall do whatever you want. I'm going to find you a place. You'd root up a pigpen on your own. A trough. With hot and cold running slop. Su-eee.

She has a copy of the *Times-Picayune* turned to the classified section. The French Quarter has plenty of apartments available. The turnover is large: young artistes and quasi-artistes and those who fancy themselves artistes come and go with pistonlike regularity. And the older ones—those whose art has enabled them to sketch Yankee tourists and sailors on liberty for three dollars a head—these move off or vanish or find liquid haven sometimes in the cadaver tanks at LSU or Tulane Medical School. The permanent residents—club owners, grocery owners, hookers and pimps—none take up much room. Space in the Quarter is valuable. Time not so much. Even a blank wall on St. Peter Street can be rented to some artiste-in-training who wishes to display his wares to the passing camera-bangled gawkers from Cincinnati and St. Paul.

—I see a little place on Royal, Mrs. Nieman tells them. —Ninety a month. Two bedrooms, living room. Balcony over the street. It looks good. Youall horse around a while and meet me back here. I'll keep this hound with me.

She stands and brushes powdered sugar from her tight tan skirt. It pulls close across her belly, molds her thighs and hips. Billy Bob swallows his coffee noisily and elbows his last *bagnet* onto the floor. Jeremiah gobbles it before Billy Bob can recoup, then chases after Mrs. Nieman.

As she swings out beyond cover of the awning, Billy Bob snaps his eyes off her with an effort. He sneaks a guilty look at Christopher. But Christopher is paying no mind. He is brooding on his freedom. He has spent a week looking for Mary Ann in Bossier and Shreveport. To no avail. He has come out in search of himself, has fired off his chastity, ground obedience into powder, and sits with an aching head wondering how long it will take his mother to ask what he's up to; how long it will take to figure out the answer for himself. And whether, in fact, Billy Bob does look like Charlie Nieman.

—I thought I might cat around some, Billy Bob says. —About time for a beer. I thought I might go over and look up and down Bourbon Street. I ain't never seen it.

—You go ahead, Christopher tells him. —Go ahead. I think I'll look for a job. I need something to do.

—What do you know how to do?

—I could teach catechism, Christopher says glumly. —I'm a licensed exorcist, acolyte, and subdeacon, too.

—What's an exor . . . ?

—He casts out devils.

—Oh. If you was on the level about that, you'd have your work cut out. This here is the meanest part of the meanest town south of New York City. More sin in a square block here than in all of northern Mississippi. You could fill the river from here to the Gulf with devils. . . . You could . . .

Christopher shakes his head. —I was only kidding, he says. —I don't believe in any of that crap. You can't cast anything out. We *are* the devils.

Billy Bob looks at him with profound sympathy. —An' the only god is a shot wad?

Christopher's head snaps up from his cold coffee. —All right. That's all right. It's as good a god as you can likely dream up.

—You reckon you can jack off Jesus? Billy Bob asks, his voice assuming that peculiar distant hollow unctuous tone that flows from the grain of an unpainted pine pulpit. —Flog your mule, and away with the Lord, he says more loudly. —Skin your cat, and that's that.

Christopher glances around. A few people have noticed the increased volume. One man with a copy of *The Denver Post* spread before him is beginning to grin, turning in his seat to listen. A waiter with a silly slash of black moustache is beckoning nervously to another.

—It's your metaphor, he says to Billy Bob. —Don't get excited over it.

—I *am* excited, Billy Bob begins. —I get excited. I can't help it. Jesus Christ comes down to cleanse, and all this cocksuckin' world turns Him away. What does it take? What's He got to do to find youall's hearts?

Now Billy Bob has turned from Christopher and is talking loudly to the assembled drawers of coffee and hewers of donuts who stare back at him mesmerized. —Youall want a sign? What do you need, a sign? All right. Take this here feller with me. A preacher turned against his call. A man with Jesus' seal set on him who done give the kiss of betrayal. And me? A sinner under God's sun who's done wrong enough to wilt the grass where his foot falls. Heaven and earth risin' up against me. A stranger amongst my kin. Who's made an abomination of the love of man. Take a good look at both of us. Gamblers, sinners, fornicators. Ready to rob a grave or shame a heathen. The Jonah sign, that's us. The Jonah sign . . .

Christopher cannot move. He is like a small wolf in a large trap. He is not angry with Billy Bob and at first cannot understand why he is not. Then the synapses close: he had expected this. Not from a red-faced boy out of Mississippi carting around his own strange burden of woe. Not in an outdoor café. But somewhere sometime someone was bound to do it. And probably often. In dreams or visions (or dream-visions) Christopher discovers himself standing in a supermarket or St. Mark's Piazza, the Place de la Concorde or the Columbia Restaurant when suddenly an ancient anchorite clad in brown, long beard cold and white, dark piercing eyes, comes toward him moaning and gesticulating, crying out within the hearing of all, *Bad priest, bad priest*. Pedestrians and pederasts, housewives and hussies stop and stare at him. Not with anger or hatred, but in horror. As if, before their eyes, he had been changed into an enormous insect, as if the transcendental sign of his failure shows stark and glaring on his forehead.

He stares at the wooden tabletop, paralyzed eyes following the patterns of crusted sugar and spilled coffee running into cracks, oozing off the table's edge and falling to the floor.

When he raises his eyes, the two waiters have Billy Bob hustling him toward Decatur Street, and Christopher follows after them in the wake of nervous laughter that rises and tiptoes from one coffee-and-sugar-stained table to the next.

&~ &~

On Decatur Street, between a brewery and a dealer in imported foods and fancy groceries, the Staff-o-Life Bakery nestles amist that ghastly and peculiar sweet stench of modern mass-produced, chemically-preserved, gummy-textured bread. All New Orleans swallows the glutinous indigestible product of this place, and behind the faded brick façade of the building, carefully renovated numerous times to retain its old-fashioned character, all the latest machines gobble tons of Midwestern flour and excrete the viscous mounds that pass for basic sustenance in a progressive city, in a modern land.

Every day, thousands upon thousands of these loaves, untouched by human hands, machine-mixed, machine-baked, machine-wrapped, are stacked into brightly painted trucks. Drivers are carefully trained to watch for old ladies at intersections, to slow down in school zones; warned to smile continually if they want to keep their jobs (bread is a happy food, the advertising people on the account insist) . Only one or two of the drivers are conscious enough to know what they might really be smiling about. These trucks broadcast the loaves around New Orleans every morning except Sunday. On Sundays there is no fresh bread in New Orleans. The chemical preservatives must counterfeit until Monday sees the truck fleet on the move again.

The trucks are parked at ground level. Above is the baking and packaging area. On the third floor are offices. Below the garage is a storage area for flour, monosodium glutinate, and various arcane elements and additives which guarantee a half-pound of Staff-o-Life to supply the consumer with fifty-five percent of the thiamine he requires daily, thirty percent of the riboflavin, fifty per cent of the niacin and forty percent of the iron. On the lowest level, beneath all the rest, in a dark and noisome subbasement, are repair facilities for Staff-o-Life trucks. The equipment is antique. In one corner, amidst chunks of differentials, covies of old spark plugs, shards of body metal, lie an anvil and a small charcoal furnace used to forge parts as recently as the late war. There are five unshaded 250-watt bulbs hung at peculiar intervals to dispel the gloom, and across from workbenches and a tool cabinet with door broken loose from its hinges, is the grease pit.

This pit, the ultimate depth of the Staff-o-Life operation, is permanently awash in an inch or two of filthy water. The water level is remarkable. It does not vary. The oldest employee of Staff-o-Life can remember attempts in the 1880's to pump and bail out this pit. An hour after being drained dry, the pit was again several inches deep. No deeper or less deep than before. Nowadays the pit is bailed out only when grease and oil make footing impossible. For the rest, its occupant must cope. Cope with cigar butts from previous occupants, crusts of bread and fragments of canned meat, a pair of jockey shorts green with age and petroleum, the crotch rotted out. And, at present, the stiff and bloated corpse of a rat floating, bobbing in the greasy scum. No one has explained what the rat was seeking at this depth.

Usually there is work enough for three or four men in the Staff-o-Life subbasement. The trunks are old, the drivers, for all their smiling, are frequently villains at the wheel, swine on the clutch. Transmissions disintegrate; rear axles snap. Valves carbonize, plugs are rarely good for more than 50,000 miles, even if engine smoothness does not matter. There is, then, plenty to do. And only one present occupant to do it.

It is the present occupant's own fault that he is alone. Only a year ago, there had been two other colored men floundering around the dim garage under the weak glare of two 200-watt bulbs. One, fat and lazy, always shirking his fair share of the labor, claiming to have diarrhea or coughing blood (in fact, tobacco juice), was spending as long as an hour a day in the reeking jakes for colored males upstairs. Naturally enough, he was discovered, one day, sprawled on the toilet, his fat legs spread, one hand clutching his sex, a copy of *Esquire* with its fold-out Varga girl folded out in the other. He was stone dead. Heart attack. Possibly overwork, someone said. His wife was given a recompense by Staff-o-Life to forestall discussion of the working conditions and hours in the pit. The wife was not prone to argue.

For a day or so, the executives at Staff-o-Life cast about for another cheap mechanic. But a young assistant manager, eager to rise, to increase his share of dough, noted that the repairs were being turned out just as regularly, just as rapidly as before. And there were no more complaints from the Negro baker's helpers who, in recent time past, unable to use the toilet, had taken to pissing in hallways, sinks, and who knows where else? Mixing vats are huge, and while the batter is whipping, left strictly alone.

So that left two: the present occupant and an ancient Negro with a most peculiar accent who, while grinding valves or lapping pistons, would tell stories of Anthony Fokker's factory, of a beautiful plane with three wings called the DR.1, painted red with black crosses on white grounds. The old man would grin and tell of women in Hamburg, and how little 200,000,000 marks would buy in those days. Once, a day or so before he vanished, he had told the story of a crop duster in East Texas brought down by the finger of God—in the form of a Negro Baptist church steeple. Crazy, huh? It seemed crazy enough to the present occupant. Maybe, the old Negro had said, maybe we're all crazy. Maybe God's crazy.

Two days after the old man vanished, a colored doctor over on Perdido Street had called the Staff-o-Life office about him. Gone? Not there any more? No surprise. An old nigger eaten up with cancer, prostate rotten with it. Strange old airplane mechanic. Would probably turn up in the tank at Tulane Med School. Too bad. Late that evening, both the Negro doctor and the Staff-of-Life personnel man heard of an airliner which exploded over the Gulf on the first leg of a flight to Frankfort. Forty-two people lost. Too bad.

And so the present occupant was left alone. To the surprise of even Staff-of-Life's assistant manager, the trucks kept rolling. If anything, the number of breakdowns increased. But the repairs kept pace. For a week, a month. For six months. By which time no one could remember that once three mechanics had been down there. The present occupant was doing very well.

One morning, the junior assistant found a dirty piece of paper on his desk. It was the inside wrapper from a pack of cigarettes. Tinfoil on one side, exotic scratchings on the other. He and two secretaries managed to decipher it finally, and in due course three more light cords were added in the lower depths, and the bulbs were changed to 250 watts each. The day after, another message, scrawled on a bit of paper sack, arrived. It said: *Thanx you.* There was no request for a raise, no mention of increased work load. After all, with the new bulbs, you can see to work in the pit all night. If you want to. The trick is endurance, and the present occupant knows something about that.

◄§ §►

—I'm sorry, Billy Bob is telling Christopher. —I mean it. I wish to God I didn't have a tongue to shame you like that. It wasn't none of my business to talk like that. Me least of all people on God's earth.

—It's all right, Christopher says. —Don't worry about it. I know what you were trying to say. I only wish I knew what I'm trying to say.

They are on the upper end of Decatur Street now, passing a brewery and a grocery which deals in exotic merchandise.

—You don't believe in anything?

—I don't know. I don't even much care. I want a quiet room somewhere with a few books. No, that's what I had. Maybe I need a knife fight and a nigger woman.

—You come to the right place. You ought to be able to exorcise them things up without much trouble.

They pause in front of a brick building with a brass plaque on a dark walnut door. Through a nicely curtained bay window, they see a girl typing invoices and letters. The plaque reads:

STAFF-O-LIFE BAKERIES
INC.

—I think I'll try here, Christopher says almost to himself.

—Try?

—For a job. I need a job.

—I thought your mamma had more money than Ed Crump.

—I don't need money. I need something to do.

—You want to work?

—I've never worked. I never made my own bread.

They look at the plaque, and laugh.

Billy Bob touches Christopher's shoulder. —You're right, ole buddy. It ain't no good livin' on somebody else's bread. You ain't full grown till you've eaten your own.

There is a rear door to the place. It is in an alley without bay windows or brass plaques. This alley has all its original charm. No one has attempted to restore it. The filth underfoot, the sagging brick walls leaning into a plank outhouse full of garbage buckets, a broken orange crate with a gunny sack draped across it, a scattering of German words and phrases scrawled on the wooden fence separating alley from garbage yard of Staff-o-Life Bakeries (*du kanst mich ficken und zu . . .*).

But the door leads not into a hallway or office. Rather it opens on a dark stairway that falls steeply into gloom as dense and impenetrable as if the world ended somewhere near the bottom.

—I don't think you can get there from here, Billy Bob says, swallowing. The place is spooky. The alley is enough to put him off. These murky stairs are too much.

—I'm not looking for an office job. Maybe they need somebody to fix things. Maybe they need somebody on the delivery trucks.

—Maybe they need 'em a gravedigger, Billy Bob whispers. But he begins walking downward after Christopher, carefully testing every sagging step with his toe before placing his weight on it. It looks like a place for Judgment, he thinks. And he is not ready. Not even half ready.

—You don't have to come, Christopher says over his shoulder without force. —You could go get that beer.

—What beer? Billy Bob asks, his throat almost too tight to breathe, much less drink. —I'd give a pretty for a gulp of fresh air.

Deeper. The stairs twist like a body in pain. There are certain sounds. Rats, perhaps. Snakes? The air becomes fetid past believing. Surely some revelation is at hand. After stumbling past two landings, a locked and disused door and a bricked-up passage reminiscent of the poorer catacombs, they reach bottom. It is a dirt floor, but dirt is the cleanest thing around. The walls are thick with cobwebs, the ceiling hanging with strings of web and moisture and disintegrating plaster. On one wall, as they turn a final corner, Christopher sees a tattered and crumbling calendar. It has a picture of General John Pershing. The date reads 1921. Billy Bob glances at it and shudders in disbelief.

Ahead, at the end of the noxious corridor, they can see a single naked light bulb swinging gently like a forgotten minor god, bleeding pale light onto a floor littered with automotive junk.

—Look, Billy Bob says as they issue from the dim passageway into a wide shadowed room. —That's a planetary gear. From a Model-T truck. And look. Over there's a part of a Durant.

—You reckon we've found where the old cars go to die? Christopher asks him, not really in jest.

—Looks more like the devil's garage. Don't you reckon he owned the first Model-T?

Across the dim expanse of the room, they can hear a faint and irregular clatter of metal against metal, as if a ratchet were being turned slowly, wearily.

—Why don't we go along upstairs? Billy Bob asks. —You ain't gonna get a job down here. This must be where they keep the garbage. Ain't no man in his right mind gonna work down here.

But Christopher has discovered the source of the cranking sound. There is a red-and-white bread truck parked in a patch of faint light falling through a single barred window on the far side of the room. Under the truck, he sees a scuttling shifting light, moving one way, pausing, then moving again.

—Look. Something . . .

Billy Bob scratches his head. —Nothin' with any jobs to pass around. If it had jobs to hand out, it would have gotten rid of its own first off.

—Hey, Christopher calls out tentatively, the sound of his own voice hollow and mournful in the gloom.

—Huh? something answers from under the bread truck. —What? Who there?

—Wow, Billy Bob whispers. —They must have that bastard chained to the wall.

—There's all kinds of jobs, Christopher says without force, watching the light under the truck, seeing something struggling to crawl from beneath it, hearing labored breath and a splash of water like Leviathan lumbering upward out of a pool.

What Billy Bob Stoker sees at first is nothing. He strains, along with Christopher, trying to squint out substance of the voice from amidst the shadows. His flesh creeps, and he knows for certain that the wrong sound, sight of the wrong thing could send him scrambling back down the damp spider-ridden passageway and up those ramshackle steps to the other world. Not that Billy Bob is superstitious. If he still had his .38 pistol, he would try anything to be found in a subbasement. But this is an old place. For all he knows, they have wandered into somebody's private snake pit or alligator wallow. And besides, if nobody can prove there is any such thing as a haunt, nobody has demonstrated that there isn't.

Christopher touches his arm. —See?

—Naw. I don't see a thing.

—Not a thing. Something between us and that dirty little window. Just a dark shadow. Getting bigger. Behind the truck. Like a shadow without anybody connected to it.

And, coming around the truck into what passes in this dreary cellar for plain sight, a huge and ungainly figure, black as a negative of the sun, covered in filthy rags, arms long and dangling, feet shining, almost luminous with water, face a vacancy except for rows of white teeth and two great staring eyes pink as a flamingo's wing. Billy Bob holds tight. But not for long. Christopher is paralyzed. The figure, like some rough beast, slouches toward them to be recognized. A dozen feet away, it pauses, stares at Billy Bob staring at it, scratches its head and moans. —Bugger, it wails plaintively, pointing with a long twisted finger. —The ole Bugger Man . . .

Which is enough and more than enough, and Billy Bob, already backing up gingerly, turns, falls across the skeletal rear axle and differential of a 1935 Ford V-8, clambers to his feet, and heads for the passage yelling for Christopher to follow or be damned.

The apparition watches him go, seems to sigh with relief and sits down heavily on an old orange crate covered with dirty sacking. Christopher still studies him, fear draining away. He is not concerned about damnation. Either it is or it isn't. If it is, he is doomed. If not, he may as well learn something for his long and difficult descent.

—Thought he'd come for me, the occupant of the garage murmurs. —Reckon he'd come all the way from Mississippi after me. Always figured he was a devil. Had to be a devil out scoutin' the land for his partner. Keepin' a lookout for his boss.

All of which means nothing to Christopher. Except that this peculiar troll in the bowels of New Orleans has recognized Billy Bob, and fears him. Which is a nice and interesting inversion of things. The creature piddles with an old gear shift, drops it and picks up one foot, shedding the glistening overshoe as he does so. He seems to count the toes, probe the instep and sole as if the foot belonged to another. —Hurts, he says finally. —Hurts all the time. Ain't nothin' on earth can make 'em stop hurtin'.

Christopher squats down in the place he has been standing. There is something here, and he wants to find out about it. It is as if he has been brought face to face with the nervous system of the universe. What keeps a creature in this God-forsaken cellar? Even a black creature can improve on such a demi-hell.

—This . . . is your job? Christopher asks cautiously.

—My job, the cellar's occupant avers mechanically. —I does this most of the time. At night an' on Saturday an' Sunday mornin' I does other things. They lets me off them times. Mostly. Except when they got a lot of fixin' to do.

What the present occupant of this cellar is not going to tell Christopher is that he does not know how to get out of this place. When he came, years ago, he was only a boy who had worked in half a hundred cotton gins and fishing camps, general stores and lumber mills for day wages. It is not customary to ask the age, past employers and social security number of a young Negro you are paying thirty-five cents an hour. As a matter of fact, some of those past employers had not even asked his name.

But Staff-o-Life is a forward-looking firm. A secretary had spent almost two hours prying arcane information out of the cellar's present occupant, and he had signed payroll-deduction forms, health form, employee's compensation-insurance form. Now, without any clear idea of what those documents had been, he suspects that he has signed some sort of indenture, and that if he does not appear for work, they will come for him. He does not want to be come for. Once his papa had signed a paper, and later, claiming he had not fulfilled the paper's demands, the sheriff had come for him. And taken him away to Parchman for a year and a day. On his return, the old man's chest was no good, and, less than sixty, he had wheezed his life away inside six months of his return. It is a bad thing to be come for.

Christopher tries another tack. —You know that boy who came down here with me?

—Don't *you* know him? the dark creature asks, amazed. As if all heaven and earth were privy to Billy Bob's name, character, reputation, and prospects.

—He's . . . a friend of mine. From Mississippi.

—Ummm, the occupant hums. —What youall doggin' me for? I kin take care of myself. I ain't goin' easy. You tell him that. You hear? Or are you another one? Is you up to that stuff too?

—Up to? I'm just looking for a job.

—Down to. If you know Bugger Man, you know what I mean.

—. . . Only a few days. I met him in Shreveport.

—Shreveport, God knows. Poor niggers in Shreveport. Ain't that a nasty shame? Ain't it enough colored people in Mississippi to keep him over there?

—What did he. . . ?

The creature frowns and reaches for something on a long narrow worktable beside him. Christopher squints to see that it is a preposterous cob pipe black with use. The cellar's occupant stokes it, fires it, and settles like a lump of dark putty onto his orange crate. —If you don't know, I expect I got to tell you. No tellin' whut ole Bugger got up . . . his sleeve.

The dark creature seems taken with this last phrase. He hunches and laughs, gesticulating with the vile pipe, weaving from side to side. Like a minstrel nigger. Yowsah, yowsah. It's a lonesome ole town.

—Ole Mississip, he drawls. —It ain't a place. It's a thing that gits hold of you. Like a bellyache you done had so long you miss it when it's gone.

—You love . . .

—Shit, I hate it. But I need it. You can't get by, and you can't do without. Sorry when you're there and sad when you ain't.

—But Stoker . . .

—Over to Poole County. He was a deputy. He tended the jail. He come along one day and said he got religion and wanted to minister unto his brother. Wanted to bring the love of man into that Poole County jail. Sheriff like that. High sheriff name Joe Reynolds. He like it, bein' a God-fearin' man in charge of that jail. Looked good. High class. Can't go wrong wif God.

The dark man almost doubles over as if he had suddenly contracted the bellyache he had mentioned. Christopher cannot tell whether he is laughing or crying. Maybe both.

—Naw, you can't go wrong. Ole Bugger kep' things down. Ole Bugger kep' things down, the lord of the cellar says again, remembering. —You ain't never seen the like. That crazy sonofabitch got it so a nigger wouldn't even overpark or jaywalk in spite of the fact that it ain't any law about parkin' or walkin' in Poole County. Shit, them colored folks was walkin' around wit a mouth full of tobacco juice afeared to spit it out on the open highway. They wasn't a chicken or a shoat stole while ole Bugger was on the job. That crazy sonofabitch even had 'em tearin' down old cars and gettin' rid of the metal instead of leavin' 'em where they quit. He had 'em paintin' their houses and dressin' the little school-age niggers in store clothes so he wouldn't think of them if something went wrong and it come to carryin' folks in to question on suspicion.

—You mean all the colored folks turned up model citizens? Christopher asks.

—That crazy sonofabitch had 'em shaped up, the creature says. —I was visitin' my grandmother who was a Hinds County nigger and as old as St. Helena's breastbone. All the neighbors come by to report, and my granny would sit and smoke and cluck and cry shame on damnation. She couldn't figure how the sheriff could allow it, and this one ole boy come by and told her, what the hell. You know damned well what happens to a nigger man who lays wit a white woman even if the woman kneels down and begs for it. So what do you reckon is gonna happen to a nigger man who's been laid wit by a white man—even if he was in jail and outmatched and helpless as a Junie bug in a frog pond? So you know it wasn't anybody gonna go up in broad daylight or even in the dark of night and say, Hey Mr. Sheriff Reynolds, your crazy sonofabitch of a deputy done put meat to damn near every nigger man in Poole County. I reckon you know. Or if you don't know, you ought to be able to speculate. You ain't from Colorado or somewhere.

Christopher shrugs and frowns. —Somebody ought to have put a stop to it. You can't just let it go on forever.

The present occupant examines his fingernails. Greasy. Broken and uneven. He frequently examines them as if he expects they might miraculously improve. —Somebody did put a stop to it. Ole Bugger Man finally fucked the wrong colored man. Somebody did go see old man Reynolds. But that was only on account of she got so damn mad she was kinda crazy.

—She . . . she?

—Some boy's wife. He come home after a stretch for simple burglary. She was hot and ready, and he just kinda giggled at her and asked if she'd push a weenie up his tail. She come apart. Then, after a couple of days, he come home with his nose split open and two teeth gone, and she got word he was standin' around the package store in town talkin' up a unusual proposition. At least unusual for them plain country niggers. One of 'em whipped him pretty bad. I reckon all of 'em would have if they could of figured what he was talkin' about.

—So she went and told the sheriff . . .

—Ole Bugger Man fell like Lucifer. Except for all the devil tried to do, no preacher I ever heard claimed he was cornholin' archangels. Feds come for Bugger, too. He beat it over here to Louisiana.

—Do you reckon he still . . . ?

—I dunno, the occupant says. —I expect a nigger's safe enough around him now. I hear tell he give it up. I hear he done even give up preachin' the love of man. Only preaches God now. And Him crucified. Reckon he might turn to corpses?

Christopher is bewildered. Billy Bob has never made a pass at him. Is Billy Bob a fag? Or something more exotic? —I thought you couldn't cure a queer. I thought if he liked . . .

The creature frowns as if Christopher has lapsed in taste. —Shit, he says. —That boy ain't queer. He's just a Protestant. It ain't no sense in you bein' narrow-minded.

—He never tried to proposition me.

The present occupant does not suffer fools gladly. It is his reasoning that if white men consider themselves so goddamned good, they ought at least to understand things better than a Negro. In this Christopher disappoints him. This white boy is a real meathead. He is a fair tool, but simple. The cellar's denizen believes in the law of gravity because, on his first day in the pit (he was nineteen), a pair of vise grips, carelessly handled, fell and broke two teeth. He is not sure that this would constitute proof to Christopher. If he were a half tone darker, the present occupant would adopt him, put him on the Horse, or get him a steady frig. No scene. Christopher looks like a good paleface. But he wishes the boy would come off this queer bit. In the hierarchy of grand offenses against nature and nature's presumptive God, sodomy is a quiet unassuming and mild enough aberration. It is not, *not*, homosexuality really, the present occupant considers. Christopher's repetition makes him nervous. After all, how would he know so much about Billy Bob Stoker's background if he (the present occupant) had not suffered at least that fool—though with indescribably less gladness than usual.

Christopher's eyes widen. It would seem the vibrations are coming through.

—Sometimes, he says, —I don't think I know anything.

The creature's eyes roll. His smile is that of a man relieved.

—Now you on, he says kindly. —You don't know for shit, but you in there swingin'.

Christopher staggers to his feet. He has to get upstairs, and fast. Just to make sure upstairs is still there.

—Hey, the creature calls after him.

—Yes . . . what?

—If they gives you a job . . .

—Yes . . . ?

—Make sure you gits number nine. It got a good transmission and them brakes is new. Don't let 'em lay number five on you. The devil couldn't pilot number five. You hear?

—Yes, Christopher calls back, plunging for the stairs.

—Thanks. I'll remember.

Mr Christian Blackman

He remembers, vaguely at least, a time before this garage, this pit, this Jonah sign had engulfed him. Long ago. Blue skies and flat fields along the river. Cotton higher than a boy's head in wet years. In dry, great clouds of dust blowing over the tranced Delta. Fishing. Or sitting in the yard outside his father's cropper shack watching the wagons rumble past with sweating men riding bales back from the gin. Or rolling a hoop taken from a barrel. All very well in the summer. But there was winter too, and he remembers that. Days of squatting amidst the thin and fragmentary blankets in a bed shared by him with seven brothers and sisters. Freezing and hungry, the fireplace hardly worth stoking up for the little heat it gave. What made them endure? God knows. And won't tell.

But that was all long ago. And endurance is getting a little old for Mr Christian Blackman. He is tired in the bones and tired in the soul. His feet have been tired for a dozen years, and almost every finger on both hands has been broken and badly set. When he holds his hands out in front of him, the fingers point in every direction but straight ahead. When for a day or two he is free of dysentery, he finds himself constipated; if his belly gives him no trouble, his liver pumps bile into his throat. He has had, in various sequence (sometimes together) tuberculosis, whooping cough, mumps (at twenty-seven), buboes, scabies, rickets, measles, eczema, warts, pimples, low pains, shooting pains, boils, fading pains, syphilis, the crawls, pip, impetigo, pneumonia, yellow pustules, open sores, soft chancres, hard chancres, the grope, and something without a name that made the meat slough out of his nose. He has lost women, good and bad, and the only one who had stayed with him longer than a week, who could stand grease and oil and hours, had given him a case so bad that the spirochetes gobbled sulfa drugs the same way she put away bon-bons.

Mr Christian had tried half a dozen times to begin again; to find a new job, a new life. But nothing turned the trick. There might be curves and twists, loops and spirals, but the road was cold and lonesome and always ended up in the watery grease pit of Staff-o-Life Bakeries, Inc.

Though he had wept and fasted, wept and prayed, the grease pit was inexorable, ubiquitous. And Mr Christian lived with the midnight blues. He has, for a dozen years, since his feet began to hurt in the galoshes, felt himself turning mean. There was no more give to him, no more laugh and lie down, fuck and forget it. He felt anger in his heart and hard evil thoughts in his mind. In days past he had gone to Mass. His mother had asked that as he had knelt to pray a prayer he did not believe in beside her dying-bed. But it was no use, because when the priest, in his gold or scarlet or green vestments, turned and intoned a prayer, Mr Christian found he could not say *amen*. His tongue would tangle, or his nose would clog. His eyes would water or his mind wander. He could not manage to ask any longer, and he knew he would not receive.

Only in the present had he given much thought to being black. He knew hunchbacks, cleft palates, clubfoots, one-eyes, harelips, paralytics, amputees, folks with bad luck and Jews. It was all the same: you got dealt a twisted leg or somebody knocked your eye out down on the docks, and you lived with it. Being black was a congenital defect. Not as bad as a hunchback; worse than a harelip. What you did was make do. You prayed and did your best, kept clear of white men as best you could and refused to admit white women existed. A white man was like a runaway truck or lightning or any other natural hazard. Leave them alone and they mostly leave you alone. Tacks on the road, a rollerskate on the stairs, a copperhead in the cellar, wasp nest in the attic, white man on the street.

Mr Christian's attitude toward white men had not changed. But he had begun to study his own color. Like Shylock, he had begun to notice that his blood, his bone, his flesh, his ills, his fatigue were all human—the same as any other man's. The discovery was depressing. He couldn't blame the grease pit and all the rest of it on white men. That was too simple, too obvious. He didn't believe it. Anyhow, old Whitey had his own problems. He knew a paleface or two with problems worse than his. Some were winos who had to beg other white men for the price of a quart of Gallo, a gallon of Virginia Dare. He knew a poor broken-down bastard who lived in a shack near the river. The old man had no legs, no hands. He sold pencils in the Quarter, moving everywhere on a flatcar with rollerskates nailed to the bottom. Better black hands than no hands at all.

No, the white man was, to melt a metaphor, a red herring. Like the white whale. The real villain, the author of Mr Christian's suffering and misfortune, was clear enough. He might hide behind Mr. Whitey; he might pull off his vicious jokes under the cover of natural phenomena. Fools will curse bad fortune and call lady luck a whore. They will even shrug at odds and talk about statistics.

But then fools are always watching the quarterback when the right half has the ball. Mr Christian would only grin at this idiocy and picture the real source of his trouble. Only one phrase described it all, and that phrase was going out of style. Act of God. Exactly. Just so. Act of God. Who else could be the Cosmic Villain who cleft palates and hared lips, clubbed feet and blackened skin? The Devil? If so, then the Devil and God must be brothers, lovers—or the same old rogue. Any way you sliced it, it was still baloney. And God Almighty stuffed the skin.

That High-Up Sonofabitch, Mr Christian thought. That Blue-Sky Our Father with His doves and candlesticks and commandments and canon laws. All an enormous con game. And the one-eyes and the clubfoots, those without hands and those with hook noses and black skins without a past and even less future? They were supposed not simply to bear it all in good heart (as became a man, Mr Christian, no sniveler, agreed) but to bow and scrape and pray and send bouquets of love to that

Bastard Beyond the Blue who created some men specifically for agony and sorrow.

It took Mr Christian a long time to sort it all out. It took a couple of years, because Mr Christian found it hard to concentrate on good and evil, guilt and innocence from under the transmission of a GM truck. The grease and oil seemed to dim his vision. There were no stars or pastures to inspire him. Only the worn lubrication points of a bread van over his head, and the grass that grew in pavement cracks in the alley off Decatur Street where he squatted on a broken orange crate and ate his tasteless sandwiches (still cheese or tuna fish on Fridays. From habit or poverty. Or both). But the years ground by, and Mr Christian concluded his conclusions. He knew at last where responsibility rested; where human suffering began, and what power made a monster of the white man and a laboratory rat of the Negro.

Mr Christian did not call the resulting dark mood metaphysical despair. He was no philosopher. He was, by then, a deeper and more committed believer than ever before. Of course there was a God. Yes, there *is* a God. Most assuredly. There has *got* to be a God. Because if there was no God, then vengeance would be impossible, Mr Christian realized with a shudder. But surely God lives. If He were ill, Mr Christian thought with a kindly smile, it would be necessary to nurse Him back to omnipotence. In order to torture and degrade Him when the Way should present itself.

      ✤

And so, *Laus tibi Christe,* Mr Christian Blackman was again most careful to present himself at Mass each Sunday morning. He would alternately stand, kneel and squat in the rear of St. Louis Cathedral opposite Jackson Square (for in those days, wondrous to recall, a black man, whatever his condition, however adamant his belief, no matter his charity, was obliged to keep well back. It was not lawful to sit with the whites—whatever their condition, etc.). He would be found there, in whichever posture, with head bowed and eyes closed. Only rarely would he look up, his red-rimmed eyes weakened by long days and nights in the grease pit, focused intently on the priest's hands as he lifted the host after consecration, or the ciborium, displaying to the people the lamb of God who, he contended in a dead tongue, taketh away the sins of the world.

Then Mr Christian would smile faintly and duck his head again, waiting patiently for a sign, an indication. Waiting, in cold truth, for God to make a slip.

But even patience, that least kinetic of virtues, that slothful beatitude, wears hard on a soul already scraped thin by the world. In the term of his waiting, Mr Christian had contracted, as a by-product of his crafty virtue, a loathsome and wearying vice. One night at a party he had stumbled into, after a dozen drinks and some puling tears, some less than senseless thing had offered him a shot, had popped him almost before Mr Christian realized what was up. And now, even more lonely, more forsaken than before, Mr Christian rode the Horse. Powder-white horse, coal-black rider. Who, in the mad glory of half an hour's shadowless career, was suited in Sir Modred's inky armor riding not against dragons or for the sake, Lord knows, of pale virgins, but, full of power and a new variety of righteousness, riding to defy the Foul Fiend. Whose name, besides Light-bearer, Adversary, and Legion, was Almighty God.

Sometimes for the hair-thin portion of a second, Mr Christian Blackman, full of miraculous junk, could discern Him through misty pale clouds. His robes were the color of chalk, His long hair and beard hard and crystalline as snow. Around Him blessed winged thugs with the faces of bookies and cops and heelers, ladies' club secretaries and Newcomb coeds, hands full of cash and juice, orders and invoices. The face of God? No, that eluded him. The Horse flagged and fell away from heaven. The air thickened, and Mr Christian's heart collapsed as he saw the carbon of his armor turn back again into dark flesh, his mailed hands become black again with all the fingers askew. And under him the Horse would die. Back to the wretched earth, and twenty bucks for another mount.

To pay for his stable, Mr Christian stole things, sold stolen things. Ran odd jobs here and there. Very odd jobs. He pushed the same pony he rode. Not without guilt: shamefaced and

sorry, knowing that the ride was not worth the price, but knowing too as he sold his bags to other colored men that it was as
good a ride as they could find, and that however high the price,
it was only a little dearer than that they paid for only standing
still.

So he pushed for Mrs. Mailer. And there was another pair of
hooks, too. When he came up sweating from under the bread
trucks, when he had peddled his stuff, he would wash quickly
and find a certain cab. From it he pandered the long streets:
Bourbon and Royal, Chartres and Toulouse. He sent custom to
a house on Conti Street where a Yankee Jew kept half a dozen
girls and made movies of what he called "short subjects" on the
side. This Boundoch had asked Mr Christian to strip down
with one of the buck-toothed, long-breasted white girls and become a short subject. But Mr Christian shrugged him off.

The last connection was with a scary foreigner from Mexico
or Bessarabia or God knows where. Corpulent and clothed in
strange dignity, he kept a place on Royal Street. This foreigner, Dr. Aorta, smiling occasionally behind his thick glasses,
hands moving softly across his enormous belly, dipping like
fugitive sparrows once in a while to caress his crotch, or upward
to touch his slabby cheeks, the folds of his neck, would walk
before dawn and after dark in Jackson Square. Mr Christian
did not like the man. He was terrible. Fat as a Hinds County
sheriff, cold as a Yankee sport, soft and plausible as a priest gone
wrong.

But he paid Mr Christian for passing the word that Dr.
Aorta corrected mistakes. That no mistake a woman could
make was beyond the doctor's skill. Sometimes he would be
paid to carry one of Boundoch's girls to the doctor's place.
Sometimes he would take a girl from Dr. Aorta's to Mrs. Mailer's for a week or two. And then on to Boundoch's house. It
was like blood circulating. And while the cells moved, there
was always a Horse in the corral.

What did Mr Christian remember? He remembered snow
on the ground once near Poplarville, Mississippi. He could just
recall the thick Gulf heat that ran over his body like syrup as
he lay near the great Gulf on a beach where whites rarely came,

near Bay St. Louis. He could remember too the sweet stench of his father's work clothes lying beside the washtub, the tinny rattle of the family's radio (won to the envy of half a hundred other black families—and a few white ones too—in a church raffle at a congregation to which Mr Christian's people did not even belong), and his father's heavy breathing when he would awake in the middle of the night on the pallet between his brothers and sisters. He could not forget his father's hard asthmatic breathing, or the night when, half-awake, he heard it stop suddenly, not to resume again.

For the rest there were sawmills and dishwashing, lawns and crop-making. A sister buried beside his father (neither grave marked except with an ephemeral coffee can full of flowers that refused to thrive), and a brother vanished without a trace along the Atchafalaya River, prey to cottonmouth or copperhead, popskull or white man.

And at last the Staff-o-Life Bakery. The garage under it. The grease pit below that. Now it was hard to remember those other things, the grass, the snow, wind and the sound of a woman's laughter or a man breathing hard in his sleep. It was all less real than the transmission he had rebuilt last Wednesday—or was it Thursday? Or the bearings he had packed yesterday after-noon. Sure, it was yesterday.

Mr Christian had seen a movie once. About a dead black man from Haiti or Cuba or thereabouts who was brought back to something like life and obliged to obey the man who had brought him back. Sometimes, in the darkness of the garage, he would remember that movie and hunch his shoulders, twist his face, roll his red-rimmed eyes and make claws of his maimed hands. He would stalk from the grease pit to the tool cabinet and back like a great misshapen dead thing on some awful mission. Sometimes he could not remember clearly, or discern for certain whether he was, in fact, the son of King David Black-man, or (at least as likely) that poor zombie raised in amnesial stupor from the grave to work a certain term in this dark pit. Was he Mr Christian recalling a zombie picture, or Mr. Zombie remembering a show about someone called Mr Christian? When he mounted the Horse, he was clearly neither, but rather

Mr. Jesus riding to judgment, and falling from his steed; he was simply Mr. Shit, lying helpless as calf droppings, his straw eyes and weed body spread and suppliant as dung on a stable floor.

Or maybe (and this he seriously considered when he found it hard to concentrate on God, and the vengeance he sought) it was after all a crazy movie made by actors long since dead, and even now he (Mr Christian) was only a celluloid ghost acting out over and over again some idiot mime without meaning or sense in a dark and empty theater where even the projectionist has gone home a dozen years before.

Chapter Three

Billy Bob Stoker is wandering toward the river. It is not a conscious direction, but he is getting closer with every miserable pace. He cannot think clearly. The same old fear that has driven him from home (albeit no farther than a friendly sister state) is stalking him again. As if that dank subbasement and its suboccupant had brought to the surface certain memories he has spent two years pressing downward. His own flesh gives him the creeps, and as he walks through the wall of midday heat, passing lovely stenographers on their lunch hours and young men in silk suits and dark glasses looking for one or another kind of business, it is as if Mr Christian, wrench in hand, were stalking him. He cannot remember that blurred red-eyed face, but he knows where they must have met before. He winces, thinking of Christopher's hearing about those days. Surely vileness and sodomy shall follow me all the days of my life. Only a fool supposes yesterday can be canceled. Or lived down. Or atoned for. Or forgotten. The past isn't dead. It isn't even past. It looms like a black zombie just beyond sight. Until you try to live as if it weren't there.

He is on Canal Street now, watching the streetcars jangling past, the people hurrying toward a thousand various destinations. How many people die in New Orleans every day? How many destinations are not reached? How many pasts slouch along behind these people, invisible, like assassins of guardian angels? The past will pounce, Billy Bob thinks, and turns almost automatically into a bar with a Greek name where he can smell draught beer.

It is cool and dark inside, and the bar looks to be old and solid: mahogany or oak. There is only one neon sign advertising a local beer. Over the bar mirror is a tattered fragment of an old poster. A pack of cigarettes has an old-fashioned helmet on, a Springfield rifle in hand. *Lucky Strike Green Has Gone to War*, it says. Equipped like that, Lucky Strike Green probably died in the first wave. Green, L. S., killed in action.

Billy Bob drains his beer and signals for another. The bartender is fat, Greek (or an Italian trying to pass), moustached, wet-lipped and oblivious of his two or three customers. He talks quietly, harshly, to a girl in sweater, slacks and enormous earbobs who sits at the far end of the counter. The girl is a classic: she looks like the mother, sister, daughter and niece of every hooker who has ever milked a trick east of Austin and south of Louisville. Hair a bizarre and fraudulent red. Fraudulent only in terms of appearance. It may well be natural, but no one will ever believe it. A drained and totally dehumanized face neither pretty nor ugly, sulky nor smug, plain nor fancy. Only a face so totally limited in expressive and communicative possibilities that one could imagine her shell-shocked without much effort, and could more easily be convinced of her capacity for human emotion if he were talking to her on a telephone.

Her face is freckled, and beneath these numberless dots are the pink or flamingo blotches so characteristic of certain redheads. Her neck, her arms, her hands are the same, and Billy Bob knows for sure enough what the rest looks like. He knows, before he looks that her fingernails are bitten to the quick. He glances down the bar between cool bracing gulps. Check. He knows her legs are thin, shapeless, her feet narrow, long, prehensile. Glance. Check. He is certain before he hears it that her voice, country Southern, will be flat, monotonous, without inflection or the natural rise and fall of emotion.

Billy is not a student of human nature. If he were now thinking of what he is thinking, it would amaze him. The girl is ordinary beyond all probability—as if this Greek bar had suddenly become a point in space-time where prototypes are as-

sembled and boozed up before being launched forth into the
world. Billy turns his head toward her again. Ten to one she
squints, even in the sullen red-lined darkness. And blinks rapidly, the velocity of flutter (totally nonvolitional) increasing
when she is nervous or apprehensive, or when she is questioned closely on any subject beyond her preference in weather,
whisky, or current jukebox selections.

Somehow, as he toys with his second beer, Billy sees this
pitiful hooker in half a dozen ways simultaneously: first, as an
astounding compendium of parts that he has seen for years in
various combinations, but never all together. Second, as a
comic character required to make a bar a bar. Without such
girls, a bar tends to become a restaurant. But he sees her as
something human, too. Not very human, if you get to weighing
things. But other than animal. Not a light bulb or a fixture
despite her pointlessness. Not even a bar fixture, really. A poor
skinful of dull hope and somber foreboding. Something that
could be injured, something subject to pain—even mental pain.
Like Billy Bob himself, unable to forget the Negro down there
who has told—is telling—Christopher a story—stories—so fantastic, so vile. Billy Bob ducks his head downward as if Christopher were staring up through the concrete and along the several blocks between down there and up here. The girl rambles
on, the Greek or pseudo-Greek wiping glasses, picking his
nose, certain of where and when and how and for what time
and price this one-sided conversation will end. Or consummate.
The Greek irritates Billy Bob. He does not like the way the
fat aproned man takes everything for granted. He would like to
see the girl throw her half-shot of cadged bourbon into his face.
Even a prototype has the right not to be totally understood,
calculated, figured up and dismissed before the event. Billy
Bob can feel, over the distance and past the intervening walls,
Christopher doing the same thing to him. Mad dog. Degenerate. Gobbler. Pervert. Ugh.

The Greek draws Billy Bob another beer without being
asked. He does not even look across the bar as he sets it down
and ambles, fat-assed and proprietary, back over to the Typical
Example, who gabbles on when he walks away, raising volume

only a little, and who neither pauses nor even draws fresh breath as he returns, but only lowers volume again and rattles into new suburbs of inanity as if bed, board, and tomorrow's light depends upon her nonstop pitch till the Greek shuts her mouth with something or other later in a room back of the bar.

◄§ §►

Mrs. Nieman has hit paydirt. It is a small place, but more than sufficient for a young man—or a pair of them. With even room enough for an occasional visitor. Like Mrs. Nieman.

She stands on a small wrought-iron balcony overlooking Royal Street. Down there moves a cab with a fractured fender, a Negro woman on a bicycle, an elderly white man with a huge sack thrown over his shoulder. Out of the cab's left rear window protrudes a leg in a plaster cast; out of the colored woman's basket the tail of an enormous catfish. Whatever is in the old man's sack is struggling desperately, pausing to get its breath, and then renewing the fight.

A breath of cool air materializes from somewhere, and Mrs. Nieman shivers. Someone has stepped on her grave. She feels Jeremiah's nose searching the tan warmth of her calves, pushing diffidently at her skirt. She glances down into his strange monstrous colorless eyes and smiles. His maleness, however beastly, is some sort of continuous compliment.

In the hallway outside, a large man in a rumpled black suit moves up the stairs heavily. His balding head moves from side to side like M-G-M's lion. His eyes are cloaked in thick steel-rimmed glasses. He pauses at the open apartment door, not looking in, his head raised as if he is listening or sniffing. Then he plods on. It may be that the passage of his body stirs the moist air, and sends it fleeing outward from him.

◄§ §►

Billy Bob is not drunk. In this climate it is very difficult to get drunk on beer. What you consume, you lose quickly. Only a very low tolerance for alcohol can explain drunkenness on half a dozen beers. Rather Billy Bob is out of his senses. The beer and the darkness, his recollection of Christopher standing across from that spooky nigger, the memory of Mary Ann Downey which has plagued him since he awoke in Shreveport a week and a half ago to find himself on the floor, Christopher in bed and the girl gone—all this makes for pungent sauce in the drained heart, the desiccated brain.

A small neat Jew has entered and studies the bar and its occupants as if he were handicapping a provincial horse race. His expression is kind, quizzical and disengaged. He could own the bar, or lease the jukebox (which has not been played in several hours now) or be a drummer for Gilbey's gin. It would not even be much of a surprise if he began walking along the bar and amongst the empty tables passing out small slick cards of invitation to a revival and miracle rally out on the Jefferson Davis Parkway Saturday and Sunday evenings. For some reason no Yankee sociologist has yet plumbed, Southerners fancy converted Jews turned Baptist preachers. A saved Jew can make the difference between a couple of gummy, Psalm-singing evenings, and an honest-to-God floor-stomping wall-bending soul-saver of a revival. If you want to bring in the people, put your money on a Baptist named Lowenstein.

But Benny Boundoch is borsch of another choler. He makes a daily stroll through certain bars to see if anything likely in the way of alien gash has drifted in. As he steps up to the bar near Billy Bob, the pseudo-Greek looks up, nods, motions slightly with his shoulder toward the girl, who is still talking, who has not paused for longer than it takes to kill a drink since she came in and found a more or less stationary bar. Benny studies her. The kindly old lepidopterist: catalogs, prices, determines market value and stamina against bed, board and electricity. Then he rubs his nose and shakes his head. In this business attrition is always a problem. But not that bad. He can still muster nine hides, any one of which can screw this poor little crease right into the floor. What you can't sell, you don't buy. Some things are the same whether the New is York or Orleans.

For some reason this exchange of glances enrages Billy Bob. He does not know why, but he has had just enough beer to dispense with self-searching. This Greek or whatever down the bar is a sonofabitch: the latest in a long line of sonsofbitches who have inherited the earth. Billy measures the distance with one eye closed, and throws his most recently emptied mug sidearm. Billy Bob has a remarkable arm. It develops tremendous velocity, and the Greek or whatever goes down like a broken mast. Not a sound. Even the empty mug falls silently to the rubber mat behind the bar.

The little Jew is not flustered. He steps to the bar, leans over it, and studies the Greek. After a hot day's fitful fever, he sleeps well. Boundoch shakes his head. These things happen. The girl, her talk paused but still potential, inevitable, stands on the rung of her barstool and stares over at her sometime auditor. She frowns slightly, shrugs, and throws down the rest of her drink.

—Has any of youall been to St. Louis, Missouri? she asks finally, fracturing the silence.

—Wow, Boundoch says slowly. —What did you put on that thing? I saw it break just before it hit him.

—Aw, Billy Bob grumbles, almost embarrassed, his anger cooled, thinking how absurd it is to deck a man for following life's conventions.

—You ought to pitch for the Yankees.

Billy Bob rouses, turns to face the Jew.

—For who? What? You sawed-off little bastard . . .

—I mean the Pelicans. Chicks? Sports? Boundoch smiles, and smiles, watches Billy Bob's hand fumbling among the other empty mugs. He knows a gaffe when he has committed one. Even as survival motifs scatter like spooked rats through the channels of his brain, art sounds its clarion. Despite the adrenalin, he is thinking of a mad mad orgy that takes place in a baseball park with this huge healthy peasant in the leading role. Maybe a kind of baseball game–Black Mass combination. When you get a hit, there are these lovely nudes serving as bases. You get to stomp across them. With cleats on. If it's a homer, you slide all the way into this gorgeous redhead on the plate. At the end they lynch the umpire and throw pieces of him into the crowd. Call it *Bats and Balls?* No. *Take Me Down at the Ball Game?*

—Let me take you down . . . the street and buy you a drink, Benny says. —I think we better get out of here. Cephopolis is going to wake up.

—I've lived in Cincinnati, Ohio, too, the girl says, reaching a long arm out to snag a fifth of rye off the back bar. —There was this horse-breeder in Fulton, and we . . .

—I've made that show, Benny says absently, tugging at Billy Bob's sleeve, pulling him toward the door as a vast and inutterably sad groan issues up from the floor behind the bar, and the girl, surprised by the sound, pushes her glass away and begins drinking straight from the bottle.

๙ ๖

This is the Café du Monde again. A wonderful name. The world's body is represented here—complete with wens, tics, broken limbs, bad eyes and bandages. It is possible to see the café as a kind of aid station on the edge of a battlefield called Vieux Carre. Things are tough in there; nobody wins, and the walking wounded come here for rest and rehabilitation. Perhaps there should be a Red Cross banner flying over the awning out front. But there is nothing of the sort. Except, in the souvenir shop next door, an ancient cane holder full of Confederate battle flags. Which tourists from California and Maine perversely purchase and carry home, for what purpose God only knows.

Mrs. Nieman and Jeremiah sit in the twilight watching the fading shadow of Andy Jackson through the fluttering green interstices of summer trees and shrubs. She is sipping coffee and nibbling a *bagnet*. Jeremiah is still worrying her legs. Christopher drops into a chair across the table, automatically defending his crotch from Jeremiah's happy assault.

—Well? his mother asks.

—I got a job.

—I got an apartment.

Both of them smile, and their hands meet midway on the table. The exchange of triumphs warms and refreshes.

—Tell me about the apart . . .

—No, Mrs. Nieman says. —You'll see it in a little while. I won't be seeing the job. What are you doing?

Christopher hunches his shoulders. —Driving a truck.

—Here? In town?

—Delivering. Bread.

—You mean in a red shirt, watching out for school children, smiling?

Christopher cracks his knuckles loudly. It is a nasty little habit he began as a child. He nurtured and perfected its volume and intensity when he discovered his father despised it. He does it still when aggrieved or frustrated. It takes the place of gross language. Sometimes. Sometimes it has taken the place of a fist fight. Or self-mutilation. He cracks each knuckle separately but equally, with clarity and a certain panache. There is style in it.

Mrs. Nieman frowns slightly. —Stop it, she says without heat. —Or I'll kick you in the shins so hard your eyes fall out.

Christopher stares at his hands and sulks. —I know why you do that, his mother says, —so don't. Tell me about the job.

He shrugs. —I just get there about five-thirty and drive all over the Quarter. I take bread to twenty-five or thirty little stores. I get finished about two-thirty or so.

—Every day?

—Except Sunday.

Mrs. Nieman smiles again, and leans her elbows on the table. It crosses her mind that this boy has no greatness in him. For years he has risen at five-thirty to attend Mass, then to celebrate it. Now, his old life fractured and scattered behind him, he manages to find another occupation which makes the same demands. At a comparable salary. There is some mark upon him. He is doomed. Treadmill, squirrel cage. Motion without movement. Journey without destination. As if the journey's motion were its purpose. And who knows?

Mrs. Nieman shrugs. Jeremiah rolls on his back and coughs derisively. —This nigger, Christopher begins. —I met this colored man at the bakery. He knew Billy Bob in Mississippi.

—That's fine, Mrs. Nieman says. —Maybe he could come up to the apartment.

—No, I mean . . . they wouldn't want to see each other. You see . .

—Horseshit, his mother says softly.

—No, it's not that he's a nigger. It's that Stoker used to be a deputy sheriff, and in those days . . .

When he is done, he orders fresh coffee and studies his mother's face. She is smoking quietly, squinting slightly as the smoke curls and weaves around her head. He cannot tell what she is thinking. The corners of her mouth are drawn up into what, on another face, would be a quizzical, possibly a cynical, smile. But his mother is a separate species, and her smile, like the vague tightness at the corners of her eyes, is more a response to things in general than to any specific enormity.

—Don't sound healthy to me, she says finally. —You reckon that boy's all right?

—Mr Christian—the nigger—says it's religion. He says too much Protestant religion makes you morbid. You get to misunderstanding things. Things get out of perspective.

Mrs. Nieman's mouth corners climb a notch or so, her eyebrows following suit. She looks like the Cheshire cat. —That sounds reasonable, she says grinning. —I always had a suspicion that religion was best in small doses. At long intervals.

Christopher's blush almost warms up the coffee. —All right, he says.

Mrs. Nieman is working with that grin, but it will not be quenched. She spreads her hands Hebraically. —I was thinking of your father, she says lamely.

St. Joan at the Alcázar, Christopher thinks, groaning inwardly. The ultimate flagellant. Is it more unnatural to poke a colored man than to desert your family and travel 4000 miles to die? Or be dragged into the priesthood through the throbbing knothole of Grünewald's grisly imaginings?

—Everybody's peculiar, Mrs. Nieman says, the smile at last under control. She pauses and sips her coffee, one eye on Jeremiah. As if she expected some mysterious grossness from him. But he is an average hound.

—Yes. Like you said this afternoon. We all make mistakes.

His mother's eyes narrow, and she studies him, his hands below the table's edge.

—Are you popping those knuckles again?

—Yes.

&♥ ♥&

What moon there is stands beyond the river, apparently faltering and about to collapse on Algiers or Westwego. Billy Bob is not sure where he is, but the cool river breeze does wonders for him. He can smell that fine, faintly rotten odor of fresh water and dead fish. A few early lights glimmer on the river, and he recalls for no explicable reason how his mother's grandfather, a truly ancient man, veteran of some obscure Mississippi cavalry company, used to describe the river as he stood staring out at it during the siege of Vicksburg. A few lights here and there. A campfire or two across the way. Perhaps the turtlelike smear of a Yankee gunboat up at the northern bend. Billy Bob squints, looking for campfires and spots an oil flare across the way. No gunboats, but one long dark barge shoved by a clucking wallowing tug.

Beside him, Benny Boundoch is thinking of other things. The Staten Island ferry. Manhattan the night of V-E Day. Broadway stoked up again, burning as usual. He recalls the rise in business as Johnny came marching home. Prepared, initiated as it were, by Paris and her exhibitions, her inimitable enormities. Those were the golden days by any measure. In the quietude and detachment of this exile, Boundoch considers the glory of what he has known. Things were once very good. They will be good again. Only it's now. How to survive the now until then. Maybe a little show. He has the girls. And this great country carcass could turn the trick. If he will turn the trick. Boundoch is no novice. He knows how to move. They have dined and drunk, and now they are walking in the general direction of his place. The girls will be waiting. Given the run of nine choice cunts, this dinosaur will go along. What kind of monster turns down first-class hide? Not this kind of monster, Benny thinks.

But Billy Bob, back from Vicksburg, at least half sober, is

beginning to wonder how come the free dinner? What for all these drinks? This walk by the river? He is not particularly suspicious by nature, but his mind has been dredging these channels all afternoon. Do you reckon this little guy is some kind of? Maybe that damned nigger has published the disasters of his youth throughout the city. Maybe the dinner and drinks and this walk. Do you reckon this is . . . a *date?* Billy Bob almost falls off the pier. Ugh. His fist bunches and he considers beating this little monster to death and throwing his body in the river. If there were sharks. But catfish take weeks on a body. And if even a Mississippi sheriff can bring a man in on fingerprints, the New Orleans cops can probably run you down with nothing but knuckleprints. Maybe better to shove him in front of a car. Or cut his throat and drop him in a manhole.

They reach a point where a long ill-lighted street meets the Bienville Street Wharf at right angles. Benny turns away from the river. —My place is down here, he says diffidently.

All things considered, diffidence is the worst possible tack. Better he should growl, menace, threaten, draw out a bloody dirk and point. But Billy Bob is a prize: the perfect body. And so Boundoch is soft-spoken. Wow.

Billy Bob's problem is no longer one of analysis. If something looks like a duck, walks like a duck, and quacks, it is a duck. Or something bound and determined to be a duck, trying to be a duck. By analogy, Billy Bob figures, it is possible to identify a fairy. They may not sport wings any more, but then you wouldn't look for a devil to be horny nowadays. He would probably have a gray-flannel suit and a Bronx accent. So with this soft-spoken little queer. The problem is how to dispatch him. Why not walk away? Against certain ingrained rules. Especially if this little creature assumes Billy Bob to be one of the Flight. Only annihilation will suffice. Billy Bob is looking for dark alleys, vacant lots, deep ditches, uncovered sewers.

—We can have another drink, Benny tells him soothingly as they walk below street lamps just beginning to flick on. —There are some people I want you to meet.

Billy Bob's eyes widen. What is awaiting him? The whole crew of the gay ship *Peter Pan?* He pauses under a light and sees above, beyond the light, a muted streak of lightning. Summer storm.

—Come on. We're almost there.

Billy Bob shrugs. He will probably have to butcher his way out of this, leave some mauve apartment smelling of lilac or lavender ankle-deep in blood, waist-deep in delicate corpses. But he needs a drink. Surely he can get a beer or two down before the thigh-slapping begins. Maybe even wait out the worst of the rain. Something is giving way within him. He has been too much bullied by the world these last few days. Beginning with that dice game that cost him a scramble. He should have cracked Christopher's head like an eggshell, given the remains to Jeremiah. It has been downhill ever since, and he lacks the will to walk off, to punch his way out. Things pile up. Enough grains of sand can crush a giant.

So Billy Bob slouches up the steps of a run-down attached house with long shutters and a dark, dark doorway, behind Benny Boundoch like some rough beast, his hour come around at last, and nothing but spookish horrors up ahead. Even as they reach the door, the sky caves in and dollops of rain fall like paving stones. They are soaked before Benny can turn the key.

—My God, honey, the first one calls out, pulling open the door even as Boundoch fumbles with the key, —you gonna catch your death out there.

Benny's smile lights up the foyer. Ulysses is home. It is meet and right that wayfarers should be so greeted. By now, the second one, in blue shorts and something like a loose brassiere made out of soft feed-sack material, has hold of Billy Bob. It looks like a girl, a good-looking skinny mean-eyed brunette. But Billy Bob is no hick. He has heard that everything in girl's clothing is not a girl. He steps back, shaking his drenched head like a water-shy hound. Great Jesus, it looks like a girl: Forget the body: those eyes, that tiny cruel little mouth. Like a wasp sting on her lower lip. The way she moves. And those hips. If this is one of those transmorphadites, he'll eat his . . .

Down the stairs come three more. Billy Bob feels like a poor undeserving Christian who has stumbled into the Moslem heaven. These have got to be girls. Then what about Boundoch? This slick smooth-talking Jew with a mouse's warm eyes, small hands and feet, and apparently a money tree out back. What about these girls?

Then one of the new girls reaches the foot of the spiral stairway.

—Well, God Almighty, she says, embracing Billy Bob like a long-lost mark. —Are you follering me for the FBI?

Billy Bob cannot believe it. Everything snaps into sudden and perfect focus. These are girls all right. And this lucky little Jew has the world by the tail. The best part of its tail, anyway.

—Where's your ole buddy? Mary Ann Downey asks him.

—Well, Billy Bob begins, and leaves off, overcome. He stands, dripping head down, shivering with pleasure. He is not the sort to consider at this point how close he came to stomping Benny Boundoch to death and caching the remains in the nearest barbecue pit. It is better to think how old Benny can be made into a good friend: the kind of friend who might even give a friend exclusive rights in certain areas. Maybe even a job. Make a friend every day, Billy Bob decides.

—I was sorry to scoot out on youall, but I woke up thinkin' of Christopher's mother. Some god-awful old crow comin' in there to the apartment. And there we'd be. Me and ole Chris. The priest with the hole in his robe.

—Huh, Billy Bob snorts. It is no use trying to explain Mrs. Nieman to this girl. She is a pathological mother-hater. There are better things to do with her than argue. —She come down here with us. To get us started.

Mary Ann smiles crookedly, glancing at Boundoch. —Looks like you're started, all right.

They are in the parlor now. It is a phantasm of old Queen Anne and late Victorian gargoyle furniture: screens, plush chairs, marble-topped tables, a frowsy and brittle titmouse under a bell jar, red velvet hangings, a copy of *The Angelus* and two mute pastoral catastrophes by Watteau framed in worm-gnawed walnut-stained cypress. The mantel is from an old downriver plantation house, the triumph and chef d'oeuvre of some psychotic millwright slave. It resembles the bridge and superstructure of a steamboat circa 1884, as seen from the vantage of frenzied trappers in a pirogue about to be swamped. The fireplace below contains a brace of fake logs which glow in electric anticlimax when one presses a switch ingeniously hidden amongst the loops, whorls, struts and rick-rack of the mantel.

Benny has changed into a Dubonnet smoking jacket with gold epaulets and kelly-green frogged buttonholes. A few customers sit here and there in the room which seems in size to rival the reading room of the British Museum. A phonograph is playing somewhere, and one of the girls begins a casual strip in the dim light of fringe-shaded, globe-shaped lamps. She bumps prettily to the crowd at large, and grinds on the hand of a Latin type who grins sedulously, showing a gallery of alien teeth, some gold, some platinum. Billy Bob sits on the edge of an enormous chair with dragons creeping all over it. He is not comfortable, but Mary Ann's presence keeps him from bolting. He studies her and wants. The phonograph plays Stan Kenton. June Christy eases through the brass:

> . . . *whisper to the wind*
> *and say that love has sinned* . . .

Benny Boundoch sits like a Mandarin, his hands caressing the beautifully tooled cover of a copy of *Justine* in German. Bound in some odd skin almost pink in color. It is the gift of a local friend and colleague. Benny treasures it.

The girl is nude now. Her dance has passed from the social, through the esthetic, past the aphrodisiac to the beastial. The music is "Blue Prelude": much drum, a low tenor sax; some trumpet man who should be punished or rewarded.

> . . . *all the love I could*
> *steal beg or borrow*
> *couldn't heal all this pain*
> *in my soul* . . .
> *What is love but a prelude to sorrow,*
> *with a heartache ahead for its goal?*

A few more men have come in now, a few more girls come down. A small bar at the end of the parlor is functioning quietly and efficiently, and Billy Bob has downed a pair before he even realizes he has been served. The girl, still ostensibly dancing, comes by and sits on his hand. Before he can move it, she is away and pressing her breast into someone else's drink. Billy Bob raises the hand as if he expects some fingers to be melted off. He shifts among carved dragons, trying to find easement for his crotch. There is none, and when Mary Ann, drinking too, and brushing off a few customers, comes to share the seat with him, the situation becomes critical.

—Listen, he breathes, —you reckon we could pass up the entertainment and go somewhere?

Mary Ann smiles and kisses him. —You talked to the boss?

—Well, no. I mean, have you got to get his okay to leave the room?

—He owns the store. You don't want to get caught shoplifting.

—I want to get caught with my . . .

—Watch it, Mary Ann says, as if she has memorized the speech. —This is a high-class residence. No loud talk, no rude talk, no common talk. You got to conduct yourself like you was at home.

—My God, Billy Bob says, —don't that last part hold back business?

The nude girl has given up dancing and is sprawled in someone's lap. Several others are gathered around handling her in one way or another. She is handling in return. The temperature rises, and outside there is thunder and a burst of new rain against the heavily draped windows.

Boundoch plays the bonze. He watches everything, occasionally making a frame with his fingers and peering through. The room is perfect for color. Things are coming along. Billy Bob slouches up to him, walking with awful clumsiness as if he were carrying an egg between his thighs.

—Say, Benny, you reckon . . .

Benny reckons he is within a pinch and a tickle of being ripe for the proposition. But ripeness is all. Even a speck of green might start old John Calvin rearing up into this country boy's mind. Better let the flesh have its way. Mary Ann has all the tenderer aspects of a succubus. If Billy Bob is star material, a night with her will blast him into nova. So cool and inch by inch, the bonze figures.

—Yes?

—I wonder if I could take this little lady . . .

—For a walk?

—Well . . .

—How are you fixed? Benny asks soothingly. —You've got a little money, don't you? A house like this costs a lot to keep going. You want to help us along.

—Sure, but . . .

—No money?

—Well, I just come into town, and what with fooling around and those beers . . .

—No money. Broke.

Billy Bob shuffles uncomfortably. Where he comes from, if you're not good, Sandy Claws sure as hell doesn't come. There have been a couple of Christmases when he was left high and dry with nothing but BIRDSONG and a few carols from inside the Baptist church. Now he is face to face with a new kind of Sandy, and again he seems to be up a stump.

—I reckon, he mumbles.

—No money, Benny says meditatively. —Do you suppose you could work out your keep? Like selling magazines to get through college?

—If it wasn't nothin' funny. I mean against . . .

—Nature, Benny concludes, remembering a story in *The New York Times* about the fall of Dolls, Inc.

—Yeah, Billy Bob brightens, thinking perhaps he could steal or murder or fire barns to stay with Mary Ann.

—All right, Benny says in mock impulsiveness. —All right. I'm going out on a limb. I want a good strong boy around here. I want somebody I can trust, somebody Mary Ann can trust.

Billy Bob almost loses his footing. He reaches for Benny's

hand and for another drink simultaneously. —You can count
on me, he cries, —you can sure as shit count on me.

—All right, Mary Ann says sharply from behind. —What did
I tell you about that kind of talk? You just can't help bein'
crude can you?

The nude girl giggles, but it is impossible to tell just why.
Her current friend seems to have opened his fly, and she is
bouncing up and down like Judy being punched. Benny
watches the other clients, but there is nothing to see but garden-
variety lust. One of the old-timers, well dressed, diffident as only
a respectable citizen in a brothel can be, is quietly asking if
there might be a girl in a Viking costume complete with horned
helmet and a length of chain anywhere around, and about the
price of a ticket to Valhalla. Benny smiles and nods, mentally
searching the prop trunks in the attic. They had been purchased at a sheriff's sale in New York by an old friend, an un-
crowned queen who owed a favor. They are unused, for the most
part, upstairs, waiting only to be called into technicolor splen-
dor again. Benny's day will come. Movies will be bluer than
ever. How do you balk the grandson of a Polish grenadier?

᥊§ ᠔᥊

In the dark hallway, Billy Bob and Mary Ann have reached
the first turning of the second stair. His hands, hungry as birds
of prey, are investigating her breasts, her thighs. Uusually this
would seem bad conduct. A girl likes some savoir faire. But
Billy Bob is breathing like an asthma patient in a chalk mine.
Mary Ann looks backward and down at his dark sweating face
and sees there mingled expressions of hope and despair. Above,
on all sides, there is darkness, and the narrow landing is close,
fetid as a tomb, but the size of love. She stumbles at the second
turning and his hands are upon her, twisting, turning. From below there is music sharp as severed tin, and from outside, from
the distant river, the long mournful dirge of a tanker shambling
north to Baton Rouge, its bow troubling the water like an old
man's ruined mouth. Mary Ann looks over his shoulder at the
curving stairway above, feels his body seeking hers, his insis-

tent hands worrying her brassiere, her skirt. She is not struggling now, and what had seemed absurd only a moment, only a
stair's turning before, seems all at once just and right and her
hands lock behind his head, her fingers move in his hair, and
she lifts her hips to aid him at first, then to receive him, and
her eyes close to open again high above a bright pasture, a wilderness of sun and pine and live oak sprinkled with honeysuckle and a mist like silk, cool and full of flowers, and she can
hear only the dimmest harmony as she mounts higher and
higher to where the birds are and beyond, and can hardly hear
him saying, —Oh honey. Lord, honey, Lord. And she is fading,
fading like the soft and immeasurable hum of a biplane beyond the horizon, and pressing herself as closely to him as
flesh will allow, she thinks amidst the mist and the flowers and
sun, *little girl, little girl,* and the universe is emptied of stairs.

Benny Boundoch

&s;

I remember those goddamned lousy winters, that's what I remember. Sometimes you'd be trucking down Madison Avenue down around Twenty-fifth Street, passing delicatessens with pastrami, turkeys and kidneys and things in the windows and all of a sudden this car makes a corner and slosh, you get a chest full of melted snow. The cabbie laughs and shifts down, and the rest of the way home you're asking God because you still at the moment believe in Him to send that sonofabitching cabbie to the bottom of gehennah. Which is hell.

Always the lousy snow and my brother Lester saying, come on, Benny, you're late you don't make no money. What's money? I'm twelve, maybe fourteen. Stick ball, hustling a little, pick up a few cases of bottles for the deposit. Mabe once or twice break a drugstore across town. Those winters were awful. I worked for this guy down near Pier 80 who leased the back end of a fur warehouse. This guy made shoe polish in big vats and sold it around to the barber shops and the box-boys. He even sold some to the Catholic Archbishop and chancery or something I don't know what they did with it. Anyhow he had me bottling the stuff. Not cans, see. Bottles. These square funny bottles with long necks and lips at the top and a little #7 cork jammed in. Christ, you never saw anything like it. This was just after prohibition and you could buy these bottles, quarts and pints, by the thousands for almost nothing. They looked like they were for medicine and now they weren't any good to anybody anymore.

And after I finished a six-hour day after school, that god-awful lousy walk back uptown. Subway your ass. If I'd used the subway and bought a hot dog every day, I wouldn't have had any money left. So I walked twenty-two blocks up to where Lester kept books for the McCahey Ice Cream Company which was by then an honest-to-god dairy outfit since beer was legal again. I waited outside till he got done and then we'd walk another nine blocks and catch a ride with Poosh Tuminello who lived in the building with us and charged only twenty cents a week for Lester to ride to work and back and threw me in on the home trip free because, shit, full or empty, he had to drive the same distance.

So we'd sit in the Model-A and drive uptown. Nobody talked. It was strictly a business deal. The dago didn't like kikes, and yids didn't go for wops. Silly, but like that. We just climbed in and said good evening, cold, or warm or whatever it was, and Tuminello let out the clutch and we rolled. To tell the truth it wasn't as good as the subway. Because this big silent dago was some kind of fresh-air nut. He drove with his window down and his sleeves rolled up and his big meaty arm out the window. My God, I'm sitting behind him and it doesn't matter which side of the car I try. I tried taking it in the face head-on, and I tried taking it in the back of the neck sitting over behind Lester, but it was terrible either way. It didn't matter how cold it was. Once I froze my ass off back there, but no worse than usual: only paralyzing like always. Then when I get home, it said on the radio that the temperature was four above zero. That stupid lousy wop.

We didn't have any money. I mean we weren't on relief, but if Papa said let's go to a show, or in summer, let's go to Coney, Mama had to go to work on her fingers to see if we could go and still eat. Those were tough days and three of us working didn't clear enough to go far. My sister couldn't work because she was too little, and Mama was too tired to do much after she took care of us. So Lester and Papa and me did what got done.

And I guess it would have gone on about like that forever if it hadn't been for one especially cold winter, and what happened to me because of it.

When I remember, it was like the house that Jack built: one thing following on another, so that if you looked at the start of it and the end of it, you thought, come on, something like this doesn't go to something like that.

It started with the bad winter. Ten and fifteen below, and snow and a wind blowing off the river like a hurricane. And one night after Christmas the temperature drops to twenty-one below. And the next morning the dago's car has got a broken block. He starts it up, pulls into the street, and a piece of it falls out. It starts steaming in a minute, and the dago is screaming to St. Anthony, and my brother stood at the window of our apartment with a cigarette and no expression on his face, shrugged and came back to his coffee.

—He saved four bits not buying antifreeze, my brother said disgustedly. —Jesus Christ.

My father sliced his egg. —You can't blame him, he said. —It never got so cold. It never got more than a few degrees below. So why waste fifty cents?

—So now he owes two hundred for a new motor.

—A poor man has to take chances, my father said, spreading his hands, raising his eyebrows.

—Fuck that, Lester said.

—Lester, my mother said sharply. —I won't have it. I've told you I won't have that.

Lester closed his eyes and held his coffee cup between his hands. He felt like he took a lot. He looked at me tiredly and got up.

—Come on, punk, he said. —No ride today.

—You mean we're gonna walk both ways?

—Naw, Lester said, —We're gonna try the subway. I got a dime. You wanna take a chance?

So that afternoon when I was finished washing the shoe polish off, I walked up to Lester's. I figured maybe one more subway ride.

—You crazy? I ain't the U.S. mint. I don't make dimes. We got to wait and meet a friend of mine. When he gets off work.

This friend of Lester's lived way uptown and could drop us off. Only he worked late, and even after he was done working, he didn't go home. There was this bar in the Village he had to make.

—Part of the job, Lester told me. —He has to scout after hours.

—Scout?

—Look for talent. He kind of works in entertainment.

His name was Maury Rosenfeld, and he looked like a fat Eddie Cantor. Pop eyes and his wide pasted-on grin. Nice suit, but the shirt collar was dirty and the shoulders of his jacket looked like he'd been out in a blizzard. He manicured his nails. They looked a lot better than my mother's and sister's. He was kind of bluff and muscle-mouthed. You could hear him laugh all the way across the street even with the traffic. He rubbed my head as we walked into Sheridan Square.

—I didn't even know you had a kid brother, Les, he bellowed.

Lester shrugged and faked a smile. —Saving him, he said.

—Don't save the good wine, Maury roared. —You want to let the kid move around. What does he do?

—I work in a dump pouring shoe blacking, I told him.

He pursed his lips and shrugged. —A cute kid, Les. He could do better.

—Forget it, Lester said. —You got the whole fucked-up world to choose from. Let's get on over to the dump.

It was a dump. A run-down little place you had to walk down into and then turn almost around toward the street again to see the sign. It read:

THE COBBLER'S COCK

There was a picture of this shoemaker with a big rooster on his bench. The shoemaker and the chicken were both staring down into the guy's lap. I remembered Lester telling me they named it The Jockey's Strap, but the cops make them change it, and even now they wouldn't let them have the sign up on the street.

Inside it was dark with the usual beer signs and glasses and the rest behind the bar. Only the bartender had an orchid in the button hole of his shirt, and they poured the beer into what

looked like brandy snifters. It was weird: there were workmen
at the bar, still in overalls and caps, but laughing like girls and
patting each other on the ass. There were those young guys
who probably clerked in banks and stores uptown. Now they
were drinking beer and fooling around, and once in a while
dancing with each other between the tables till the bartender
with the orchid yelled at them: —All right, no fagging. If you
can't be nice, go on out on the street.

Everybody laughed except Lester and me. Lester looked embarrassed and I didn't know what the hell was up.

—At first we wanted to call it The Golfer's Balls, the bartender was telling Maury, —but you know how far that got.

—There's a cafe in England, right off the town square in
Petersfield, Maury said, —called The Blue Peter.

—Say, the bartender brightened. —That just might . . .

Lester kept running his finger under his collar. Two guys at
a table near the door kept looking at us and smiling. Finally
one of them kind of beckoned to me. Me? Yes, you, he signaled.
Well, I started over. Maybe it was somebody I knew. The place
was so dark I couldn't have recognized Lester till I was almost
on top of him.

—Christ, Lester breathed, and grabbed me by the coattail.
—Sit on the stool and stay put or I'll break your goddamned
arm.

—Those guys . . . I started.

—Guys, hell, Lester said.

—. . . Then we thought maybe we'd call it The Tinker's
Tool . . .

Maury was back beside Lester. —They'll start coming in
pretty soon now, he said. —You can tell one a mile away. It's
like farm boys coming into a pool hall for the first time.

I got up again and started for the back of the place where
there was a red light over a door. One of the guys at the table
who had motioned to me started to get up too. But Lester had
me by the ear before I could get clear of the stool.

—I got to go to the toilet, I said.

—Not much, he said. —Piss in your pants.

—Aw, come on. You're acting crazy.

—Listen, he said. His face was serious in the gloom. —I'm telling you. Don't make me beat your ass. Stay in your seat. If you got to shit, hold it. There's no other way.

I shrugged. Sometimes the strain got to Lester. But you don't want trouble with your brother in public. —What's your business? I asked Maury.

Lester covered his face with his hands. —You could call it stocks and bonds, Maury grinned. —Kind of a chain-store deal.

Then Maury was turned back around toward the door where these young guys a little older than me were coming in. They were both kind of thin and watery blond and looked like high-school girls with short haircuts and big adam's apples. And they had this kind of sick smile. There was an older guy with them. He looked like some kind of Roman with a round haircut and bags under his eyes like sleep was out of fashion.

—. . . Somebody suggested The Butcher's Meat, the bartender was saying.

The cut-rate Caligula comes up and pushes in between my brother and Maury. He stares at the bartender's orchid like it was either a rat or the silver star. You can't tell what he's thinking. Or if he's thinking. He reminded me of a story about fantan players in Hong Kong. Faces that don't do what faces are supposed to do.

—It's a new world every day, Maury said. —In this business you've got to keep ahead.

—Don't start no philosophy, the new guy said. —Why don't you treat me like I was some kind of rancher? Keep the market stable.

The two blondies were at a table moving their hands like waterbugs. You could feel the others along the bar and at the tables looking them over. I was only so stupid. I saw what the Roman rancher meant. Fresh meat. The bartender is smiling like something hurt him. He took one of Maury's hands and rubbed it.

—You have to live on the edge, don't you? You can't just come in and drink, can you? Do you know what a license costs me? Do you think they give me a license for the same price as that frog across the street?

—Toad down the road sounds better, Maury said innocently.

My brother had been throwing drinks down like he hoped to use them to tell time in place of the watch he couldn't afford.

—You could call this place The Sissy's Secret, he belched. Nobody laughed except Maury, who laughed at everything. Who probably would have gotten his kicks at the Crucifixion. Or who, as it turned out, could have directed it and made the back-street massacre of a couple of thieves and a righteous loud-mouth into the greatest artistic atrocity this side of an un-censored de Sade on a forty-million-dollar budget.

—It's like a screen test, Maury said. —Only more so. If your customers like 'em, my customers will like 'em. This is con-sumer research.

—Jesus, my brother choked. —Consumers.

—Why don't you act like I was deBeers, the rancher was say-ing. —You don't shit the syndicate. If you want a diamond, you pay the price.

—Everything is fine, Maury told him, signaling drinks all around. —You've got some nice little jewels there.

We all turned around some to see the jewels' progress. The table was slowly being surrounded. Wolves around a campfire. Red eyes. Tongues. Meat. One big heavy man with a hard rubber face and eyes like a dimestore Madonna was gesturing to one of the gemlike boys. His hands, parodying grace and delicacy, made me want to either puke or break his fingers one by one with a beer bottle. Another one kept trying to draw at-tention with his strange barren profile. He would turn his head one way and then the other, seeking the best angle, trying to outline his face against the soft orchid light from behind the bar. This one I wanted to bust very much. I sat on the stool looking like a high-school kid and thinking what I could do with a broken bottle. Down through skin and meat to the gris-tle of his long smooth nose. It gave me shivers down to my butt to feel that imaginary bottle grinding against his real nose.

—. . . The Postman's Pouch, one of them said. My brother shook as if someone had dropped a bottle of roaches down his vest. Lester had all the right instincts, and if you can admire somebody for the way he feels about things, then my brother was admirable. Except everything was ready-made. What he had against queers was what everybody has against queers, which is that queers make them uncomfortable. Like cripples or niggers or idiot children. People hate to have to be near somebody who lacks when they have. They feel threatened. Which is why they like to see other people get smashed. Most of them, secretly, would love to punch a queer's face in. Or trip a cripple. Or string up a jig. I don't know about the idiot kids. They have homes for them. But the nurses probably all have hard faces and have to be watched constantly.

With me it was different. I hated the queers because they all had money. I hated the fat rubber-faced cocksucker and his partner with the pretty profile because they were tossing around twenty-dollar bills like toilet paper, while I knew Andrew Jackson was on a twenty only because Lester told me. He told me Franklin was on a hundred, and I took it on faith. What else? So I wanted to tear holes in these fags. But in a cool indifferent way. I just wanted to tear holes where their wallets were.

—I'm gonna eat you all up, the wolf said. The bartender was smiling like a society matron and telling Maury a story.
—Eat, eat, eat, Red Riding Hood said. Don't anybody fuck any more?

Some scattered laughs. My brother looked at me. He was about past being stoic. He shifted on his stool and started to get up. I knew what he had in mind. Stuff the ride. He'd just as soon walk as wait for this sodom streetcar. But I wouldn't. I was really wondering some more how much you could get off one without even fighting. Just doing the opposite. Lester would fall through the bar and blat like a holy horn if he knew what his kid brother was thinking. New angles . . . tough games. Maybe a long close look at a twenty for doing either nothing or next to nothing. It was a cinch that I'd never earn a sawbuck pouring shoe polish. Or any other way I could figure. You were lucky in those days to find a twenty in one piece by robbing a liquor store. And that kind of twenty could cost you twenty, anyhow. So this looked like it. Why not try the circus? Who's afraid of chartreuse animals?

Maury was either finished or tired by then. He heaved himself up from the bar.

—You're a tough customer, he told the rancher-cum-diamond merchant. —If you can save your property bring it around in the morning. It looks all right. We'll see if it can work.

The Roman rancher was weary. He finished his drink. —Sometimes I think about the flower business. Why knock yourself out?

—The pansy business, my brother mumbled.

—That's uncalled for, the bartender hissed. —Live and let live.

My brother got up, shrugged, some kind of defeat sketched into the curve of his shoulders.

—I think I'll take my life in my hands and make a stab at the toilet, he said to no one. Maury laughed. The bartender wiped a glass viciously. —That's *really* uncalled for, he muttered.

As soon as he was out of hearing, I turned to Maury. —How would you like to put me on the payroll? I asked him. His eyebrows shot up. Maybe it was that my voice was still changing.

—Lester would kill me, he said with real humility. —He'd jerk off my balls and cram them up my butt. Slowly.

—Lester, I said, —is exciteable. But Lester is okay. He'll come around. He'll have to come around. They all come around after a while.

—Anyhow, Maury mused almost to himself, —what can you do? What do you want to do? I mean, those movies . . . you want to . . . ?

—No, I told him. —No. What I want to do is scout and maybe join the sales force.

—But almost everybody is . . .

—Look, I said, —you must have things to get done outside fairyland.

—Sure . . .

—So that's it. You could call me your straight man.

Maury smiled. He looked like a worn old Peter Pan who

has lost his immortality pills. Lined and creased. But gay.
—Say, he said, —you got something.

—So have you, I said.

Then Lester showed up and we headed for the door. On the way out, I heard the bartender talking to the diamond merchant.

—A picture of a turkey on the block, and this big sexy guy with an axe. And you call it The Gobbler's Goal.

&ent; &ent;

Have it your own way, if there's a way you like to have it. But I can tell you it beat pouring shoe polish.

By the end of the first week I'm a prince at home. I come home Friday night with a fifty-dollar bill. Ulysses Grant. Next greatest American to Benjamin Franklin. At least in those days. Later on, I got to be a McKinley man myself. Anyhow my father just looked at it. I laid it down on the dining table in front of him.

—You've turned to crime, he said. —Bootlegger.

—Booze is legal, I said. —I just got a raise. They put me in charge of the bottling. They said maybe later they'd put me out to selling the stuff. I could make a lot of money.

Lester caught hold of me later. —I don't know what you're up to, he growled. —But don't hurt 'em. Don't hurt the old man. Think of your mother.

—Think of your scruffy ass, I told him. —I'm gonna put us all in Westchester. Don't cross up my luck.

—You'll put us in the penitentiary, he said. —You've got to be stealing government checks out of widows' mailboxes. You're too young to be pushing; you're too young for a gun. You're too young for bank jobs. If you tried to pimp, they'd laugh you into the river. You can't be running numbers. Nobody would trust a kid. You're either stealing checks or running off those fifties on your play printing press. What's going on. What's up?

—I'm a night watchman for the Ark of the Covenant, I said.

—Smart little prick, he snarled, slapping me alongside the head.

But old Lester came around. That's the first thing you learn. They all come around when you've got the coin. A month after I got started, Lester was borrowing money from me. For the market, he said. He thought he'd try the market. So I slipped him fifty one week, and began giving him fifty a week regular when it started rolling in. It was an investment. What are you going to do with two hundred skins a week when you're fifteen? You can't even buy a drink without getting a hard time about it. So invest. Give the brother a chance to come on.

The work. Oh man, that work. It all happened in the basement of a building down behind Pier 86. You went in the back, and down, and down. Finally there was this door. Old time iron-bound door. With a sign that said: DOLLS, INC. Inside there were a few broken-down puppets and things in the dark front room where we did the paperwork and bookkeeping. Behind that front room was hell. One hundred percent unadulterated hell.

Usually when you went in, they'd be shooting. They shot around the clock. Because the market for exotic films (that was Maury's name for them) is enormous. You got to keep the cameras grinding, and the ideas bumping. And the fresh talent moving in. You don't want any fat or wrinkles, any sharp angles. Everything has to be young and fresh. Or at least look that way. You want girls who look not only like they've never done it, but never heard about it. Preferably who look like they can't even believe it when it's happening. For most of the girls we used, you had to count on acting talent. Most of 'em couldn't even remember the first time—or the last time—they'd been at it. The one way to get that expression of surprise and horror was to bring in the pony. When they saw that Shetland coming with a hard on, almost all of them looked wild. And then, just like it was scripted, some of them would smile. Fast thinkers. Cute pony.

I didn't mind the straight fuck shows. They didn't interest me a whole lot at first, but they didn't make me sick. The first show I worked was pretty high-budget. Called *Roman Gang Bang*. Thirty people. Every known kind of heterosexual encounter including multiple-blow job by one girl and musical screwing, from girl to girl, by the emperor. Who was a tailor from the garment district trying to get money enough to go to law school. He had good muscles and a fine dong. Only he insisted on a mask. He said he couldn't afford to be known. It might prejudice a jury someday. Maury thought the mask brought down the tone of things. Made it like wrestling.

—The Phantom Fucker, Maury said. —Doesn't that sound elegant?

—It could make a title, one of the writers said.

Maury stared at him. All the writers were sluggo. One of them was trying like hell to get out of this back to his father's grocery, a little dago joint that catered to charge-account types —mostly black. They could pay by the month—if they didn't mind ten percent tacked on every can of lima beans and every hamhock. But there was a mortgage problem. Somebody was doing to the grocers what they were doing to the niggers. Big ones eat little ones. And so on.

The other writer, the one who handled all the queer stuff— the drag and flag—was even funnier. He was trying to make up his mind to be straight or go gay. Which was no decision to speak of, if you saw his scripts. The Italian is an advertising man now. It works like his old man's store, only with different victims. Mr. Undecided writes for television: only the plots are all real psychological now. But any shrink could make the obvious substitutions and see that he's cribbing his own old blue-movie stuff. Only now it's green.

Anyhow I learned fast. I made all kinds of contacts. I met the stag-club owners, the smoker promoters. I worked with the hicks who came up from Des Moines and Omaha and Knoxville to set up a monthly supply of hot prints for the Legion post or the Grand Lodge. Jesus, what a bunch. The actors, I swear to God, were a better class than the spectators.

Anyhow, it got better and better—or worse and worse, depending on how you look at it. I got up to almost three hundred skins a week. We started getting a good name, a real reputation. I helped place some of the scenes. Then I wrote a few scripts. Finally Maury let me direct a show. I wanted to call it *A Breast of the Times*. But Maury said it wasn't hot enough. He

liked *Pussy Wants a Corner*. We argued for a week, and when
we were both worn out, I changed some of the parts, some of
the action and called it *Take the Gay Train*. It was okay. About
a Southern colored guy who comes to New York and gets
queered. And likes it. And a Southern white girl who comes up
and goes les before she loses her slotcover. There was a social
message in it: how easy it is for primitive people to go wrong in
a big city. Lots of action, lots of characterization. You really felt
for those people. You wished happiness for them. What good
is a film if you don't get involved in it?

After that, I did *A Time to Shove and a Time to Lie*, *The
Cocksman*, *Around the Girls in Eighty Ways*, and this mad story
of an American girl tourist lost in the Alps who is found by a de-
ranged St. Bernard. She no sooner drinks his brandy than he
nuzzles off her ski pants and rapes her two or three times. We
called it *A Piece of Ass in the Brenner Pass*.

Five years in that basement. By the end of five years, I'm a
co-owner. You could say a vice president. The tailor is a success-
ful attorney in Queens. Some of the girls are dead, a couple married to admirers who saw them in the movies. One has gone
on to Hollywood. A fine blond. I knew she had star quality.
You never needed to bring out the pony on her. She could act.

Lester and the old folks have moved out to Westchester. Like I
said, you can go anywhere if you can pay for the ticket. They
like it out there. They cook steaks on the patio. The old man
had the first Oldsmobile with hydromatic drive. Lester is still
socking it away into the stock market. He's been buying automobile and steel stocks all during the Depression. Now all that
paper is on the way up. Lester wasn't asking questions. He
was too busy counting the money—half of which was mine.
Anyhow he'd gotten the law-school bug too. He started going at
night in 1937. I wonder if he ever came across that tailor.

So it went just fine. I had monogrammed shirts and silk underwear. I owned a fur shop and a music store. You could contact a lot of girls who came in to price coats or buy Cab Calloway records. Some of them wanted mink stoles pretty bad. So I
had this wear-while-you-earn plan. Handing out fur coats at
retail value cut down our overhead. One kid from Jersey just

took her salary in payments on a piano. Then, after she'd worked that out, she took lessons at the store. By the time her bloom was gone, she was pretty good. I put her back across the river playing intermission piano in a little club I'd bought. There was a kind of special bar at the back of the club. For fairies and drags. It didn't have a sign. But the crowd called it The Bellman's Dong. Money coming in out front; talent-scouting in back. If you think things out, you can make everything work together. That's how it's got to go: nothing wasted, nothing hanging. Everything has to plug in.

The truth is, I thought the money I gave Lester was money down the drain. But by the time Hitler took the plunge, we were worth a couple of fortunes. I got one of the last Rolls-Royces to come across. Lester had a Lincoln Continental with push-button doors.

—Long way from Tuminello's lousy car, I said to Lester one evening.

He was pouring Haig & Haig and putting it away two ounces at a time, three drinks an hour. He's already out of law school by now, and in Pelham, Palham, Griswold and Croon, one of the big outfits on the Street. He's worth almost as much as one of the partners. He's married a little Gentile girl from Philadelphia and put up a fifty-five-thousand place next to where I stayed with the folks. But Lester couldn't stand prosperity. A straight man. Cursed with the straight man's sense of how instead of what. By now it's almost eight years since we walked into that bar to beg a ride from Maury. We're stalking around in $250 suits, and Maury is a sad-seamed, sometimes almost hysterical old fag who still talks like he owns Dolls, but who knows better and never crosses me. Who is so far down the road toward whatever home for overripe fruits there may be that the new princesses laugh at him when he shuffles over and lays down one of his 1920's-style propositions. It's the land of silk and money but the gay blades can see who weaves the cloth and signs the checks. The unboys know Maury couldn't get up enough to bankroll the filming of a good feel, much less a transvestite epic like *Clothes Make the Queen*, or *Drags in Rags*. The money up on the Street came to me. And now we needed it.

Because now the pictures were going six and seven reels. Some of them even had plots. And characterization. There was more violence, too. It was my own idea to have a show where nobody does anything sexual to anybody. It was a big thing, and took some writing, some thinking. But the time was right, and so I sunk a quarter of a million in *The Big Gash*, a war movie where all the actors were naked, and killed each other with knives or swords. You could tell the good guys from the enemy, because we put big swastikas on the chests of the bad ones. And an American flag on the good guys. Just before we finished shooting, we ran in a few boys from Chinatown with rising suns. On their asses. This got us a lot of attention. One of the American Legion posts uptown bought—not rented—a dozen prints. An enlistment gimmick, somebody said.

But here's Lester pouring that Scotch down like a priest with a bottomless chalice.

—What does it all mean? he asked nobody, shooting his shirt sleeves out of his cashmere jacket. —Where are we going?

My brother is a Jew. What else can I say? If you drop manna on him, he takes it to the chemist for analysis.

—What's it all worth? he groaned. —We make money, we spend money. But what's the use?

I was getting bugged. This is my brother who, for all the lines and angles of his character, in spite of his being the prince of squares, is a shrewd boy on the Street and figures to be a good lawyer. If he doesn't cut his throat and wrists on a sliver of highball glass. But what can you do? If I took his $200 jacket and his twelve-year-old whisky and threw him out in the street, he'd be a happy man. Give him a ten-dollar bill and let him get started all over again. Then, about every ten years, when he managed to climb back up to his place, I'd have to rob him again. And let the whole mess start over another time.

—It means what you want it to mean, I told him. —It means that if somebody hands you a C-note, you tell him it's not the right plate number. It means that you're not a man. You're some kind of suffering machine, and all the money and luck have turned you off. You think it's immoral.

Lester was sobbing. Great tears coursed down his cheeks. He finished his whisky and fumbled for more ice cubes.

—I don't know, he choked. —I don't know. I wish to Christ I was a lousy bookkeeper again. I don't know where all this came from.

He waved his hand around the room vaguely. His elbow knocked my Utrillo sideways.

—What's going to become of us? Ho did you get the money? Me, your own brother. You do tell me anything. How can I enjoy money I don't know it comes from?

—Bureau of Printing and Engraving, I said, completely hacked. —Through thousands of dirty Irish mitts and hot Jew paws and fine Italian hands. It's like a lottery, and we got all the winning stubs.

—Where did we get 'em, Lester pleaded. —How? Have you hocked our souls?

Too much, I thought. The boy is going lame inside.

—Your soul is okay, I told him. —Your soul is the greatest. Don't sweat the money.

Lester couldn't stop. Always before he'd been able to sheer off before he got himself worked up. This time, after eight years, he was too far in to stop.

I thought for a minute. I got this image of our new flick in mind. One which featured girls and muscled guys being raped and tortured and executed by the Gestapo (years later I found out how lousy our writer was: the Nazis had more imagination in their trigger finger—and the one right next to it—than our writer had in his head. I should have sent him to do research). All this tying down and stomping naked tits, guys with their balls in a pillbox. We were thinking of sending a few prints to legit distributors claiming it was a smuggled documentary.

—Well, Lester said, —where does it come from?

—Stocks and bonds, I said. —Just like it ought to. Nothing but stocks and bonds.

Lester was whipped. He knew better. He remembered when and how hard the money had started rolling in. But he was still whipped. Probably because that old-time Jewish conscience was already corrupted a little. Money doesn't roll off anybody's back. He wanted—needed—to know. But if he needed a lot, he wanted only a little, and so when I gassed him one more time he spun in. And that was that. He never asked me again.

But Lester was the kind of Jew who couldn't go quietly to pieces or gently down the drain by himself. Moses carried a whole race of people with him into the desert. For a couple of months, Lester just brooded. He drank at night and stalked around the offices of Pelham, Palham, Griswold and Croon like Marley's ghost looking for a Scrooge. All the spirit was drained out of him. I didn't know what to do about him. I was still pretty young, and I didn't know all the signs, or how to read them. If I had, things might have even been worse. Though God knows how.

What is happening in those two months I have no idea of. Because I don't know or maybe have forgotten that lawyers know private detectives. And that private dicks do lawyers favors. So what is happening is that Lester, coming unglued himself, is being a Jew. He is loosening bolts, shearing pins, putting sugar in gas tanks, sand in transmissions. All very sneaky. He has got this private investigator named Peter Spurt, who is only a pistol permit, two friends in the Ninth Precinct, and a sniff of airplane glue this side of a cell himself—Lester has this creep on my tail. And I am like the lamb. Thinking the whole world is kindness and uncut whisky. Thinking that goodness will follow me at least a few more days of my life, and that mercy won't be needed. Meanwhile this Peter Spurt, pocket full of Lester's stock-market cash and his own war surplus .45 cartridges that go more or less with his hocked Smith & Wesson which he last fired from a fire escape in the Bronx on New Year's Eve of 1937, is off the Lepage's, and sniffing along behind me like Bulldog Drummond after a Boston bitch in heat. Wow.

You have got to understand that in those days security is minimal. War on. And anyhow the Watch and Ward Society is long out of business. You lay a bill a week on a police lieutenant, and this reinforces a cop's natural tendency to live and let live, till a still small voice from on high—like the Commissioner's office—whispers that sacred word: Duty.

The bill a week is no bribe, not for protection. It is honestly for nothing. Except to assure that the vice squad is not giving any answers before questions are asked. For a bill a week my boy didn't volunteer. But if he was to get drafted, we both understood he wasn't a slacker.

This was cheap, and about as good as you could buy. You could spend more and get less. So after a few years of wincing inside at unexpected knocks on the studio's outer door, I forgot it. You can live in a bear's cage with some edge if you once get used to it. You see that the bear can eat you any time. Any time at all. Then you forget it and get on to living. If you can't beat 'em and your situation won't allow joining 'em, you got to forget 'em. If Lester had just learned this, we'd have been home free for another decade or two at least.

But not my brother. He's got to *know*. When he itches, he scratches off great pieces of hide. This time I'm the flea, and it feels like the continent is breaking up under me. Because, shitkicker though he is, keystone noncop and all, this Peter Spurt can operate.

It's not a hard operation. Too many people know about it. There's no way out of this. You got to have casts—including a lot of extras and even a few really dirty stand-ins for the chewing and crawling, the domination and degradation bits, for the rubber-hose and barbed-wire stuff. And cameramen, process people. On and on. I don't know who Spurt picked up on, but he got the whole scene. How long, who, how much. All he missed was the why. But then for all his head full of horseshit, Lester was no philospher, and anyhow, he knew why every time he snaked sadly into one of those old nasty ill-gotten Savile Row suits or picked up a dinner tab for ten at El Morocco.

There was no confrontation. Lester is a creep—he and Spurt should have gone into business together to ferret out evil-doers—but he isn't a showgirl at heart. What he knew he knew, and talking to me about an end to it all, about straightening out my crooked way, about the horrors of perversion and the cheapening of sex (which is obviously the cheapest thing on earth unless merchandisers get hold of it—and even then, you got two good hands) would have only made things worse.

Does Abel tell Cain? I might have been tempted to lay a yard or two on this boy Spurt, have him bail out his .45 and then wrestle with the ethics of hitting a current client. If Spurt goofs out, you can buy burns all up and down the East Coast for less than I made in a week.

But none of this. What happens is that one afternoon between flicks I'm over on Long Island checking out a location for some outdoor shots. Sea, sand, clouds and mixed perversions by Negroes and whites. A potboiler, really, but still good for a giggle in Omaha or Dallas. And on the way back I call in to see if my sheet-metal man has finished the new things: an iron maiden with a hole cut in it just below the waist, and a thumbscrew not intended to screw thumbs. Maury is there and gets on the line so fast I can't even find out about the equipment.

—Hello, Benny-boy. How's tricks?

—Tricks is cheap and time is short. What's with you?

—Seen the afternoon paper?

—Paper is to wipe the ass. What do I need with paper? Did they bomb Manhattan since I left?

Maury giggles. Not like the old laugh he used to have. Not like that night at The Cobbler's Cock. Now it's a mean little old-lady laugh, and you know you'd never hear it unless somebody had broken off his own fingers or eaten a live rat.

—No, baby, they've bombed you.

—How would you like a punch in the cunt?

—Grab a piece of the afternoon paper, baby. And before you shove it, take a look at the banner.

—I'm going to buy the whole third run of the *Times* and make a two-hour feature out of stuffing it up yours if you don't come off the cute and tell me what gives.

—Your brother blew the whistle on you.

That was enough. It was like I'd been watching a frame of film that was blurry, out of focus. And hadn't been able to see who was doing what to who. Maury's words snapped the lens. Telephoto. It was Lester. And he was fucking. Me.

Maury waited a minute. I didn't say anything. In my mind I was watching Lester make his peace with God or the D.A. or whoever would listen to him read Spurt's notes from the un-

derground. The focus is fine-edged as a ripper's razor. Only
I've got the wrong script.

Maury can't hold it any more. His voice is like old wine. He's
opened my guts, so now he tapers off for the details. He
doesn't want me to hang up.

—Benny baby? You there? You still on your feet?

—I'm coming over and cut whatever you've got out. And
hang 'em around your neck like the crown jewels.

—Wait. I'm only started. The D.A.'s office is a mess.

—Let the D.A. fire his scrubwoman.

—No. It was Lester made the mess.

—So let the D.A. push Lester's face in it.

Maury's voice is a pattern of restraint. Underneath all the
control is the exultation of a man (or whatever) who can
smell the blood of his persecutor, and is headed for it with slices
of rye bread.

—He can't, Maury coos. —The D.A. can't. Because Lester
hasn't got a face. His face *is* the mess.

That's Maury's counterpunch. It's pretty much downhill
from there. It seems that Lester collects the dirt from Spurt,
jams it all into his dispatch case and then sits in the D.A.'s reception room for two hours like Job in the refuse. When he finally
gets his day in court (or as near court as he was going) he
walks over to the D.A.'s desk, tells him that God sees the truth
but waits, throws the dispatch case down, pulls out a corroded
old Smith & Wesson he'd borrowed, and blasts his poor be-
fuddled head all over hell's half-acre. And by now, by the time
I am talking to Maury, there is a bench warrant for me—and
cops on the way to Dolls, Inc. Which Maury seemed to have forgotten. He was too busy contemplating the bust of Benny Boundoch. I mentioned the cops.

—Sure, he gurgled. —But I'm just passing by. Just came in
to buy a doll or see an old friend. And when they ask who the
big cheese is, why Benny baby, of thee I sing.

I hung up. It was all right. Everything was fine. In ten minutes the cops would be talking to Maury, who, in his waltzing
senility, was living it up over my bad luck. And forgetting that
Dolls, Inc. was incorporated in his name, not mine. So that,

failing to get me, the D.A. wasn't going to let all that evidence go to waste. Maury would have a home in his declining years.

As for Lester, that was all right, too. I mean what he had done. He had only blown the bridge across which all the goodies came. No more cashmere suits and Rollex watches and Bentley convertibles (even if and when the war did end). A little wife wondering how long before the trigger-pull her wandering Jew had lost his brains. My mother and father sitting in that expensive living room with one son a corpse and the other a notorious trader in human degredation, which for them would be half again as bad as a mere suicide.

And me. Fucked and damned well fucked. No way to get to a bank. Maybe six or seven hundred in my pockets, and a thousand at the house. Which might as well have been located in the fashionable section of Mars or that half-acre of hell around the D.A.'s desk.

It's LaGuardia Field for me. Fucked and forgotten. Yesterday's Bonoparte of the Blue. Today's hot number flashing in every precinct and APB all over the state. But maybe not the airlines just yet.

⋖⋗ ⋖⋗

—Where to, sir?
—Who cares? A long one. For a vacation.
—New Orleans? In twenty minutes.
—Do I need a passport?

Chapter Four

Mrs. Nieman has a secret. She is cool, calm. Her vision of life is dryer than ever. Nothing is quite the same. Even her son's defection from the priesthood fails to take precedence in her thoughts. All she can remember is that peculiar, utterly golden moment three weeks ago when her doctor, hands full of records, X-rays, cardiographc tapes and lab reports, shook his head, real tears in his eyes, and asked: —Why didn't you come sooner?

It is, he has told her, a hasty heart: a syncopated heart. It murmurs, coughs, pauses and begins to beat again. Mrs. Nieman has almost fainted behind the wheel of her car. Once, in Shreveport, going into town on the Market Street viaduct, she has felt the world falling in around her like the collapsing walls of an Inquisition chamber. When she had recovered, the world was sorted out again, its parts resettled, and the whole of it from bright sun in a china-blue sky to grease-stained concrete overpass seemed to shimmer with some unique and precious aura not like anything she has known. At night, she is alone and perhaps dreaming of her late husband (it is assumed he is late: he was last heard of ten years before, one of those few American souls who vanished in Spain serving not with the fiery hearts of the Abraham Lincoln Brigade, but with the Falangists, Franco's cold-eyed Fascists who matched their leftist foes pound for pound in bleeding flesh, lie for lie, betrayal for betrayal) running through a hail of Loyalist machine-gun fire, relieving the Alcázar. And of his brother Charlie, who had vanished less eccentrically on a hunting trip into the fastnesses of the Arbuckle Mountains of Oklahoma only a year or so afterward.

Sometimes she awakens to find that her sullen heart has stopped. As if a P.O.U.M. bullet has found it. As if, under the olive trees or amongst the geological monstrosities of the mountains, she has fallen, felt the last fading strum of her blood's course, and now, at last caught in the mute inglorious avalanche of death's passage, has risen from her flesh and hovers in the warm expectant air, a long and soundless summer dark above her tenantless body, still golden and beautiful as her son remembers it, as her late husband feared it below a Spanish wall, as Charlie adored and envied it in whatever cheerless place he found beyond the mountains.

And then, as suddenly, she has felt, like a single drop of water dripping from a tap supposedly turned off, the heart's purposeless pounding start again. Like an uncertain wild bird thrashing in a cage, its tempo has increased until, even in the velvet Louisiana summer evening, she has sweated and felt her body's chill liquor drench the sheets below and above. She is dying and she knows it, and she knows that she cannot know when the water's source will cease forever, when the bird will fly.

Mrs. Nieman has been two weeks in New Orleans now. She has stayed ostensibly to visit for a while with Christopher and help him set up an apartment, to while away a dull summertime.

She has, in fact, come to tell her son good-bye in various unspecific ways, to bring him to terms with that peculiar and immitigable loneliness even the oldest orphan feels. And if luck or fate or fortune or God will have it so, to die in his presence, to have from him whatever kind of crippled blessing a priest gone wrong can give to a bird in flight, to water flowing finally underground.

The night is ended now, and the first tentative probings of July sunlight have begun to inch across a wide green awning over the second-story balcony. Mrs. Nieman walks slowly to the French windows, her soft beige negligee trailing behind.

Christopher sleeps in the bedroom. He sounds as if he is sobbing in long irregular periods. Like a child. His mother listens and frowns.

Mrs. Nieman tries to remember those dark ferocious evenings long ago when she would mount the stairs slowly, a little drunk, leaving Charlie stretched out below on a sofa or the floor. When she would find her small son asleep, curled around the newel-post, stains of recent tears on his cheeks, sobbing in this same unsteady rhythm.

She steps onto the balcony above Royal Street where no cars yet move. Her breasts, still firm and perfect, her arms still slender and flushed their length with blood (from that questionable heart) feel against the tan unblemished patina of their flesh a faint morning breeze perfumed, cool and whispering altogether of life and strength, of the wonder of youth in the heart. She opens her gown to taste this dawn, and a passing Negro on his way to work in the grease pit glances up, cannot believe what he sees and quickly averts his eyes in case it may be so.

There is much to be answered for, Mrs. Nieman is thinking. There is so much the body has craved, so much given it. And what the body has spared, the heart required. It is as if each one of us, despite ourselves, passes through life like a conscience-less juggernaut, smashing into others, crushing, being crushed. Mangling and being mangled in our turn. Even the survivors are terribly scarred, and none dares look behind at the wreckage strewn in his uneven path. Mrs. Nieman closes her gown and shivers, though the breeze is no cooler than before. She is done with so many things. So much remains undone. It is a shame, she smiles, considering, that we can take no pleasure in things done that cannot be undone; in things undone past doing.

What should she say to Christopher, a priest for a little while and now something else, neither a priest nor man? He rests for a moment. He has traveled. Yet the trip is hardly begun.

Mrs. Nieman feels her fraudulent blood move fresh and vigorous within her breast. It is done with mirrors. It is an illusion. What seems to be right is wrong. What appears wrong is inscrutable. She wonders in passing if there might not be an Adversary, a fiend, a devil. Who stalks the corridors of some irreproachably sanitary asylum like that thing of Poe's that drifted from room to room, a mask of plague obscuring its features, pestilence oozing from its robes. She believes for the space of an instant, and thinks those corridors are in her heart.

Then she sees the sun clearly, and an Italian vegetable-peddler passing on a mule-drawn cart sees her precious nakedness, sighs loudly, kisses three fingers and waves to her with a wand of green onions. —*Cara mia,* he coos, and does not understand her tender frown.

ᥕᥩ ᥲᥩ

It is early morning, and almost anywhere in the state outside New Orleans, the air is sweet enough to send a Paris *parfumeur* to an early and envious grave. It is an odor of completion, not of expectation. Instead of pointing to the sullen blaze of coming day, it recollects the cool soft hours gone, the darkness beginning to curdle now under a vengeful sun.

But this is still New Orleans, and the odor is of rotten vegetables, diesel fuel, stacks of newspapers, cheap cooking oil and burned coffee. If despair and hatred and the directionless fury born each day in large cities had a characteristic stench, it would be strong enough here to gag a maggot.

The city uncoils, and along the alley behind Staff-o-Life Bakeries, Inc. Christopher Nieman is half walking, half stumbling to work. His eyes feel like slits in a Klansman's sheet. His tongue like a shirttail. Only a few days of late sleeping, and the habit of fourteen years falls apart like a plaster statue of St. John the Divine caught in a rain of blood.

It seems clear enough that man is depraved, God or no, Christopher is thinking. Vice is as easily begun as falling into a bed, as hard to break free of as pulling a tooth barehanded. Man is prone to evil; he would rather get hooked on marijuana than help an old lady across the street.

As he reaches the garage door (not the subbasement; the parking garage, which is street-level at the rear of the building) he almost falls on his face over an orange crate. While he untangles himself from the rubble and wipes the alley grime from his red and white uniform (which is designed to attract attention and remind motorists of something Christopher has already forgot), he hears an old lady's voice at the subbasement door. Deep in shadow, there she is: small, fragile, silver hair perfectly coifed, a basket of gardenias on her arm. The very kind to help across a street. She seems, however, to be selling marijuana.

—You want Mary Jane, okay, she says indifferently. —You swung by the hemp once, you can do it again. You ain't Captain Marvel.

Someone at the top of the stairs mumbles a long sentence which concludes with one word Christopher can make out. It sounds like *shazam*.

—You bring me some trade, you get fixed. Wishes ain't Horse.

—Lissen, I'm dyin' like a dog, someone in the doorway croaks. —I feel like I been walkin' on my guts. Like they was strung out under my feet. You know what I mean?

Mrs. Mailer is not moved. —Hang your guts on the wall and snap at 'em. You hustle up some black marks or a sprung cunt, and I'll dose you.

—Jesus, the voice almost sobs.

—Try sniffing the back of a postage stamp, Mrs. Mailer calls over her shoulder as she sees Christopher and vanishes down the alley.

Mr Christian Blackman looks like a man dragging his saddle. There are spurs in him, demanding he run six ways at once. Christopher is ready to catch him when he falls. But somehow he manages to put both splayed thumbs in his belt and hold on. He swallows hard. He scratches up a weak smile for Christopher.

—Lissen, he says, —don't never get no cravin' for licorice unless you owns the candy store.

And vanishes unsteadily back down into his lair like a vampire sensing dawn.

∾§ §∾

The truck handles well enough, and Christopher's route card and New Orleans map take care of the rest. He stops at store after store carrying in light bread, cracked wheat, sweet rolls, chocolate-chip cookies, hamburger buns, hotdog buns, brown 'n' serve rolls until the smell of baked goods begins to turn his stomach. Most of the grocers ignore him, but at the far end of Bourbon, when he services a small Italian grocery, the proprietor studies him with a long careful unembarrassed Sicilian stare. Christopher wonders if he is prescient, if the wop can feel or sense somehow the dregs of a ruined priest beneath the bright idiot-vestments of a bread routeman. *Corpus Domini nostri Jesu Christi*, he thinks, as if to heighten the man's suspicion. He places each loaf of bread in its place with careful, almost practiced precision, the rolls and cookies just so. But the Sicilian is not placated. He stares until Christopher is done and presents him with the receipt list to sign.

They exchange no words, but as Christopher reaches the door, he almost collides with a tiny fat woman clutching a missal and a brown-beaded rosary.

—*Jesu*, the woman exclaims, more distraught by the chance bump than she has any business being, Christopher thinks. As he almost runs back to his truck, empty metal basket banging against his leg, the Sicilian and his wife, fresh from Mass, stand in the grocery doorway staring after him. Fortunately, for the sake of Christopher's sanity, neither makes the sign of the cross. Christopher settles in his seat and guns the engine. He has the nervous structure of a race horse with a wooden leg, he thinks. But these Italians. Having invented the Church, they have ways to know. The wop has his reasons.

He remembers the morning he had celebrated his last requiem Mass. For an old Italian, Silvio Carlotta, who had lived so disconcertingly long that only one of his children—and his third wife—had managed to survive him. Some of the grocery-store Italians, envying the old man's success in the wholesale-produce business and his fantastic ability to outsmart Old Mortality, had hinted to the pastor that perhaps there had been something of the demonic at work.

—How'sa come da competition die an' he don' die? Two generation a Scarlottis under ground (much crossing and an instant of pious eye aversion) and he'sa still eat lika da wolf.

Father Brophy had shrugged. —Old age isn't a sin. The Scarlottis were unlucky.

Gross understatement. The elder Scarlotti, watching his oldest son fall off a produce stake-truck, suffered a stroke. Lived four years like one of the tomatoes he had so often hefted, fatswathed eyes cold with profit. The oldest son with a broken neck. Not quite a vegetable. All man—from the neck up. But less than satisfied with that, he (the eldest son) by an act of will unparalleled in modern medical history had used his lumber legs to knock a glass off the night table. Then he had rolled out of bed and with ingenious single-mindedness had cut his throat on the jagged base of the tumbler. Two years later, ambition driving him to recoup the family fortunes, the younger son had branched out into meats. Pork was his undoing. Going to the source, he had roamed through the backwoods of northern Alabama. One evening, fortified against the autumn chill by a quart or so of Chianti, he had fallen into a hogpen while the owner was inside blessing his own family's meat. What the hogs left was dutifully shipped back to Alexandria by the farmer—in a closed and sealed coffin.

Back to the funeral of old Carlotta. Christopher had reached the Preface, trying very hard to ignore, to put out of mind the snuffling and occasional caterwauling that burbled up from the congregation.

—*Vere dignum et justum est* . . .

It is right and proper. But then the widow Carlotta, who would normally have rather fallen directly into limbo than disturb the altar, shrieked like a cougar. Several of the pallbearers kneeling or sitting in the front pew gasped. One spoke aloud. —Jesus Christ, he choked.

Christopher had heard people moving, shuffling toward the rear of the church. He had not wanted to turn. He bowed low. —*Sanctus, Sanctus, Sanctus.*

No bells. Not even the muffled abortion of bells that untried altar boys, surprised or wool-gathering, often made him in return for his Holys. Then the hand of one of those altar boys, no neophyte, but a faintly whiskered nineteen-year-

old from the school. —Father, if you please. —What? —The
. . . body. The old gentleman. The people are leaving.

—*Diaboli,* someone crooned hysterically from the congregation.

—What I tell ya, one of Scarlotti's supporters drawled softly.

Christopher had turned, covering the chalice, and descended
the steps. One. Two . . . three. One pace past the Holy Spirit,
he had paused above the coffin. Inside, the old Italian had
turned black. Not simply swarthy. He had been that and more
even alive. But as black as Satan's instep, and the creased and
countercreased waxy surface of his face was beginning to sag,
to fall away. There were open crevices at the corners of his
mouth, and the mouth itself had fallen open. There was something dark and almost translucent deep inside. The breaks at
either end of the mouth gave the old man what even charity
could not fail to recognize as an obscene grin. And above, his
eyes, so carefully closed at the moment of death, had opened
in thin slits to complement the terrible smirk.

One of the popes, he thought. Or was it Elizabeth the first?
Total corruption. The lead casket almost burst. Most loyal fleeing from the charnel stench.

—Father, the altar boy had quavered.

—Close the coffin, he had said. —Just close it. Never mind
the people. Then we'll finish.

৹§ ৪৯

Afterward, one of Scarlotti's retainers had approached him.
—You go on and say it. There'sa no devilish intervention. It
don'ta mean nothin'. Go on.

He had shrugged. —I'm not going to tell you anything. It
was a natural phenomenon.

But not with the kind of dogmatic unction any good biologist
—much less a priest—would be expected to bring to such a
pronouncement. If God could be climbing in and out of the
wound watch of creation, why not the Adversary, partner in
human destiny.

In the months after, he had received almost $400 for

Masses in behalf of old Carlotta. Even when the embalmer was arrested for shady practices, even when he admitted to using, while drunk and in bad odor with his wife, everything from orange juice to cheap wine in the hapless cadavers brought to his establishment. —When she don't let me in, I get crazy, he told the police. —I do things.

He could not remember what he had done to old Carlotta. Possibly, he had said, it was carrot juice. Or vinegar. Once he had used mercury. —But it cost a fortune. And the stiff weighed twice what it ought to. One pallbearer had a stroke. I dunno. I get crazy. We all get crazy. Maybe God's crazy.

Even then the Mass stipends poured in. —Don' tell me a little beer or prune juice gonna make him smile like dat, one of the donors told Christopher.

By then he half hoped Carlotta was in hell. If he wasn't, he ought to be. For indirectly harassing the clergy. —Breakdown of the tissues. It happens to all of us. Some later, some sooner. God knows what that insane undertaker pumped into him.

—Ole Scarlotti go into da grave, he looksa lika baby. Same undertaker.

—Maybe he filled Scarlotti with whitewash. Or Jergens lotion. Scarlotti was lucky.

◄§ §►

Even as Christopher is beginning his appointed rounds, light falls in Benny Boundoch's house of varied fame. The sun's immodest klieg spots Mary Ann Downey nude and adorable, lying with Billy Bob Stoker, limbs intermingled, breaths rising in paired rhythm from dreamless untroubled sleep.

It is the sound of a church bell that awakens Mary Ann, and she comes out of it mean and contentious. Because there is a dream that comes often in the dusk before morning, and it troubles her now as much as long ago. There is a small girl running and a man falling out of the sky, impaled on a tall spire that looks like a clawed finger. Then the steeple becomes in fact a finger, part of an enormous hand. And the falling man, arms outspread, a deep gash in his side, is swallowed by the hand, and there is the distant hollow sound of a bell while clouds like tufts of cotton, cotton boles the size of clouds drift and fall about the girl, and she vanishes, annihilated by white.

Mary Ann sits up, stretches, disentangles her legs from Billy Bob's, and gazes with mordant incuriosity out the tall old window beside her bed. Far below, an old Italian peddler turns from selling a stalk of green onions to a Negress in one of the houses across the street. He looks up and sees Mary Ann, whose body, uncovered and catching the sun, momentarily paralyzes him. —Hurry, the Negress bawls, noticing Mary Ann, who smiles and like a monarch to the manner born, extends her hand, one finger raised in acknowledgment of the comment from below. —Twice in a morning, the old man sighs reverently as Mary Ann fades out of sight. —It's a good day already.

◦§ §◦

Downstairs Benny Boundoch is awake and mopping his forehead. He will never get used to New Orleans weather. It is impossible to stay neat, well turned out. The humidity wilts collar, bundles seersucker jacket, melts huge dark patches of sweat into shirt. Tie looks like a flayed eel; socks fall away from ankles. In the morning he looks like a million in newly minted dimes. An hour later, he could pass for one of those Marines who climbed up Suribachi with nothing better in mind than to plant Old Glory there. Every minute spent in this overgrown plague-hole is a battle with humidity, heat, insects. After two years in New Orleans, he is still astounded when customers come to the house during lunch hours (called here, dinnertime) and screw happily till the dock or the office or the store calls them back to duty. It is hard enough for Benny to get going at night. Only mad dogs and Southerners get their gun in the noonday sun. Apoplexy should be the national disease. But nothing kills a hick. Rednecks are immortal. The only way they die is to wear out.

Boundoch remembers a number in overalls, workshirt, red bandanna, and some kind of jerky railroad cap. This one has watery blue eyes floating in flaming whites, a neck like a strangled goose, a very rock of Gibraltar for an adam's apple, and not a scrap of hair on his head. A genuine creature. He had to be seventy-five, and ninety would be within reason. He had purchased three girls for an hour each, and left faintly disgruntled, mumbling about skinny thin-blooded women. And something about Lillian Russell. When women were. And men could. Too late Benny had bolted out onto Royal Street looking for him. The ultimate movie: *Great Granpaw*. How great? The old bugger takes one after another, wearing them out, tossing them away. At the end, he turns facing camera, grinning, waving his ancient tool, gesturing come on. But no dice. Gaffer is gone. Opportunity comes but once. Or twice. He has lost his creative edge in New Orleans. What a falling off. From secret Sennett to public pimp. But he also stands who only serves.

Somehow Billy Bob's presence has turned Boundoch on. He has found his subject. He sees the title frames: a whip, an iron maiden covered with dust, perhaps a skeleton immured next to a rotting cask of Amontillado, a portion of human torso under the terrible tension of the rack while dark hooded figures with points of insane light for eyes move in the shadowed background bearing crooked crosses and statues of a leering virgin. And in huge black gothic letters:

THE INQUISITION

Boundoch sips weak Yankee coffee and sees scores pass in technicolor. Bloodshed, the putting down of heretics. Debauchery: godless priests and nuns profaning their souls' temples, their vows, and even sacred vessels. Orgies beyond belief. Harrowing sequences in the lowest depths of the Grand Inquisitor's castle. Eyes plucked out, breasts pinched off with red-hot tongs. Rapes, slaughters of innocents unparalleled. Babies skewered on bayonets—pikes, that is. Final scene with young priest Billy Bob called to the question for defending gorgeous young heretic nun, Mary Ann, who, in medieval fashion, he has been harmlessly sleeping with. Both guilty, of course. Smashing climax: Billy and Mary Ann both crucified back to back on a cross of gold. Souls, rising from horribly mutilated bodies, kissing, feeling up, floating to judgment naked and alone.

Dozens of bit parts, plenty of space for special effects, sub-plots. This could be it. This could be the start of something big. Planning, casting, equipment, sets. A world out there waiting. Hold tight, world.

Boundoch lights a cigarette and sees his name swirling in the smoke. Fear. Sex. Violence. What else is there? That, Benny muses, is the trinity. He begins to write memoranda to himself, and the rising sun shapes a shimmering corona around his well-barbered head.

ᐊᔥ ᒉᐩ

—Horseshit, Mary Ann answers sweetly, scrabbling amongst dirty clothes in a corner of the room.

—Now, Billy Bob says with pained dignity, —I mean it. If I didn't mean it, why would I say it? Ever since that first night I saw you. I wanted to break down the door and take you away.

—What you did was get too drunk to piss a crooked stream, she says, finding a man's white shirt. Slightly soiled. —You was so far gone, you couldn't find your ass with both hands.

—I was nervous. You made me nervous. I didn't know what in God's name was goin' on. I just wanted to grab you and run.

—Horse*shit*, Mary Ann says again, dragging on a pair of faded blue jeans. She stands erect, her bare breasts pointed toward Billy Bob, her eyes bright with abstract anger. —I've heard 'em talk as good as that from Oakie City to Tampa. Next thing you'll say whyn't you come out of this damn place and let me marry you.

—Well, Billy Bob begins, crestfallen to hear his best line preempted, —I thought maybe we could. You don't want to stay here. This is an awful place for a girl.

Mary Ann slips into her shirt, leaving the buttons tantalizingly undone so that Billy Bob's attention plays hide and seek with her tanned breasts as they alternately vanish and reappear at the shirt's gap. —How'd you like to hear how I ever got in this business? Sin and shame, huh?

—Well, I never thought to ask.

—You would have, Mary Ann says wryly.

She hustles Billy Bob out of the bed and begins to arrange the sheets. —Look, you got something goin' with ole Boundoch. He's been lettin' you stay here without even blinkin' and there was a fella there last night who pays fifty bucks to visit with me a while. So you got it with Boundoch. Stay right with him, and we'll see a little bit of each other.

Billy Bob stands naked and downcast, head bowed, arms akimbo, eyes averted. Everything points at the floor.

Mary Ann studies him for a long moment, and then, pushing a pillow into shape and dropping it at the head of the bed, she walks over and takes hold of him in an intimate way. —You're all right. I mean you ain't one of these wise-asses or else some kind of pervert. I like you fine. Don't look like I just blew a candy store out from under you.

Billy Bob's eyes meet hers, and there is a sudden and predictable change in his attitude.

—Lord, Mary Ann says, falling back onto the bed. —Jesus, it's all a person's life is worth sayin' something nice to you. . . .

But Billy Bob's face is buried in the shirt's opening, nuzzling her flighty breasts, and the burying is only begun.

~§ §~

Now the day is full: overhead the sun squats like a bronze gong awaiting one great blow to fall into the city's streets. Christopher, just finished with his morning run, walks down Bourbon's nastier end, passing bars and fleabag groceries, junk-shops with signs in front reading *Antiques,* a laundry run by Korean twin brothers, a realtor specializing in French Quarter real estate: more especially in ponce properties from which more than rent is forthcoming. Next to a praline shop guarded by a make-believe mammy in red calico and yellow polka-dotted bandanna, a jukebox sounds from a shadowed door-way:

> . . . *on the wings of a snow white dove*
> *God sends His pure sweet love* . . .

There is raucous laughter, and Christopher thinks for a moment of the small Christian boy passing through a Jewish quarter with the Host in his mouth. Found in a cistern, throat cut, eyes wide. And certain Sons of Belial gathered around the house . . .

> . . *I can't feel at home*
> *In this world any more* . . .

It is a peculiarity of his mind, Christopher thinks, pausing to light a small cigar, that every undirected word he hears seems somehow aimed at him. *The wicked fleeth when no man pursueth.* In the last several days he has felt as if he were the center of the universe, as if everyone he passes knows what he was, what he is. As if every eye is fixed on him, every hand raised against him. Out of the bar, a new sound:

> *My devotion* . . .
> *Is endless and deep as the ocean.*

Even the terms of secular love turn to his condemnation:

> . . . *and like a star shining from afar*
> *Remains forever the same* . . .

But of course nothing does. If a man were to love this morning, he will be cool in the evening's shadows, only to love again some other one before whatever dawn there may be. Even stars wink, Christopher thinks.

On a telephone pole outside the tavern someone has painted in painstakingly small script: GET RIGHT WITH JESUS. Christopher shivers as if the whole Wehrmacht had goose-stepped across his grave, as if some monstrous inquisitor were stalking him in the city's dingy streets. Two small Negro boys rush past him rolling hoops, shrieking. One runs full tilt into the other. —Mothafucka, the aggrieved one in torn striped polo shirt yells. —Mothafucka, the other in a cut-down Army shirt roars happily. —Gone cut ya, the first snivels, finding his hoop's rhythm again. —Bull*shit,* the second keens, already half a block away and bearing down on a little old lady with a tray of flowers who sidesteps him with remarkable alacrity and sends him sprawling with an almost invisible kick. —Motha, he yells, then, seeing her face, subsides and scrambles to his feet, moving off, waiting for his friend.

Christopher is moving again, thinking now in a strange and disorganized pastiche of Mary Ann, Billy Bob, Mr Christian. Huddled masses, he thinks, drawing up short at the second word. On a light pole to his right he sees:

It Is No Secret

Passing, he looks backward over his shoulder. He can see the rest of the message on the pole's far side:

What God Can Do

He does not run, but walks rapidly over into Royal Street where his truck is parked, hardly even looking as he crosses in front of traffic, every car of which may well be in God's hire, for all he knows.

&ea; &ea;

By noon, Christopher is done and has his truck back in the garage. Something sends him down into the subbasement where Mr Christian sits amongst the scattered pieces of an ancient transmission like Job on the refuse. His hands shake like gulls over garbage. There are tears in his eyes, great streams of dark liquor coursing down his black cheeks as he tries to reassemble the greasy puzzle. It is useless, and finally he takes hold of his right wrist with his left hand, trying to guide a worn gear into place. The quivering seems multiplied by two. Mr Christian drops the gear and rubs his crimson eyes with dirty fists. Then he fumbles a brown cigarette out of a pack. It takes him a while to get it to his mouth. He cannot light it. Christopher strikes a match, and Mr Christian draws long and leans back against the crumbling brick wall.

—I hates you to see me this way, he says weakly. —I ain't usually like this.

—You reckon I can help? Christopher asks him.

Mr Christian grins. —You got fifty bucks?

—No.

—You know a girl carryin' something she'd like to get rid of?

—No.

—Maybe you seen another fella up there along your route looks just about like me?

—No.

—You can't help me.

Christopher squats across the old transmission. He wants to say something. Be of good cheer, Master Christian. Play the man. But his tongue is like a weed. He wishes he had a hundred-dollar bill.

Mr Christian's face is buried in his hands and he rocks back and forth like a man bereaved. —I don't exactly what you'd call hurt, he whispers. —No. It tingles some like I had hold of a hot wire. And sometimes it feels like somebody had stuck a fishin' line up my ass and caught hold of my tongue wit the hook. And then they gets to reelin' it in. Right now it's like they had out my eyeballs rollin' 'em in salt.

—That's bad, Christopher says inanely, wishing he had an amputated hand or a clubfoot to show Mr Christian. Price of an easy conscience.

—Yeah, Mr Christian answers, shivering in the preposterous heat.

—I been tryin' to think of how my feet hurt to take my mind off all this, Mr Christian says finally. —But it ain't no good. The sonsabitches done hurt without stoppin' for six years. Just now they feel fine.

—Oh . . .

—My feet never felt better, Mr Christian giggles, raising his tear-filled eyes to Christopher's. —Ain't that the shits?

Christopher rises. He feels rank, covered with an odd subspecies of sweat that will not give way before soap and water. He has been down here at least three days. Bearing the good news. The transmission is no nearer fixed than when he came.

Mr Christian wriggles like an eel. —I heard something, he says.

—What? A rat? I didn't hear anything.

—Somebody told me somethin'. Said you was a priest. Said you done threw over your burden and took to women and good times. Said you was Bugger Man's honey.

Christopher sits down heavily, without volition. He has been trying to find the gnat that nips him every time he sees Mr Christian. Even as Mr Christian finishes, Christopher zeroes in. It is Grünewald. Matthias Grünewald's bloody beastly Christ. Mr Christian looks like that same pulpy wreck; as if he were the corpus left on the cross a week instead of three hours. The lax jaw, the brutal hopeless eyes, the lips ground into a permanent smirk of total knowledge, splayed fingers on help-less hands. In a week of tropical sun, the body would blacken. Father Madden's monster risen again. He is ugly as judgment, and out of his mouth come accusations of monstrous sin.

—No, Christopher tells him. —No, they were lying. I never . . .

—Never took no vows? Mr Christian asks in a tone between disbelief and disappointment.

—Yes, took vows, but . .

—An' went back on 'em?

—Yes. No. I was a child then. It was a childish thing.

—Never had no woman?

—No. Yes. Once I knew this girl . . .

—Found damnation 'tween her legs?

—We were drinking. I don't know . . .

—Drinkin' too.

—But that . . . that other. About Stoker. So help me God.

Mr Christian stares at Christopher placidly. He shakes his head slowly. —Don't swear on God. It ain't no good. You done the rest. You'll come to that. Man goin' down the ladder don't miss a rung. Maybe goin' up. But he don't miss a rung goin' down.

Mr Christian cackles and weaves from side to side. —Reckon you'll come down to this here, too, he says. —Reckon ole lady Mailer's gonna give you a pony. First one is a cheap ride. Any good stable do as much. Let you try the Horse. At first you

pace, and then you trot. And then you come on down. You ever
see a horse come down a ladder?

Christopher cannot break away. It is as if the walls of the
basement are closing on him. He stares at the grease pit. A few
feet away Mr Christian's head, still oozing tears turns like the
needle of a broken compass.

—I never had anything to do with Stoker.

—I never said you did wrong. Somebody said. Word in the
street.

—My God, Christopher trills, thinking that on top of everything else—he changes the figure instantly—beside everything
else, a sodomist by repute. And he had come from Alexandria
to walk up and down in the world. To be some kind of man.
Some kind, so the word in the street.

—Congratulations, Mr Christian says at last. —You done
right. Almost right. You done half right. Maybe you can do all
kinds of right.

—What? Christopher begins. —What?

—You on the lam. Headin' for tall grass. Big hound snufflin'
after you. Takes some kind of man to eat God's bread and then
slam the door on His fingers. You a hard case.

Mr Christian is still shivering. He cannot control his hands
and Christopher fears he will stab himself with the rusty screw-
driver he plies aimlessly.

—I made a mistake, Christopher begins absently. —I was
only a kid. They asked me to promise, and I thought: Well, all
right then, I promise. I thought if I promised, it would come
out all right. That what I said I'd end up really meaning. If I
believed everything, it would be all right and I would even
believe what they didn't—couldn't—tell me. Do you see?

Mr Christian wriggles exquisitely. It is a measure of past
suffering that he can talk some kind of sense while his body is
in hell. It is a quality reserved to angels and demons. —Aw, he
cuts Christopher off, —you ruinin' it. You ain't right. You
comin' on like a man in love wit a whore. Nothin' but excuses.
Why don't you just come up wif it? Say, I hate you, you Blue-
Sky Bastard in a white sheet. Feels better to say it out than fool

aroun' tryin' to get shut of Him wif one side of your mouth and talk Him out of doin' you bad wif the other. Anyhow, it don't do no good to talk decent to Him. He ain't got no heart, no feelin's. He's just a thing up there. He watches all the time. He's got His eyes on us now, listenin', figurin'. He's got all the cards, all the chips. Owns the table. An' He plays a mean game. Ain't nobody walkin' out wif nothin'. You come in flat and howlin', and they carries you out flat and quiet. In between, you *got* to play. Old Sacred Sonofabitch up there, He deals you a lyin' woman, two accidents, an' a run-in wit the sheriff, and then He lays the Horse on you. Or maybe He deals you a pansy heart. An' you play till He gets sick of watchin' you. Then He cashes you in and you see 'fore the lights go out you ain't got nothin'. Not a chip. Not a shoe or a vest to carry wif you. And that's it.

—Then? Christopher asks, almost against his will.

—Then you dead. An' you go to hell.

Christopher wishes he had found another way to spend his lunch hour. He nibbles a salami sandwich on Staff-o-Life bread. It is warm and miserable. Flavorless, except for the faint tang of his own sweat, and the ubiquitous stench of Mr Christian's cellar.

—You believe . . . ? Christopher begins again. —You think there's something up there?

Mr Christian pauses long enough in his writhing to fix Christopher with a red-eyed stare. —I ain't no damn fool. It's bad enough knowin' He's there. Where you reckon a broke-up nigger like me would be if I didn't believe in Him?

—But you hate . . .

—Yeah, yeah. I hate. What keeps me goin'. If I didn't know He was there, couldn't feel them cold terrible eyes on me when I works way into the night, almost hear that sniggerin' and gigglin' when I gets like this . . . how could I get by if He wasn't there? Reckon what I'd do if this black skin and these no-good hands and these shakes and feet hurtin' every minute of every day, if all this wasn't but a accident. Oh God, I'd pour a quart of bad whisky down my throat and a gallon of gas all over me and light up a big cigar.

Mr Christian's eyes are filled with grateful tears. —But it

ain't no accident. It ain't bad luck. I do believe. Yes, I believe.

He is roused now, and his voice, ragged, strained through phlegm and pain, wraps around Christopher like a narcotic mist. Christopher recalls the days just after his ordination when, if he ever believed anything, he believed that God was close, that God was aware.

—I do believe He lives, Mr Christian almost shouts in something like ecstasy. Then his voice drops, his head lowers, and he squeezes his hands between lean shanks. Tears fall on the dismembered transmission, and shimmering on the ancient oily metal, retain their shape, their integrity.

—An' one day I'm gonna have me a piece of Him.

But Christopher is bombed. He is trying to scramble through a sudden grisly downpour of words that have erupted in his mind. Memory is having a field day. In it there is much of madness and more of sin, and horror the soul of the plot. He recalls fragments of a sermon: *God sets spies on us; He looks upon us Himself through the curtains of a cloud, and He sends angels to espy us in all our ways, and permits the devil to winnow us and to accuse us. And He cannot want information concerning our smallest irregularities.*

—Say, Mr Christian breaks in, his face slowly brightening, as if some measure of relief has been vouchsafed him. —You could do it. You could. Ain't nobody could do it easy as you. For you, it wouldn't be nothin'.

The horror, the horror, Christopher is thinking. If this poor monster is right, it could be even worse than Christopher has guessed. It is one thing for God to be dead, never to have been at all. But suppose He lives. And is a fiend. Some poet, Christopher tries to remember. Old Nobodaddy. The Devil has defeated God, usurped omnipotence and wears the mask of the Almighty. Prodding man onward to destruction as if it were salvation, never happier than when all belief is extinct, and a man is without even the defense of his own gut-chilling fear. Deals have been made, Christopher is thinking. There was that day in heaven when Something pretending Godhead passed the time with Something called the Adversary. *Hast thou considered my servant Job . . .* indeed, hast thou considered.

Christopher drops the remains of his sandwich which promptly vanish amongst the refuse at his feet. He hears Mr Christian, who has been talking without pause.

—You could get a whole cupful for me. You could walk in and they wouldn't think nothin' of it.

—What? Christopher is asking him, shaking his head, banishing the agonized grinning zombie-head of Father Madden's —Grünewald's—Christ, his own personal adversary for so long.

—We can get Him. You and me. We can't kill Him. Ain't no way to kill Him. But we can shame Him. How'd you like that?

—Like what? Christopher asks, rising from his orange crate, almost knowing what Mr Christian is about.

—Get me a cup of them wafers, get me some of them little white Jesuses. You could go to the St. Louis Cathedral in your black suit and get 'em and bring 'em down here. Then we could take 'em and . . .

Christopher is backing away toward the dark corridor, but Mr Christian pays him no mind. He is still flexing his hands, one against the other, his voice low and gentle as he describes what he has in mind for those sacred hosts Christopher the infidel, the heresiarch, the recreant, will obtain for him.

And even turning in the dark hall, one hand on the door, trying to see some point of light amongst the tufted cobwebs where spiders operate continually, amidst great flakes of dirt older than his purjured orders, in the poignant static heat, Christopher feels a sudden chill as if distant wings are beating, fluttering above a lake of ice. The taste of Staff-o-Life bread is bitter in his mouth, and going up those numberless stairs wearies what once he called his soul.

&~ &~

Mrs. Nieman is rubbing Christopher's back. He lies in his shorts sprawled on the bed. As she rubs oil into his knotted muscles, he tries not to think. But her hands are smooth and wonderful, and he thinks of Mary Ann. That is profitless, and he turns it off even as he feels the result of her instant's imagined visit coupled with his mother's massage.

Somewhere across the street he hears a fulsome Italian voice:

. . . there's no tomorrow . . .

It has been a musical afternoon, and he is sick of it. Of course there is a tomorrow. And one after that. But how to fill them? Again, Mary Ann appears before him. This time he does not cast her into outer darkness. He dallies, and even as he does, his mother cracks him firmly on the behind and kisses his neck.

—So there. You're a new man. A new life.

Christopher shakes his head. —How about a beer? Driving a truck, you get to liking beer.

—Sitting on the balcony with a beer. In your undershirt. Staring at the windows opposite. With your chest hair sticking through your undershirt. Gee, Mrs. Nieman says, —you got some new life. If you get promoted to manager you can sit out there with a beer . . .

—I know. And a white shirt on.

—And your chest hair sticking out the buttonholes. Gee.

Christopher nurses his beer like a sullen moppet in a Dickens fable. It is very hot, and Mrs. Nieman tries to cheer him. No use. He is not trying to be difficult; he is just hung. And late for his afternoon's work. Mr Christian has drained his energy.

—Maybe you should go find a girl, his mother suggests, turning on her portable phonograph. "Rainbow Rhapsody": Glenn Miller. Early 1942. Too lush, too fleshy for the hour. Like a quart of Crème de Menthe for breakfast. Christopher shudders.

—It's no good. I'm broke. I can't do anything.

—Money is only the second thing a girl wants. If she's healthy. What you need is a little . . .

—Boy, you said it.

—. . . confidence.

Christopher sips his beer and thinks of the afternoon ahead. He will deliver 1500 loaves of bread. People's sandwiches, and toast, dressing and bird food depend on him. Some trust.

—I should have stayed where I was. Three meals and a room, and all you had to do was make signs. And listen to dirty stories.

—How come you don't believe in yourself? his mother asks,

abstractedly, one ear snagged in Isham Jones' "For All We Know."

—I don't believe in anything. You never believe in yourself. You believe in something else. Because we know how weak and useless we are. It's absurd to think we can do anything, change anything. Maybe something else working in us . . .

—Bullshit, Mrs. Nieman says kindly. —You can do what you want to do. I never wanted anything I didn't get. Mrs. Nieman feels suddenly tired. Her heart beats perfunctorily. She is thinking about death. They say he is a lover, and comes to ravish those who think of him too much. —All you have to do is want.

—I want something.

—That girl?

—Mary Ann? Sure. I guess so. But something else. Something tied up with her. Something she has.

Christopher sounds like a cross between a voluptuary and Count Dracula to his mother. Things are simpler for her. She thinks: You want life. Or you don't, and finally the desire is registered somewhere, the cells and the bones and the nerves come to realize, and what you want you get. It is the nature of things. Christopher worries her.

Christopher sighs and shakes his head. The beer is flat and Staff-o-Life awaits him. He has 1500 promises to keep before he sleeps. Alone. Without benefit. Perhaps he could buy prints after Aretino and paste them on the sun visors of the truck. Mr Christian could procure him a dose of some kind. The advantage of living, he thinks, is that there are a million awful remedies for every ghostly malady. The dead have to lie still and dream of their failures. Christopher squints at his mother and shudders. There is something he wants to tell himself, but it is something he refuses to hear. Big men and small boys differ chiefly in exterior measurements. The phonograph snarls politely and it is Benny Goodman's "Undecided."

. . . so whatta you gonna do? . . .

Mrs. Nieman lets her robe fall from her shoulders. She wears only bra and panties and Christopher feels barrels of water, cold as the Bodensee, sluice around him. Her breasts, her small waist, almost smother him. She is unconscious of it, guessing, he supposes, in her simplicity, that nothing seeks its own past, that going home again is something you cannot, and there's an end on it. Tex Benecke and the Miller Band. Something very new:

> . . . *aware my heart is a sad affair,*
> *There's much disillusion there . . .*
> *But I can dream can't I . . . ?*

Mrs. Nieman lies down on the bed and stretches her long tanned legs, each smooth muscle from ankle to hip turning, pulsing, tightening and loosening again. Christopher is not given to spontaneous nosebleed, otherwise his bread suit would be a mess. He would like to pray, but he has forgotten, and anyhow, there is no sacramental charm against the demon who is blowing his spine cold, his loins unbearably hot.

—Come over and sit here, his mother says lazily. Christopher squints. Is she Asmodeus' accomplice? No. One knowing word or glance and he will rend the temple and cut his throat, play Mr Christian: curse God and die. He is beginning to believe something. It remains just beyond his grasp. There are perhaps eight veils. Conceivably nine.

But Mrs. Nieman is covered with perspiration. She feels that lethal tango moving in her breast: three or four beats and a long dragging pause before the next. Her arms, her legs feel like old lumber; the room turns on some hidden axis. The open French doors, the table, Christopher and his beer all move around her slowly like satellites of a cooling sun. —Come over and sit here, she whispers again, not trusting her voice. She is not ready for the last excursion yet. There can be no excuse for deserting a troubled child. Death is only an alibi. She breathes slowly as Christopher's hands touch her, as she lifts her lovely insentient arms to circle his neck.

Christopher kisses her closed eyes, his own breath as short as hers, his will perched amidst dancing angels (and others) on the head of a collapsing pin. He kisses his mother, knowing that any instant he may topple and his embrace be of another kind. Which he desires and does not want. Which, God being venerable bugbear and not in fact even there, is permitted; which, if Jehovah lives, will not be overlooked.

His arms are around her waist, his lips on her breast. And Mrs. Nieman smooths his uncombed hair, thinking of his father, who, even in their marriage bed, claimed her love like a sullen, ill-favored child. Are we brought to bay by chromosomes?

Down in the street, someone has run up onto the curb, hitting a pushcart. Words pass.

—Goddamn you, someone shrieks. —Goddamn you to hell.

Christopher's head snaps up. Within the wet vestment of noonday heat and his own passion, certain old circuits growl and clack beneath the rust of abandonment. He looks down, and sees that his mother is asleep. But how could anybody sleep in this heat, this sticky unimaginable heat that ravels his backbone and churns his loins?

Between the act and something like a dream, Mrs. Nieman feels his hands withdrawing, regrets the moment's passing even as, her pulse finding foxtrot rhythm again, she realizes what, beyond his unhappiness, had stirred him. What, beyond her lurching heart, had oiled her with sweat.

She hears the door open, calls faintly after him. —I'll see you later, hear? You're going to be just fine.

Only silence, and then the doorlock smoothly engaging, the muscles and nerves in her taut belly easing, her fingers loosening in the pillowslip. —You hear?

And from beyond the door, as if from beyond all seas, mountains and the deserts and forests between, the softest, most distant of replies.

—Yes.

&~ &~

Back to the Café du Monde. After all flights, inevitably back to the Café du Monde where everything begins and any number of things end.

A girl with freckles, slacks and bizarre earbobs leans on her elbows over a cup of coffee and stares into the street. Her eyes are some approximate blue, and there are bits of scarlet polish scattered along her chewed nails. She is kind of thinking about St. Louis, though not really, on account of a boy at Fort Hood who kept her until his unit headed for the Pacific and after him two policemen in Dallas swapped her around the studs on the night patrol before they sent her on into Louisiana (writing ahead to police in Bossier City that there was a wild trick falling in).

The trick fumbles with her reddish hair and gazes out toward the street. An old man in a golf cap waves a newspaper: something about Nuremberg Trials. Frick's Diary. Jodl pleads. Von Schirach. She drains her coffee and starts to walk down the steamy length of the French Market. When she rises, she finds herself sick. Not quite throwing-up sick, but sick. What she needs is a doctor. You can't play squat-and-shoot-it without losing sooner or later. With her luck, the life in her belly is probably one of those cops. All the way from West Virginia, a thousand flops between, and now she has a gutful of howling tomorrows and nobody to cut them out. Whisky and coffee do barrel rolls in her belly. A Negro walks by, stares just a little, his eyes tight and squinted against the afternoon sun. One thing: if you're hard up against it, a nigger'll give you a kind word. More than that no-count Greek sonofabitch in the bar. Even as she turns, she finds the Negro turning back toward her, infinite compassion in his red bleary eyes. Trouble knows trouble, she thinks. —Little girl, he says.

⋅§ §⋅

Mrs. Nieman has Jeremiah under control. He no longer tries to wriggle up under her skirt. Now, with a length of clothesline for a leash, she can walk him in the afternoons when the heat's worst damage is done. On the way downstairs, a skinny redhead accosts her with a piece of dirty envelope in hand.

Mrs. Nieman points one flight up. Apartment 10. Just above. Where the man with thick glasses and the mechanical walk stays. The girl thanks her and climbs again. Not going up to wash and iron, Mrs. Nieman thinks. And not too much good for anything else. But then old B-B eyes isn't Leslie Howard either.

Down near the river Jeremiah pees cheerfully, sniffing, darting to the clothesline's end, squats and scratches. Thunderheads gather to the north and rumble. But it sounds like fraud to Mrs. Nieman. You get used to the weather. You come to know when it will rain and when there will be clouds and thunder and nothing of substance afterward. They turn away from the river and the street goes gray with cloud, then begins to color again, the sun rolling up shadow like an old rug. They pass a house in Conti Street and Jeremiah pauses, sniffing acutely. Then he bolts. Down an abbreviated alley, around a corner, under some kind of stunted miserable berry tree, into a wooden door indifferently hung in a crumbling brick wall. Jeremiah sniffs the door, his colorless eyes glazed with anticipation. It gives way, falling backward on a single hinge, and as it does, Jeremiah gives one final yelping lurch and pulls free of Mrs. Nieman's tether.

Mrs. Nieman hesitates. Beyond the door there would appear to be some kind of garden. She can see what looks like a tall rosebush. There is grass, and a curve of stone that looks like the edge of a pool or fountain. God knows what Jeremiah has found within. When a hound goes bad, there is no telling what he will run to earth. Finally she steps past the collapsing door. Her heart beats faster, but regularly. Her steps are careful. She does not mean to die for somebody else's dog. It is a garden indeed, and Jeremiah has found some peculiar game.

The naked man who lies splayed out on his face beside the fountain might be dead. He might be drowned and fished out of the pool and laid on the grass while the police or next of kin are being summoned.

Except that the pool is only a foot deep, and as Jeremiah's nose sinks into the grass at his side, trying desperately to turn him over, the naked man curses volubly and tries to kick the hound, turns over his own way, and grabs a large beach towel all at the same time.

Kneeling next to him, bottle of suntan oil in hand, a girl stares quizzically at Jeremiah, half in recognition, half in uncertainty. She is nude too except for the briefest of G-strings which only accentuates what it fails to seclude. Her skin is already so dark as to defy the sun, and her tan is perfectly even over high smooth breasts, down her flat belly, along the round of her hips and thighs.

—Would you . . . get that . . . sonofabitch . . . off me, the man growls as he rights himself, still fumbling for the towel.

—He's your sonofabitch, the girl tells him, her head turning suddenly to find Mrs. Nieman staring at her.

—Oh goddamn, Billy Bob Stoker coughs, getting the towel at last, and blushing three shades redder as he spots Mrs. Nieman. —Yes ma'am. Good to . . .

Jeremiah is beside himself. His master's. Yes. His very self and voice. —. . . see you, Billy Bob grins, cuffing Jeremiah across the snout.

—Ain't no use hurtin' him, Mary Ann says. —Natural to make over you, ain't it?

But Jeremiah has no sense of proportion. He continues to fawn and flounce, roll and scuffle, tongue lolling, eyes wide and loving, yelps tremulous with pleasure. He throws himself at Billy Bob's head.

—How's . . . you mother. This time he clouts Jeremiah with his fist. Agonized howl. Brief retreat.

—That ain't no way to treat a dumb animal.

—You want some? Billy Bob roars, almost losing his towel.

—Any time, Mary Ann snaps, suntan-oil bottle poised. —Any time at all.

—Yes ma'am, Billy Bob says to Mrs. Nieman, smiling wanly. —How's ole Christopher?

—That's . . . ?

—Right, Billy Bob finishes for Mary Ann. —Ole Christopher's mama.

—Jesus Christ, Mary Ann says, pop-eyed. She stares at Mrs. Nieman unbelieving. —You don't look like anybody's mama. You don't hardly look like his sister.

Mrs. Nieman smiles. In a way, surprised reactions like Mary Ann's keep the heart bumping along. After all, she thinks, it is a ridiculous heart. Older than its container. A damn poor match. —Thanks. You must be . . .

—Uh huh. Mary Ann Downey. I was kind of down on it in Shreveport. I mean I ought to of stayed and thanked you. But I didn't know . . .

—Hell, we both tried to tell you, Billy Bob puts in.

Mary Ann shrugs and pushes Billy Bob over. She begins massaging him with the oil.

—We didn't know where you'd gotten to, Mrs. Nieman tells Billy Bob. —Christopher wondered if you'd gotten your head pushed in.

—Aw, naw, Billy Bob grins, wriggling as Mary Ann's hands press into his thighs. —No ma'am. I was kind of lookin' for a job. I mean I couldn't live off youall. I had to find something to do.

Mrs. Nieman smiles and looks at Mary Ann. —Do you like the work?

—Aw well, Billy Bob blushes. —*This* ain't the work. I got me a job with this feller who makes . . .

Mary Ann's fingernails almost meet in the flesh of his thigh. —. . . picture shows, Billy Bob finishes.

—Picture shows?

—I'm gonna be in a movie-picture. All about Catholics and those bad sonsabitches in the requisition burnin' good Protestants and hangin' Jews. One place they take this Jew-boy and cut him . . .

—It's a historical religious picture show, Mary Ann says modestly. —My boss says Billy makes them Hollywood fellers look like a bunch of cock . . .

—Robins, Billy Bob finishes, trying to move Mary Ann's hand down a little. She is working hard and working high. It is inconveniencing him. But, absorbed in talking with Mrs. Nieman, she pays him no mind, only slapping his hand and going on with it as if they were upstairs and alone.

—Uh, Billy Bob begins, feeling the towel begin to take on a life of its own, like a rigged table at a seance. Jeremiah sulks, lapping from the fountain without pleasure.

—Uh, did ole Christopher get that bread-truckin' job?

—He's up at four, Mrs. Nieman tells him. —And split-shifting at that. Carting bread around is a lousy job. Not like the movies.

—You reckon, Mary Ann asks musingly, —you reckon Boundoch could put Chris on? I mean to help with making things the way they really was? I mean, with him, bein' a priest, wouldn't he know all about those days? All that killin' and bishops screwin' and . . .

—Naw, Billy Bob cuts in, trying to hold down his towel and snake out from under Mary Ann's competent hands, which have zeroed in on his lower belly and thereabouts and have, of their own volition, shifted purpose from relaxant to stimulant. —Now, say, would you . . .

—Lay still, Mary Ann snaps, still caught up with the idea of helping Christopher. —Listen, Miz Nieman, Christopher is all right. I mean maybe he ought not to of cut out from that church and all, but it ain't no use stickin' with somethin' when it goes bad. He's a nice-lookin' boy. Maybe he could even be in . . .

—Naw, Billy Bob says depreciatingly. —He wouldn't want to get into this business. Unhappy memories. You want to make him feel evil?

Jeremiah is ready for one more try. In the old days, he had run with shoes and sticks, even old paper bags, and Billy Bob had laughed and thrown him squirrel entrails, or whatever there was. Maybe a return to those good old days. But what to grab and run?

—You could ask him, Mary Ann goes on.

—Naw, Billy Bob repeats doggedly, watching his towel rise and levitate in the middle, too far gone even to try escaping Mary Ann's unconscious professionalism, or fend off her delectable hands. —Naw, he wouldn't . . .

—You're so goddamned smart.

Mrs. Nieman feels like a tennis scorekeeper. Too many things to watch. She would like to speak to Mary Ann alone. One good massage like that would make Christopher. Into a new man.

—I could ask him, she tells Mary Ann.

—I'd like to see him. I'm obliged to him. He's a good man.
And a good man is hard . . .

Jeremiah sees, considers, pounces. He has a corner of the
towel before Billy or Mary Ann even know he is moving. He
pulls it away, prances off, and squats waiting to be chased. Old
games are the best games. He has often been chased. But rarely
caught.

—Jesus, Billy Bob howls, undone, exposed to one and all. He
scrambles crablike after Jeremiah, trying even in extremity to
minimize his shame, and in so doing snags his source of shame
and pride in a patch of grass burrs.

—Arghhh, Billy Bob gargles, trying to free himself as Jeremiah cuts and capers, muzzle wrapped in the bright towel.

—You oughta be ashamed, Mary Ann says, still seated, her
hands folded primly. —Seems like you could play with that dog
after Miz Nieman . . .

Billy Bob is seated too now, trying to cover himself with one
hand. Picking burrs out of his parts with the other. Jeremiah
runs at him with the towel, pushing him over on his back, snag-
ging the towel around his master's head. Billy groans and lies
still, neither covering nor picking any longer.

Mary Ann shrugs apologetically. —Some people are common, she tells Mrs. Nieman. —There ain't a thing on God's
earth you can do with a right-down common man.

Mrs. Nieman, who has not felt so well in a long time, still
contains her smile. She tries not to look at Billy Bob, caught between pity and admiration. —Christopher would like to see you,
Mrs. Nieman says finally.

—You could tell him to come by . . . naw, maybe not.

—You could meet him. After work. If you can get out
for a while.

Mary Ann bristles —I can get out any damn time I want out.
You tell him to come over to the Bethel Bar. You tell him to
come after work. I'd like to see him. You know . . .

Mrs. Nieman is smiling now as they walk through the gate
into the alley. —I bet I do. He reminds you of somebody.

—Yeah. Naw, not really. I mean not his looks. He don't look
like anybody. Just one night in Carthage I saw this man talkin'

to a girl. He makes you feel like . . . hell, I don't know. You just get to likin' him.

—I know, Mrs. Nieman says, shivering slightly. —You can get to loving him.

—What do you reckon makes some people like that? I don't feel like that. I mean like people just want to love me. I think they want my . . . But you just want to treat Chris right.

—I always thought he was sad inside, Mrs. Nieman says. She has not always thought that. Not exactly, but it is as close as anything else.

—Um. So you want to make things easy on him.

—Can't do it, Mrs. Nieman says. —Not really. But a good try is worth something. He likes you. Mabye more than that.

—Um.

—No dice?

Mary Ann frowns, concentrating. —I don't know. We ain't much alike. You take Stoker in there. He ain't worth a shit, but I know everything he thinks ten minutes before he thinks it.

—Pretty comfortable.

—You better believe it. With Chris, you don't ever know.

—It's better to know, Mrs. Nieman almost whispers. —I guess.

—Um. You tell him to come on by the Bethel Bar, you hear?

—Yes.

ᵉ§ §ᵉ

Dr. Aorta has no use for midday. He likes early morning when, for a moment or two, he can sit in Jackson Square and pretend it is the Bois de Bologne. At such moments his heart rises. The past is recaptured. The odor of verbena or hedgerose or honeysuckle recalls those bright days of 1940 when Paris belonged to him, when the least boring days of his career still lay ahead.

But by ten o'clock, there is no room for illusion. The rising stench of vegetables rotting and gasoline fumes, the blast-furnace heat brings with it other memories. They do not disturb him. One is disturbed only if it is possible to believe things might or should have been other than they were. Which kind of thinking implies absurdity in series and in parallel. It is, Dr. Aorta considers, bad enough to live with an unslakable thirst of boredom without adding to it the salt of self-delusion.

So in the afternoon he remains in his apartment, usually sitting in front of a large block of ice across which a cheap fan shakes and twists and perhaps cools a little. He sits in darkness stripped to a pair of ridiculous jockey shorts over and around which his fat tends to settle in pale bluish folds. He still wears his glasses and behind them the ambiguous pupils of his eyes resemble tadpoles swimming at random in shadowed pools.

But this particular afternoon is different. He has business. On an outsized table in his kitchen, under a less than immaculate sheet, lies the body of a young woman. She has red, brittle hair, brownish at the roots. Thin arms, negligible breasts, pale skin beneath countless freckles, and large bluish veins lacing across her body in every possible direction. She lies unconscious, her mouth open, revealing bad teeth. She breathes heavily and it has taken a large dose of anesthesia to put her out.

If Dr. Aorta were given to expression, he would, at this moment, be registering disgust. Medicine at best is a nasty job. It is a calling which reveals with awful clarity the nature of humanity. There is, Dr. Aorta muses, no poem, no oration, no epic which can dignify a bad case of hemorrhoids. Metaphysics is washed away in the slime of sinus discharge. And the most basic claim to meaning is blasted when a woman offers her parted legs to be rid of the life which stirs between them.

Dr. Aorta pours half a snifter full of Hennessy and relaxes in the gloom across from his fan and block of ice. He wipes his hands absently on a neat full-length apron which does him for medical togs (it is the same outfit he wore in medical school long ago; identical to his working costumes at Ravensbrück and Dachau. Not a surgical garment meant to protect the patient from infection: rather a butcher's garb to shield the clothing of the carver from blood, bits of flesh, the fluids and jellies connected with corpses, experimental animals, etc.) .

The girl in the kitchen moans slightly, and Dr. Aorta's head turns. He nearly spits out an order before he remembers that there is no one to obey it.

Time passes. He sips his brandy and remembers a luncheon
at the Imperial Hotel given for certain graduates of British
medical schools who were about to leave England for the col-
onies, for other countries. An elderly doctor, member of the
House of Lords, had spoken. Something about carrying the message from London to every corner of the earth. That Britain
cared. That her facilities, her wisdom, her technical superiority
were, after all, only given her by the All-High in trust. To be
used for the welfare of the less fortunate.

Dr. Aorta had enjoyed the old man. He had listened with
rapt interest, something approaching glee, while an Indian on
his right hand and a Lithuanian on his left had alternately
sniffed and mumbled under their breath. It had been a lovely
performance. The old man was a fabulous clown; all the better for his grotesque seriousness. Almost, Dr. Aorta had considered, as deliciously absurd as his father. Dr. Aorta recalled
his own thoughts running in ironic parallel to those of the long-
winded noble old doctor. That medicine is the most bizarre
of callings. For there is no success. The patient always dies. If
not this time, then the next. If not of that complaint, then of
another. And behold the man, the one to be saved by your
skill. Who will as surely waste his life as did his father and his
father's father. For in all man's endless scrawling, only a line
or two is sure, and these the words of Solomon: *Vanity, vanity.
All is vanity.* Life is as vain as death, and the law of the universe is that nothing matters, never mind. That man and galaxy
are driven by entropy. Life is an itch; an instant's inexplicable
interruption in the long actionless dream of a silent universe.
And man goeth to his long home. Then shall dust return to the
earth as it was.

But in the time between, there must be . . . what? Amuse-
ment? Diversion? Perhaps one might pretend that he himself is
the God that is not. Granting life, denying it. At his whim, at
his own untutored pleasure.

While the old man ground to his labored conclusion, Dr.
Aorta thought of chess and war, of priests and musicians. And
thought finally that the best game of all is surgery. He glanced
down at his own smooth hands in which lay the difference be-

tween death and a bit more life for thousands. He thought of the femoral artery where an instant and a fraction of an inch separated death from life. There would surely be times, places, when the temptation . . .

—Forever and ever, the old doctor finished, —and especially in our time.

Indeed. In our time. The boredom would be broken. In our time.

The girl moves on the kitchen table, sighs, and is silent again. Dr. Aorta rises irritably. She is a cow. The anesthetic should keep her totally immobile for another hour at least. As he reaches her side and gives her a small injection, temptation moves him. But it is no longer prudent to be arbitrary. Although no one in the city has the slightest interest in whether the girl lives or dies, there is here, as in England, a repulsive and meaningless penchant for order. Every corpse must be tallied, and an explanation supplied. What the law notices, the law must explain. There is no feeling behind the impulse. Neither love nor justice. Like surgery, it is a game and those who play it pass the time. It is neither doubted nor believed in. It is simply done. Dr. Aorta walks back to his brandy and ice cake and fan, considering with something like a grin the chief exception: capital punishment. Which is, finally, as arbitrary as his own past doings and those of his colleagues. Although few executioners admit taking pleasure in their work, it too passes time.

The heat presses in. Finishing his brandy, Dr. Aorta yawns, cleans his glasses and moves back into the kitchen. Time to work. One must respect, if nothing else, his own ability, his capacity to shatter the mindless flow of things.

The work does not disturb him. He rather likes it. Each time his curette peels away another formless futureless life that will not be lived, he recalls the past and thinks that the purpose of his late confrères and associates in Germany was simply abortion on a grand scale. They had set out to cleanse the world's body, to carve from its purposeless and teeming uterus the inferior scum which grows and flourishes and takes space, air and sustenance from those who have the right to live. If the mechanics of abortion are repulsive, its end is sound: cosmic surgery. If the operation failed in 1945, it will be attempted again another time, by other surgeons. Meanwhile, even on a modest level, the procedures, the mentality must and shall be preserved. Dr. Aorta finds himself wishing for disciples and shakes the thought out of his head. This is not the time for missionary zeal. It is a time for prudence, to watch and wait.

The girl stirs again; her mouth opens and closes like a fish's. Her hair, dripping and kinked, glares sick and unreal against Dr. Aorta's sheets. —Mr. Bailey, she mumbles.

—*Was ist?*

—I never wanted those for only hope. Mr. gone plum wants holy tones. You want me tiny sin or place . . . we went that night? Won't you. Come home?

Dr. Aorta shrugs and places his tray within reach. Usually, Mrs. Mailer is there to help. But she tends to keep up a running commentary, spiked with observations on the decline of modern morality, her own past in the context of the these times ("a lady alone . . . ain't got no fucking chance") and Dr. Aorta bores with exquisite ease. When he is bored, moreover, he becomes irritable and even simple operations are botched when one is irritable.

Outside, the street sounds merge and flow like zany liquids freed from hydraulic law. Dr. Aorta begins his examination, trying to screen out the sounds. A car backfires and from a vast distance comes a woman's hysterical laugh. There is a baby crying somewhere, soft ragged wheezing staccato. Dr. Aorta frowns. Possibly a serious lung infection. He smiles slowly. It is a law of nature that the stupid will die and their progeny with them. No work of man can save the stupid. Statistically, with the passage of enough time, Dr. Aorta is thinking, the world belongs to us. By default.

He is frowning again. The girl is three months gone and then some. She is, moreover, a mess inside. The tissue of her uterus is fragile, and for lack of nourishment, lack of even primitive hygiene, and from general misuse, her chances of carrying a child to term are almost nil. She would be lucky to produce a cretin, Dr. Aorta thinks, pouring antiseptic to reduce the

stench. Still, it is an interesting technical problem. No doctor,
bound by the reactionary safeguards of a hospital, would go on;
both diagnosis and prognosis would point toward a conserva-
tive mode of treatment. But there had been, according to reports, a surgeon at Ravensbrück whose technique had made
abortion possible up to the end of the fifteenth or sixteenth
week. Dr. Aorta had read one such report. The operation had
been performed on a Slavonian Jewess, who had survived four
months, the doctor risking all to save her from the gas chamber
until his success had been proved. Dr. Aorta had long wondered
if the doctor had used some drug to slow the rate of blastula-
tion. Duplicity is not beyond scientists. If one could impede
the cell growth rate, then it would be possible to abort far beyond the accepted limit without real risk. But this case: if one
might see, if one could handle his scalpel with almost microscopic control, the fetus could be detached, and the rest done
easily enough. If the wall was not cut; if its tissue was of normal
strength and resiliency.

As Dr. Aorta begins, he hears again that mélange of sounds
from the streets and apartments around him with particular
clarity. As if the outside, moving in metaphysical space, were
at his shoulder, observing without concern or interest. From
far off, a woman's voice:

—What have I duune?

Time passes. This heat is enough to irritate the Buddha,
and from beyond the hot wrought-iron balcony of his apartment, the idiot world creeps in to plague Dr. Aorta and blur his
concentration. A cornet blares from across the street.

. . . how great the Lord,
how great the Lord . . .

Dr. Aorta wipes his brow with a clean towel, and begins
carefully maneuvering his scalpel. At first the progress seems
good. There is no fetal activity. The ambush proceeds. A
mosquito swings past his ear, but that special charisma of the
professional keeps the doctor's attention centered with perfect
aplomb. The cornet wavers, strikes a false note, and stops.

A voice replete with the most Southern of accents coughs out:

—Sonofabitch. You goddamn well know it. You feather-fuckin' sonofabitch.

Then that woman again. *Angst* and jeopardy: —What *have* I duuuuune . . . what have *I* . . . ?

Dr. Aorta is half finished when he feels it. Before the tissue collapses, the trained nerves feel it. What has been firm begins to go flimsy, and within a microsecond, the knife is withdrawn. But that is at least a millimicro second too late. Before he can remove his hands, there is a single rigid spasm from fetus or uterus, and he feels an incredibly smooth fluid rushing like engine oil from a broken crankcase. His fingers, even cased in rubber, detect its heat and the ugly force of its flow. He takes out his hands, purses his lips, and stuffs several of the freshly laundered kitchen towels into the fast-filling aperture. There is not equipment for transfusion. Which makes not the slightest difference, since all the blood in Jonah's Leviathan could be pumped into this subject, only to flow as quickly out her ruptured and irreparable tissues.

Dr. Aorta sits down opposite his largest fan. Time passes. He sips a little brandy, removes his glasses and squints his eyes tightly. He is irritated almost to the point of expressible anger. The cornet blubbers once more. —*Scheiss,* Dr. Aorta spits. The girl moves, tries to turn on her side. Dr. Aorta glances at his wristwatch, approximates the seconds since his work went sour, and gazes at the ceiling. Possibly six, seven minutes more.

—All the where it's okay warm, the girl lisps, her tin-can voice suddenly melted into the soft edgeless wonder of a child's. —I once knew all you could see up in it. High. You can see it cream and a little pool. Oh sir, get the doll a roofing.

She is quiet again, but her eyes are open, and it is just possible that she has some idea of what is happening to her. Dr. Aorta has great respect for the body's things. There are signals and ciphers. One can sense ultimate occurrences. Even if one is clearly, absolutely *Sklavenvolk*. One could possibly scream.

He fills a syringe quickly and moves to her side. Breathing rapid and shallow. Pulse beyond manual detection. Yet her eyes are open, clear, starry. Bright as those of a child at the edge of the circus grounds, or a girl who has just heard a palmist's sweetest lie. She is looking at Dr. Aorta with an expression of total and concentrated rationality—a way she has almost certainly never looked before.

I— love you, she whispers.

—Shut up, Dr. Aorta replies just as softly, reaching for her arm. But even as the needle touches her flesh, those trained nerves of his stop him from wasting an expensive lethal drug. Her eyes, still locked with his, begin to glaze, to collect that strange distance that seems frost rushing to cling at windows behind which there is no warmth because the tenant has vacated. The sincerity in them fades, and is replaced by terrible objectivity of lifelessness. The palmist's trailer has vanished. The circus has left town. Dr. Aorta breathes rather more deeply than usual, squeezes the syringe back into its lobeless bottle, and finds his glass of brandy still cool. He has logistics to consider now. Transportation of meat. He considers his failure, and thinks after a moment that no failure has taken place. On any level. The man at Ravensbrück was clearly a charlatan. The old Spanish woman a myth or a mountebank. Fourteen weeks would defeat a Napoleon of surgery. One may keep trying, but it is pointless. Nature deals a close deck. Only absurd luck can outdo nature, and luck is the instrumentality of slaves. Now as to transportation. Of meat.

Chapter Five

Christopher's shoulders sag as if he were bearing a heavy burden on his back. He moves uncertainly, his hands, his arms and legs numb as he imagines Mr. Christian's must be. The door of the Bethel Bar is narrow, but there is, deep in the gloom, a dart of red glimmering like creation's first tentative fizzle. As he staggers into the cool and total darkness, he hears from an archaic jukebox, glowing red as an old timer's pipe, the word:

> . . . *same old story* . . .

A light shines in the darkness, but Christopher cannot comprehend it. Squinting, he sees it taking form: another word. SCHLITZ. The beer that made Milwaukee.

> . . . *as time goes by* . . .

He stumbles against the table, but in his fatigue it does not matter: he has no way, and therefore wants no eyes. He stumbled when he saw. Somewhere a voice is calling, but the words are blurred and misty. His throat is dry, and there hangs about his garish costume the stench of bread freshly baked and recently delivered.

> . . . *jealousy and hate* . . .
> *woman needs man and man must*
> *have his mate* . . .

That no one can deny, Christopher is thinking as he orders an ale and feels the tension and bone-tiredness begin to flow away. As the day's grinding misery drips away, he begins to feel faint. Holding his ale, he tries to step carefully through the gloom, hoping to find an empty table before he falls out. A table finds him, and he sprawls across it, barely managing to set down the ale before it spills.

—Thanks, Mary Ann says. —Ain't you gonna have one?

—Uh, Christopher gurgles, the last of his strength trickling out through his legs. —Yes, I couldn't carry. But one at a time.

Mary Ann's face rises out of the darkness, each feature, each adorable curve of cheek, smooth flow of forehead, the soft oval of her lips seeming to move toward him like a lost garden reforming, taking shape again in shadow and mist. Christopher feels as if someone has plugged him into a high-voltage line. He sees on an imaginary screen huge shaky block letters: COMING ATTRACTIONS. TECHNICOLOR. Preview of *The Beatific Vision*.

—Boy, Mary Ann whispers, —you look like hell. They got you in a sweat-shop?

—No, Christopher says, feeling for a chair, almost sitting down on air. —No. Healthy outdoor work. But you. I wanted to see you.

—Yeah, Mary Ann muses. —Drink some of this here beer. You been goin' too strong. Your eyes look like a couple holes pissed in a snowbank. Don't you ever get a tan?

—No. My father. He was very pale. His hands looked like something from under a rock. White.

—Your mother ain't pale. I never seen a woman with a grown-up son look so good.

—You. You look kind of like her.

—Me? Naw. I'll never look that good.

—Yes. You. To me you . . .

—You like your work?

—Like it? No, it's work. Something you do, and they don't care what you think or feel. You don't have to think or feel anything. They don't care. If you think or feel anything, you might mess up.

—Hey, Mary Ann crows cheerfully, —that's kinda like my work.

—You're working here?

—You mean this bar? No. I got me a nice unhealthy job inside. Night work.

Christopher feels a sword slide through his green-bean ribs. Into his potato heart. Naturally, of course. She is not likely to be a teller at the Hibernia National Bank. What is likely is almost always so. Given time, it is absolutely so, Christopher thinks. The jukebox clanks and stutters. Ted Weems, much bass, clarinets, a drummer working double time. There are no lyrics, but Christopher knows what they would be if they were there:

> . . . *what does it matter*
> *if my heart breaks* . . .

—You get up real early, huh?

—Yes, Christopher tells her. —You sleep late?

—Yep. Late as I want to. Late as that bastard Billy . . .

—Billy Bob?

—He's got him a job where I work. It's nice to have somebody I know around.

—Sure, Christopher says. —It's a bad thing to be by yourself.

—I been by myself a lot. You never get used to it. I used to hate the trailer with my mama and Gene. Always yellin' and carryin' on. But it gets so the quiet is even worse. You get to thinkin' even a yell or a bottle through a window is better than just lyin' on a bed in Oklahoma City starin' at the ceiling. You know?

—Yes, Christopher says, thinking of ceilings in Shreveport, New Orleans, Alexandria, London, Brighton, Lewes, Horsham, and those vast and terrible ceilings in the waiting rooms of Waterloo, Kings Cross, Paddington and Victoria Stations. For no conceivable reason, he thinks of Michelangelo on his back for years. Staring at the ceiling of the Sistine Chapel. Adam slouched alone, one hand languidly outstretched as if he did not especially want to live. That other groping downward full of ages and events, seeking a channel, a creature to bring history to life. The upper hand. Fumbling where it listeth. Did you ever see an arm, white damask to the wrist, come sliding through a ceiling in an Oklahoma City hotel? Christopher thinks. Guess what the hand did then?

—You can't talk your way out of it, can you? Mary Ann asks rhetorically, finishing the ale, waving to the bartender.

—No, you can't. You can't talk your way out of anything.

—So you got to have somebody.

—Somebody to love.

Mary Ann shrugs. —Naw. That's too much to ask. You do the best you can. Anyhow, lovin' somebody is like puttin' your finger in a electric fan. It ain't whether you'll get cut. It's just how bad.

—Maybe not always, Christopher tells her softly, paying for a pair of fresh ales.

Mary Ann drinks deeply and licks foam from her lips. She throws her head back, sending a gale of dark hair shaking in the gloom. The jukebox glow catches the luscious line of her throat, turning it crimson for a moment. —You know, she says quietly. —You know the same as me. There ain't any way to love when it's just two people. There's got to be something . . . I don't know. Maybe something else they both love that makes them love each other. I seen a lot. I seen all kinds all over. Two people together can be lonely too. Not as bad as by themselves. 'Cause they got each other to fool with. But you don't get full that way. You still got empty places. Like where you see a cistern, and you can't tell if there's anything in it. Maybe it's almost full. Or maybe not a drop. So you drop a stone. And if you hear it splash right off, you know it's full. But what if it don't sound? What if you wait a long time?

—It's got to make some kind of sound. At least the sound of one rock hitting another one.

—No. Because this one is inside somebody, and maybe the rock you drop is a word. Maybe you say, "I love you."

—I love you, Christopher whispers.

—And you don't hear anything for the longest time, Mary

Ann goes on. —Till finally you hear—you think you hear—a tiny splash like a mouse falling in a well. Then nothing at all. So you never know for sure if you even heard anything or whether you just wanted to so much you made yourself think you did.

—And anyhow, Christopher chokes out, —anyhow, even if you really heard it, the water is too far down. Too far to reach.

Mary Ann places her chin in her hands. —You know, I like the way you understand things.

—Thanks, Christopher says, signaling weakly for more ale. He drinks the last of his present one and holds the cool glass between his hands like a ship stanchion in heavy seas.

—Hey, Mary Ann begins again, brightly, emerging from the unaccustomed journey into metaphysical badlands. Persephone with *carte blanche* from Pluto. —You come across that creepy doc who lives over by you?

—Creepy . . . ?

—Dr. Aorta. He's a friend of my boss. Lives in that building with youall. He'd make the flesh crawl on a bronze mule. Talks with some kind of accent. Got eyes like somebody dotted his eyeballs with a fountain pen. Big thick glasses.

—No, Christopher tells her. —I haven't.

—You watch him. He looks like a feller I knew in Wascom. Took dope and set in this gin mill all evening long playing one-eyed soldier with kids from over in Marshall and Longview. Till something riled him. One night he killed two kids, a girl who worked the bar and a deputy sheriff. It's that goddamned dope. You can't never tell what a dope fiend's gonna do. Runs after death like it was livin'. You just stay clear, hear?

—Sure, Christopher says, about to cast what bread he has left upon her waters. Even as he tries to draw beginning breath, she rises. —Listen, Mary Ann, he starts. —I want us . . .

—Sure, Mary Ann says. —I'll see you around. We'll drink some more and watch the world go round. You be good, she finishes, and before he can realize that she is gone, there is across from him only the wine-dark gloom, an empty glass, two ale bottles, and the filmy recollection of her hands, her arms, the perfect lines of her face, the softness of her mouth. The hand has withdrawn through the ceiling. The jukebox babbles and croaks:

> *. . . I'm a long-gone daddy . . .*
> *long-gone lonesome . . .*

—Yes.

❧ ❧

Mr Christian shivers as if he were working in the lower depths of a salt mine. But it is one hundred degrees at least, and the magneto between his quaking shanks tilts and quivers so that even gross work is impossible. There is a smoldering cigarette butt between his lips, and the smoke burns his eyes. But Mr Christian is beyond misery. He thinks he is probably dying, and that will be just fine. On the other hand, it seems unlikely that the Celestial Cretin would take him now, before agony and ignominy are perfected. "I got plans for you, boy," he seems to hear, and bobs his head not in acceptance but in calm acknowledgment of the warning. The very best part of it all is trying to figure out what the Right Awful Rat's Ass might have up His sleeve for the next humiliation. His ingenuity must be infinite, Mr Christian thinks, just like His power and His meanness. He can do anything He wants to a man. But man's capacity to suffer is finite. You can't do but so much and a man collapses like a deflated gas bag. Mr Christian makes no big thing of endurance. He just means to go hard. No cut wrists or bullets in the head. No dives off the bridge to Algiers. When he goes, he means to have God's ankle in his teeth. And since Mr Christian is not infinite, not praetermean or supercagey, it is taking him a long time to reckon a way. He is not ready yet, but somehow Christopher figures in it. A former employee ought to be useful in getting to the Boss.

He hears someone coming down the dark treacherous steps. As often as he has heard that sound, each time it comes again he wonders if it might be Michael with the fiery sword or maybe Satan himself coming to do the Heavenly Hulk's dirty work

for Him. One day it could be. Satan, naked and woolly. Black
certainly, and covered with shit. He would come, a preacher in
Mississippi had told him once, discovering Mr Christian a
Catholic—he would come stinking like all the goats in creation, both clawed hands at the ready. And he would know his
own even as his own would know him. Then, in a blur of
smelly furry motion, he would grab Mr Christian, black papist,
and shove him bodily up his horrendous ass.

All this is absurd, of course. But when you are small, with
kinky hair and huge white eyes, and told such by a tall terrible
man with clawlike hands and a smell of his own none too good,
hardly anything is too absurd to give you the creeps. And some
of those creeps are residual.

—They wants you, a voice tells Mr Christian out of the shadows beyond the door of his private pit. —They sent me for you.

—Wow, Mr Christian squeaks, ready to toss the magneto
right at the first furry belly he spots. —Haul ass, you motha . . .
You tell Him to come on His own, you hear?

—Aw, the small colored boy says, tossing his cigarette into
the reeking water-filled grease pit, —Doc ain't comin' down
here. He say you come on to his place. Worth a coupla bags.
Soun' like he got the wind up.

—Sammy, you little fart, Mr Christian sighs, ready to embrace the boy in his relief.

—Well, I tole you. Don't you go sayin' I didn't tell you.

As the boy leaves, Mr Christian's trembling hands give way
and the magneto falls on his right foot. The pain is blinding,
but he hardly notices it. Spared again. It may be that Satan
started down the stairs, only to send Sammy on when he found
out that he was expected. Scratch loves surprises, recognitions
in his victims. He has, perfidious like his Patron, the mind of a
nasty child.

Upstairs clouds are gathering. Mr Christian's galoshes seem
appropriate *in potentia*, at least, and the humidity does not
trouble him. He has lived too long like a disadvantaged mud-
puppy to notice it. As he nears Dr. Aorta's apartment building,
he finds he has brought the magneto with him. Things are beginning to fall apart. How long can the center hold? The body's

mortality is no matter to him. He has lived with the falling apart of his flesh for too long to consider it. But now the mind shows signs of crumbling. Maybe Horse is kicking out the stall slats. Or whisky. The old ailments, not content with hands and feet, lights and liver, are aspiring to the last meaty stronghold where his mind has managed to endure all previous assault. Mr Christian shivers again, not for Horsepower but from some shameful disabling thing called fear.

Dr. Aorta is sitting in his parlor when Mr Christian comes in.

—The black, Aorta says to no one.

—Ugh, Mr Christian mutters. Dr. Aorta's presence gives him multiple and extensive creeps. When he is somewhere else, the doctor's image seems no more than that of a fat ugly alien white man whose face is a mask of expressionless contempt aimed not at Mr Christian but at everyone. He may well be God's agent, Mr Christian reasons, since he is clearly a hater of mankind.

—I have something for you, Dr. Aorta says with punctilious courtesy.

—Yeah, Mr Christian answers, veins twitching, but his metaphysical ears pointed for some monstrous trap.

They step into the kitchen and Dr. Aorta pulls a sheet off his long table.

—Sho, Mr Christian says. —That's for me, huh?

Dr. Aorta ignores the ironies. Some of them even escape him. —I want it disposed of.

—Yeah, Mr Christian says, studying the thin white corpse without interest. Meat is meat. Somehow a dead white looks deader, more vulnerable, more beyond help than a dead Negro. Somewhere, he thinks, pulling out and closing squeaky spiritual drawers, there has to be pity left in him. He knows it is there, but it seems not to be forthcoming. The girl's hands are folded under her body as ambulance drivers usually handle corpses. Her eyes are closed, but her mouth is slightly open, and a dark substance seems to be running down the corner of her jaw like a thin fissure in her pallid flesh. She has almost no breasts, not the slightest tinge of sexuality left at all. That is sad, Mr

Christian thinks, remembering how, when his father's body
had been lifted from the bedstead, there had remained behind
a trace of feces and the light stench of urine on the worn
bleached-out sheets. He had looked at these mute reminders
as if they were his patrimony. As things have developed, perhaps they were.

—There are no marks, no fingerprints. Once you have gotten rid of it, there will be no problem.

—Yeah. This ain't exactly my line.

—You have a . . . line?

—Yeah. I got lots of lines. I got irons they ain't even stoked
fires to put 'em in yet. But this here is Marshall Fields' line.
When he loses one, it stays lost.

Dr. Aorta does not seem to be paying attention. He drops the
sheet and stifles a yawn. —I tried to find this other one, Fields.
He is absent. No one sees him today. His cart is vacant.

—Yeah. He been known to lose himself for a couple days.
Doin' God knows what.

—So you have the job. One bag. Two, three days of good
time.

Mr Christian is almost turkey. He wants it. He needs it. But
he has wanted and needed all manner of things in his life, and
sublimation is as much a part of his nature as the wanting or
the needing, and a more familiar part at that. He is considering
chances against risks against pleasures against the clear and present duty of his vendetta against the Almighty. Ummm.

—Uh-uh, he says finally. —I don't need no piece work.
You want me to go dumping white women for you, you gonna
have to put me on the payroll. A spoon a day.

—The other, Fields, does it for fifty dollars. A hundred for a
hard case. You want thirty-five dollars a day for one job.

—I don't even want the job. It ain't my line. But if I go to
spreadin' out my line, I got to get me an edge. I'm tired of hus-
tlin' and pushin' and fixin' without an edge. Every sonofabitch
from Rampart to the river got him an edge. If you don't want
me regular, just don't call me at all no more. Man ain't got an
edge got nothin'.

Mr Christian amazes himself. He is not a profit-motivated

creature. Why the dealing? Is he afraid? You bet. But not of the job. He sees with sudden clarity that his fear is of ultimate failure, of losing the only game he cares one hoot in hell about. He needs an edge. So he can go after God in earnest. And he has begun to smell death about himself. Not lurking or fixing to pounce. Only strolling in the outskirts of his being, clawed hands in pockets, whistling an old hymn. Maybe it was death instead of Satan who came down those stairs—turned into Sammy. Or maybe death and Satan are the same. Anyhow, Mr Christian bows his neck like a mule and waits for Dr. Aorta to answer.

But Dr. Aorta is recollecting the peasantry of Baden and Westphalia. Forever seeking a patron. Electrons desperate for a nucleus, lacking which, they have no identification. This black believes he wants heroin or money—a steady job. What he wants in fact is someone to think for him, someone to make decisions for him.

—Yes, Dr. Aorta says at last. —You are right. From now on you come here each evening to see what I have to do. I will see you are paid. You will have a patron.

Mr Christian's eyebrows come up. Patrons? This is something to think about. Maybe it is one of those cosmic hints that the Ineffable Idiot drops on His victims from time to time. Patron. Like a saint. Maybe Dr. Aorta is one of His angels, given special orders. It would be wise to stay close. You know not the day or the hour. And the night cometh when no man can work.

—So you will move this now, Dr. Aorta gestures at the sheeted figure.

—I ain't got a car, Mr Christian tells him.

—Look, Dr. Aorta says, moving to the balcony and pointing down. Mr Christian's eyes bulge. It is a truck. A bread truck. With STAFF-O-LIFE in large letters printed along the side.

—Wow, Mr Christian exclaims. —That won't get it. I works for these people. I know the man runs that truck. You don't want to get him into this.

Dr. Aorta begins to feel irritated. Every peasant has, at bottom, the mind of a petty bureaucrat. There are always difficulties, each one insuperable.

—I don't care about the work or the man. You can drive that truck. You can carry this away in it. I don't care how you do it so long as you do it.

Mr Christian considers for a moment and then begins to tuck the sheet around the body. This fat man is getting angry, and that would be bad. Anyhow, the truck is a good idea. Fast hot-wire; a quarter against the ignition poles. A quick drive to the river, a few old parts from the subbasement tied tightly around the sheeted corpse with good rope. The magneto he has left outside in the hallway. That should do. Who watches bread trucks? Nobody. What will Christopher have to do with it? Nothing.

Down the numberless stairs and out. The girl is stiff and Mr Christian cannot decide if this is good or bad. A department-store mannequin? Who is prurient enough to cover one with a sheet? One question could put Mr Christian out of business altogether. But he is not much concerned. It will not happen that way. Not here. Not now. Not drastic enough. The State of Louisiana would house and feed and clothe him for the re-mainder of his natural life. Or give him a ride on the lightning if they were of a mind to charge him not only with transporta-tion of meat, but with the criminal conversion of that meat from its previous condition. He lowers his burden and lets it stand, more or less, on its own feet.

At which point Mr Christian finds himself in the narrow dirty foyer only a step from the street. It is twilight now, and the sky, having passed from yellow to violet to the most deli-cate of grays, is beginning to go dark blue. Only an occasional workman with an hour of overtime behind him passes on his way home. Aacross the street, an elderly blind couple walk arm in arm as if the sidewalk were cobbled with eggs. They hold a small feist on a leash. Mr Christian squints at them and sees the feist run into a light pole. It is blind too. Mr Christian shifts his burden and laughs a little louder than he intends. Or per-haps the foyer, the stairwell, and the long corridor running to the rear of the building where there is a small and untended courtyard with one desiccated mimosa tree and the twisted stalks of dead spring flowers act as some kind of spooky echo chamber.

Even as Mr Christian hoists his burden and pushes against the door, someone blunders against it from the other side. There is the briefest of duels, before Mr Christian stops pushing and prepares to floor the incoming traffic with his ungainly parcel. Let them figure it out. Tough, Dr. Aorta: patron saint found and lost in an hour. The human condition is an outrage.

—Say, Christopher says. —What're you doing wandering around with a dummy under a sheet?

—Ah yeah, Mr Christian laughs, as if a dose of broken glass were going down or rising in his throat. —Sure. I got a gal . . .

—Who drinks whisky and gin, Christopher laughs. Not much more brightly than Mr Christian. —I got one living in a house by the side of the road. Being friendly with men.

—Who wants a dress.

—Makes her own?

—Oh yeah. Uh . . . , Mr Christian mumbles, feeling his bundle up and down. Pretty stiff. Not stiff enough if Christopher decides to give her a feel. He looks a little drunk.

—Uh, you reckon we could use the truck? She don't live far.

Christopher sits down on the bottom step, his head hanging between his knees. —Why don't you take that thing to the city dump . . . ?

—Lord, Mr Christian coughs, thinking that surely he is surrounded by agents of that Sacred Sonofabitch. They see all, know all. Reckon do they tell all?

—Naw, I guess maybe the river . . .

—. . . and buy that girl a dress?

—Money, Mr Christian chokes with partial relief, trying to cover or overrun that last word. —I ain't got . . .

Christopher fumbles in his pocket. —I'd give you half my cloak, but . . . I've got ten dollars. You reckon you could buy a dress . . . ?

—Why don't you just lemme drive this thing over to her? Cheaper. Anyhow, that girl loves to work. You never saw a girl loves to work like her. Sew, cook, stoke coal . . .

Mr Christian, already twelve hours past post time, is a sham-

bles. If this thing isn't resolved soon, he is going to be confess-
ing war crimes and treasonous deals to Christopher, to hell
with the seal of confession. Enough is enough. Wow.

Christopher lumbers to his feet. It is dark outside now, and
there is no one in sight except one old Italian wearing a beanie
or whatever they call those flat round hats, going past with an
empty vegetable cart. —It's a good day, anyhow, Mr Christian
incredulously hears him mutter.

Aboard the truck, Christopher drives adequately, if not
well. He is rocky and sad. Only some spirit of kin with Mr
Christian keeps him functioning. His hands grip the wide wheel
automatically, and the necessaries of handling the truck take
care of themselves. They had better. Because, nine or ten—
more like fifteen ales—away, he is thinking of things past. Of
Mary Ann, only hours past, who cannot love him; of his mother,
who might love him as he loves her. And of pseudoloves, quasi-
loves and semiloves. He remembers breakfast on the screened
back porch years, eons ago. It is bright summer, very early. His
mother is still abed, but his father sits across from him, having
prepared orange juice and cereal for himself. There is nothing
for Christopher. It is a morning larger, more portentous than
bright sun, early bees and a few hummingbirds among the
flowers might indicate. Christopher's legs swing free an inch
above the floor, and he is entranced with the deep green shadows under some oaks at the rear of the yard. He is gingerly
picking his nose, and wanting orange juice terribly.

—*Introibo ad altare Dei,* his father says.

—*Ad Deum qui latificate, juventutam meum,* Christopher
answers mechanically.

—This is an important day, his father tells him. Christopher
tries to ignore the puffed flesh around his father's eyes, those
soft repulsive hands with fingers the color and shape of grubworms you turn up in garden soil. He does not love his father.
He wonders if grubworms love their fathers.

—. . . entering God's service, his father is saying, as if it
were a recruiting pitch. —Do you know that this is a blessing?
I wish I could go this morning. But they won't let grown people
serve Mass.

—Why? Christopher asks as he assumes he is expected to do.

—Because God wants only the young, the pure of heart.

Christopher rolls his snot into a ball and flicks it away. An instant later, he hears a tiny ping as it hits the screen somewhere.

—How come the priest is old?

—Priests are different. Inside, they are still young. They stay childlike always.

—Ummm.

Christopher brakes for a light and discovers himself wishing for orange juice. He wonders if perhaps his father had not loved him after all. I confess to Almighty God, to Blessed Mary ever virgin. . . . Children are not simple, Christopher recalls. Only adults are. Too simple sometimes to tell what they feel. Grubworm fingers and pasty unlovely faces and the burden of a wife poorly served and a God beyond serving can choke a heart. Christopher feels something old and round as a Spanish olive rise in his throat. The ale, probably.

—Which way do we go? he asks Mr Christian.

—Ummm, maybe down by the river. Go on down Decatur. I'll show you.

Christopher watches telephone poles pass. Each one brings to mind the cross of Lorraine. For He so loved the world. . . . It is the ale and the multiple cracked emotions of hours—or years—past. He feels the bite of nails in his hands, and the choked unutterable need to petition or thank. Something. Somewhere. But there is only the dreary line of storefronts and warehouses on either side of the narrow street, and feeble lights above that are not stars. And Mr Christian, who drums quiet intricate patterns on his knee, his face impassive, his eyes closed against their motion and the world through which they move.

—She likes to make things, Christopher muses aloud.

—Oh yeah, Mr Christian hums. —She. Do. They. All. Do. They make: we break. And that's how the world goes round. Any questions?

—Here's the river. Peters Street. Which way?

—Oh yeah, Mr Christian sings low. —This is fine. This is okay. That will be just fine. Just a walk and a stalk. Can't go wrong.

—I'll take you there.

—Naw, Mr Christian insists gently. —I can walk it. I want
to sneak up and surprise her. You know how a girl likes surprises.

Christopher shrugs and pulls over. They open the rear of the
truck and Mr Christian quickly shoulders his burden. As he
begins to walk, he stumbles, falling to one knee. Christopher
helps him up, noticing that the sheet has begun to unwind,
so that one pale freckled plaster hand shows.

—It's not a dressmaker's dummy, Christopher says irritably,
the ale pinching him suddenly.

—Naw, well . . . Mr Christian is wondering if he should
drop the meat and strangle Christopher. It would be easy. But
no. Return evil for good. And kill a child looking for himself
before the day of revelation. No, that would be bad. It would
please God. God could use it: show the angels that all the suffering heaped on this Christian was more than justified. Not
Almighty bad temper: justice before the fact. Ah Lord, how
careful a man has to be lest he fall into God's hands, into the
way of His plan.

—It's a mannequin, Christopher observes shrewdly. —Anybody can see it's a mannequin.

—Yeah, Mr Christian says quickly, without the vaguest
notion of what Christopher is saying. —Sho. It's a mannykin.
You got me there. That's what she asked for. My gal says, man,
go find me a mannykin. See? I didn't have no choice.

—You sure you can find the place? Christopher asks.

—Oh yeah; you go on along. I'll see you tomorrow, Mr
Christian almost whispers, the burden heavy beyond words.

Christopher lets out his clutch, waves and begins to pull
away, still looking backward as Mr Christian vanishes into the
gloom toward the river. He is almost back to the garage before
he begins to wonder why anyone would put freckles on the arm
of a mannequin.

ᴥᶳ ᶳᴥ

Benny is on top of the world. He has, spread before him, half
a dozen books on the Inquisition, from Lea's history to *The Pit
and the Pendulum*. It is an embarrassment of riches. A man

could make movies forever with this stuff, each one a master-piece of depravity, and never get through the first twenty years of it. There are orgiastic heretics, witches, masochistic rites, incredibly brutal repressions, counterattacks by heresiarchs butchering inquisitors, torturing the faithful. It is as if God had driven the whole world mad, and exacted half its blood to make it sane again; as if old Moloch had stormed heaven on the sly, bound Yahweh hand and foot, jammed a galaxy between His jaws as a gag, and then began issuing fiat in His name.

More to the point, the reading has almost erased a lingering dark place in Benny's psyche. He had wondered long, below the threshold of wondering, if indeed God is not. Not a doleful concern; one that hardly ever floundered to the surface except in moments of great stress or peculiar happenings like the death of his brother, those nights beside his limbless grandfather, who laughed at some private joke which seemed cosmic at least: as if the old madman could see down (or up or to the side) to the place where his torturers had begun—barely begun—their bleak and ghastly terms of retribution at the hands of the Elohim, the relentless ghosts of Israel and Judah.

But now he sips scotch and considers his girls. Thinks of the Mississippi yap he has hired and of the possibilities open before him. The way he feels just now, he would use the Ark of the Covenant for a shoeshine box, and a ciborium to hold the polish. It may well be that there was a God once. But He was probably caught and roasted in a Spanish or French auto-da-fé, or else the Protestants finished Him off in Germany or England. The goyim are blood-mad. This is why you can't sell decent shows any more—the old movies, plain old sweets-of-sin shows full of naked men and women doing what they normally do. Even garden-variety degeneracy hardly gets off the ground. You got to go the distance.

Benny has been pricing leather garments for his girl-inquisitors. Nuns in leather clothes. With whips and knives and broken bottles. Someone has told him leather goods are dirt cheap in Munich now, but even Benny finds that a little too strong. How would you know what kind of hides they were? But then, he thinks, maybe that's an angle: the girls whirling around Billy Bob Stoker's naked straining body, whips and chains and stuff, perfectly planned by some choreographer. And each girl only partially covered by fragments of human skin. Because . . . Boundoch leafs through one of the books: yes, here. Mani. The goyim did it to Mani. Founder of some kind of dualism. Lived third century. Crucified, skin stuffed with straw and hung above gate of Susa. Nice crowd. Cute religion.

The scenario is coming along nicely: Stoker is a friar who falls in love with Mary Ann, the nun. They make it, are caught *flagrante delicto*. To the rack, scourge, fire, noose—all manner of suffering. But in the end, they are put in room slowly filled with water and screw with love till drowned. This is, well handled, enough to make an archbishop choke, a cantor cry. It will be called, he has it now,

The Question

Manifold implications. Will you? Will they? Did you all? Is there? And Jesus turns not a hand or a wing to help. Ghostly agonies. Only sex, only love (which is to say again, sex) has any meaning. Jesus is a fraud. Venus is the end. A strong show. The blue (and all other colors) movie that dares put *The Question:*

Is God Dead?

And answers it.

Benny sits in his patterned silk robe thinking. It is good. Let there be lights. Camera. Action.

And meanwhile one of the girls, he decides, downing his scotch and pressing a button on a table beside the bed. On which there is a short quirt, some oxblood shoe polish, and a few ocean-smooth pebbles of a certain size.

Chapter Six

It is almost eight o'clock, and yet Mary Ann lies abed. Billy Bob is downstairs sullenly trying on a brown friar's robe. The room is dark and Mary Ann stares at the water-stained ceiling. The walls are newly painted, the furniture tasteful antique. But Benny saved a dollar or two by letting the ceilings go. As a result, the wide brown whorls look like portions of God's thumbprint. The idea does nothing for Mary Ann, who is sick unto death.

She cannot understand it. No drinking, plenty of good food and exercise over and above her bouts with Billy Bob. Clean living. And still she feels as if she had swallowed a cage of unnaturally active rats. She is reverting to childhood when, racked with dysentery or one of the other disorders common to sharecroppers' (or crop dusters') children, she would freeze, moving neither toe nor finger nor eyelid, breathing in long slow sustained inhalations, hoping the sickness would pass. She hates to vomit. She knows people who do not mind it. Once there had been a spic in San Antone who ate and drank like a hog, who would then go out back and tickle his throat, and come in, legs shaking, wet-eyed, but ready for action. Spics are a different breed of pup. The mere thought of throwing up makes her sick. And, already too sick to believe, she is trying hard to think of nice things until the seizure passes. But what is nice? Billy Bob is all right. The little kike downstairs, after that first bad night, has been fair enough. Gee. Christopher. How about Christopher? Nice. But thinly nice. Nice is soft and giving, and

yet strong and able. Umm. Christopher is half of nice. So
something to eat? Ughhh. One more mistake like that, and it's
cookies all over the bed. Maybe a boat ride on Pontchartrain?
With waves, and the boat lurching? Arghhh. No means of movement is nice just now. All spatial displacement is too much.
Temporal: try to remember. And there before her, with full
color and well-recollected sounds, is her father's body, lying
easy in the thick grass, his eyes cool and quizzical, fixed on passing tufted clouds as if a packet of Answers were about to fall
from one. And a thin shimmering thread of blood running
down his jaw and into the parched grass.

Mary Ann tries to lean over the bed's edge, but she does not
make it. In the room next door, a phony blonde awakens to
hear a fantastic medley of sounds as if someone were crying his
heart out while being strangled by an amateur.

ᦿ ᦿ

—I'd as soon forget this, Billy Bob is saying to an old drab
who does Boundoch's cooking and cleaning, and who is playing
at seamstress just now. She pulls up his cowl and covers his head
with it.

—Why don't you shut up? she tells him, mouth full of pins.
—You got a job and I got a job. You got to wear this shroud and
I got to make it fit. It ain't no sense givin' me a hard time.

Billy Bob wriggles, fingering a long piece of knotted clothesline wrapped around his waist. —Jesus, this robe is sticky.

The drab grins. —Offer it up.

—Huh?

—Tell God you're sendin' all them prickles up to Him . . .

—Wish to hell I could.

—. . . in reparation for your sins.

Billy Bob turns toward her. —You reckon that does any
good?

The bawd grins on, studding the hem of the robe more or
less regularly with pins. —Shit, I don't know. Who knows anything about God?

—I got a friend . . .

—You mean that little chickenshit priest on the lam?

Billy Bob frowns. —What do you know about ole Chris?

—I got a friend . . .

—Why he's a . . .

—Runnin' out on Jesus. It ain't no sense in it. Bad enough to leave a woman with kids. You better know his ass is gonna . . . burn.

—Ouch, Billy Bob roars as a pin goes beyond the fringe. —You really believe in hell-fire?

The woman lifts her eyes to his. With a shock, Billy Bob realizes that she is human, a person. Her face a pale raisin against the wine drapes of the parlor, seems for a moment that of someone aware that she swims in banalities toward some mystery. —If I didn't, you reckon I'd still be around?

—Huh?

—I'da slit my throat the first time I offered it to a man for free and he laughed and pushed my face in.

Billy Bob fingers his robe. —So you found Jesus.

—Found me. Layin' over to Pirates Alley. Some feller had hit me over the head and stole my purse.

The old woman pauses, staring out into the rich morning light, watching as the sun inches along a table, burnishing bookends, turning dingy doilies the color of champagne. —Used to be I worried about my ass. Then I had bad dreams of runnin' into one of them fellers who likes to take you down and cut yer throat. Now I worry about my money.

She helps Billy Bob squirm out of the robe, watches without emotion as he fumbles into his trousers. —So I came to that night and my purse was gone. I didn't have a cent. Not even a room. Last place I worked laid me off. If you can't give it away, you sure as hell can't sell it.

—When did you come across Jesus?

—That night. That self-same night. When they took and laid me out and went off with my purse. I come around and saw how it was, and I said, I been walkin' the off side, Jesus, but I mean to do right if you'll help me. So I started walkin' and went inside the cathedral there next to the alley. It's Catholic, but it's all right.

—I guess.

—It's all right, the beldam says, pushing a gout of colorless hair out of tired eyes planted among elephantine wrinkles. —I went in and kind of spread out in one of them pews up to the front. I got to watchin' that little red light and prayin' and puttin' aside past sins. And I looked down in my shame. And there was my purse.

—Empty, Billy Bob says with the certainty of long experience.

—Sure, the old woman agrees. —Empty. Except for a C-note tucked down in the lining. They got maybe four, five dollars. Jesus saves.

—You owe Christ a bundle, Billy Bob says, pushing his shirt down past a tight belt. —It is no secret.

—An' I been payin' him back with love.

Billy Bob grins despite himself, staring down at the old bag of rags and righteousness. —At five dollars a trick, huh?

She rises, quickly angry, all her person drawn back. —You, she says brittlely, —are a fuckin' heathen.

—Naw, I'm a monk.

—You gonna pay, she warns with a long red finger.

—Naw, gettin' paid.

—Comes a settlin' time. I'll see you in hell with this damn slanderous garment all afire and glued to your ass. The Lord won't suffer no goats in . . .

Billy aims a casual kick at her head, but she scuttles, hands and knees, into the kitchen, leaving an imprecation hanging like a crooked cross in the sunlight beside him.

⋅§ §⋅

Benny has his equipment and most of his cast. His nerves are tight as a bird dog's the night before season opens. *The Question* plagues him now. Does he dare use outside locations? He would like one love scene on the Pontchartrain beach; Billy Bob and Mary Ann walking in habit, spotting one another; recognition, slowly begin stripping off robes so they meet buck-naked and fall together in instant ecstasy. Water flows around them, waves beat one upon another up the virginal sand. Gulls

wheel overhead, crazy, diving, turning, wings a symphonic ac-
companiment to the divine madness below.

But he still needs people. Genius will not people a stage. He
has flop-house friars and gay torturers, the ladies of his own
nunnery, but he wants class. Class shows. You can tell class a
mile away. He wants a mother superior for Mary Ann's convent; a venal but smooth priest for Billy Bob's abbey. And an
Inquisitor. Somebody to ask the question. This is going to cost
money. But you got to spend it to make it. He finishes a ham
sandwich, blinks at his hurrying watch, and is on the run again.
There is talent in the streets. You have to seek it in the high-
ways and byways. Find it where it is.

&> &>

Mr Christian's eyes are closed. He is riding high. The work
is easy. Transmissions heal themselves under his hand. He
touches an axle, and it is whole. At his feet are covies of spark
plugs, renewed; a horn which was mute, and now can sound
again. Mr Christian prances and weaves, boxing with one of
the overhanging lights, sending mad phantom shadows scuttling for filthy cobwebbed corners. He hears everything: Traffic
above. Squeaking of ancient stairs where ghosts clamber up and
down. Metal falling against metal as he brushes against a shelf.
A June bug struggling against odds in the wash of the grease
pit. He can smell old oil and new tools. From somewhere the
piquant reek of carbon tet mixes with a synthetic paint thinner. Over all the sweet fetid overpowering stench of baking
bread: like burned flesh a day or so later. Foul and funny Mr
Christian feels. His supply is assured. All things are made new,
and he is equal to all things. Now he is armed again. The whole
armor. Plans can be made without desperation. Money can be
gotten. The Supernal Shit had better tremble: Christian Blackman has found benison. The Black Knight is clanking in his
chapel. There will be a crusade, and at its end, a blissful piss
in the grail. Wow.

But at his back, his superhearing picks up a sound on the
stairs. Not the constant subaural mutter of wood growing old,
beginning or continuing to give way. No: the higher shriek of

stairs burdened with more than time and their own weight. His supersmelling detects, past grease and fractions of gasoline, turpentine and kerosene, the scent of a known creature. His lightning mind flicks through the thumb-stained cards of memory. Not a white man. That kid again? Aorta's dark messenger? Some other nigger. Hmmm. Oh no, not him. What would he? Mr Christian Blackman's supermind reflects in less time than it takes a bullet to cleave a false heart. What? How? Yes. *Habeas corpus:* he has the.

The Negro is small with a jolly head of grizzled wool, broken gray. His face is unmarked, sweet and virtuous: eyes wide and full of unspent glee, cheeks smooth and hairless, mouth full and creased at the corners from much smiling. He knows the ways of men and is not shaken by them. His name is Marshall Fields. He is a ghoul.

Mr Christian sits down on his burlap-covered orange crate. The kingdom is dark of an instant. The armor fades and cracks. He can barely see his visitor's face. The words are blurred. Oh gracious Lord, he needs another fix.

—I've seen 'em dumb and I've seen 'em wise, Marshall Fields says. —I've seen 'em young and I've seen 'em old. I've seen 'em ever which way you *could* see 'em. But you in a class by yo'self, Blackman. It ain't nobody like you.

—Sho.

—Naw, I mean it, Marshall Fields says scornfully. —You know what I got in my cart upstairs?

—Yeah.

—Right. You know where I got it?

—Naw.

—On the river. I got it off a feller lives alone in a shack. He reckoned on keepin' it till it wasn't no more use, and then tossin' it back in. But I got it off him. On account I reckoned you wouldn't want it lyin' around.

Aw God, Mr Christian moans.

—Wif a Staff-o-Life truck inventory slip stuffed right in the mattress cover it come out of. Boy, I seen 'em smart and I seen 'em stupid. How come you tryin' to do work you don't know nothin' about? You ever see me with a wrench in my hands?

—Naw, Mr Christian sobs. —I never did. What you reckon to do with it?

Marshall Fields takes out a long crooked stogie, turns it over lovingly between his fingers, lights up with a kitchen match drawn across his pants, and draws on it with deep pleasure. He squats across from Mr Christian and turns his head slowly. —'Fraid it's gonna cost you. Things is tight. I gets stopped every now and then. They could be up there right now goin' through my cart.

Ughhh, Mr Christian strangles.

—How much did that Yankee give you to get rid of what you didn't get rid of?

—He ain't a Yankee. He's a Arabian or somethin'.

—How much?

—He give me a regular job. I gets a dose a day. However much I need. And a little money.

Marshall Fields makes a cathedral with his hands, fingers raised into arches for a roof, thumbs wiggling easily. —I reckon it'll cost you the dough. And the dose.

—Lissen.

—Naw. I seen 'em cute and I seen 'em nasty, but I never seen one didn't have to pay for bein' stupid. I got to do what you set up to do. I got to put it somewhere, don't I? Don't I?

—Yeah.

—I got to do the whole business. From here on, it belongs to me. If it goes wrong, they gone be lookin' for me if they look for anybody.

—Yeah.

—All right. You just gimme what you got as you get it.

—I can't get by without . . .

—I'm gonna take care of you. Every couple days you gonna get what you need. Just not a hog's ration. You gonna have to scrape by on short stock till you find a smart piece of business to make up for messin' up.

—Yeah.

Mr Christian slumps staring at the filthy floor. The shadows press in. He wonders if he could take the top off Marshall Fields' head with a tire tool.

—Forget it, Marshall Fields tells him softly, blowing a long wave of blue smoke toward him. —Even if I was dumb enough to let you, you'd have two of what you couldn't handle when you only had one.

Mr Christian glances up to see Marshall Fields scratching his dark belly between two shirt buttons. Tucked into his trouserband is an ancient Smith & Wesson .44. It looks plenty used. —Yeah, Mr Christian chokes.

—I don't wish you no harm. I got myself to see to. I don't want no trouble. I got into this to do you a Christian charity. You want to keep your profit and just let me dump what I got in the alley here? Or take it back over on Royal where you got it?

Aw, naw, Mr Christian squeals. —Naw, we got to handle it right.

—*We* got to do nothin'. I wouldn't let you walk five feet with me. This whole thing is a caution. I want you to stay on your own side of the street. Peddle if you want. Hustle, that's all right. If you want, you kin go to killin' for a price. But don't go playin' undertaker. You hear me?

—Yeah.

•§ §•

Mary Ann is sicker than ever. She is walking down Canal Street now, and her stomach has settled. But what she knows keeps small chills running up and down her back as if a fever were just beginning to break. She did not believe the first doctor, and so paid good money to a better one out on Jeff Davis Parkway. Another examination, another rabbit. Same answer. Now she is thinking of Atlanta. Or Chicago. Somewhere a long way off, away from this miserable town. She thought first of Carthage, but you can't go home again. Especially when you don't know where home is. Her last letter to Gene Autry had come back: *Addressee unknown—no forwarding address,* or something. She imagines the trailer hooked to an anonymous car, grumbling through the night toward that unknown address. With her mother, head lolling as the road turns, Gene squatted expressionless, eyes fixed on the darkness outside the small grimy rear window. Under the big bed, her father's tool-kit full of aircraft wrenches, and a filthy rabbit's foot on a key-chain. On one plywood wall near the door, a hand-written schedule of jobs for the summer of 1943. Mary Ann feels as if she were crying, but her face does not change; there are no tears, and she knows why.

✥ ✥

Christopher is sitting in the alley out behind Staff-o-Life. On a sagging orange crate covered with croker sacking. He is study-ing his hands, traces of grime under his fingernails; the dark beginning of heavy calluses at the base of each finger, on the heels of his hands. He is thinking of nothing. He is too ex-hausted for lucidity. Certain images drip through his mind like curdled molasses, but he assents to none of them; neither ac-cepts nor rejects them. He feels like the father of murdered children at a police line-up. What is to gain by identification, by classifying, by denominating? It is the bones and meat of the world that killed my baby. His hands, stained long ago with chrism, flex and tighten, and the sun, creeping down moldy brick, touches his bowed head. He is something like sleeping now, while visions of olive trees dance downward from amongst angular rocks toward a long sandy shore. The stutter of trucks passing in the street becomes distant thunder; laughter of shop girls out on Decatur is the skirl of birds. His head hangs. He travels without pleasure. He has not shaved today and the collar of his Staff-o-Life shirt is crusty with dirt and sweat. There is a feverish seedy look about him. He sleeps without ease, dreaming of empty places silent and shadowless.

Mr Christian Blackman hates to rouse him for he looks so peaceful there. But there is no choice. Things are coming un-glued; the world's cancer has metastasized. Dr. Aorta wishes to see Christopher. He knows about their trip in the bread truck. He has almost smiled. He has handed an unwilling Mr Christian two bags and ordered the bad priest brought before him. What can you do? Between Dr. Aorta, Marshall Fields, the bulls and an empty stable there is scarcely room to breathe, much less treasure friendship.

Now Mr Christian stands contemplating Christopher, his own ruined hands folded before him. Nothing looks so innocent, so helpless as a sleeping white man. Hard to imagine they are deadly, that there is a thing in all of them which can be turned on. But not off. It must have to do with consciousness, with waking. Asleep they look like children. Awake, they are mostly insane. This one sleeping like a dirty worn-out kid doubts the existence of God. What can you do with a man who doubts old Dirty Daddy?

Mr Christian shakes Christopher's shoulder gently. —Lissen, he says, —wake up. You got to go somewhere. The man wants to see you. Come on. You got to go. Lissen, wake up.

⋅§ §⋅

He has seen them easy, and he has seen them hard, but Marshall Fields has never failed to plant a stiff. He knows a dozen places within a mile of any given street corner in downtown New Orleans where you can make a safe deposit. There are huge trash containers, incinerators, old sheds not opened since the last war, whichever one that was. There is the river, but it is not a trusty accomplice. Nothing keeps a corpse down. The dead seem harder to suppress than the living. You can frighten a man into a cellar for twenty years, but his body will roll up into sight a day or so after you have weighted it with chains. In wine-dark moments, Marshall Fields has wondered if, down below the river's oily surface, a corpse leans and twists, bloated fingers fumbling with the chains or rope holding it in loveless embrace to auto springs, old anvils, batteries or discarded bathroom fixtures. Even in hallucination, it is an awful spectacle, and mornings following such visions, Marshall Fields has considered giving over his calling. It is a corrosive way of making a dollar—worse than straightforward assassination. Despite his expressionless face, every new commission puts a ball in the pit of his stomach, a steel ball large enough to use on an iron billiard table with a copper cue. He has certain enemies in the Quarter, several police officers who would give their retirement pay to lay at least one carcass to his account, not to mention the reception of stolen goods, trafficking in narcotics and so on. No man, especially a black one, is beyond fear. Not really. A man may pride himself on being so far out that not even a .38 Special slug can call him back. But this is mere fustian and vainglory. Every man plays the game, and no matter how hard or careless or nearly catatonic he may seem, there is within him that tiny room, some niche or crevasse where a child shivers and shrieks, fearing that last confrontation from which nothing human escapes forever.

But such moments are rare. The distinction between lubberly amateurs and hard-eyed professionals begins with a capacity to suppress abstract, overly metaphysical thought—what The Writer has called horseshit.

We are now passing the Court of Four Brothers. Marshall Fields grins to a Negro standing out front in something like a uniform. The Negro raises his eyebrows and shakes his head. In nine years, four night deposits have been made in the courtyard, amidst vines and flowers and trees. The diners, squatting around their gingham-covered tables, strewn with cameras and postcards and outsize purses and mammy-dolls, are always amazed at the luxuriant growth around them. Amazement is the child of ignorance. There is an explanation for every phenomenon, but some are best foregone.

Marshall Fields pushes his outsized cart onward. There is a place on Ursulines Street, an enormous courtyard. Two deposits. None since 1940. An old woman owns the building. She pays Marshall Fields a small amount to cart away trash every day, rather than wait for the casual coming of the city collector. Marshall Fields thus has a key to the courtyard. It should be possible to rest his stiff in the garage where a 1924 LaSalle has been parked without being moved since the husband used it to asphyxiate himself during the last week in October of 1929. Something troublesome had come down by tickertape from New York.

Under the car, the sheeted object is almost invisible. Tonight Marshall Fields can dig a nice hole under the smaller mimosa. Interesting scientific fact. There are three mimosas in the courtyard. Two are tall and in the spring covered with blossoms, later heavy with fuzz and pods. One, planted at the same time, is smaller, less flourishing. It stands almost in the middle of the courtyard. Marshall Fields studies it. He has wanted to do something about that tree for a long time.

ᵃᵇ ᵇᵃ

Christopher is standing before Dr. Aorta's door. He is also licking his lips, flencing his hands like a distracted Uriah Heep. Not from anything so simple or straightforward as fear. Christopher is past fear of what can be done to the body. Or thinks he is. It has been too long since he gave the body that kind of solicitude. For years he has feared other things: arrows that fly at midday; business that stalks in darkness. He remembers how, as a novice, he had one day realized that he was becoming a glutton. He had moved out of himself, as St. Ignatius instructs us, and looked back to see himself construing Greek mindlessly, and considering tea: the possibility of hot buttered scones, or biscuits bought fresh from the baker in Eastbourne. Tarts, full of Belgian strawberries, possibly. So many things to delight the eyes. Then close the eyes. Let each crumb and morsel rest on the tongue before chewing it slowly, swallowing. And even when the belly is full, there is at least room for more warm tea to sluice down the scones or biscuits or tarts. And later, dinner: roast beef and marrows and Yorkshire, with bitter, and more tea.

Until, looking backward from out there, Christopher saw, dully puzzling over Greek constructions, a beast with a thousand mouths and a belly the size of hell's forecourt. He put away Koiné and found the *Spiritual Exercises. While eating, reflecting on the life of some saint or other pious contemplation, or some spiritual business he has to do, that having his attention fixed on such matter, he will take less sensible pleasure in his bodily food.* After a week or two, he had contained the beast, cut its intake as well as its filthy pleasure. More subtle a beast, more difficult to handle than the serpent between his thighs. No cold beer bottle chills the gut's scratchings, or the brain's connivance. Till he found another passage in Loyola: *Chastise the flesh; that is to say, cause it sensible pain by means of haircloth, or cords or chains of iron upon the body, by scourging or wounding oneself, or by other kinds of austerities. What seems to be most suitable and safe in the matter of penance is that the pain should be felt by the flesh and not penetrate to the bones, so that it may give pain, and not cause infirmity. For this purpose, it seems better to scourge oneself with small cords* . . . Until at last, one winter morning, he had been discovered by the prefect of novices kneeling in the snow before a frost-covered statue of the Sacred Heart, a small cord in his hand, naked but for a pair of trousers, back covered with freezing blood, ribs showing for lack of food, in pain to the bone, dissolved in tears before the effigy of Him Who Suffered.

Now he is at the outpost of some awful new perdition. He trembles with a fear older, possibly, than the sun which burns outside, transforming the hallway into a dark oven.

He knocks one time, and hears a voice within, distant and blurred. As he opens the door, he finds total darkness. Nothing can be seen. He hears low breathing, something like a sigh. At the left side of the room, long windows open onto a balcony above the street. Christopher gasps as he realizes that the outline of the windows, the shape of the room, so far as he can see it, is identical to his own, one floor lower.

—Ah, someone says. —The priest. You have my message.

—Mr Christian told me you wanted to see me.

—The Negro. Yes. He told you. Come up by the window here. I like the dark. You cannot see over there.

—People say it's cooler in the dark, Christopher says, aware of his inanity.

Now he can see Dr. Aorta's dark motionless shape. Dr. Aorta is naked except for a pair of shorts. His feet are in a washtub, and he lifts handfuls of crushed ice at intervals, passing the chips over his pallid skin. —You think of cool and dark much, eh, priest?

—Priest? I don't know . . .

—Never mind, priest. You can pretend to the grocery clerks and the people in the streets.

—I don't know . . . , Christopher begins again, his voice tiny and uncertain. —In this heat, everybody thinks . . .

—Stop it, Dr. Aorta cuts him off with bored finality. —Look down into the street.

Down at the corner of St. Peter Street, opposite Lou Webb's stand, Mrs. Mailer is trying to sell gardenias and tiny turtles emblazoned with various legends on their shells: SEE N. O. —PARIS IN USA, or NEW ORLEANS—LAND OF DREEMS. A small gray-polled Negro is pushing an outsized cart past the corner. Looking up, he sees the blur of Christopher's face, raises a forefinger and thumb joined and grins like a mad conspirator. Mrs. Mailer sells a turtle to a young man with a reddish crewcut, dark glasses and a Hawaiian shirt. He puts it in his shirt pocket and slouches away, a spotted Catahoula hound padding behind him.

—The woman knows, Dr. Aorta says. —Everyone knows. The Negro knows. You think you have hidden something. Not so. You have nothing hidden.

—Know, Christopher squeaks. —What do you know? You say . . .

—Nothing, Dr. Aorta smiles in shadow. —I say nothing. But even in the darkness it shows. Like a scar or a bad smell.

—What?

—The mark on your soul, Dr. Aorta shoots back with quiet glee, his massive edgeless bulk lurching back and forth, both hands dragging up shards of ice, laving his white flesh with it. —Ineradicable mark. Priestly character. To carry into hell with you. No knife, no fire. No surgeon skilled enough to take it away. It festers and rots for all eternity. Blessing to a servant faithful; utter horror to a Judas-priest. O God of Israel, you will suffer.

Inside the room it is more than hot. It is as if the sun's awful effluvium has managed to obtain material entity; now it flows around Christopher's legs, washes up his calves to engulf his thighs. His feet itch and sting. There are a hundred spectral gnats feeding on his back, beneath his arms. Something fetid reaches his nostrils. His fear has faded, has begun to curdle into a strange and heady despair.

—Ah, Dr. Aorta continues, —the church is lucky. It profits by your betrayal. There is no use in you. When you were ordained, the ninety-eight wounds of the Savior began to bleed again. The bishop should have been eliminated.

Christopher considers, for the space of a second, leaping for Dr. Aorta's throat. It seems in that instant that a red corona is pulsing and throbbing around the doctor's shadowy bulk. Christopher knows suddenly and profoundly what it means to lust for blood, to wish another not simply dead or even annihilated, but in a condition of permanent and excruciating agony. He would like to get his thumbs into those depthless eyes; he would like to ram a dull and rusty knife into the soft belly, and twist it slowly, feeling flesh and organs and viscera giving way, the rush of warm blood over his hands.

But Dr. Aorta's voice begins again. —Why do you stiffen? What does it matter to you? You are only a Jesus-shouter gone wrong. Is it not so?

—You know about me, Christopher almost shouts. —But I know you. I can tell. You're . . .

—A displaced person, Aorta finishes for him. —A man without a home. A victim of the war. Do you attack a man for that?

—You were one of them. It's all over you. I can smell the death on you.

—Your imagination is overexcited. Do you have hallucinations, visions of doing awful violence? A doctor, a psychiatrist, perhaps. Do you feel God is searching you out, spying on you, waiting the hour of vengeance?

—What you did to the Jews, Christopher croaks, out of breath, emptied of fear and hatred alike.

—Jews? I *am* a Jew, Aorta smiles. —You hate Jews? It is a sign. Irrational.

—No, people around here know, they hear things. They say . . .

—Hear things? Ummm. Like seeing things. Very bad. Are you part of a nest of paranoids?

—The Jews . . .

—Ah, Dr. Aorta yawns. —The Jews. Your concern for the Jews is admirable. A stiff-necked people. Outcasts. The eternal sufferers.

Dr. Aorta sips his beer and sets it aside, licking his lips. Out-

side the heat has begun its daily decline. The sun, falling slowly
like a punctured Zeppelin, begins to illuminate the room.
Christopher sits huddled on the edge of his chair like a rumpled
and soggy bird.

—Did it ever occur to you, Dr. Aorta begins casually, —to
wonder how many of those martyred Jews would have been
manning machine guns or piloting Stukas in the invasion of Po-
land or on the beaches of Normandy if we—they—had chosen
another scapegoat?

Christopher gapes. He stares at Dr. Aorta, feeling suddenly
that the doctor is not a man, only an abstraction as formalistic,
as conventional as Scratch with spearmint tail and twisty horns.
But, of course, the thing about devils is that they tell the truth.
Sometimes. Part of damnation, Christopher thinks with sudden
feverish lucidity: to taste eternal verities, only to have them
slide off the tongue and be lost again. Devils cannot remember.
It is their punishment to remember nothing except what is of
no consequence.

Dr. Aorta is rubbing his head. His hair, of an imprecise and
lambent brown, is quite thin. He has considered having his
head shaved. But it would be too conspicuous. Anyhow, there
is something Benedictine about shaven heads. Or is it the faint
recollection, already fading, of those other shaven scarecrow
heads gaping upward out of eternal darkness, which puts him
off? But those heads, those ragged mummies, stacked like cordwood, are dust, those strident banners folded. *Den Töten zur
Ehre.*

He remembers his trip to the compound and shed noted by
Krankowytz in his last moments. Children in sackcloth. An old
creature of indeterminate sex squatted near a shriveled corpse
of sex no more certain, rending its rags, damp earth running
through its fingers into the ruin of its hair. A long line of prisoners from Eastern Europe standing in cold drizzle outside unpainted barracks. One old man, remains of a rabbi, his skullcap
askew, eyes turned upward unblinking as rain, all heaven could
provide, falls into them. Across the road, a concrete blockhouse
gas chamber and two ovens. The gibbet for public executions
of attempted escapees (seldom used) or particularly noxious

Semite elements. Blood-ditches near a shooting range where SS officers come occasionally to practice marksmanship on moving —or at least animate—targets.

The children like wizened dwarfs, playing with sticks, shaven-headed little men. One old woman, hair falling out, eyes infected, squinted almost shut with iritis. Hands warped like starfish dropped into hydrochloric acid. Mouth lax, tongue timidly exploring lips cracked as old leather. No, Dr. Aorta remembers thinking. Not her. Not the chic plump Jewess who, even in middle age, with hair streaked fashionably, had charmed guests with her warmth, the wonder of her table. As she spoke sardonically of the Catholics, no one had paid attention to the slight arthritic swelling of her hands. Her eyes were not affected by the candlelight of her salon. The woman stood at a section of barbed-wire fence, her twisted hands caught like bird claws between its spikes. She stared out, her eyes stopping on Aorta, moving on and then back again. But they were empty.

—Prisoner's number? Aorta asked a guard, pointing at the woman. The guard approached her, spoke, listened and came back.

—71633, I think, Herr Oberst.

—You think?

—She doesn't talk plainly.

The old woman still stared out, her jaw loose, the toothless cavern of her mouth like a hole descending to that rusting gut from which no Jonah returns. It could not be, Dr. Aorta considered. She had had two gold fillings in front, and a platinum inlay. No, it was all absurd.

—Go on, he said to his driver.

Just then, from beyond the barbed wire, he heard a strange quacking voice, neither male nor female, but like some monstrous and intricate wooden device made to produce an almost human sound. Without emphasis or shading it said: —*Deutschland über alles,* and spoke no more.

&» &»

—The Jews, Christopher is beginning again, as if he is making a confession instead of an accusation.

—What? Dr. Aorta asks, rising from his washtub of ice, waving his arms like giant pinions, stepping into the center of the room, standing posed before Christopher like an obscene outsized mushroom.

—*Jawohl*, he goes on, as if there has been no pause. —The Jews. You would have had another million loyal German soldiers to kill. Which would have turned the tide at Stalingrad, at Normandy. Even at the Belgian breakthrough. All of which, short of victory of the Reich, would have added another hundred thousand American graves to the butcher's bill. Your government—our government—should decorate any surviving Gestapo and *Schutzstaffel* they find. If any indeed survive.

—You survived, Christopher grins hideously, almost drunk on wave after wave of horror. —You came through.

Dr. Aorta pulls on a pair of shapeless pants and a frowsy shirt. He smiles wryly, remembering the camp commandant who had attempted to escape with him. Near the Swiss border, they had been stopped by an SS *Einsatz* company. Those of whatever rank who could produce no orders of transit were summarily executed. Except, of course, doctors. You do not shoot doctors. You must have doctors. He remembered the commandant standing before a bomb-shattered garden wall trembling and sweating in the April chill like a boy caught in his first attempt to creep through a girl's window. But this was more serious. He seemed suddenly very small in his colonel's uniform. His dry lips moved compulsively, imprecisely, as he tried to explain his defection, to apologize for the lapse, saying in a voice which broke frequently into falsetto that he would not do it again, that it was wrong and he was sorry.

—*Ja*, the SS captain had said, glancing at his Walther pistol to make sure there was a round in the chamber.

The commandant fumbled a rosary borrowed from one of the young soldiers who formed the firing squad. The commandant, it appeared, was crying. Doubtless, Dr. Aorta thought, he is considering the sorrowful mysteries.

Even as the commandant went on speaking in a monotonous earnest voice, promising to do better next time, so that it was difficult to tell whether he was addressing himself to the SS captain or the Christ whose sacramental he pawed desperately, the short concentrated bursts of machine-pistol fire cut him down like straw. He fell, eyes still wide, lips still moving like the cartilaginous mouth of a fish swallowing, desperate for oxygen. The SS captain asked Dr. Aorta for a light, drew deeply on his half-cigarette, and strode over to the commandant. He studied the body for a moment, smoke leaking in a twisted unhurried skein from his relaxed lips. Then he fired one shot into the commandant's forehead. The body bounced and lay still as dung on a stable floor. A few hours before, that bullet-riddled carrion, its skull burst, its fingers twisted in a blood-soaked rosary, had been an ageless tyrant luxuriating in his power. Now he is garbage, Dr. Aorta thought. *Den Lebenden eine Mahnung.*

—My rosary is fucked, the young soldier groaned, his machine pistol probing the commandant's sodden wreckage. —What's it good for now?

—The same thing as before, the SS captain said, flipping his cigarette butt toward a staggered line of freshly chipped circles in the garden wall.

The SS captain had put Dr. Aorta in the back of an armored car. There were, altogether, only ten or twelve soldiers. Their uniforms were fresh, their boots only a little scuffed and muddy.

—We guarded an airbase, the captain told him. —Der Führer likes to keep elite troops at the airbases. He does not trust Göering. What if the Luftwaffe should mutiny?

—What is left of the Luftwaffe to mutiny? Dr. Aorta asked him as they drove deeper into Bavaria toward what had once been the Austrian border. The captain laughed, smoke pulsing through his open red lips. He was a fresh green-eyed young man who looked like an athlete. Absolutely nonreflective. A system of responses. Dr. Aorta made a mental note not to offend him.

—You're right, of course. But our colonel had no intention of pointing out the obvious. The last officer to complain that he was not being utilized ended up in Yugoslavia. We heard they had crucified him—I mean the guerrillas—on a boxcar. Nothing else. Just nailed him to a boxcar. It was an ammunition train, and the Ami Air Force was coming in.

—So finally they decided we were of no use at the airbase. Now we patrol the roads. Looking for deserters.

—I am not a deserter.

—No, of course not. You're a medical officer. Very good.

They smoked, and Dr. Aorta had almost finished his foul-tasting Belga when he heard a rattle of small arms.

—What the hell, the captain yelled, moving up into the open turret and looking around. —My God, Amis. What the hell are they . . .

The armored car pulled into a farmyard and the captain began firing his machine gun. Empty cartridges spilled down on Dr. Aorta. The Americans had been moving along the northern Swiss frontier. They were looking for a rumored last bastion of the German forces, called the National Redoubt. It did not exist, but while the Russians took all of eastern Germany and Berlin itself, the Americans were snuffling after it.

Dr. Aorta looked out through a slit in the side of the armored car. The road they had been traveling was arched over by trees, lined with spring flowers and tufts of grass. The trees, leaves freshly sprouted, kept the narrow road in semidarkness, and only an occasional side road leading into a pasture or farmyard broke the wall of green. It was hard to decide who had been most surprised by the sudden meeting.

But it was not hard to tell who had been most injured by it. As Dr. Aorta stared out the slit in the armored car side panel, he discerned an American jeep turned sideways in the road, its occupants spilled out, sprawled in grotesque postures like dolls dropped in haste by a fleeing puppeteer. The jeep was burning at the rear, and tracer bullets from the captain's machine gun had ignited cans of fuel carried on the side of the jeep. Beyond it was a troop carrier with a .30-caliber machine gun firing sporadically in the direction of the armored car. On either side, in the heavy grass, American infantrymen fired ineffectually with rifles and light automatic weapons.

Above, the captain was cursing and yelling to his driver,

while he continued to fire bursts of machine-gun fire over and around the burning jeep.

—Goddamn you, get us turned back into the road. We're broadside to these bastards. Get us back in the road. We can cut them to pieces.

—*Du kanst mich ficken,* the driver shouted back. —We're stalled. They saw us first and opened fire. They must have hit something. This thing won't turn over.

—Make it turn over, the captain screamed, his voice rising to falsetto. —If they have a . . .

They did indeed. Dr. Aorta saw, beyond the smoke of the jeep and the haze of cordite from the gun, several of the Americans fumbling with a long black tube. It was a rocket-launcher.

—Sonofabitch, the driver yelled. —They've got one. They've always got one of everything.

—Get this thing . . . the captain began, but it was a little late. Even as he shouted, the driver and his seatmate bailed out of the front seat, hit the roadside and rolled clear of the armored car. While the captain, screaming something about treason, tried to depress his gun to fire at them. As he did so, a soldier, one of those who had sat patiently in the rear of the armored car awaiting orders, stood up.

—This is absurd, he said. —Let's get into that farmhouse.

—We fight here, the captain roared hysterically.

—This is absurd, the soldier said again, firing a burst of sub-machine-gun fire into the captain's back, missing Dr. Aorta by fractions of an inch.

The bullets struck the captain from behind and below. The momentum lifted him above the armor-plated shield of the tur-ret, and as he rose, a score of American bullets struck him, spraying blood, bits of bone and flesh down on Dr. Aorta, and knocking what was left of the captain clear out of the armored car.

—*Wo gehen Sie?* Dr. Aorta called to the soldier.

—*Zu dem Teufel,* he answered,—if we don't jump.

Dr. Aorta cannot remember jumping. But when the rocket struck, he was rolling into the farmyard, geese squawking, a pig running over him. He had, in one hand, his small cardboard valise. In the other, he found a Walther P.38 laid aside by the captain when the firing began. He followed two of the soldiers into the empty house, and placing the pistol under his suitcase, squatted near an overturned chair while the soldiers knocked out windows and began firing into the shadowed smoky road.

The fight lasted perhaps twenty minutes. The Americans were brave enough, running into the farmyard, hurling grenades, firing rockets which buried themselves in the thick stone walls of the farmhouse, spraying chips of rock down on Aorta and the others. But it ended. The farmyard was littered with bodies. Occasionally one moved, and the SS soldiers fired into it briefly.

—Dumb fools, the young soldier who had killed the captain said. —They all want to win the war by themselves.

He set his submachine gun down, took off his helmet and wiped his forehead. His two companions set down their guns and drew out cigarettes. —Well, that's the end of it, one said.

—Indeed, Dr. Aorta replied, lifting the Walther and opening fire on them.

⋙ ⋘

And so, on foot, into Switzerland with a suitcase containing an astounding collection of curiosities—including almost twenty-five kilos of pure heroin. Worth, conservatively, 1,000,000 pounds sterling. Most of it sold for 100,000 pounds and happy to make the sale.

To Madrid, from whence certain special flights could be chartered. To Egypt, to South Africa, to Latin America. Fare: from 5,000 to 500,000 dollars, depending on what sponsors of the flights found in customers' luggage, taped to their bellies, sequestered in a tube up the anus, between toes, sewed into articles of clothing. They had dealt in barter: two Rubenses and a sort of snuffbox by Cellini for beautifully forged papers; ancient correspondence from divers parties including Innocent III planning the Fourth Crusade, nine grams of radium, and a relic of St. Gregory the Great, in return for plastic surgery and certain hard currencies. It had been a seller's market all the way, with Allied Intelligence people digging and delving, and Spanish authority driven up the wall, torn between vast amounts of money to be had for the most trifling service or for simple refusal to squint at a questionable passport, and the constant pressure of agents of the victors, who, at best, had little use for a *Falangista* regime, and might well make trouble for it in postwar settlements.

But Dr. Aorta, a kind of cosmic junk peddler, had got to Argentina still well supplied with Swiss francs—which were used heroically to corrupt not only neutral officials, but Allied agents as well. From Argentina to Mexico, meanwhile in contact with pen pals in Egypt, Turkey, Sweden, and even the United States, where hatred of Nazism, like all other fads and fashions, finally withered in the glow of endless frozen dinners, autos, clubs, hemlines rising and falling, gardens, golf dates, assignations, and other overriding considerations.

At the end of much waiting, Dr. Aorta managed, with the help of some 25,000 francs, to enter the United States with truly superb papers claiming Rumanian citizenship: Aorta now a displaced person fleeing the Communists (true enough: MGB or NKVD or its politically dependable descendant has a dossier on Aorta, complete down to a photograph filled with luxury and money and sunlight, a backdrop of mountains and larches and overwhelming green, an open powerful expensive chromium-trimmed sports car; a woman's face hatless between a rich scarf and a seal coat, ageless and beautiful, cold, serene and damned; beside her a handsome youngish man smiling in the brown and silver of an SS major's uniform, hat in one hand, leash to sleek well-fed shepherd dog in other. Dog killed in air raid. Hat and uniform tossed into ditch 3.7 kilometers from border between Austria and Liechtenstein; woman denounced at strategic moment for flaw in maternal grandfather's bloodline. Leash still in trunk stored in Royal Street apartment. Dr. Aorta is a displaced person: *Homme sans carnet*—which, barring details, is true enough. A man who walks to and fro in the world, and up and down in it, whose life has the substance and meaning of a faggot's smile.

—I came through, Dr. Aorta repeats. —Of course. I know how to survive.

—What for? Christopher asks suddenly. —What do you survive for?

Dr. Aorta shrugs. The discussion begins to bore him. —If you have to ask that, you would not understand the answer. You are unhealthy, morbid. Guts of polished crystal.

—I'm not an animal.

—No? And why not? You are an animal. Your feet, your belly, the hair in your armpits, the juices in your mouth, your excretions, your lusts—all beastly—and yet, God forsaken, you want to believe that your mind, your soul, whatever absurdity you invent, is more than the sum of sweat and hair and digestion and urine. You are an animal, and a stupid one. In another time and place . . .

—You'd liquidate me?

Dr. Aorta winks benevolently. —I would hope you return to your sacred duties.

—Huh?

Dr. Aorta's face goes suddenly cold as he switches on a lamp of low wattage. —So that you will be out of the way. So that I can have some small assurance that you will not breed and reproduce your kind. Make bread into saviors. Leave alone the genetic stock.

As Dr. Aorta squirms into a shapeless tweed jacket and adjusts a soiled scarf at his collar, Christopher tries to frame some kind of response, something to rescue the wreckage of his dignity. Counteraccusation is no good; the Jews are played out. Dr. Aorta cannot be touched. There is no place, no sad or tender or frightened place in him. Christopher feels all at once that ghastly and indescribable distinction between those who win and those who lose, those who survive and those who are swept from the earth's arena like sprinklings of butchered kine. He begins to succumb to that malaise that begins the process of self-loss.

—The world is full of disasters, Dr. Aorta grumbles, —and all of them are men. Rights of man, declarations of independ-

ence. Filthy drivel by assemblies of fools and weaklings determined to keep man a craven domestic beast, to bore him into
oblivion. There is a better law, a higher law.

—What . . .

—The Athenians. You remember? To the Melians. Somewhere in Thucydides. No, you don't remember. The Athenians say: *You know as well as we do that justice, as the world
goes, is only in question between equals in power, while the
strong do what they can . . .*

—. . . . *and the weak suffer what they must,* Christopher finishes as if on cue.

—So. You are not ignorant. Only foolish. You know the
words. You simply choose to ignore them. Even in religion, it
must be some kind of offense, some sin to know and yet ignore.
Why do you deify mistakes, stupidity?

Christopher opens his mouth to give answer, but he knows
he has none. He is remembering a small boy trying to mem-
orize the Mass, his paunchy unsmiling father listening to the
endless Latin responses, asking over and over again, when do
you kneel? When do you rise? When do you change the missal?
When do you bring water and wine? It was too much for a small
boy who found daydreaming (of his mother and himself in a
quiet garden surrounded by high shadowed mountains) as
close to concentration as he could come. It was too much. Mistakes were bound to happen.

So, in the private chapel of the school, Christopher served his
first Mass alone, without assistance or witnesses. Old Father
Gamow (who was gone in eye and ear, and as it turned out, in
tongue as well) was the celebrant. Christopher did the prayers at the foot of the altar without a flaw. The introit, moving
the missal for the Gospel—all went forward with that mindless
lock-step precision Mr. Nieman considered the only proper way
to serve the God of Abraham and Paul.

Until the preparation of the chalice. Somehow the lockstep
fractured. Possibly because Christopher had never been so close
to the altar before. The altar cards, instead of blurred rectan-
gles, were covered with Latin prayers, illuminated with Byzantine pictures of Savior and Virgin, law-giver and dove. There

was the ineffable tabernacle, Christ's small golden home. With
a tiny lock which, if you squinted, said Yale. The crucifix and
tall candles, the sweet austere odor of flowers and incense and
tallow. Christopher was unsettled. He stood like an anxious
dwarf, shifting from one foot to the other, his new black shoes
shiny and incongruous under the frayed red cassock and outsized surplice. And then, holding a cruet filled with water and
one with wine, his eyes large and mind distracted by the
nearness, the almost palpable immediacy of Him, Christopher
did it. As Father Gamow leaned against the altar, chalice ex-
tended to Christopher, face warm with the perpetual informed
smile of advanced senility, Christopher managed to pour water
twice. The old priest, noticing nothing, turned back to the center of the altar. Christopher knew. He realized even as Father
Gamow turned away, nodding and shuffling, and he almost followed the priest, almost plucked at his sleeve. But at last he replaced the cruets, and returned to kneel at the foot of the altar
while Father Gamow, smiling and smiling, prepared to consecrate and consume a chalice full of tepid water. Christopher
was petrified. What should he do? Could he, between offertory
prayers and canon, possibly during the preface, slip up behind
the old man and pour a jolt of wine into the unready chalice?
Would it be worth it after all if, slouched in ancient piety over
the altarstone, the old priest should catch him, and there before
God, the angels and the saints, shake him, bawling out in that
angular Flemish accent: —Boy, what you do? God's name,
what you do here?

No. Christopher was no Prince Hamlet. So the water, untainted with wine, was consecrated and reverently drunk while
Christopher keened the confiteor to himself and thought in ten-
foot red gothic letters:

—*Domine, non sum dignus.* Lord, I am not worthy.

He remembers wondering afterward how deeply the sacrilege
had scarred his soul, whether giving a priest only water and no
wine was a sin reserved to the Holy See. He wondered if he
could confess it. Blasphemy against the most precious blood;
by extension against the Sacred Heart, and thus against the
whole of the Mystical Body. Souls in purgatory who would have

been released by that particular Mass still groaned and rolled in attenuated agony. Whole clouds of grace dissipated, falling on rock and fruitless soil. God's mercy clotted in the church's pinched arteries; His love and justice aborted in that bootless chalice.

—I am not worthy, Christopher whispers mechanically.

—Exactly, Dr. Aorta whispers, sitting down opposite him. —There is nothing personal in what I say to you. It is abstract. You are valueless. What have you done? What will you do? If you were a steer, you could be eaten. If you were a guinea pig, certain experiments could be furthered by using you. But, as it is. . . . Dr. Aorta spreads his hands. The world is strangling, running toward collapse with *Sklavenvolk*. Human garbage which refuses to admit the truth of its nature.

—Sometimes I feel, Christopher begins, —sometimes I feel . . .

—Yes, Dr. Aorta answers. —To end it. To find your own gibbet, adjust the nails, and flee to that kingdom for which you consecrated your life and then found you could not serve. Is it because you hate God? Because you do not believe in Him?

—No, I feel . . .

—Ah yes. What you feel has no place in the world. You are not of this world. Your kingdom is not of this world.

—No, Christopher agrees. —I can't find the . . .

—*You* are the stateless person. This world belongs to us. You are a usurper, Dr. Aorta smiles gently, a tutor pleased that his dullest student begins to understand. —You foul the working of destiny. Like an insect falling into complicated electrical equipment.

Christopher slumps. —Could I have a beer? he asks.

—Yes, Dr. Aorta says. —You can have a beer. You like imported beer?

—Yes.

                              ❦

—Don't come near me, you sleazy sonofabitch, Mary Ann says through her white even teeth. —I'd as soon kill you as look at you.

—Aw, Billy Bob begins, unbuckling his belt, feeling, as he watches her slip out of her dress, need and desire in merged and equal portions.

—Fuck you, buddy, Mary Ann retorts, stalking to the window, to watch sullenly as that evening sun goes down.

—Yeah, Billy Bob answers, pulling off his pants.

—Listen, Mary Ann tells him without turning from the window, —you know what you've done to me?

—Honey, I want to do you good, Billy Bob says soothingly. —I just want to do what's right.

—You sonofabitch, what you done is knocked me up. I'm fixin' to have a goddamned baby.

—Come on, Billy Bob says, his trousers limp in his hand. —You're kiddin' me.

—Somebody done it. The doctor says . . .

—Lord, you gonna have . . . Billy Bob begins. —You're gonna be the mother of my child?

—Ummm, Mary Ann answers, remembering her first night at Boundoch's place, that night in Shreveport with Christopher. —I don't know. People ought to be more careful.

—Uh, Billy Bob asks tentatively, —whatcha gonna do?

Mary Ann tosses her head. —Shit, she says, sprawling on the bed, nude but for her brassiere, —how do I know? I been too damned mad to think about that.

Billy Bob strips and lies down beside Mary Ann. —Listen. Don't you reckon we could get married? I mean this high-society stuff is okay, but it don't stick to the ribs.

—I got somethin' stickin' to my ribs, all right.

—I mean, wouldn't you like to settle down and get a place? —Naw.

—Well, maybe a little house-trailer.

Mary Ann bursts into tears, her face buried in a pillow. —Don't you talk no house-trailer to me, you low-class sonofa-bitch. I'll stay right here. Who asked you for anything any-how? Why don't you get your drawers back on and get out of here? Just leave me alone.

Billy Bob feels like a wolf in wolf's clothing. Has he brought this little girl to tears and desperation? He rises from the bed, only to discover that he cannot, practically speaking, get his drawers back on. So he rummages in the narrow closet, finds his monk's robe and struggles into it. Downstairs they are serving supper, and the cook likes to see him in his robes. She says it reassures her, and Billy Bob wishes he knew exactly what she means.

&ᵇᵂ

Sundown, and lights begin to appear in the Quarter. Some have never been off; a neon sign shines day and night before the Bethel Bar, for example, because the owner, once in the Navy, has heard that electrical apparatus lasts longer if it is never turned off. Upstairs, a desk lamp goes on, and off again—much wear and tear on circuitry. Street lamps flicker and take hold as Marshall Fields pushes his outsized cart past Bethel, around the corner into Ursulines, and pulls up short in front of a certain brick wall and battered garage door which, in darkness, is easy to miss. All brick walls and old garage doors look the same at night.

He removes the rusty padlock and eases himself into undifferentiated blackness. A pen-sized flashlight reveals the old La Salle unvexed, majestic in its dusty fuelless decrepitude. He reaches under the old car and slowly draws out his draggled charge. The sheet is filthy, and the lower portion seems soaked in some liquid discharge. The sheet's contents seem fairly stiff. Marshall Fields is about to step into the courtyard with his spade when one hand touches something peculiar, something alien. His ear detects the crackle of paper, and his eyes, already wide with sudden and absolute apprehension, light on a modest square of expensive buff letter-paper appended to the sheet by a single dressmaker's pin. Marshall Fields has seen them plain and he has seen them fancy, but not in thirty years of ghoulwork has he felt his own blood thudding so behind his eyes. He has been shot at and missed, shit at and hit all over, but this is new. He has never found a note on one of his tricks. His has been a sullen art; run silent, run deep. No communiqués required or solicited.

Amazed to find his hands trembling, hardly answering the imperative of efferent command, Marshall Fields unfolds the message. It is written in a flowing script so regular, so perfect, that it gives the impression of high-priced engraving, as if it were a form letter. But it is not. Unsigned, undated, it says:

> No, don't put it there. I don't want the other tree tall. I think I may put a terrace there with a table and nice wrought-iron chairs. But thank you anyhow.

—Jesus Christ and the Holy Ghost, Marshall Fields moans, scrambling to his feet, stuffing flashlight and note into his pocket, pulling his spade and the draggled sheet with its rigid contents behind him, looking neither right nor left as he emerges from the garage and begins piling things into his cart, as if the Eumenides or at least five homicide detectives of the most upright and unpurchasable character were closing in upon him from the caves of destiny or the purlieus of downtown central.

◄§ §►

—You've got to be kidding, Benny Boundoch groans.
—Here I take you in. I make you prosperous. You were a dog, and now you turn on me. You, Benny goes on, spreading his hands, staring up at the dining-room ceiling, then down at his empty plate. —You've ruined my star.
—Huh?
—How can I torture her nude if she's bloated with a lousy kid? How can she squirm on a rack with her belly a foot high?
Billy Bob has never had much use for Boundoch. He is too small, too neat, too clean. His eyes are like tiny dark shoe buttons, his hands as delicate as a sparrow's claws. And now he is talking about torturing Mary Ann.
—If you was to try anything with that little girl . . . he begins menacingly.
—Oh God, Boundoch slaps his forehead, drops his chin onto folded hands, his elbows on either side of the plate. —I got a movie to make, he says in a pleading tone. —I just want to make a movie. You're in it. You get to hustle her.
—Listen, Billy Bob starts again, less than reassured, —about this here movie. I been thinkin' about it. I come to wonder if

it ain't against God. I mean, it looks like you was runnin' down religion and family and everything else.

Boundoch is gifted with great patience. All his heritage and rearing points to patience as the key of success. In any case, what choice is there? He would weigh maybe 160 covered with tar, feathers and a coat of ice. He is confronted with a shaggy Southern beast, horrid with golden-red hair on arms, legs, face, and back of his hands. Hair even erupts at the top of his monkish robe. His woolly eyebrows give him the appearance of some terrific zoo specimen on sabbatical. Billy Bob weighs at least 220, and, Boundoch suspects, has killed more Negroes than he (Boundoch) has eaten sirloin steaks. Formerly a deputy sheriff in Mississippi, he will not bear head-on arguing. Better try a flank.

—Look, are you a religious man?

—Sonofabitch, I reckon. I'm a Southern Baptist. Saved over to Mount Hebron Church out of Wildwood, Mississippi. And saved all the way. Except I done backslid some. You can't stay clean. Didn't you ever think about it? Sin. What can you do? You shut your eyes and it comes in your ears. Stop 'em up, you can smell it. There ain't no way on Christ's poor bleedin' . . .

—Yeah. Sure. You got it right. Well, this movie is just what a minister would go along with, see?

Billy Bob frowns. He has seen the first draft of the scenario, and it did not much read like a sermon. This little Jew bastard is funning him. Maybe he should succumb to that recurrent impulse and break his neck for him. —How do you figure that? Billy asks suspiciously.

Boundoch is thinking fast. He cannot read minds, but he can sense distrust or hostility a hundred yards away. He has long supposed it was racial equipment. But then he thinks of his grandfather. Take no chances. You got a lot more to lose than your chains. Like arms and legs. Eyes and a tongue.

—Look, he says, —this show is about the Catholics, right?

—Yeah, I reckon.

—How come there's a Protestant Church?

—On account of them popes and all that business they did before the war.

—War?

—The Confederate War. The Baptist Church is plenty old.

—Sure, Benny whispers, slumping over his cold coffee.

—Yeah. Anyhow, this movie takes off the gloves. No holds barred. It tells the truth about priests and nuns, about popes and bishops. The whole scoop about the lousy Church and what it did to the, uh, Southern Baptists. Before the war.

—Ummm, Billy Bob mumbles. It seems hard to object to this. When you get a chance to punch the Whore of Babylon in the belly, plain religion approves it. Like shooting Lincoln or setting fire to a Republican's barn, it is a moral obligation.

—All right, Billy Bob says at last. —I'll go along with you. Except you got to promise two things.

—Sure, Boundoch answers, trying not to show the full measure of his relief. —Sure. What?

—First is you got to promise not to do anything to hurt that little girl; no stuff that might hurt her.

—Sure. Okay. What else?

—You got to let me have a copy of the movie when you get done with it.

Boundoch shudders. He can imagine trying to edit a high-class fuck-fest with Billy Bob Stoker of Mississippi as censor and artistic adviser.

—Look, it costs. It costs plenty to make prints. You'd have to pay for it.

—All right, I will. But I got to have a copy.

—What for? What are you going to do with it?

—I'm gonna send it back over to Mississippi. I got a friend over there.

—Listen, you've got to be careful where you send it. You don't want us all in the can.

—Naw, don't worry. This feller is a preacher. It'd just be for showin' in churches. Don't you reckon it might do some good?

—Yeah.

⋖§ §⋗

—So now, Dr. Aorta begins, handing Christopher a piece of cheese, a thick slice of buttered bread (not Staff-o-Life, which he finds inedible, but heavy-crusted, tender-centered French bread baked by some Central European Jews in Metairie) and a glass of beer. —So now we talk about reality.

Christopher is not much disposed to an encounter with reality. He cannot focus his attention. Certain shadows, long forgotten, keep rising and combining in the theater of his consciousness. He sees Jesus Christ nailed to the clapboards of a barracks in Bavaria, half a dozen SS troops dicing for his garments. Dr. Aorta, in Roman dress, washes his hands in a basin of blood, reaching then for surgical gloves made of the hides of Holy Innocents. And himself Barrabas, chosen over and over again, to be freed, to be turned loose while his Savior bleeds and suffers, to be cursed with life when life is death. And Mr Christian, broken hands woven into ghastly parody of Dürer, singing in low cracked Negro falsetto,

> *Were you there when they crucified my Lord?*

—You want money, Dr. Aorta is telling him as he munches cheese. —A bad priest needs money. When the people find out in such a town as New Orleans, when they know for sure . . .

—They don't want me to deliver their bread, Christopher muses —Some of those Italians . . . they look at me like they thought . . .

—You are Satan?

—Yes, Christopher says, drinking the beer and stuffing a mouthful of bread after it. —Like I was the devil. Superstitions. I don't know.

—Fools, Aorta says perfunctorily. —Oafs. Even an Italian should know Satan owns; he does not work. The devil is an aristocrat. He hires.

Christopher shudders and finishes his cheese. The room is cast in deep shadow now. There is only one small lamp burning, and from outside there is the sickly odor of garbage and gardenias, of scorched rubber and stale cooking oil. Somehow the melange seems good to Christopher. He wishes he was out amongst the refuse, the rotting vegetables and smoldering trash. The streets are cool now. It is hotter here in Dr. Aorta's apartment than outside.

—I think I better . . .

—Go? Oh not yet, Dr. Aorta cuts him off with a touch of the imperative. —Not just yet. I have a thing to tell you.

—To tell . . . ?

—Perhaps to ask. Tell first. I must tell you that what you have done is known.

—Done . . . ? I don't know how they could . . . nobody knows me here. Nobody from Alexandria . . . nobody is here from Shreveport . . .

—Ah, I mean the other, the . . . disposal. Last night.

—What? Christopher falters, uncertain, yet apprehensive.

—You assisted the Negro Christian. You drove him to the river.

—I drove him. He wanted a ride.

—*Ach* so. By doing it you committed an offense under the criminal code of Louisiana. Accessory after fact. You helped the Negro Christian dispose of a dead female.

—The sheet. That dummy . . .

—You have become part of a modest apparatus. You and your bread truck.

—Oh Jesus, Christopher groans. —I didn't want to . . . I never meant . . .

—Come now. You sound like a minor functionary at Nuremburg. Even if you did not know, even if you want no part of it, play the man. It is more embarrassing to be taken for a dupe than hunted as a monster. If they come for you, tell them yes, you are part of everything. Tell them you have sold children for unspeakable purposes, that you have eaten the internal organs of human beings. Tell them you wish to burn whole populations alive . . .

—Oh Jesus . . .

—Tell them anything that will astound them, force them to turn on you in outrage. For a moment, for a few seconds you will feel like a god. A terrible lie is better than a half-witted truth.

—You're insane, Christopher almost shouts, his beer glass falling to the floor and shattering there. —You're crazy.

Dr. Aorta's eyebrows raise, his muddy pupilless eyes widen. —I? No, priest. You are feeble-minded. You stumble into things like a blind man, like an idiot. I function very well. Of course, Dr. Aorta says, staring at Christopher benevolently, —of course, we may be able to help one another, if you are not ready for a grand gesture.

—Help? Christopher asks. —How? What can you do for me? What can I . . .

—I can keep what I know quiet. I can instruct the Negro Christian who depends on me, and certain other persons to see that no word of your action is spoken. And you may be able to do small favors for me. Your truck is a convenience. What does one look for in a bread truck?

—Bread, Christopher answers woodenly.

—So that the Negro Christian could easily place small parcels, various things, in that truck. He is not clever, but he will obey as well as he can. Do you know how to obey?

—I don't know . . . anything.

—No, you obey badly. You swear on the blessed wounds of your God, and then betray him. But you do not want to go to prison. Hell, if there were such a thing. But not prison. And, above all, you do not want to die. Do you?

—No, Christopher says. —No, I want to live. I don't know how, but I want to live.

—Of course you know how. Even an animal knows. How to live is not to die. If you do what I tell you, you will never die.

—Never die, Christopher laughs almost hysterically.

—I mean, not now. Not of some accident with your truck. Not of gas in your apartment. With your mother.

—Mother . . .

—Or in traffic you will not die. So far as I can help. You will even make money, certain things . . .

As Dr. Aorta speaks, there comes a mad and uproarious knocking at his door. Christopher turns to see Marshall Fields staggering into the room, an unutterably filthy sheet-covered burden on his back. Dr. Aorta's expression does not change, but his lips tighten, he seems to grow more pale. He is not accustomed to his minor failures returning. Such resurrection, he thinks, is evidence of a disordered universe.

—I seen bad days and I seen good, Marshall Fields bawls, —but I'm goddamned if I ever see another day like today. I quits this assignment. You done it; now you clean it up. I done tried, and the whole business turned on me. I ain't used to that. It used to be you picked 'em up, you found a place, you planted 'em and that was that. But it ain't like that no more.

Marshall Fields lowers his burden to the floor, grabs a half-empty bottle of beer and drains it. He has a story to tell.

Chapter Seven

It is that alley again and the darkest part of the night. Behind the Staff-o-Life bakery, Mr Christian is leaning against the crumbling brick wall shaking his head, his shoulders slumped, his legs almost buckling at the knees.

—Aw naw, too much, man. Fo'get it. Lissen, just fo'get it.

—Can't fo'get it, Marshall Fields repeats for the fourth or fifth time. —Ain't no way to fo'get it. You done fucked up to start, and you been fuckin' up all along.

Mr Christian covers his eyes with splayed fingers. The Horse is gone, the stall door swinging ajar. He thinks he may be dying. But he is afraid not. It could go on for days like this.

—Lay off, Christopher tells Marshall Fields. —What did you do? You brought it back. You found it and took over and loused around and brought it back like an albatross.

—Never mind the poetry, Dr. Aorta mutters impatiently. —We go in.

—Naw, Mr Christian says one final time. —You can't do it this way. God.

—We can do it this way. It is the best way.

—We better get out of this alley, Christopher tells them, —or it's not going to be done any way at all. The bulls are only stupid, not deaf.

Dr. Aorta reaches for Mr Christian's arm. With amazing dexterity he inserts a hypodermic needle and presses the plunger.—The key, he says sharply.

—Wow, Mr Christian answers. He hears the thunder of a
thousand hooves in the distance. They are on the way, every one
with a saddle and wings, too. It will be a high ride and handsome. —Why not? Why. Not.

—This goddamned thing gettin' heavier, Marshall Fields
grunts, pulling the filthy sheet behind him. —I swear to God
it feels like somebody done embalmed her with mercury.

Christopher shivers in the darkness. He feels just now like
one who has been judged and sent on. He has not even the will
to turn and run. It is as if he belongs here. Not because of Dr.
Aorta's threat, but for judgment. Someone in Sussex had said
the damned choose hell, that having won their place in chaos,
no offer from bliss would draw them forth. It sounds like Calvin, Christopher is thinking. All in all, the universe is an image
of providence. Everything is where it belongs. Nothing can end
in the wrong place. For all the torment and agony, they go
where they want to be. To hate God is to hurt. But to love Him
is to hurt. So every soul chooses its hurting-place.

—You gonna have trouble, Marshall Fields is telling Dr.
Aorta. —It ain't been used in thirty years.

—Shit, Mr Christian laughs, —it ain't even there. Youall
both been chewing crazy pills. It ain't nothin' down there I
don't know.

—Lissen, Christian, Marshall Fields says, —you got a big
vein on. So fo'get it. I know every flowerpot in this Quarter. If
I say it's down here, you better believe.

—This is what should have been from the beginning, Dr.
Aorta says, pointing his penlight down the dusty stairs. —Even
burial is an invitation to trouble.

—I been layin' 'em down for twenty years, Marshall Fields
answers defensively. —Ain't never had one come up.

—Cause that old lady on Ursulines liked good healthy trees,
Mr Christian giggles. —What you reckon happen to her husband?

—I been wonderin'. There's a good-sized oak out behind
the mimosas.

—The river is as bad as setting it in the chair of the chief of
polizei, Dr. Aorta is saying to no one in particular .—Absolute

immolation is best. What does not exist cannot stand to your condemnation.

—Um, Christopher murmurs, wondering about that.

They manage to get down the long tortuous flight of stairs at last, and move into Mr Christian's private chamber.

Marshall Fields is fumbling amongst old paint buckets and dusty unused tools against a far wall.

—Ain't nothin' over there, Mr Christian mumbles, irritated by this invasion of his dark kingdom.

—Shit, Marshall Fields says, trying to remember where the old door is. —Somewhere here. At an angle from that stinkin' pit. They put up shelves. I remember the old man used to work here. He was some kind of foreign nigger. He had 'em put these shelves. Somebody gimme a hand.

Christopher helps him pull one of the shelves away from the wall. Sure enough. There is a door behind it.

—Ha, Marshall Fields laughs, turning toward Mr Christian. —Reckon you know everything?

Lèse-majesté. Mr Christian kicks at an old tire sullenly. Nobody likes a smart-ass.

—Get on with it, Dr. Aorta insists. —We spend too much time at this.

The door, its knob no more than a right angle of wrought iron, yields easily enough. Beyond it is total darkness.

—We will need wood. Crates, planks. And paper. Bring whatever you can find, Dr. Aorta tells Christopher and Mr Christian.

—An' some gasoline from upstairs, Marshall Fields puts in. —Lemme have about five gallons.

Mr Christian shrugs and moves back toward the stairs, boxing with his own outsized shadow as it prances across the wall, over tools and broken parts. A feint, a jab. A nice right cross. He is good with his hands. Everything moves like oil on glass when the Horse is under him. All creation divides into those in the saddle or under it. Just now Mr Christian is riding, pennons flaring in the breeze, down a sun-smeared road toward Roncevaux. All the horns in hell cannot recall him. Wood? Paper? Okay. Just so. Live ten thousand years, effendi.

Meanwhile Marshall Fields has rigged some kind of torch out of a length of pipe wrapped in old rags, dipped in waste oil. He has passed into the far room and planted his flaming brand in a ring fixed to the ancient brick as if it had been meant for just this use.

—Some ole Spanish made this place, Marshall Fields says formally, as if he were some bizarre guide through the mysteries of the Escorial. —An' look here. Just take a look at that.

Dr. Aorta and Christopher squint into the center of the dark room. The floor is so thick with ancient dirt, brick dust and mortar long decomposed that Marshall Fields has left a trail of footprints behind him. The walls are completely bare. Except for a crumbling piece of paper attached between two bricks by a thick nail. It is a calendar, pages falling apart from the edges inward. The large type still shows, even through an overlay of dust and cobweb. It says August 1914. There is a large circle around the fifth, and a scrawl in pencil that Christopher cannot read. He steps into the room and moves closer. The words, seeming to fade as he reads them, written in blunt small capitals say: SACRED HEART BLESS EVERYBODY NOW.

—Ah, Dr. Aorta is saying behind him, —lovely. Just right. Exactly right.

Christopher turns from the calendar to see what Dr. Aorta so approves. It is large and square, its bulk so filling the center of the room that it seems a part of it rather than something added. It is an oven. Large enough to accommodate almost anything that one might need to burn.

—Used to bake here long years ago, Marshall Fields is saying with the air of discoverer, guide and proprietor. —Then it got too small for 'em so they burned garbage and junk in it. Then the city got to takin' care of that and they didn't have no use for it. So they just left it. Cheaper than tryin' to pull it down. You can see that. They built that thing to stay. My daddy did the brickwork.

—The steel, Dr. Aorta says. —It looks like good material.

He goes closer and rubs the fouled surface of the iron door. Great flakes of rust and petrified grease fall away. There is lettering on the door.

—Ought to be good, Marshall Fields tells them. —Come from some foreign place. Best ole oven money can buy. See there?

Christopher moves closer, next to Dr. Aorta. He tries to make out the raised lettering:

STEIGMEIR INDUSTRIE. FRANKFORT. 1870 DK 69174

He hears Dr. Aorta's laughter even before it begins to wash around him, echoing in the shadowy room, flowing around the walls and over the squat furnace and back along the musty corridor where someone can be heard struggling with an armload of lumber and a half-filled can of gasoline.

&~

Boundoch pours a cup of coffee and passes it across to his guest. When he has a problem, he calls in an expert.

—What do you think? he asks Mrs. Mailer.

—What do you think I think? she answers, leaning back in the fancy brocaded chair expansively. It has been a long time since she was last entertained in a high-class parlor. —I think it'll cost you five bills.

—Hey, five bills. This is cooperation? You people sell them to me and then make twice as much when they need fixing. What kind of a deal is that?

—Like G.E., Mrs. Mailer answers smoothly. —Like Westinghouse. We don't issue no warranties. You didn't ask for no service policy, did you?

—Look, Boundoch tells her in exasperation, —I got a movie working. She's got to get cut. This flick could be worth a nice piece of change.

—What you gonna call it? *Belly High?*

—Listen, that's funny. How about taking one percent of the gross? I need working capital, and that way you make maybe five times five bills.

Mrs. Mailer shrugs. —Sure, I can ask him, but it won't do any good. Doc wants it on the barrelhead. He needs working capital, too. This scrape scene isn't but a side line.

—So he makes a pile on the sniffers. Okay, so tell him it's time to diversify. Listen, tell him you make it quicker and safer with a movie. Like if they catch you cutting or pushing . . .

—If they catch *him*, Mrs. Mailer cuts Boundoch off, —the rap is the same no matter what he goes in for.

—What?

—He got in some trouble in European politics or something. You know how funny the laws are over there. So whatever he gets snagged for, it's all the same.

—So. Five bills.

—Five. You got her ready to go?

Boundoch spreads his hands. —Jesus, I haven't even talked to her about it.

—So talk. I'll come back tomorrow and take her over to the place.

—Listen, Boundoch cuts in, —I don't want any more funny stuff. You know what I mean?

Mrs. Mailer frowns. —What?

—The cunt from Mobile. Last year. I never told you about that?

—The fat one?

—Not fat. Firm. She had some regular tricks. Till I got her back.

—We cut her. That's what you paid for.

—I didn't pay you to put her on the stuff. She left with some Mexican who swore he owned a poppy field in Chihuahua.

—Oh, Mrs. Mailer lisps. —I forgot. I meant to tell you. We run out of chloroform.

—My God, what an operation.

—This ain't Bellevue. It's just a small home-style outfit. You want everything neat, take your hides over to Charity. Maybe Tulane Medical School will give you a special rate.

Boundoch shrugs. Things are what they are. It is a world without order. Only art makes it worthwhile. —So I'll get her ready, he tells Mrs. Mailer.

—So do it. You want to give me the five bills now?

Boundoch shakes his head. —When I get her back alive without a habit.

—You don't trust nobody, do you? Mrs. Mailer says accusingly.

—I did once, Benny muses. —I trusted my grandfather.

—Don't worry. She'll be fine. He'll just clean her out. Say, you want him to . . . take care of her?

—Sure I want him to take care of her. You think I want he should throw her out in the street?

—I mean he could fix her. So you wouldn't have any more trouble like this.

—How much?

—Couple hundred more.

—Forget it. When she finishes this movie, she can sign up somewhere as a brood mare. Just take care of the problem. Leave the future alone.

Mrs. Mailer shakes her head. —You don't build no loyalty like that. A girl don't want to feel like her boss is using her.

—Wow, Benny whistles.

—You want a bad name?

—No, Benny says with exaggerated seriousness. —You can put the hook on my wallet, but don't fuck with my name. I might need credit.

Mrs. Mailer arranges a gardenia on the shoulder of her frowsy dress. —Listen, I got no time to mess with you. You want a straight cheap-shit job. That's what you get. When do you want to deliver her?

Benny shrugs. —Like tomorrow. Maybe I ought to check with the doc.

—You can check with me. I get paid to keep him from being checked with. What time tomorrow?

—Evening. I need her in the morning. Maybe I could drop by the apartment and ask the doc . . .

—Maybe you can drop dead. Don't you know anything about business?

—No, Benny tells her, his mind creeping back to *The Question*. —No, I'm an artist.

—Bullshit.

—That's one kind, Benny signs off.

❧ ❧

The first attack had come in late afternoon while Christopher was out. Mrs. Nieman had managed to get to the bed somehow, leaving the roast to cook past rareness to perfection, to well done, to a cinder and beyond while she lay listening to the tentative rhythms of her wrong heart. She had taken one of her pills, swallowing it without water, eyes fixed on the ceiling, on a small patch of water stain. After a little while, the stain began to acquire a character of its own. It was, at its center, a small garden in a valley among mountains that kept it in almost continual shadow. The very smallest of gardens, and yet full of levels and turns, sudden surprising vistas. And then Mrs. Nieman came to see that it was not a small garden after all: it was enormous. Big as Versailles. Only the valley was larger still, and the mountains were so huge that it was impossible to comprehend their size. They stood on every side, tall, cold as all space; great vertical limits not only to passage from the valley, but even to imagination itself.

But the garden; full of every flower she could name, and as many more that she could not. And all blooming at the same time. Blooming at the same time, and filling the chill unmoving air, the garden's dark silence with a slow tide of perfume, a single discrete odor containing within it every scent: roses and lilies, gardenias and magnolias, daffodils and carnations—the whole spectrum of blossoms' scent, every one flowing and washing over her like mysterious minor currents within the body of a great river.

And she shivered. Because for all its beauty, the garden was cold, Lord, cold. A tiny fountain stood between two thick plantings of lilacs, its spray arching upward in the unalterable twilight, and floating toward her, its touch perceptible only because, like a mist of pure alcohol evaporating, it left her flesh chill, her soul dark and ravished.

Which, she sees, is all the kind of morbid horseshit you expect out of a hypochondriac. Now Mrs. Nieman rises slowly, one last glance cast disgustedly at the miserable water stain on the ceiling of the room. She stands, hearing again traffic in the street, the temporal currency of voices and auto engines; a laugh from down the hall. And she smells suddenly the detestable stench of her roast, long since reduced to charcoal. What a lousy.

And it strikes again. Like a Stuka attack, a naval bombardment, or an artillery barrage timed on target. She says, thinks, feels nothing. When consciousness begins to return, her chest feels as if all enemy action had scored direct hits on the command post. She is lying face up on the bed. Which is luck and luck alone. Had she been on the balcony, she would have ended up through the roof of a car. Yes, Lord, it's a good day.

This time the water-stain garden is more than an impression. She can feel the cold rock of the outrageously tall mountains. The grass is smooth and chill beneath her feet. Each blossom stands out in singular relief, as if a certain curl or turn of petal and stem were some surrogate for personality. There is no wind, no sound, even of rustling leaves. There are only the long paths shadowed by trees and shrubs and the mountains beyond all. And the certainty that she is alone, absolutely alone, here. No one has been here before, and no one is coming. She will be here always, and the weather will never change; it will always be that strange luminosity of twilight when day's final glare is gone, and the vague edgelessness of night has not yet risen. It will always be like this. The endless beds and borders of flowers are hers alone. The trees and the perfume, the colorless sky, and the distant mountains. All of it is unalienably hers. Forever. She will get used to the chill motionless air, the grass stiff and cold beneath her feet. She has only to strip off her clothes, forget all that has gone before, and enjoy her garden. Forever.

Mrs. Nieman is fully conscious now, her eyes bright, fixed on the stained ceiling. Or somewhere beyond it. Her robe has fallen open. Her matchless breasts rise and fall quickly, to some distant adagio. Her legs are parted as if to receive a lover, the shadowed perfection of thighs and belly leading upward and downward to the world's dear place. And there are tears of some kind in her eyes.

⋞§ §⋟

They are still at it. Only the subject has changed.

The coffee is hot and black, and Benny is drinking it compulsively. He listens to Mrs. Mailer's droning voice.

—This stretch along Pontchartrain. I had a bad time finding it. But there are trees and a long strip of sand going down to the water. Plenty of room. He can see her against the trees, just coming out of the woods, see? And they start walking toward each other, then running.

—He's pulling off that rope, and then getting out of the robe all the time he's running, Benny says intensely, lapping his coffee.

—He's breaking his goddamned neck trying, Mrs. Mailer drones. —And she's coming in her nun's dress, pulling off the hat, opening the front of it.

—Do they have fronts?

—This one has a front.

—You got to be authentic.

—You got to be reasonable. You want it to look silly?

—But if . . .

—You got the camera on his back, over his shoulder. If he looks like a pelican walking on hot coals, it don't hurt. Anyhow, he's too horny not to be clumsy. But she's got to look right. You see?

—She's a young girl. Promised to God.

—Right.

—But love. She saw this guy, this monk, while she was shopping for the convent.

—Right.

—And she can't help it. She's afraid. She's afraid of God. afraid of the chief nun. She's terrified of the Inquisition.

—Right.

—But she's got to have him. She feels love. She never had a man, but she knows what it's got to be like. She can feel his mouth, she can feel his body . . .

—She can feel his ass, Mrs. Mailer yawns. —You're gonna push this thing too far. Nobody's born as dumb as you want her to be.

—He's dumb, too. Same story. Just a little kid, a bright kid when he goes into this monastery. He doesn't even know what she's got down there. He just feels this thing . . .

—Wow, Mrs. Mailer sneers. — What happens when they come

together out on the sand? How long will it take them to figure out what to do? Or even how to do it? That ought to make a nice scene.

—Listen . . .

—Maybe you could have directions printed in big gothic letters on her belly.

—You don't know what art is, Benny grumbles disgustedly.

—I know what money is. I know who pays five bucks to see a fuck-fest. You go arty, and you're gonna have to run it at Radio City.

—Listen, one of these days, when things stop being crazy and repressed, they might run *The Question* in every house in the country.

—What kind of house?

—Every good movie . . .

—With *Snow White and the Seven Feebs* for a second feature? Jesus.

But Benny is thinking about tomorrow. And tomorrow. About the scenes in dark terrifying chambers, on a long deserted stretch of beach. Love and torture, fear and tenderness. Precious moments of life amidst absolute terror. This is all at second remove for Benny; he has never experienced anything like it, but he imagines it must be that way if you do not grow up perverted and depraved. Someone has observed that a virgin yearns for experience; a whore for innocence.

Mrs. Mailer tosses her head back, drains the coffee left cooling in her cup. She tries to waste nothing, not even words. In a world full of Boundochs, things rarely work out that way.

Boundoch watches her red wattled neck rise from a high lace collar. Her throat undulates in vague and awful parody of a kooch-dancer's belly. Benny wonders how she would look stripped naked, chained to a rack, four nude Negroes, masked, and their bodies oiled, turning the great ratcheted wooden wheel, muscles straining, grunting, chanting some monstrous heathen hymn. Suddenly a beautiful blond girl, body blindingly white, gauded in gold ornaments, steps from the shadows with a wide-bladed golden scimitar, and gently, affectionately cuts Mrs. Mailer's throat. Gouts of blood, a blanket of steaming gore blots out everything: rack, Negroes, girl—all glisten crim-

son. Great God, the colors. Who would have thought the old har-
ridan had so much blood in her? But never mind. Evil, every
boot-black knows, into the mind of God or man may come and
go, so unapproved, and leave no spot or blame behind. It is all a
dream, Benny thinks, in the mind of a limbless Pole who smiles
away long years in candlelight. Man is a midge flitting through
darkness, seeking the lamp on the D.A.'s desk, a place to lay his
burden down.

—I got four niggers for tomorrow, Mrs. Mailer is telling him.
—Bad boys from over in Algiers. They'll cost you five bucks a
day. Cheap as dirt.

—Wow, Benny starts, as if she had been reading his mind.
Are bitchery and witchery all of a piece? —What do I need
with them?

—To tote and carry, Mrs. Mailer drones. —To set up and
take down. But most of all to see you get your dirty show on the
road in peace. Or did you figure you could get a permit from
the mayor to keep people away from that stretch of beach while
Stoker and his slut screw for art?

—Sure, Benny says. —That's a good deal. You'd make a great
producer. You know your stuff.

—When I had stuff, Mrs. Mailer answers wearily, —I knew
it.

She rises from the table. —Keep the niggers well off where
you're shooting. Don't tell 'em anything.

—Huh?

—Jesus. For five bucks a day, they don't need to know enough
to put you in the penitentiary. Anyhow, if they saw what you're
up to, they might get nervous. Everybody wants to be an actor.
You might end up having to change your script.

—Oh, I see, Benny begins. —You mean . . .

—Unless maybe you'd like to call the show *Gang-fuck by
Quartet of Moors.*

—Oh . . .

&§ ¦֍

It is hot as the hinges of hell, Christopher thinks. The room is
knee-deep in chunks and fragments and slats and slivers of
wood, bales of old newspapers, the gasoline. Marshall Fields

and Mr Christian are stripped to the waist, sweating freely, looking as if they had been dunked in olive oil. Dr. Aorta sits in the doorway on a swaying orange crate watching Christopher and the others stoking the dark squat furnace.

—Seem like you can't satisfy him, Mr Christian mutters. His Horse has slowed to a trot.

—Dr. Aorta? Christopher asks.

—Aw shit, I mean this here oven. We been pilin' stuff in for thirty minutes.

—I don't know, Marshall Fields shakes his head and throws the seat of a broken chair in. —I seen 'em easy and I seen 'em hard. But I don't know.

—Know what?

—This here fire. I don't know it'll burn up a body. My ole daddy used to get a job now and then. He worked down in the French Market but he knew the fly crowd all up and down the river, an' once every so often they'd come up with somethin' they didn't want in the river. So real late they'd bring it out to the Market, back where my daddy run the incinerator. Lord, he'd be four or five hours late comin' home. Said it just wrinkled and went black. Said it cracked and started fallin' off the bones in good-sized pieces. But you ended up with them roasted chunks and a bunch of bones on your hands.

—Absurd, Dr. Aorta says from the doorway. —You have to stay at it. Everything oxidizes. Charcoal and calcium dust when it is done. What remains can be poured into a gutter. You will see. The rest is smoke going up and not coming down again.

Christopher wipes his eyes and stares into the lurid flames spouting from the furnace. He has been tossing fuel into that Baal-like mouth with the unconscious precision of a machine. He has felt some indefinable pleasure in the joint effort with Marshall Fields and Mr Christian. Strange things are done in the name of solidarity.

—Up in the truck, Dr. Aorta is saying, —there is a . . . *Schmiedehammer* . . . what do you call this? A large . . .

—Sledgehammer, Christopher answers absently, throwing an armful of barrel staves into the furnace.

—You will need it later.

Mr Christian and Christopher exchange glances in the fitful red and yellow light flaring from the oven door. Mr Christian's steed is a plug by now, and Christopher is feeling sick. Not puking sick, but that special subspecies of soulsmertz where being itself seems more of a burden than it can possibly be worth.

They go on pushing wood, cardboard cartons, shattered crates, a Tampax display, bits of show-window decorations, an outsize plastic Santa Claus and eight tiny papier-mâché reindeer, an unframed photo of Franklin D. Roosevelt edged in black, with a brush moustache penciled in above his broad and kindly smile, a thatch of hair crudely drawn down over his lithographed eye, some burlap sacking, even a few reels of ancient crumbling film.

—Lissen, Marshall Fields begins, —it ain't gonna be hot enough. You just gonna roast her.

—Not your concern, Dr. Aorta snarls, glancing at an expensive watch on his wrist. —Push in the wood and paper. It requires longer without coal or coke or oil, but it can be done. Anything is possible.

—Maybe we should wait, Christopher begins.

—Shut up, priest. When we are ready, you will put your blessing on her. It will be fitting. What you can give is what she deserves.

Christopher turns away. Marshall Fields and Mr Christian and Dr. Aorta stare at him in silence. Above the crackle of the fire, there is a peculiar rumbling sound. Dr. Aorta stands quickly, one hand disappearing beneath his shapeless jacket.

—What . . .

—Nothin', Mr Christian says. —Only water. It's done started to rain. Whenever it rains, the gutters carry it down here. It comes down here, down the drains till you can't hardly hear yourself think.

—Ummm, Dr. Aorta says, relaxing again.

Christopher listens to the thundering drain superimposed over the fire's mounting roar. It would be possible, he thinks, to grapple with Dr. Aorta at this moment, to beat him to death with a chunk of wood or a tire iron from the other room. Or to wrest his pistol from him and commit suicide with it. Or begin to scream until the tissues of the throat collapse, or Dr. Aorta opens fire. Or beg mercy of a vanished Jesus. Or run upstairs into the street bearing the thin corpse, sheet stripped away; running on under the rain's flail searching for a policeman, who, in the absence of all else, might make things, if not right, at least the kind of glum and ordinary wrong to which Christopher is accustomed, the kind of wrong a coward—and perhaps a traitor—can bear.

—Ain't gonna get no hotter, Marshall Fields announces, tossing a final bale of old newspapers into the fire. The headline on the top paper reads: *Allies Prepare to Assail National Redoubt.* There is a map with black arrows and cracked patterns of military positions outlined, a tiny swastika on one side; British and American flags on the other. The headline and its map wilt, twist as if in agony, and fall into whitening ash amidst the soaring flames.

—All right. We begin, Dr. Aorta says suddenly. —Lift it. All of you help to lift it.

Mr Christian and Marshall Fields grab the sheeted object at the top, Christopher gets hold of the unbending legs. Marshall Fields guides the head and shoulders through the furnace aperture.

—Come on. Shove, he tells Mr Christian. —This thing is heavy.

—Man, this is awful, Mr Christian answers, pushing halfheartedly. He helps Christopher jam the stiffened lower limbs past the iron door.

As the feet pass them, a portion of the filthy sheet falls away, and Christopher sees, or thinks he sees, for a fraction of a second, a large callused foot, and a thick hairy ankle, clearly black. He glances across at Mr Christian in sudden and absolute terror. But Mr Christian, five shades lighter, the color of ashes in the rain, is staring at the closing furnace door, swallowing as if he had a chunk of iron the same size caught in the lower reaches of his throat.

&ep; &ep;

—Did you see . . . ? Christopher begins.

—Yeah. I seen. Shut up and lemme alone. My feet's bad

and my head feels like a lodge-hall fulla Holy Rollers.

—Who . . . ?

—God knows. Somebody done swapped on ole Marshall Fields. Let it be. It ain't your problem. You done what they tole you. They didn't ask you for no topsy.

—Huh?

—Topsy. Cutting 'em up when they die.

—Oh.

They are walking up Bourbon Street. Both of them are in need. A drink or several for Christopher. Something stiffer for Mr Christian, whose steed is down in the fetlocks. They are triangulated on every side by bright neon. Signs proclaim that Honey Chile, the Body Beautiful, can be seen inside. No cover. Two-dollar minimum. Another place, its door rimmed in red, has a placard in a glass case which says simply

24—Hostesses—24.

Something between rain and fog is falling—or rising, for all Christopher can tell. It touches them lightly, but chills their heated flesh. Mr Christian looks as if he is sweating. Cars and signs, doorways and windows blur in the mist. Streetlights lose their definition, and the neon tubes grow and become fuzzy like earthworms suddenly turned caterpillars. Christopher thinks of Impressionist painting, the posters of Toulouse-Lautrec. Mr Christian thinks of a good jolt. He wishes to that hateful God above who is busy making fog that he had hit Dr. Aorta for another bundle after they had got done in the Staff-o-Life subcellar.

Christopher and Mr Christian realize suddenly that they have been walking purposelessly. Both of them want a place to stop. Coffee at least. But there are not many places in New Orleans where a white man, even a cursed priest, can sit down across the table from a black one, no matter how much hard luck he has to talk away.

—Reckon we could stop by Jimmy's Tip-Toe Inn?

—What? Christopher asks.

—Nigger dump just off Rampart.

—Would they throw me out?

—Aw naw. They don't care who comes in. Long as he drinks and stays quiet. Once in a while they get a fella from New York or Chicago comes in drunk and sits down to show how he don't think he's no better than a colored man.

—Gee, Christopher mumbles. —What for?

—I dunno. Jimmy had some bad luck with them people. One of 'em come in and bought drinks for everybody till he passed out. And when Jimmy went through his pockets he didn't have but twelve cents, a picture of some movie-woman naked, and a Los Angeles driver's license that was expired. Next one come in paid for his drinks ahead of time like Jimmy asked. But then he tried to pick up Jimmy's kid.

—Sonofabitch.

—Worse than that. Jimmy's kid is a ten-year-old boy.

Christopher shrugs. —Reckon we better go somewhere else.

—Naw. Anybody can see you ain't gonna do anything.

Christopher ponders that, and is not overjoyed with the implications of it. But then he is not joyous over much of anything. There have been times in the last week or so when he even remembers St. Magnus Martyr with something close to nostalgia. It is a tough row to hoe, he thinks. And sometimes it seems the choices are all extreme. You can bury old Italians who turn black in their coffins or weigh six hundred pounds. You can listen to Mrs. Blood's god-awful confessions. Or you can groan for a tan-skinned red-lipped girl who has no use for you. Or assist a lunatic burning bodies, and not even the right body at that.

—Come on, Christopher says, turning the corner, heading toward Rampart. —You're right. I'm not going to do anything.

Chapter Eight

As mornings go it is a good one. For Benny's purposes, it could hardly be a better one. The palest kind of sunlight falling through a thick mist along the lake. He has staked out his Negroes to forestall interruptions. The kitchen crone serves as wardrobe mistress and make-up crew. Benny has rented an old 35-mm. camera and is ready to direct and shoot simultaneously. There is no sound equipment. Sound can be dubbed later easily enough, and when you are not working with both picture and sound at the same time, you are less a hostage to the compounded miseries which nature and fate have in store for every creative genius.

—You're walking out of those trees, Benny is telling Mary Ann. —You come out with your head down, sad, lonesome. It's a shortcut to market. To buy the convent food. Like your life is missing something. A dimension is lacking, see? All you've got is Jesus.

—That's crazy, Billy Bob breaks in, scratching under his friar's woolley habit. —If you've got Jesus, if you've really got Him, what could you . . .

—Pussy, Benny answers shortly. He finds it maddening that amongst all of nature's slings and chance's arrows, he should be plagued in addition with theological debates carried on by country Calvins. —Cock, in her case, he tells Billy Bob.

Billy Bob sneers. —You think somebody with Jesus would trade Him for a mess of . . .

—Ass, Benny finishes for him. —You're so damned religious.

How come you keep looking for Jesus under Mary Ann's skirt?

—I don't have Him, Billy Bob almost sobs, huge and faintly absurd in his frock, like a Reformation leader fresh out of the old dispensation, still shaking from his new vision, looking for a change of clothes. —I thought I did. Lord, that night I reckoned I was saved. I went down to the water and I believed in my soul Jesus was come for me.

His head droops. Even Benny can see this is for real: a nut hurting. Benny's eyebrows raise. He thinks this is type-casting with a vengeance, and at the back of his mind there flickers briefly the notion that a man can be lonely, afraid, bereaved of something that does not exist. Unless, of course, Benny thinks frowning, there exists a real correlative for every longing, which is absurd.

Billy Bob looks at Mary Ann, who has been studying him, pink tongue-tip between her teeth. —Did you ever have Him?

—Have who? I've had . . .

—Jesus. Did He ever come into you? When you was little? Did your mama and daddy ever tell you about Jesus?

Mary Ann is adorable in her weird mixed habit made up of garments belonging originally to the Carmelites, Sisters of Charity, and Daughters of the Cross. —Not much, she says gently. —My daddy flew. He didn't have much time for nothin' on the ground. My mama didn't pay no mind to anything but him. I heard a preacher once up to Minden, Louisiana. He told all about the promise of Abraham.

Billy Bob shakes his head. —Ain't none of us but lost out here.

The old bawd is kneeling in the sand, pinning up Mary Ann's skirt. —Speak for yourself, she mumbles through a mouthful of pins.

—Come on, Benny says, tired of the gabbling. —We've got a movie to make.

Scene opens. Camera on Billy Bob, hooded, hands folded, walking barefoot on shaded sand, rays of first light diffusing around him. His eyes are cast down. He meditates, eyes large with secret knowledge and pain that passeth understanding.

He is, for all this quietude, wrestling with angels. Light and darkness war within him. He is moved to wonder about the truth of all he knows. Strange things are in the wind. Is Mother Church, in fact, a harlot? Is priestly celibacy of Christ's teaching—or a snare and a delusion perpetrated by centuries of wicked prelates? Hypostatic union? Salvation by grace alone? What of the Sacrament? And, mainly, that celibacy bit. Something transcendant seems to tickle his manhood. He wonders what it all means, as he scratches interesting, possibly lewd signs into the sand with his toe.

Camera rises from quizzical look at peculiar marks scrawled in sand with toe. Rises to examine distant line of thick close-growing oaks covered with bizarre strands, bangles, sashes and twists of gray Spanish moss. Trees shadowy and ill defined. Sun not yet high enough to illuminate vague hint of movement within or beyond them. Some sylphlike uncertain tremor that seems for a moment to take form, only to dissolve again as the camera's anxious eye attempts to fix it.

This hour of dawn is a holy and mysterious time, or so Benny imagines his monk from Mississippi whispering on the sound-track. He shudders and makes a mental note to look around for someone else to do the voice dubbing. Mary Ann's will do: Southern accent for a cunt is fine. Billy Bob's is a horror. Actually, Benny recalls, Dr. Aorta has a fine voice. Deep, assured. A kind of special quality you might expect in a religious man. He thinks it might be worth a try. Everybody has a streak of ham in him somewhere. He hopes to use Dr. Aorta as one of the masked Inquisitors in a later scene anyhow. And . . .

Benny's face lights up. Sure. That's it. He can use Aorta for the Grand Inquisitor. Only he will dub in Billy Bob's voice. A blood-thirsty sadistic medieval cardinal or whatever they were. With a Mississippi accent. Benny closes his eyes. It is not arrogance for creative genius to recognize itself in action.

Meanwhile, back in the woods, that gauzy vision is beginning to take shape. Billy Bob has fallen to his knees on the sand, head down, is praying for this chalice of creeping inexpressible venery to pass from him. He covers his face. God is far away.

Camera rises fitfully, uncertainly from Billy Bob's monkish

agony. There, coming past the final barriers of moss and shadow, is an apparition not calculated to allay gross visions. Yea, she moves across the sand upon tiny sandaled feet. She is swathed in the dark motley of some multiconvent. But the habit is caught tightly at her waist, and the flowing skirt is hiked up to her thighs. To make walking in the wilderness easier, Benny has proposed.

She pauses, seeing Billy Bob in the throes of anxious prayer. Her hands loose the folds of her skirt, release the tight cinctured rosary around her waist. Modesty takes its last trick. She breathes deeply, the sound of that single breath breaking Billy Bob's passionate meditation. His eyes raise, catch hers. Each bumps deep into the other's soul. Benny's camera grinds on.

As if, Benny likes to describe it, in a dream, Billy Bob the monk rises to his feet. He smiles, granted this visitation. God is no closer, but this child—no, this young woman. Mayhap she is a messenger. But no matter.

And this vision from the moss-strewn trees. Is she petrified? Not exactly. Rather she sees before her the incarnation of what has been on her mind for several years, despite the advice of her confessor and frequent appeals to every likely saint from Michael to Jude. She burns now, recalling, despite innate modesty, how it has not been possible to lay this phantasm of lust. Perhaps she will lay it now.

The monk lifts up his arms, holds them out to this precious vision. The sleeves of his robe fall aside to reveal strong firmly muscled arms glowing golden red as fresh sunbeams kindle the curly hair of his wrists, outline the thickness of his biceps. He wonders what message this angel may bear. Will she give unto him some heavenly remedy for the hot thigh, the itching groin, the mad specters of flesh, the parted lips, the white teeth, the rounded limbs which have reduced his monkdom to a shambles of alternate sensual groveling and terrified resignation? The worst of both worlds. Now surely some revelation is at hand.

Indeed. As if in trance, this dark-eyed harbinger approaches him. But what? In the name of His bloody sweat, what does it mean? For she removes her starched white headdress, veil and all, and tosses it aside. It falls amongst briars, and is lost to sight. Her hair, long and richly brown, catches the sun's fumbling beams, enlarges them, and broadcasts a radiance of its own. As she comes nearer, her hands move slowly at her waist, loosening the age-dimmed rosary passed on to her from some anonymous dead nun of the convent who held world, flesh, and king of evil at bay with its rough ugly beads. The rosary looks like a slender articulated serpent lying on the cool sand.

And, God's wounds, the obscuring habit falls away from her shoulders. Billy Bob the monk staggers back as the enveloping robe slips lower and lower, revealing her smooth breasts, brown nipples warmer than buds on the trees nearby, hips and thighs round and rich as tan marble. His eyes widen. Is this the message? What is he to make of it? Satanic influence? Is she but another, a more delectable and convincing chimera? Or is Monseigneur telling him that Love is the Thing? That mind and archaic fear have conspired against heart and body, but that at last he is free? Could it be that what the world calls sin is, in fact, the chiefest virtue? Once, he recalls (according to Benny, who wants this thing to rise above the level of mere gash-game), as a novitiate, a fellow student laughingly suggested that Satan had won the war in heaven, that all moral teaching of restraint, of humbling the flesh, was the unnatural raving of an impotent fiend who somehow had stormed the mercy seat, had cast down the god of love, appropriating His name and place, even His strength, to reign over unwitting man. But such memories dissolve as she comes near. His hands, as if controlled from without, tear at the rough wool of his holy garb. His robe forms a crumbled pattern, dark and ignored, against sand the color of sun-warmed flesh.

Benny backs away slowly, letting his camera touch the tree-tops, lurch crazily amongst the leafy branches, curving over toward the quiet water of the lake, covered with bright golden wrinkles, flashing coins of rich sunlight.

Then back suddenly: they cross the last few feet and instants of space and time between, touch, kiss, hands moving over each other's bodies. Then, as if it were a slow-motion demonstration of sumo, their legs intertwine, and the beautiful nun falls backward slowly, gracefully to the sand. Her naked monk falls too, his body moving between her legs as they reach the warming earth beneath. Her hands frame his face. Close-up. He smiles and whispers some inanity. Her eyes are closed. Her heels dig into his back, bringing him closer. Pan in on her face. Eyes open as he penetrates, lips part, white teeth, bit of pink tongue. Pain, but heavenly pain. It hurts beautifully. His eyes are glazed, hands move up from her hips, along her sides to cup finally over her trembling breasts. Her head arches backward, long hair trailing in the sand as she feels his first surge. She draws from him as gladly as he gives, something inside her shouting with the voice of a high wind (so Benny has it noted for dialogue), *This, this, this* is a sacrament.

Well, why not? It is, Benny thinks, his own groin swelling in sympathy, a hell of a lot better than swallowing motor oil. Maybe hers is holy. Maybe this is holy. How about maybe everything is holy? Benny keeps the camera going. How about nuts?

—Okay, he calls out as he closes the shutter slowly to a pinpoint and changes from telephoto to wide-angle. —Okay, that's plenty. You can stop it.

But neither monk nor nun pays him any mind. They seem to believe in, if not the Method, at least the follow-through. Mary Ann bites Billy Bob's ear, her hands moving from one part of his body to another. He buries his head between her breasts, kissing, rooting. They roll over, Mary Ann suddenly dominant. She seems to be an accomplished roughrider.

—Listen, that's enough, Benny calls out again, his own temperature beginning to rise. He sheds his seersucker coat and sets his camera aside. Next is a beach scene and they have to get on with it. Mrs. Mailer has given no guarantee on how long the Negroes will contain their curiosity—or whether they will give warning or take to the woods if trouble should crop up.

At his side, the old bawd sits on a piece of cypress log. She watches Mary Ann and Billy Bob, her head moving from side to side as if watching a peculiar sort of tennis match.

—Jesus, she croaks. —Even with religion, it makes you want some, don't it?

—I don't know, Benny chokes. —I don't know. I don't have any religion.

The old baggage smacks her lips and hikes her skirt. —It does me good to see them young people havin' a good time. Don't hardly anybody have a good time any more. Nobody got the grit to stay with it. Look at 'em.

—Yeah, Benny groans, unbuttoning his shirt, pulling off his tie.

—I never had nothin' as good as that boy. When you look back, it's awful to know you never really had the . . .

Barring certain uproarious endearments, it could be a wrestling match, or a fight to the death between a Spartan and an Amazon.

Benny is trying to picture the next scene. Believe it or not, he makes a frame with his fingers and stares out toward the water's edge. There is a fairly long section clear enough . . . his crotch throbs; he hears the Venus and Adonis thing continuing back there. As he singlemindedly studies the shore, trying to ignore this absurdity behind him, he notices a piece of flotsam in the distance, a bundle of rags or the remains of a picnic lunch which eases up onto the sand and lurches heavily from side to side as new breakers roll solemnly along the beach.

—Okay, Benny calls again. —How about it? You're screwing off on my time.

—Leave 'em alone, the old crone breathes heavily. She is down on the sand close to them now, her mouth wide as a cod's, her rheumy eyes staring like those of a Bavarian peasant caught by some freakish mischance on stage in the midst of *Die Walküre*. Benny turns and cannot believe what he sees her doing.

—Stop it, he howls, running toward them, tearing at his belt and fly with one hand, reaching for Mary Ann's slender thrashing ankle with the other.

✥ ❧

Christopher is used up. When he reaches the apartment it is almost dawn. There is still the stench of burned paper and wood in his nostrils, woven into the fabric of his clothes. Beyond that, there is a deeper odor, but Christopher, hands shaking, legs ready to go under, is determined to think that the rest is no more than the smell of his own scorched cortex. He finds the bed, touches a clean sheet as if it were one more figment of his dementia. He starts to rise, to find his mother's bed, and feels his legs begin to unhinge again. This time he accepts the sheet as if it were his shroud.

Some time later, it seems to Christopher that he awakens. Refreshed. Not simply rid of the shakes and attendant horrors, but truly revived. He breathes deeply and stands up. He has never felt better. He remembers suddenly and with perfect unwavering clarity everything: that lamb sacrificed to his rifle, his father's pale fat obscene hands, his uncle's cold suspicious eyes. He remembers it all: his mother's cheek against his own as they parted at the dock, Father Madden and the tortured beast behind him on the wall. He remembers Dr. Aorta's heavy laughter and the glow of something burning, burning, behind the slitted grate in the bowels of Staff-o-Life. The time of his ordination and of his turning away are a single fused instant. Even as he prostrates himself, he is rising against that promise; as he rises, he feels himself falling before the altar until it is all one motion without beginning or end, without pause or willful determination.

He shakes his head slowly, and then walks through the darkness toward his mother's room.

—I heard you, her voice says softly. —I heard you call out. I wanted to come to you.

—No, Christopher hears himself saying evenly. —No. I've come to you.

—It's late.

—I took the wrong road: every turning took me somewhere I didn't want to go.

—Where do you want to go? she asks. Her voice is that of a young girl, lacking undertones, without the cool certainty he has come to know, to expect. It is the right voice exactly, at last.

He folds back the sheet gently, without hesitation. She lies nude beneath it, legs curled, arms crossed, hands resting on the gently curved perfection of her belly. She stares up at him in the darkness. He leans over and kisses her lips, then each of her breasts. —You've been here before, she whispers.

—A long time ago, he tells her. —I had to go away.

—Everybody goes away, she says, raising her arms to circle his neck. —And then everbody comes back. It doesn't matter what we do. We all end the same.

He lies down beside her, taking her into his arms, smiling as he thinks of a universe full of dead ends, stopped up with nullities. But only one path to find soon or late. And time enough to find it. He feels her turn, feels her lips against his cheek. —It doesn't make any difference, she whispers as he returns the kiss. —We'll always be this way. Won't we?

Something like mountains and leafless olive trees, a taste of brass and dry wine flows through him.

—I think so, Christopher says, turning to embrace her again. —I don't see it any other way.

—Don't you worry, she whispers, her voice growing softer, more distant. —Don't you ever worry again.

—No, Christopher says, slipping away in more directions than he can comprehend, —I'm through worrying.

And later, as much as centuries it seems, he begins to rouse. For an instant, he feels the chill iron of an old fear rising. But it dies even before he can identify it surely. And he awakens amidst that same certain peace. In his own bed and alone. He remembers, or thinks he remembers, what has passed, and he walks into his mother's room. He expects he will take the day off. Maybe they will go to Arnaud's or Brennan's. They will be together a lot from now on.

He stops at her door, forehead wrinkling. The room is empty. Not simply unoccupied, but empty. The bed is neatly made as if no one has slept in it within memory. The closet door hangs open, revealing its emptiness. Christopher leans against the wall, arms folded, studying the room's featureless quietude. She is gone, he knows, even before he notices a small envelope propped against the whiteness of a folded counterpane.

She is gone, and he feels as if certain of his senses have been removed with her. But he feels neither fear nor loneliness nor even the racking uncertainty which has been a part of every mood for as long as he can remember. He picks up the envelope and carries it back to the parlor and sets it down while he pulls on clean underwear. There is a half-burned cigar lying in the ashtray next to him. Christopher lights it and leans back on the sofa. That, he considers, was quite a dream. The result of heightened and morbid consciousness after the mess in Staff-o-Life's subcellar. But, he frowns, it does not feel like dreams feel afterward: nothing vague and edgeless about it. Clear and warm—not only undreamy but even in retrospect untouched by the awe and repulsion proper to unnatural acts. Christopher inhales the rank smoke of the raveled butt. He has come full circle; it may be a great crime to return to the place from whence we come.

He shrugs and opens the envelope slowly, blowing a cloud of smoke at it. His eyes skate over the page, squinting through the smoke at small, surprisingly neat script:

> . . . you need to be alone now because you know and don't know and it could stay that way on center forever. We are so scared and lazy we stay where we are even if where we are is a garbage pit. . . .

Advice to a Young Explorer, Christopher thinks. Or Façade for a Bill of Divorcement.

> . . . we have been us, which is all right for me but not for you. You have never been you yet. Us is all right afterward. I am so ashamed of the me that sent you off where those crazy priests sold you on Jesus. For a while I thought at least wanted to think okay, that will be him. But that was me lying to myself. What kind of little kid gets hung up in Jesus? . . .

Saints, Christopher thinks wryly. And disturbed children. Which could be the same thing. Or some kid so lonely that all his cells shiver. Some kid who would go for the devil if he smiled and stretched out his hand, and said, little boy . . .

> . . . if it's not one thing it's another. You can get off one sugar-tit and go right onto another one. I want you to walk your own way no matter what, and anyhow I have to go to see somebody . . .

Not Father who lies chaste till the great and final rising in a Falangist grave. Nor Uncle who will turn up one day probably confused with Indian remains by a coed on a field trip for Geology 1—unless he went beyond the Arbuckles in search of tits unsugared. Who is she after? Christopher feels, surprised by the feeling, beyond caring overmuch. He would like to believe that she has left somehow to clear a path for him. But where? he wonders, blowing a last burst of smoke into the room's shadowed corners. He finishes the letter as he stands and walks into the kitchen.

> . . . so I will see you sometime. Not in Shreveport or New Orleans, and not soon probably, but you be on the lookout for me. I love you so much I will wait for you wherever I settle and will send word one day.

Christopher pours a cup of yesterday's coffee, or thinks so. Then, tasting it, he realizes that she has brewed a new pot before leaving. So that she must have made the bed. And left this morning. Which means that weird dream could have something of crazy substance. He shrugs, pours more coffee, and walks out onto the iron balcony beyond the parlor. He sips and looks out over Royal Street, wondering which way to go. And what to do. What to look for. Below, the street is still dark. Storefronts shimmer with the multiple reflection of early sunlight flashing from above. An Italian vegetable and fruit vendor pushes his cart toward the French Market, pleased by the cool shadows, the unloaded weight of his cart. As he comes abreast of the balcony, he glances upward and sees Christopher in black trousers and white undershirt, chin dark with three days' beard, staring out over the city. The vendor squints, pauses. In days past, it has been a good window. Above, the man sips coffee from a cup held before him; his lips move, and the vendor shrugs and moves on. Some days are pure treasure. Others are hot and fleshless as the bones of hell.

◆§ ֍◆

—There's about a million ways to get killed in this world, Billy Bob is telling Boundoch. —And you're tryin' the quickest and easiest one of the bunch.

Decorum has returned, in a manner of speaking. The crone is helping Mary Ann back into part of her habit. Billy Bob, still naked, is seated on Boundoch's chest, one hand tightly woven around his windpipe, the other balled into a fist. Billy Bob has never liked this neat little Jew. There is something scary about small neat men who shrug off Jesus and make informal movies.

Boundoch is slowly strangling. He realizes that Billy Bob is not trying to kill, is only angry and deciding what to do about him. There is a chance that he can come out of this alive if he lies absolutely still, smiling and smiling, apology and shame oozing out of his face. He tries, choking, to register mollifying sentiments.

—Urgh, he says placatingly. —Urgh awough.

—Never mind, Billy Bob frowns. —Just you never mind. It ain't no sense in you losing control of yourself. Man cookin' hamburgers in a café don't go to eatin' all of 'em. What kind of feller are you?

—Kroaugh, Benny urges. He can hardly see. Things are losing their edges, going dim. To die in an alien land under the hands of a huge naked guy. He tries to turn his mind to last things, but there is a truck or a hippopotamus in his throat, and his mind drifts. He cannot quite remember what things are last.

Billy shifts his weight, still pondering what to do with this lizard. His hand eases slightly and Benny gulps air. The crone stands over them, watching Benny's face carefully.

—Reckon he's dead? she asks. —He never was worth a shit. Paid awful. Never had no respect.

—I thought you was religious, Billy Bob says accusingly.

—Sure, the old bawd answers. —I got Jesus all right. It ain't me chokin' the sonofabitch. I'm just watchin'. I'm too old and frail to keep you from it. May as well enjoy what I can't help.

Mary Ann is still naked from the waist up, prepared for the next scene. —Why don't you get off him? she asks. —He didn't do nothin'.

—He tried, Billy Bob snarls, letting go Benny's throat.

—Didn't try nothin' that don't happen every day, she tells him. —I ain't really a nun. I'm a workin' girl.

Benny lies doggo, sucking in great volumes of air. Breathing is a novelty. It is delicious, worth making a career of, he thinks. As his head clears, he becomes conscious of Billy Bob's great weight on his chest.

—Listen, he gags, amazed at the sound of his own voice. —It was . . . a mistake. I didn't . . .

—Shut up, Billy Bob tells him impatiently, still considering. Mary Ann's words sink deep. They are enough to turn a warm-hearted boy mean. What is sold is irrecoverable—except by the systematic slaughter of every purchaser. Billy's freckled shoulders slump. You can't cut off every dick in New Orleans. It is no use strangling this bush-league monster. Oh that all mankind had a single pecker.

—Listen, Benny starts again. But Billy Bob heaves himself up and looks for his robe. The world is a close place with every exit, every nook and cranny accounted for, blocked with slime. He walks down toward the beach disconsolately. Maybe the world is a penal colony and everybody in it is paying for enormities they cannot remember, committed somewhere else under another star.

—Get up, Mary Ann tells Boundoch. —Let's get this thing going. I got a appointment in town this afternoon.

—Listen, I can't . . . Benny begins, rubbing his throat, feeling of his ribs. —I can't go on. I feel . . .

—You better go on, Mary Ann tells him. —I wouldn't fuck around with him if I was you. That boy is real sensitive. You ain't never seen him really upset. You don't want that. Do you?

—Jesus, Benny croaks. —No, I don't want . . . Where's my camera? Listen, you keep him off me, will you?

Mary Ann does not like Benny. She feels a cold distant mood sweep her when he is near. Professional control permits her to neutralize the shudder she feels. But she is sorry that strangling him would be a lot of trouble. She would not mind watching.

—You've got an appointment this evening, too, he tells her. —Don't forget that. You know where and when?

Mary Ann stares at him, expressionless. —I know, she says. —You don't have to say anything else about it.

—Come on, Benny says, some portion of his aplomb returned. —We want to finish this scene. We can't stay out here all day.

Meanwhile Billy Bob walks apart, kicking sand and an occasional mussel shell along the moss- and leaf-strewn beach. He squints out across winking medallions floating and dipping on the lake's uneasy surface. He remembers, for no reason, going to a revival with his grandmother, listening to the strange crude poetry conceived in terms of a Ptolemaic universe dead, according to learned men, for almost four hundred years. And how Jesus, up from hell, down from heaven, walked upon the water, each sweet naked foot on one of those shimmering ripples. Moving forever closer to the shore where hungry, thirsty and maimed await His coming. Why do the waters shake like that, mammaw? Cause of the wind, honey. Where do the wind come from? That's God aworkin'. That's His breath that consumes and heals.

Billy Bob lifts his head and sniffs. It is a sweet breath, compounded of a hundred odors. Of things he knows, unknown things, and things he seems to have known once but cannot quite bring to mind.

As he reaches the water's edge, he raises his eyes, squints against the reflected sunlight. There before him lies the flotsam he had seen from back among the trees. Only it is not a pasteboard box or a chunk of driftwood. It is the body of a girl.

She lies in the draggled sheet as if it were her shroud, and a weeping swell runs up the shore, embraces her, kisses her cheek, goes back again and forces up the sand to bury her. And every time it parts sheds tears upon her, till at last with a kind of unresolved unwilling pace, winding its waves one in another, like a man that folds his arms or wrings his hands for grief, ebbs from the body and descends as if it would sink down into the earth to hide itself for shame of such a deed.

Arms folded across scant breasts, the sheet white as if it were freshly washed and wound around her waist to hide the secret wreckage of her loins, she lies eyes closed, thin freckled face purged of agony, composed as if her last glance had met that of a lover; as if she sleeps in certain faith of a new awakening.

—Jesus, Billy Bob moans. He kneels beside the girl, recalling some earlier meeting. It was that bar. The girl who talked and talked. Who knew Kansas City and Tulsa. Or Dallas.

Who needed some kind of work. Who had been offered to Boundoch by the dago barkeep. And he had decked the sleazy bastard with a bottle. And now.

And now she lies looking more feminine, more like a woman than ever life and powder and rouge had permitted.

—What is it? Mary Ann asks, coming up behind him. —My God. What's she . . .

—Ask him, Billy Bob coughs. —Ask that nasty little sonofabitch.

Benny is covered with cameras and equipment. He is ready to shoot. —Come on, he is saying. —This light is getting strong. It'll change quality. It won't match those last frames. We need . . . What the hell?

—Yeah, Billy Bob stares at him. —What the hell you got to say about this? Did you have that dago kill this little girl? What did she do? Say she was gonna turn you in? Maybe she knew somethin' about you, huh?

—What are you talking about? Benny gurgles, his throat still tender. —I never saw . . .

—In that bar. Where you come across me. That dago looked at you and you made some kind of sign.

Benny stares down at the girl. —Oh, he mumbles finally. —Oh, that little red-headed cunt. That afternoon. All I did was shake my head.

—You mean a shake of your head and that dago kills 'em?

Benny's eyes are wide. This plowboy, this rough beast may jump him again. —I mean I told him no, I couldn't use her. I got a good place there. You can't sell skin and bones. They want meat. I couldn't use her. That was all.

—Jesus, Mary Ann whispers, looking down, seeing suddenly and terribly some part of herself as if a piece of the future had fallen on the beach before her. —It sure was all.

Chapter Nine

High noon now in the Quarter, and hotter than the hinges of hell. Eggs could be poached on the street in front of St. Louis Cathedral. Mary Ann is walking through Jackson Park, frowning at the old general, at his unstinting élan. She wonders what keeps that brazen hand with its quaint hat from melting and running like wax. Leaving the park, she averts her eyes from the cathedral. She hates these churches with their tall spires pointing upward as if they could summon God from His heaven. It is silly to hate this way. It would make more sense to hate electric circuits or cotton planters, but hates are not chosen: one makes do with what is given.

Decatur Street is jammed with dusty old cars and pickups and stake-bed trucks. People are loading produce and unloading burlap bags of coffee, hustling barrels and boxes in and out of small warehouses. The hot moist air here is laced with rich odors, thatched with dank stench. Spices, preserved fish, sweat, dried fruits, urine, the smell of cigars boxed and cigars smoked. Somewhere there seems to be an open container of antipasto. Someone is eating rollmops wrapped in fresh French bread. There may be English mustard. Mary Ann sniffs and shivers. It is like olfactory technicolor. Almost enough to take her mind off that imaginary strumming in her belly. Last night she lay beside Billy Bob, arms wrapped around her pillow as if it were a privileged trick. And she dreamed. That what she had inside her was not a baby at all. It was a minstrel show with white suits and black faces. Dozens of grease-painted peo-

ple singing and humming. Down on the levee. A whole steamboat inside there. With a man prancing and cavorting and singing "Sewanee River" and "Old Folks" and mugging and
laughing till somebody else in a straw-boater with a big banjo
took his place and started playing

louder and louder with the interlocutor and the end men and
the line all humming or maybe even singing except not so you
could understand because the banjo got louder and faster,
its notes falling out of the air like shrapnel, and the banjo itself
seeming to grow and grow until it overwhelms its player and
goes on playing louder and faster:

Little girl . . . LITTLE GIRL . . .

It was one hell of a bad dream, and worse than that what
with waking up to a night sweat and then sick as a dog when
morning came. Mary Ann is not superstitious exactly, but with
a headful of bad recollections and a bellyful of trouble, a nightmare about some kind of monster banjo invading her bowels
seems inauspicious. Maybe that little turd Boundoch is right,
Mary Ann is thinking as she walks. Abortion is self-defense.
Getting knocked up is an occupational hazard, right? Right. If
a man got poisoned on the job, would he be honor-bound to
lay down and die of the poison? Naw. This whole thing is an accident, and the only thing is to make it right, and get on with
it quick.
Which would seem to be some kind of decision. But Mary
Ann is not satisfied. A decision ought to be taking something
on or getting shut of it without a lot of niggling ends hanging
on. This one will not lay down and be settled. It may be self-
defense or making an accident right, but it still feels funny.
Like a shoe that seems to fit, but pinches or rubs so subtly that
she cannot even tell just where the discomfort is.

Pirate's Alley is almost deserted. One thin girl wearing slacks and a sweatshirt bespattered with paint is sitting in a canvas chair next to some weird canvases. She wears a baseball cap over short-cut hair, and silver-lensed sunglasses. On the T-shirt it says *Manhattan Squash Club*. Mary Ann's eyebrows raise. The girl does not look like she could raise a radish. Her paintings, hung or leaning against the iron-fence surrounding the rear of the cathedral, don't even look like she could paint a squash.

That church, Mary Ann pauses, putting aside her sullen disgust. Ummm.

That's it. Chris. Who may be a second-rate stud and a piss-poor priest. But is all right. Not a screwing-machine or buck-nuts. Or likely to lie one way or the other. She is not much for asking advice, much less taking it. But when something keeps nibbling after it has been thought out, trying it on somebody else makes good sense. Before that nibble turns to a gnaw.

She passes the stairs to Dr. Aorta's apartment without looking, smells tortillas and something like vinegar coming from above while one voice, seeming to ooze out of the wall, asks where the extra roll of paper is. As she reaches Christopher's door, another voice, down from the ceiling, replies that there is no extra. —Use the *Times-Picayune*.

As she knocks, a third voice wells up out of the floor. —*What have I done?* Mary Ann shrugs involuntarily. God knows. Worse. What are we doing? Aw shit.

—Come on in.

The room is unlighted. There is in the South an unspoken but nonetheless real belief that even a single fifty-watt light bulb adds to the heat. Across the bar of shadowed furniture, Mary Ann sees a silhouette, feet propped on the iron balcony railing.

—Chris?

—Yes.

—I wanted to talk to you.

—Come on over. Get yourself a beer out of that tub.

Mary Ann squints at him. He sprawls in a straight-backed chair, his profile at right angle to the door. One half of his face is in shadow, the other half bright as a coin in reflected sunlight. He wears a T-shirt and black trousers. There is a bottle of beer in one hand, a cigar in the other. The shirt of his Staff-o-Life uniform is hung across a chair like the hide of a scarecrow. Christopher does not look different, May Ann thinks, but he looks like he might *be* different.

—I missed you, she tells him. —I was hopin' you'd come by.

Christopher smiles and gargles a mouthful of beer. —I lost my dice, he says. —Anyhow, I don't want to cut in on Billy Bob. He's a good boy.

Mary Ann sits down on a sofa cushion dropped on the floor near the French windows. —You can't talk to him. He ain't got but one thing on his mind. Night and day, at home or away.

Christopher smiles. —I don't expect that's his fault. It's you, honey. Something about you.

—I need to talk to somebody, she goes on seriously. —I need to in the worst way.

Christopher's feet slam down onto the balcony. —You mean it, don't you?

—Oh boy, I guess.

He pushes the chair away and sits down across from her, trying hard to ignore her breasts under a thin cotton blouse. There are tiny crescents of moisture under her arms, and beads of sweat on her forehead. Her legs are smooth and tan. Her hands, curled in her lap, draw his eyes. She is a masterpiece of composition. Wherever he sets his gaze, it is drawn, by one route or another, back to her womanhood. He reaches for a fresh beer, uncaps it and sets it between his legs.

—What's wrong? he asks gently, taking conscious care to keep his hands on neutral ground.

—Wow, Mary Ann answers, leaning back against the doorjamb. —It ain't but everything gone all to hell. In a handcart.

—Sometimes it looks that way.

—Looks nothing. This time I've done dug a hole and pulled it in after me.

—The first time I saw you, you had trouble.

—I ain't had nothing but trouble for so long that a good streak of prosperity would kill me. But this time takes the cake.

Christopher sips beer and stares at the awnings on the building opposite. Cream with black stripes. When she wants to give trouble a name, she will. Until then he will sit like the frog footman and stare. And drink moderately. Keeping his eyes off her. Christopher has not yet got a rape chalked up. He pictures himself on the Ground of Being, shouting, *I never raped anybody. I admit the rest, but I never* . . . which would surely keep him out of the sophists' circle.

Then it occurs to him that a rape more or less would make no difference. The point would never come up. They do not try you for stealing a bicycle if you shoot ten people peddling away from the scene. Dr. Aorta is right: a bad priest has nothing more to fear. Christopher sees himself amongst a mob of felons at the Judgment: he is trying to hide behind two Gestapo officers, a covey of sodomists and an arsonist whose speciality was convents, orphanages and homes for the blind. No use. He is hustled forward to the head of the line. Famous faces fade as he moves to take his place. Small brush on upper lip and hair over mad brown eyes. Bullet-head and jut-jaw. Handlebar moustache and tiny rat's eyes—who was fortunate enough to drop out of that Georgian Seminary before he was ordained. Thus losing his place to Christopher. *Never mind the petty criminals,* a nonvoice thunders. *Bring me Nieman. I want Nieman.*

—I'm pregnant, Mary Ann blurts, without changing expression.

—Oh, Christopher answers, back from Judgment. Or pre-Judgment, diving back into existence with a last wry query: does he believe in all this, or not? Leaving Alexandria, the assumption had been not. Just now he wonders. —Oh, he repeats. —That's fine. Gee. What will you name it?

—Jesus Christ, Mary Ann groans.

—No, Christopher says absently. —Why not Francis Xavier? Or Ignatius?

—You stupid sonofabitch. I ain't married. Anyhow I can't have no kid. I got all I can do to see to myself.

Moderate jolt. Christopher is back now. —A kid? What do you know? How did that happen?

—Guess, Mary Ann says, about ready to leave.

—No, sit down. What do you expect to do?

—I expect to mess around talkin' to you and then goin' shoppin' and then havin' some coffee somewhere. And then come back here. To see that doc upstairs.

—Aorta? You want him to . . .

—I don't want him to marry me, Mary Ann snaps viciously. —He's supposed to be good. He knows how to take care of things.

—Oh brother, does he, Christopher says harshly. He may get pushed out of his place at Judgment yet. —You stay away from that mushy-eyed bastard, you hear me? He's a butcher.

—I don't give a shit if he's a baker in his spare time and a candlestick-maker on the side. I got this thing in me, and every time I think about it my skin goes to creepin'.

—That thing in you is somebody. A person, a baby.

—Lay off that stuff. You done give it up, remember?

Christopher stares at her. What does murder have to do with religion? If there is no Big Daddy, do you go to killing automatically? The answer comes as quickly as the question. Yes. Not everyone all at once. But yes. Sooner or later they go to killing. No reason not to. A million reasons, but no Reason. They will not go at it like hyenas smelling blood, but when it is convenient. More and more of them. Every chance they get.

—You can't have your own flesh and blood murdered. You can't do it.

—You talk crazy. It's an operation. Just like if you had a ingrown toenail.

—You mean a baby is like a wart or a hair growing the wrong way in your nose?

—I don't know. I just don't want it. I ain't got no use for it.

Christopher opens another beer quickly, chugs half of it. —You goddamned stupid cunt. You're not supposed to use it. It uses you. Like you did your mother, and she did hers, before her.

Mary Ann's eyes narrow. He is coming close to the point that itches her. She wants him to keep going. And she wants him to stop. —How come? she asks belligerently.

—How do I know? Who knows? But it's right. You can whore

and steal and maybe kill some spic that hard-times you. But you don't get a baby cut out.

Christopher is angry. He no longer needs that beer between his legs. He is deeply pissed and could crack her across her dull head with the empty bottle. He pulls two more, opens them, and passes her one. —Drink.

—I don't reckon . . .

—Drink. You're too dumb to talk to sober. Drink.

Mary Ann drinks. —You ain't answered. A insult ain't no answer.

Christopher sees his mother's deserted electric clock. He is late for the second round of his deliveries. Tough shit. The wops will have to wait for their manna. Housewives planning hot dogs and sloppy joes will have to bake biscuits and corn-bread. Or buy Brand X. From somewhere he hears a woman's voice: —What have I *dooone* . . .

He leans back, feeling the beer moving in and taking the high ground. He needs to watch it. When he drinks, that poor mangled beast from behind Father Madden's desk comes stum-bling after him, showing its ruined hands and feet, the gash in its side deep and wide enough to hold all groaning creation in-side. Just a little more. Beer is easy to measure. Just two more and he will be as loose outside as he has been inside since awak-ening this morning.

—That's right, he tells Mary Ann. —You're right. He thinks his speech is blurred just the least bit. That will be just fine. This is not a precise maneuver. It is, is becoming, a game for a life. Which is bloody and short and often of no discernible value. And simultaneously the beginning or the end of every-thing. So we fight.

—Because it's part of you. Because it *is* you. If you go let that animal cut it out, you'll be killing yourself. Something you can't get back.

—Ummm. Mary Ann reaches for another beer on her own. —I've done had so much of me killed, I reckon I could stand losin' some more. I mean, I guess you're right. It's me. But some fine life a baby of mine would have.

—Hell, there isn't any guarantee printed on your ass when you're born. It might only have one arm.

—That's some crap, Mary Ann shoots back. —It wasn't ever a crip born in the Downey family. Or a feeb neither. It'd be fine.

—Who do you expect the father . . . ? Christopher begins. And stops. Hard. Because he is counting weeks or days or something. He hears the beast stirring and crawling somewhere in the slums of his brain. Madden's monster calling for help. Or revenge. And with a passion colder than the depths of outer space, he knows who the father is. Or may. Or might be. So that, beer aside, the game's residual precision is shot to hell. He is no longer a felon priest trying to go through motions ground into habit. He is suddenly playing for a piece of himself. And for a wife he does not—may never—have. The game is colder now. Abstractions are gone with the wind. His looseness, that fine easy control of a man gambling big with someone else's money, is knocked into rubbish. Keepsies. One day it had to happen. The secret message graven on the backside of Moses' tablets, carved in small print on that terrible wooden cross behind Father Madden's desk. *One day thou shalt play for keeps. Knowing or not, as I choose, you will be faced with a gamble upon which your whole person depends.* Heaven, if there is such. Hell or its brief earthly equivalent—the universe, all suns and the worlds thereunder.

—Ah, Christopher whispers. —I see.

—See what? If you see the clear right in this, you're a hell of a lot smarter than I am, Mary Ann says bleakly.

—No, Christopher says. —No, not the right.

Not the right. Which is only a word, but the stakes. In some vague way. The nature of the game. Why it had never been much good before, and had gone all to hell for him. Because he had not known the stakes, not even the game. Which is not played with anything so fragile and tenuous and absurd as words or even actions exactly, but with thrusts, movements of the soul toward What Is. Or toward nothingness. A game which can be played and lost and ended without the player even realizing it is in progress. Because of the dry runs, the endless and meaningless practice sessions which go on ceaselessly until no one can tell when the sham ceases and the real game begins. Which is how He wants it, will have it. You know not the day nor the hour. But one day, one hour the horseshit stops. That time, that one time, looking to a fool no different from any other time, is what everything rides on. And having lost or won, a man goes on, not realizing that he has failed or passed.

—Ah, Christopher whispers, smiling, leaning back, his face full in the blinding sun, but unaware of its brilliance.

—Boy, that beer gets to you. I can see you ain't gonna . . . Mary Ann's voice trails off. She watches Christopher. She knows that expression. Or something close to it. The way a man looks when he has reached it, felt his seed flooding out of him, knowing or not knowing as he loses it, that he is himself invaded in that instant's ecstasy. Like a man diving upward in an old biplane.

—What do you know? Mary Ann asks him suspiciously. He is just the kind to have some vision.

—Listen, Christopher says quietly. —You don't want to make a mistake this time.

——*This* time? I ain't never been knocked up before. I been careful.

—No, I mean you don't want to do wrong. Not this time. You've got to stay away from Aorta.

Mary Ann stares out into the heat. —I don't know. Either way I go . . .

Christopher is turning cagey. There is no way to tell her what he knows. He has to lie his way to the truth. Or at least use irrelevancies. Appeal to the meat.

—If you go, you'll never come out again.

—Huh?

—I saw some of Aorta's work yesterday. He killed a girl.

Mary Ann's eyes are wide. —You're kiddin'. You never saw any such thing.

Christopher shrugs. —Last night he burned her. No, he tried to burn her. It was somebody else. Down in the basement of the bakery is an oven.

—I never figured it was that chancey.

Christopher takes two more beers. —Nothing to get excited about. This skinny red-headed little whore went to Aorta to have her own baby cut to pieces. Only she forgot the baby was part of her, that it was all one life. So he did what she wanted. He killed the baby.

—And her too.

—That was an accident. It's hard to take life and split it in two when it's not made to be split. Sometimes you miscalculate.

Mary Ann drinks silently. Christopher glances at the clock. There will be consternation amongst the grocery-market crowd by now. Phone calls, bad language, loud foreign voices assailing the ears of the Staff-o-Life operators.

—It ain't enough I got to sweat havin' the kid or not havin' it. I got to sweat my own hide, Mary Ann speculates gloomily. She pauses and finishes her beer. —You wouldn't kid me, would you?

Christopher is still grinning like a dollar-forty-nine Buddha. He is astounded by his luck. Millions are born; an exactly similar number die. But how many of those ephemeral flickering spirits have ever caught on? Christopher squints, suddenly seeing something more: Calvin. Saved by election, saved by God's untrammeled choice. Not by acts, but by God's own sweet whimsy. This could be it. Saved by solving the conundrum of existence. And he who suddenly is privy to the world's meaning would yield works as a tree yields fruit. Not willfully, but out of his joy, his bounty. And knowing that he can never know for certain which of those deeds is the essential one, he would, with wry good heart, turn his whole capacity against evil, against nothingness. This is half-assed theology, Christopher thinks, still smirking like a man betting his own fixed wheel.

—No, he tells Mary Ann. —I wouldn't kid about this stuff. I saw it last night. We . . . they . . . stuffed this body wrapped in a sheet down in a furnace.

—God Almighty, like them prison camps in the newspapers. That doc is a bad ass.

Mary Ann gets to her feet uncertainly. —Which don't help

me much. I still got to work this out. I don't know that you've helped me.

Christopher rises with her, pulls her close to him. —You mean I didn't tell you, go ahead? Let him cut out your kid and maybe slip and send you off with it? Some advice. Who do you reckon would give you that kind of advice? Do you have any enemies around here?

—I don't know, Mary Ann says softly, her eyes large and dark and fixed on his. —Do I?

Christopher blinks. —Listen, he hears himself saying. —If you wanted to . . .

—What?

—To have a place. For the baby.

—If I did, maybe the Salvation Army would have a spare shoebox. Listen, ole buddy, you don't see much. I only know how to do one thing. I can't do anything else you get paid for.

—Do you want to get married?

There's a first time for everything, Mary Ann thinks, her eyes wider than ever. An outright proposal by a reasonably sober man. With his pants on.

—You and me? she asks slowly. —Us?

—That baby could . . .

—Be yours?

—Yes. Couldn't it?

Mary Ann shakes her head indeterminately, somewhat sideways, a little up and down. —I never thought about it. I guess. I don't know. The way it is, I don't expect there's any way *to* know.

—It doesn't matter. There's you, too. You and the baby. That might be worth driving a bread truck for.

She kisses him slowly, not with or without passion. He returns it in kind. A probing kiss—continuation of the discourse. Statement and question exchanged simultaneously. —Gee, Mary Ann whispers. —I like you a whole lot. I liked you that first night in the bus station. And later. You didn't know what you were doin', but you went right after it.

—I'm a learner. You don't know what a learner I am. I could scare you.

—Ummm. I reckon I'll have to fit all this into it too.

—Into what?

—What I figure to do. The baby. That nut doctor that kills girls. You and me.

—You don't want to tell me now? Christopher asks softly, nuzzling her neck, tongue tracing a line across her shoulder, his hands lightly searching, uncommitted.

—No, Mary Ann breathes. —I can't. Not with you after me and all the rest of it. I got time. I got maybe five hours before I'm even supposed to . . . see that doctor up there.

—Ah. Maybe you should stay here. I could help you think.

—No. Mary Ann extricates herself from his arms, not especially wanting to. —There wouldn't be any thinkin'. You ain't about to help me think.

—That's right. You need to feel.

—And get felt. No, I got to think. This one time. I never needed to much before. And I mean not to get where I have to again. But I honest to God got to now.

She knows it too, Christopher is thinking gleefully, his groin under splendid control. She doesn't even know she does, but she knows she can't go wrong this time. It's made in the shade. My son will be a sneak thief. Or my daughter will knit jockey straps. Which will be just fine. I'll settle for a good healthy pigeon-poisoner.

—Later Mary Ann tells him. —Before I'm due at his place I'll come by here. All right?

Christopher's hand acknowledges. She moves into his arms again, tongue seeking his. He is without qualities in this métier, but there is inspiration. He smells salvation around, whatever that may be. —Sure. I'll be here.

She turns toward the door slowly as if waiting for Christopher to call her back. —I got to think, really.

—Sure. That's right. Good thinking.

Mary Ann grins, stunning him ever so slightly. He takes a step toward her, and still grinning she opens the door and peers back around it one last time. —I'll be back.

—Should I dress?

—Huh?

—Never mind. Maybe I'll undress.

—Don't mix me up. Do you love me any?

This time Christopher grins. —I love you. Both of you.

—Honest?

—Yes.

&~

It is only one more beer and a single flight of stairs to Dr. Aorta's apartment. Christopher pauses before the featureless door. On the other side is outer space, something cold and lethal, come from Uranus and Neptune to the warmth of the inner planets. Wow, he thinks. Thrilling Wonder Tales. A little more imagination and he'd be Diabolus.

Which is silly and baroque. Except that Dr. Aorta is surely the Adversary. The other. Yang against Ying. But for a change Ying has the cards. Owns the deck. Last of the big spenders. Laying a sheaf of souls on the line.

—Come, he hears in answer to his knock.

There are three fans aimed at Dr. Aorta. In front of each one is a large bowl with a twelve-pound chunk of ice in it. The room is cool and dank. One window is open, and occasionally a course of warm air eddies through the room, hinting of the furnace heat outside.

—I want to talk to you, Christopher says.

Dr. Aorta sits slumped on a kitchen chair shirtless. He looks like a great slab of pale dough sculpted into an approximation of humanity. —So, he answers. —Talk.

Christopher steps closer. There is a looseness, a spiritual dexterity associated with ultimate things. When you cannot lose partially but must be obliterated if things go wrong, there is a sense of freedom, he thinks. Of course. It's not my game any more. It's His. I can't lose. If I go all the way, risking everything there is to risk, it would be His loss, His defeat. The only way I can lose is to hedge, to hold back.

—There's a girl supposed to come this evening. She will probably not be here. If she shows up, you won't work on her.

Dr. Aorta's eyes behind his steel-rimmed glasses do peculiar things. As if iris, pupil, all parts, merge and sort themselves out again, only to dissolve once more.

—So, he answers, amused. —You are a commander now. Has Jesus come?

Christopher stares at him. —You'll think He's come riding a New Orleans police car if you mess with her.

—So. Christ the informer. Another interpretation of the Word. Jesus the Judas. All roles become one. I may one day hear confessions.

—You'll hear mine if you fuck with Mary Ann Downey. You'll hear it in a courtroom. While they're trying you for murder.

—Murder?

—The girl we burned . . . I mean the one you tried to burn. Just that one murder. Maybe they'll check around and have some other things to talk to you about. Questions. How do you like questions?

Dr. Aorta shakes his head slowly. Worms turn, but men rarely. He squints at Christopher as if he were a mad dog. Perhaps he can be soothed.

—Ah, the girl from the house. Mrs. Mailer's friend. You like her?

Christopher ignores him. —Don't fool with her. Tell her you can't do it. Tell her it's against the law.

—Or you will speak to the authorities?

—I will speak to all authorities. About many things.

—There is no proof. Only scattered ashes. The Negroes will say nothing.

Christopher shrugs. The ground is soft, but not beyond going onward. —When they find out I'm a . . . was a priest, they're going to come looking. Then maybe I'll ask them to look at your passport with a magnifying glass. Or send your fingerprints to the High Commissioner of Germany. I'm not even counting on what you burned there last night. I'm thinking of what you burned three years ago. All over Europe.

—Sheer guessing. I was a helpless victim. I came here to start a new life.

—Then you won't mind them having a good close look at your old one. If you're telling the truth, they'll feel very sorry for you. Then you can sue me for defamation or something.

A new tack, Dr. Aorta thinks. —The girl is barely pregnant. I will do the job and send her to you in perfect health. The other one, she was too far along.

—I want the baby to live. I don't want you to touch the girl. You understand?

Jawohl, Dr. Aorta understands very well. Christopher has lapsed. Back from doubt into lunacy. He is God's benison and God's scourge again. Possibly without even knowing it. There is no use cajoling or threatening him. The madness has taken hold, and there is only one way to pacify a mad dog. Dr. Aorta knows about this kind of thing. He is a specialist.

—Well. So. The girl will come. And I will send her away. Good.

—Very good, Christopher answers. —And there will be no operation. Not even an examination. She will not even come into your apartment. We don't want all the messiness of a *fait accompli,* do we?

—No, Dr. Aorta says honestly. —We want no mess. Everything will stay neat and orderly. Your God likes order, yes?

—I don't know about that. I never asked Him. If I needed to know, I would.

A sad case, Dr. Aorta thinks as Christopher steps out and shuts the door. A terminal case. He will be preaching on the street corner soon, calling down Elijah and consecrating the contents of his bread truck. He needs help. Otherwise no matter what is done about the girl, he might feel an overpowering need for public confession. Which is an embarrassment. He must be helped, of course.

The room is dark and almost cool. Outside the sun is beginning to mellow, to lose its urgent strength. Time for a walk. To see certain people. Who can help. Of course.

Chapter Ten

↍

Mr Christian Blackman has been catching hell all afternoon. The calls keep coming down. Where is the truck? Where is Nieman? As if he knew. As if there were any way he could know. Suddenly even the lower depths are no refuge. All afternoon Negroes had come down with questions, sniffing the faded odor of burnt flesh, wondering at the stench, but with no way of knowing, even suspecting what it might be. Finally a white man had come down to grill him, holding a handkerchief across his nose, his white shirt and two-tone shoes absurd amongst the deep shadows of the subbasement.

But now it has stopped. There is a ring gear and a pinion to be reassembled, and a distributor to be wired. Nothing hard now that the traffic is gone.

Mr Christian's Horse is cantering. There had been a bag or two from Mrs. Mailer. His retainer. Half a bag in the morning, and the rest tonight. Maybe he could even pick up another slice from that doc. That doc owes him. He is tired of short rations. It seems hard times will go on forever. Nobody knows what the Celestial Cat's Ass will be up to next. No way to get to Him. Just as well try to crash into the sun. Hummm. Crash. Into.

Mr Christian lays the pinion down softly. His hands are in pretty good shape. None of those cramps. His feet hurt, and there is that permanent stitch in his side as if he had been running for twenty years. But these are as constant as the heat and dampness of his basement. He does not notice them unless something calls them to mind. Humph. Crash. Into. There is something in this. But it would take more than half a bag to get it into focus. Wait till evening. In the cool, with a bag and a half to gallop on, maybe he will crash into an inspiration. Hummmm.

&✥ &✥

There are clouds now, and it may rain. It does that here. One minute the sun will be searing brick and concrete and flesh indiscriminately. The next, huge thunderheads will materialize over Lake Pontchartrain, others floating in from the Gulf. And the city will go dark. It will be suddenly much cooler, and even the sounds of traffic seem muted. Then the rain comes. Not slowly or softly. Not small reasonable droplets. It shakes down in wave after wave of impenetrable streams, so dense that no windshield wiper can fend it off, no raincoat keep it out.

It is the quiet time now. Shady and so cool that Boundoch walks toward the Café du Monde sniffing the tranced air, head moving from side to side, up and down. He sees the boiling clouds high above, long tired rays of the sun slicing through an opening in them miles away. The day's work is done. Now for an afternoon coffee, an hour of watching sluggish traffic filter past Jackson Park. It is possible to go to sleep under that awning, to dream of international fame: King of the Blue Screen. Czar of the Underground Movies. And then to awaken in the depth of twilight, car lights lacing together. Slow groups of tourists moving down the length of the French Market.

He walks down St. Peter Street toward Decatur. There is an ice-cream parlor, a curio shop. The rest is blank doors in brick walls. A few garages. One entry long boarded up with a For Rent sign fading into gray one-by-sixes nailed across the paintless door. A raindrop falls. Just one. It is all the warning he can expect.

By the time he has run all the way to the café, skulking and staggering from one overhanging roof to the next awning, Benny Boundoch is not himself. His aplomb is gone. His neat summer suit looks like a used croker sack. His shirt is wilted, shoes splashed and discolored. It is impossible to be well-

groomed in the South. The milieu is irresistible. Things go dif-
ferently. Boundoch shivers and slouches to a table, hating the
sound and feeling of water in his shoes.

Coffee, and a single *bagnet* at a table well back from the
blowing, drifting rain. He sits like a drenched rat watching it
fall in sheets out of the sky. *The Question* is begun, but the
tough scenes remain to do. More characters remain to be cast.
He wants to test Mrs. Mailer as a prioress. What about Marshall
Fields and Mr Christian as a pair of Moors, hired by Dr.
Aorta, the Grand Inquisitor, to do the dirty work, the kind of
thing that has to be done, but which no Christian wants to
touch?

Benny squints as a single spear of late sun pierces the clouds.
The rain is tapering off, and insistent thunder fades out downriver. Now there is only the slow drip of water from the roof,
and the distant hissing of it under the tires of passing cars.
Benny relaxes and sips his coffee to the dregs. Everything seems
abnormally green. The sun is out again, but it is only a pastel
counterfeit now. His eyes light on the patch of trees and
shrubs across the street. It brings to mind stories his grandmother told of the old country. Dracula country. Benny smiles.
An endless sweep of green forest, and deep within that wilderness God knows what. He remembers his grandfather's great
pride, family distinction: he was, so far as anyone could tell,
the only blind quadruple amputee ever permitted into the
United States. There is, Benny considers, a very small quota.
He recalls, irrelevantly, his grandfather was always smiling.
Even when someone was feeding or watering him. Even when,
in family ritual, the sons and grandsons came in to lift him,
trunk only, like a grinning and shopworn Ark of the Covenant,
while the women changed bedclothes. Sometimes at night when
the ancient hulk was restless and moaning toothless in Lithuanian or Yiddish, Benny would sit with him. He (Benny) was
a small boy then, but he could remember how the old man
would grimace, his one eye (no good, but still present and
fixed wide open permanently since in some dim past, probably on that day or eon when his arms and legs were taken from
him, the lid had been cut away) glaring in the sad weak light

of a bed lamp left always burning. Benny remembered wondering why they (whoever they were: Cossacks or good Christians or playful townsfolk there in *Mittel Europa*) had left the old man his tongue.

Boundoch grimaces, recalling how Lester, older and on to things, could not bear to be near their grandfather. The old man made him break into a sweat, made the palms of his hands wet. But then Lester could stand hardly anything. The world itself was a catalog of things Lester could not stand.

He remembers with a touch of surprise that he had loved the old man. Once he had found an ancient photograph album, legends scrawled in some incomprehensible tongue under faded sepia prints of bourgeoise Jewesses in long full dresses, men in wing collars, gold studs, wide cravats—all standing or sitting stiffly, their faces marked with the peculiar unsmiling and universal arrogance of those who posed in the camera's early days. In its pages he had found a large coarsely finished print of a Tsarist dragoon, fiercely moustached, overbearing, massive thighs and calves outlined under tight breeches, powerful arms folded impassively across his chest. He had studied it carefully, poked it with one dirty astonished finger. It was his grandfather. Taken in some age past between persecutions when a Semite could serve his lord, its mute high rhetoric chilled and exalted Benny. This is what the broken shambles grinning under a soft bed lamp had been. That is what men come to.

Benny shivers, remembering, as if someone a block or a continent away has strode across his grave; as if, of all things, the fear of Abraham's God has touched his heart. But no. It is Dr. Aorta. Who smiles and draws out the chair opposite, snaps at a waiter with a smudge of moustache on his upper lip. Benny pays him no mind. His eyes are fixed on the bright dripping trees across the way. He is somewhere in Transylvania.

—Well, Dr. Aorta clears his throat. —The weather turns better.

Boundoch is risen to those distant mysterious crags. He is not here. Dr. Aorta stares at him. Is it possible he is a consumer of Mrs. Mailer's product? The doctor is not accustomed to being

ignored. He has never had that problem before. As his coffee
arrives posthaste (the waiter hurries; he prefers not to serve
Dr. Aorta. He does not know why. Ugh), he strikes the table
with his spoon.

—Ummm, Boundoch mumbles, turning at last to take note
of his visitor. —Oh, he smiles on. —You.

Dr. Aorta warps his face, trying to smile in return. At best, it is
a sneer. —The old woman said you wanted to see me. I was passing.

—Oh, Benny says again, coming in out of the woods. —Yes.
Sure. There was a job I wanted to talk . . .

—The job, yes, Dr. Aorta answers. —The girl who comes
this evening.

—Yes, that. But another job, too. Something different. I'm
making a movie. There's a part you . . .

—I hear about your movie. The woman tells me about them.
What are they for? What is the purpose?

Boundoch's eyebrows raise. How come raunchy movies? How
come drink hydrogen oxide? What a question. —Honesty, he
blurts at last. —The plain truth. No Victorian hanky-pank. I
want to show the whole human situation. All its complexity.
All its brutality.

—Hmm, Dr. Aorta sniffs. He is not impressed. The human
situation is not worth ten frames of film. It is dull. It depresses.
It begins with the mouth chewing, ends with the anus dripping.
All between is involuntary twitching.

—I've shot some classics, Benny tells him. —One called
Made to Degrade. It was a long nightmare of reduction. Men
and women into things.

Dr. Aorta watches Boundoch's excited gesticulation. What
else? he thinks. Men and women *are* things. No reduction is
called for. Horror has the function of revealing life's structure:
flesh is cut away as bricks are knocked off. Leaving the skull beneath the skin. Aorta is recalling portions of his Mexican reading. Much of madness and more of sin, and horror the soul of
the plot. Poor Kurtz.

—You never saw anything like it, Benny goes on. —The filthi-
est perversions we could dream up. I had people quitting who

had worked in Hong Kong and Cairo. We had those double-exposure bits. You'd see a dozen people in a daisy chain. With an overlay of roaches crawling around on a pile of shit.

Dr. Aorta shrugs and stares through the distance of his steel-rimmed glasses out into the shimmering street. —Why not call it *Made in U.S.A.*? he asks, mildly bored. —Children playing with their body's toys. Ugly little children. Amateur lechers.

—Not so amateur, Benny answers defensively. What does this guy know about movies?

—Amateur, Dr. Aorta barks. —Tempting one another with parted legs, and hint of excrement. Tempting God, while God is not even watching. Do you know what . . . what was happening while you were making your funny movies? Do you know?

Benny shakes his head while Aorta lights a cigarette and exhales slowly, his hands folded on the edge of the table.

—In 1934, they opened Dachau. Within a year, the little beastliness of your movies would not have brought a smile to the youngest guard. A nurse in the medical compound would have been puzzled by the attempts.

—Listen, the movies . . .

Aorta blows a long jet of smoke toward Benny. —Have you ever photographed a living child cut open from breastbone to pelvis, its viscera spread, and a Gestapo officer setting his naked buttocks down into the warm cavity? And so seated having an orgasm?

Benny's cup flops out of its saucer. His eyes glaze. —You . . . what did you say? For a moment he cannot breathe. His mind, after so long, is cinematic; what he hears, he sees. Before him two guards in coal-scuttle helmets hold a small blond girl with the bluest of eyes. There is a man in white with thick glasses and a scalpel moving toward her. Waiting, an officer in black uniform, tunic trimmed in silver, is removing his boots and breeches. Boundoch's stomach does an exotic maneuver, and he vomits quietly into his napkin.

Dr. Aorta almost smiles. —At Ravensbrück, de Sade's most imaginative fiction became the stuff of ordinary off-duty pleasure. Some of the officers discovered refinements. One colonel required that an incision of suitable size and shape be made in the abdomen of a Polish boy. Another showed the medical staff how a woman could be adapted to serve five men simultaneously by . . .

Boundoch desperately waves him silent. —No, he cries. —Forget it. I believe you. Just forget it.

This time Dr. Aorta does smile. It is a smile adulterated with knowledge. A saint must guess eternally at the world's nature and meaning. Dr. Aorta knows. —Forget, he grins. —Can you forget your nasty little games, the people who played them for you?

—No, Benny admits.

—I forget nothing. Except first principles. And names of the recently dead.

Benny sits silent. He feels like a child dressed down for furtive nose-picking. He could be jealous of a boy down the street thrashed unmercifully for setting small dogs on fire. —De Sade, he murmurs, his breath still short, the mean stench of his napkin-wrapped offal rising from the table.

—An aristocrat, Dr. Aorta tells him. —Of the old school. The oldest school. Before the intellectual buggery of the *Aufklärung* had conquered. When men feared the Host, the Jew, the Adversary. Before science and reason buried us all in a nightmare of pretended meanings; before agony and death became nothing more than byproducts of political science. Think of von Clausewitz, with the soul of a dwarf. The best he could say of pain and holocaust was, *War is the extension of politics by other means.* Which is the same as saying: *Love is the obtaining of well-cooked meals and sexual service without money payment.*

—What? Benny asks, left far behind.

—War is so much more. Almost an escape from boredom. Murder is nearly a diversion. You do not tire of murder quickly. There are so many ways . . . so many . . .

—My movies . . . Benny begins, not knowing what more to say.

—You cannot distinguish between monsters and maggots, Dr. Aorta cuts him off. —Art must be absolute. Only a few can appreciate the absolute.

—Listen, Benny says, remembering suddenly the morning's work, and what had ended it. —Out at the lake this morning . . .

—So. This morning. The lake. What?

—We were shooting a scene. And there was something on the beach.

—So. What is it on the beach to interest me?

—That girl. The skinny redhead. Tony the Greek tried to put her onto me. I heard she was full and came to you.

—Not the same, Dr. Aorta says hollowly, waving for more coffee. —Not that one. That one was taken care of and discharged.

Benny shrugs. —Then something happened to her afterward. It was the same one all right. Maybe she crossed the wrong street. There's plenty of ways to die. Huh?

Dr. Aorta's mind is doing a number of calculations simultaneously. Item: when the Negro Fields brought back the body, he had not examined it, had not so much as glanced at it. Item: Nieman, this rancid priest, this God-haunted rabbit, has suddenly acquired new purpose. As if he knew something. Item: this Jew Boundoch is unconcerned. He is not lying, and very probably not mistaken. Conclusion: what was cronic has become acute. There has been a miscalculation regarding the priest. It is unwise to depend upon a renegade priest. They are no more to be trusted than those who remain hallucinated. Now. Would it be possible to learn from Boundoch what relation there is between Nieman and the girl who is to come this afternoon? No. The question is not indicated. The relation is not important, and it would be compounding foolishness to awaken Boundoch's curiosity. There are too many variables already. But Boundoch may be of use in another way. Think. Is it wise? Why not? Things are tight. Nothing is wise except death.

—Yes, Dr. Aorta says slowly, obligingly. —Of course. She seemed underfed. I wonder . . .

Benny wants to ask. He needs to. About the part. But after what he has heard, he hesitates.

—What . . . ?

—I wonder if you know a man . . . , Dr. Aorta begins.

—What man?

—No man. No particular man. I need someone strong. Someone who would like to make five hundred dollars. Who can be counted on. Who does not mind . . . unpleasant work.

—Sure, Benny says, thinking instantly of someone very strong indeed. Who will do anything. Who wants money. Who is vicious and crazy and dangerous. A very nonpareil of unpleasant workers. —Sure. I know somebody. Do you . . . ?

—Send him here. Send him. In an hour. I will have the woman here with money. You will vouch for this man? He is dependable?

—For the kind of thing you want? Sure. Listen, I know. He likes bad work.

—Your fee, Dr. Aorta cuts him off.

Benny studies him for a moment. The doctor's forehead is covered with moisture. His hands clench and unclench and his eyes move like jelly behind his heavy glasses. —Uh, no fee. Nothing. Except maybe a favor.

—I take care of her. When she comes. I do the little operation without charge. But your man must be here in an hour. The work has to be done before your girl comes.

—No, listen, I want you to play a part for me.

Dr. Aorta looks terrible. His expression would not pass for a smile in any company this side of a morgue. —Play a part? What part? Maybe you can suggest something. This one is wearing thin. I will need a change.

—I want you to be an Inquisitor.

Dr. Aorta shakes his head. He cannot believe what he hears. —An Inquisitor? What kind of a change is that? I am tired of this part.

—No. In my picture. I need a Grand Inquisitor. I need somebody to ask the questions. You . . . you could do it.

—Your movie. You want me to ask questions? To put people to the question?

—Jesus, we're going to build a rack, an iron maiden. I've got a boot, thumbscrews. You could do it. I know you could. What you said . . . about the camps. You could show us . . .

—Yes. Of course. Send the man. Let the man do this work for me. I will think about what you say. . . .

Boundoch is ecstatic. This is too much good news all at once. His leading lady will be reamed; his leading man will pick up five bills, which should calm him. And he has an Inquisitor— the perfect Inquisitor. —Listen, he'll be here. Everything will be fine. You don't know how . . . this breaks me up.

Dr. Aorta has risen, leaving his fresh cup of coffee un-touched. —Later, he says. —I will see you later about this. It will be good. Don't forget your man.

—No, Boundoch calls after him, as he steps into bright sun-light reflected from the steaming concrete. —He'll be here.

Boundoch sips the leftover coffee, thinking ahead. There is so much to be done. *The Question*. It will be a monument. In New York, they'll know. The trade will know. Boundoch is back. He's down there somewhere still working.

&~ &~

—You're out of your mind, Billy Bob is telling Boundoch. —It ain't no job that can be done in a couple of hours worth five hundred dollars. Unless he's got one of them atom bombs and wants me to set it off under somebody.

Boundoch shrugs. —The man said five hundred. You go to the Café du Monde and find out what it is.

Billy Bob rubs his chin. He is uncomfortable in Boundoch's parlor. He would rather be out in the courtyard with Jeremiah, feeding him catfish heads or hog guts. But even the possibility of getting five hundred dollars is too much to pass up. With that kind of money, a man could vanish. Just walk out and never be seen again. And take somebody with him. —Who do you reckon he wants killed? Billy Bob muses, half joking.

—Listen, I don't know anything about it, Benny tells him. —I don't want to know anything. It's your job if you want it. I'm trying to do a friend a favor.   •

—That's mighty nice, Billy Bob tells him with a straight face. —It's good to have friends.

—So go and meet Mrs. Mailer. She'll fix you up. She knows what you're supposed to do.

Billy Bob rises and heads for the door. Benny suppresses a start as he stands up: this hick could give nervous stomach to a locomotive. It is a toss-up whether Benny wants him to succeed or fail. It is pleasant to imagine this Southern degenerate scattered all over the Quarter. But the movie. *The Question* is bigger than a fear-twitch or the ephemeral flavor of revenge. Success is the ticket. Back to the big time.

—Good luck, Boundoch calls after him.

—Thanks, Billy Bob calls back, hitching up his trousers, already pricing two tickets to Bug Scuffle, Mississippi, or at least Hard Times, Louisiana—just across the river from that promised land.

◆§ §◆

It will likely rain again. The sky is not done with it yet. There is that warm and indefinable shade of yellow over everything that makes simultaneously for precise definition and vague unreality. The air seems transformed, too. It has the rich stench of growth and decay that seems to rise even from asphalt and concrete, as if the city retains some memory of what lies unchanged beneath it, only veneered for a time with the unsavory works of a creature divorced from nature, despised by heaven.

Mrs. Mailer's thoughts are less troublesome. She has hit it big. Not exactly hit it yet. Not big. But the hit is within range. And when it is consummated, it will be big. Nothing less than full partnership in that hoard of heroin, that super snowdrift, that ten-million-steed stable of Dr. Aorta's. Mrs. Mailer does not know what has shaken him, but he is off stride, and she knows how to exploit weakness. There is no sense in trying to understand every peculiar sonofabitch you meet. Unless you want to be a headshrinker. Or need a hobby. It is not necessary to understand the roots of fear in order to twist them to your purpose. It is necessary only to recognize them.

So she waits for this country creep with a folded slip of paper in her hand. Dr. Aorta has told her nothing, simply handed her the paper, promising that henceforth he will take better care of her—better care of all his good friends. Which is kind of a gas. Friends. Huh.

Someone leans across the rail and taps on her table. It is the nigger, Christian. One of the friends.

—Merry Christmas, Mrs. Mailer tells him. —Your name came up in the drawing.

—Huh? Christian asks. —What you talkin' about?

Mrs. Mailer reaches into her flower tray and picks out two or three gardenia blossoms. Those most wilted. They go into a small paper sack. In the sack, beneath the flowers, are five bags of happy time. Enough to turn Mr Christian into Barney Google. Horse enough for a cavalry squadron.

—What's this? Mr Christian asks warily. —You done laced it with arsenic, huh? Tryin' to get rid of me.

—You're a bad nigger, Mrs. Mailer answers. —You got no faith in your friends. That's high-class stuff. The doc sent it to you. For good will.

—Hey, Mr Christian grins terribly. —That's somethin'. Cops got him an' lookin' for witnesses, huh?

—Naw, Mrs. Mailer snaps back. —He's fine. They'll never catch him. He's been around. You expect those dumb bulls to do what everybody in Europe couldn't do?

Mr Christian smiles kindly. —I don't expect nothin'. He holds up the sack of flowers. —I didn't expect this. You better not get to expectin' things. Nor not expectin' 'em either. Lissen, you seen Chris Nieman, that bad priest?

—No, I haven't seen anybody. You stay on tap, Mrs. Mailer tells him. —We may have something for you. Maybe tonight.

—Lord, did he kill another one?

—Don't be uppity.

—He better sharpen them knives. He's gonna get a bad name even with his friends.

—You're a bad jig.

Mr Christian grins. —Yeah. I rapes old flower ladies and flings what's left in the river.

He is gone before she can answer. Which is just fine. Because coming in from the street is a giant clod in blue jeans with a wide belt and a blue workshirt. He looks as if he strangles hogs for a living. Not mean-looking. Just strong and ready for anything this side of thinking.

❧ ❧

The place is almost empty. It is suppertime, and the waiters lean against the back wall smoking and talking. Not looking at each other, but out into the strange golden light that softens even the masts of ships on the river and the stark chromed lines of passing cars. The hick looks around. A bald-headed man with a wife only slightly less bald, and two children groveling under the table.

Two women in square-shouldered suits, talking animatedly in snarling Midwestern accents. Each has beside her a box of pralines, and a garish mammy-doll with red polka-dotted bandanna, white apron and a blank black face. Below two shoe-button eyes, a smile of white thread is firmly sewn.

Then there is this fragile little old flower lady. No, Billy Bob shakes his head. She probably comes from a good family down on its luck. There used to be a lot of folks like that back home. Miz Toomey. And Miz Lauderdale, whose family had a street in Memphis named for them.

But the little old lady is giving him the eye, twisting her head, signaling him to come over. Lord, what a world. It must be some kind of mistake. He has been expecting some nigger with a surplus overseas cap and camouflage jacket to sidle up to him. Or one of those wops with a big cigar and a belly to match, smelling of garlic, cheap wine and anchovies. This old lady. She looks like the president of a temperance league. Can such things be?

—I beg your pardon, ma'am, Billy Bob begins in kind formality.

—You Stoker?

His eyes widen. Yep. This is a world in which no vileness or unreason is . . .

—Are you gonna put your ass in that chair, or stand there till they close this place?

—Yes ma'am, Billy Bob gurgles, seating himself lest the little old flower lady become violent. He will never get used to this world. Nothing is the way it seems. It is mostly worse. When an old white-haired lady . . .

—Here it is, Mrs. Mailer says, sliding the folded paper across to him. —The name and address.

—What . . . ?

—Any way you like. Any way at all. So long as you do it in the next four hours.

She pushes a brown envelope across after the unopened paper. —Here's three hundred. When you're finished, come on back here. I'll have another three. He's raised it a hundred because it's got to be daytime work. Nobody likes daytime work.

—No ma'am.

—What do you want to know?

—I . . . nothin', I guess.

What is there to know? You buy a man's life like it was hog jowl except at a higher price. You pay more for day work like for extra lean. There must be something to ask, but Billy Bob cannot figure what it is. He gets up and starts back the way he had come.

—Wait.

—Ma'am?

—Don't fuck up. You hear?

—Ma'am?

—Don't try nothing funny. I got a dozen niggers who'd cut your throat for ten percent of what's in that envelope. So do it right. Doc won't stand for a fuck-up. You see that name is taken care of. It's him or you.

—Yes ma'am, and walks on into the street. There is an occasional rumble of thunder as if the rain past means to swing back again. The pavement and awnings still smell sweet. Billy Bob tries to sort out what he has heard, what he is caught up in. How about that dozen niggers? How come one of them didn't get hired? And how about the name on this piece of paper? Just a name with a man somewhere connected to it. And another man, Billy Bob, walking in the street with his life's price in a brown envelope. Which makes him think: how about that three hundred? Niggers or no, he will be out of this about as quick as he can buy a pair of tickets to Mississippi, pick up Jeremiah, and talk that damn girl into going with him.

But curiosity still scratches. Who? Who is supposed to have only a few hours left but for the fact that Billy Bob Stoker is moving on? He unfolds the paper and reads the name scrawled in a thick but spidery hand:

C. Nieman the priest
808 Royal Apt. 8

Billy Bob stops and ciphers out the words with his right forefinger. It is suddenly chill and he shudders, thinking in that instant that somewhere someone has walked across his grave. Chris is a marked man. Billy Bob is to be his Cain. What is this? Some kind of crazy joke. Wow. As he walks on, his eye catches one of those white-on-black posters they nail to telephone poles in the Quarter. It says:

WHAT WOULD

Hum. And this old lady give me three hundred United States dollars to kill a fella I know and now I'm gonna move on a lot faster than I figured before.

Then he sees the next pole with its stark conclusion of the message:

JESUS DO?

Like the boll weevil just looking for a home, Mr Christian has been poking around the Quarter for an hour when he finally sees the truck. Parked in an alley off St. Peter Street, around the corner from Christopher's apartment. With no key in it. He has been to the apartment and gotten no answer. Time to try again.

Reaching the door, he listens in silence, ear pressed against the hollow door. There is a low unpunctuated drone coming from the other side. Like somebody going *ummmm* with an occasional break, a moment of silence before it begins again. The sound wrinkles Mr Christian's forehead. He remembers it or something very like it. From a long time ago, and still it eludes him. He knocks sharply on the door, not simply for entry, but to stop that weird noise.

There is a long pause. The sound stops, begins, stops again. At last, Christopher opens the door. His face is the color of café china and his eyes rival Mr Christian's in redness. —Oh, he says, reaching his hand out. —I'm glad . . . you . . . Mr Christian is still not used to Christopher's ways. He takes the offered hand and pumps it up and down as if he were testing articulation in the elbow. —I been lookin' . . .

—I . . . there was . . .

—They sent me out for the truck. Said you was drunk or run off. They wants the truck.

Christopher finds a chair. —I was going back to work. But something came up . . . I . . .

—I got to take the truck.

—All right, Christopher says, holding out the ignition key. It is tied to a wooden plaque with a piece of woolly string. The wood has *Staff-o-Life* imprinted on it. On the other side it says, *Postage will be paid* . . .

—I don't want to do you no harm, Mr Christian says, staring out toward the balcony. He is embarrassed. They had no right sending him to do a white man's job. He is paid to fix trucks, not to deal out misery to folks.

—Don't worry, Christopher says, sitting up straight, his voice losing its uncertain random quality. —I was ready to move on. It's time.

—Ummm, Mr Christian answers, pondering a fresh pony. —I wonder kin I use that bathroom of yours.

—Sure, Christopher tells him, pointing toward it.

And rises to answer another knock at the door. Is she back so soon? Maybe Mr Christian can tell her what he has been through, what Dr. Aorta does for a living.

—Wow, Billy Bob Stoker says, grabbing Christopher and pushing him back into the room. —I didn't know if you was here.

—What the hell . . . Christopher begins.

—Shut up, Billy Bob cuts him off. —Sit down and listen. Cause you got a double handful of trouble.

—I've had a bread truck full. Have you got some more for me?

—Look at this. Billy Bob holds out the rumpled half-sheet of paper.

—My name. So what?

—Naw. Not your name. The name of a fella I'm gettin' six hundred dollars to kill.

Christopher stares at Billy Bob. —You're over the hill.

By the time Billy Bob has finished, Christopher is on top of the hill himself. —That sonofabitch. That goddamned butcher.

—You mean that little old lady? Billy Bob asks.

—I mean that fat disease-germ that gave her the money to hire you. It's Aorta.

—Jesus, Mr Christian gulps as he comes out of the bathroom. He is face to face with the Booger Man. —Lissen, you don't want me, he begins. Even the jolt he has just taken does not counteract this sudden vision. —You ain't got no use for me, he mumbles.

Billy Bob frowns. —Where you from, boy?

—Mississippi, Mr Christian answers. —Yep. Right where you figure.

—Oh, Billy Bob says, sitting down and staring at the floor. —Was you one of them boys I . . .

—Naw, Jesus naw, Mr Christian says quickly, still standing, ready to fight or run. —An' I ain't gonna be. You stay clear of me.

—I'm sorry, Billy Bob tells him. —I was a kid. I didn't mean no harm. Could you just forget it?

—You gone leave me be?

—Sure. Yeah. I'm gonna leave everybody alone. I just want to do right.

Christopher frowns, watching the two of them. Then he remembers. Wow.

—What's this killing stuff? Christopher asks. It has not registered yet. He cannot quite get hold of it. Why would Dr.
Aorta . . .

—I don't know nothin' I ain't told you. This Boundoch where
I been workin', he said I could make five hundred for a job.
This here paper says what it is. You're the job. Then this old
lady raised the price to six hundred.

—That sonofabitch thinks I might go to the cops.

—Cops, Mr Christian says, his eyes widening. The jolt is
taking hold, but he is not yet above mundane things. Cops.
Ugh.

—About last night, Christopher says. —About what he thinks
we burned.

Billy Bob shakes his head. —Youall got me comin' and goin'.
What's been happenin'? I feel like I come in thirty minutes late
on a monster movie.

—There was this girl, Christopher tells him. —Dr. Aorta . . .

—The fat fella with them thick glasses? I seen him around.

—He done killed her, Mr Christian says abstractedly. —She
come in for a cuttin', and he cut too much. Then he give her
to me to get rid of.

—And Mr Christian didn't, Christopher adds. —So Marshall Fields . . .

—And he got rid of her all right. Only he didn't know it. He
thought he'd brung her back. An' we burned somebody down
to my furnace in the bakery.

—But it wasn't the girl, Christopher says excitedly.

—Naw. 'Cause she was skinny and red-headed, and what went
in that fire was black as the ace of spades, Mr Christian adds.
—He reckon he's safe now. But he don't want ole Christopher
goin' to no police 'cause . . .

—He's got something bigger on his mind, Christopher says,
—than a red-headed girl who's dead and vanished and a
burned-up nigger man nobody knows.

Billy Bob has been looking from one to the other as if he

were at a tennis match in Bedlam. —Yeah. Only youall don't know it all. At least I bet you don't.

—Huh?

—That girl done turned up. Anyhow I bet you a five-dollar bill she has.

—The girl . . . Christopher starts.

—Lord, what come next? Mr Christian wonders.

—Out to the beach. On the shore I come across this little red-headed girl wrapped in a sheet.

—That's her, Mr Christian ventures. —I know that sheet.

—An she was dead, Billy Bob continues. —An I seen her one time in a bar. An Boundoch wouldn't hire her an . . .

Mr Christian's jaw drops. The girl who had asked him for an address. That girl. Who had been alive and chewing on Doublemint gum that first time. And dead the next. He had not connected them. He must have been down that first time. And up the next. What happens in one world takes awhile to get through to the other. Hard for a man to work in two worlds.

—So maybe Boundoch told Aorta, Billy Bob finishes. —But how come he wants you dead?

—Ah, Christopher says, —that's the part you don't know. He's got another cutting scheduled. For this evening.

—An' you got the quibbles an' told him you'd squeal if he was to go through with it.

—No quibbles. I just told him.

Billy Bob frowns. Trying to be his brother's—sister's— keeper. What's the use of throwing over the bolt of cloth if you go on doing it by the yard? —That's bad, he tells Christopher. —I mean him goin' on like that. But you shouldn't ought to go crossin' him up. What stake you got in this?

—It's Mary Ann.

Billy Bob stops. He hears Christopher breathing shallowly. Mr. Christian is beginning to grimace and hum in low rich tones. —*It is no secret* . . .

—Mary Ann. Billy Bob clears his throat. —She never said she was thinkin' of . . .

—She came by here at noon. She didn't know whether to go on or not.

For no reason he can fathom, Billy Bob feels tears begin to fill his eyes and roll down his cheeks. As if he had lost something—or someone—precious. As if someone were dead. Or dying.

—. . . *what God can do,* Mr Christian hums wryly. That Crackpot Creator has his finger in all this. You can bet your sweet ass on that. Crying and weeping and gnashing of teeth. When the fig tree bears . . .

—An' you told her . . .

—She couldn't do it. I told her she'd better not. Then I went to see him. Dr. Aorta.

—An' he wants to do it. Wants to kill . . . kill that baby.

—Wants to, Christopher says. —Not just for the job. Wants to. Likes to do it. Like a mad dog biting. Anything that gets near him. He'd do it for nothing. It keeps him from killing himself.

—An' Boundoch told him about that girl we found this morning. So he thinks you know about her. Thinks you can finger him for that one, no matter what.

Christopher shrugs. —Sounds like it. Nasty sonofabitch, huh?

Billy Bob reaches for Christopher's hand. He is still weeping like a walrus. —You ain't a bad man, Billy Bob tells him between sobs. —Ain't a fuckin' priest nor pope neither fit to stand in the same pulpit with you. You told that little girl right and didn't give a shit what happened. You done saved my baby.

Christopher's eyebrows rise. He pulls his hand loose. —*Your* baby?

Mr Christian is beyond it. He is the Buddha fourfolding along silver paths lined with golden trees. Knowledge hangs like luminous grapes in the jeweled cavern of his mind. He watches the mortals dispute. Once, when he was a little boy, his daddy had brought him some toy soldiers thrown away by some white boy in town. Christopher and Billy Bob call them to mind: posed opposite one another, moving, talking slowly. Hands, heads, lips moving with strange deliberation.

Billy Bob is staring at Christopher in mute astonishment,

trying to speak. Except that in a single and instantaneous thun-
derclap of recall, he has seen those god-awful woolly dice, that
whole evening when he had succumbed to the twin fiends of
drink and gaming, and had in his desperation, like a base Indian, thrown away the pearl. At least first crack at the pearl.
The pearl Christopher had claimed.

—I thought . . . , Billy Bob began, choking up again. Can
it be that he has lost a son even before getting him? And gained
a nephew, so to speak?

Christopher is no less glum. —So did I. That's what I
thought. I wanted to keep her away from that maniac. But the
baby. I thought . . .

—Oh Jesus, Billy Bob moans. —You ain't even thought on to
the worst part of it.

—Huh?

—That day she left Shreveport. And come down here. You
remember?

—Sure.

—That night. She stayed with Boundoch. Without takin' no
care. She said she didn't have no chance to . . .

Christopher shivers. —It wasn't that night.

—Naw, Billy Bob agrees. —It was either the night before.
Or else when I got over there. It was one of us.

—You better bet on that, Christopher answers quickly.

—So it's ours, Billy Bob presses his home-made logic. —We
both got to look out for it.

—Ah, Mr Christian mutters. He is out on the edge of a purple cloud, reigning over the dull earth and its fumbling deni-
zens. —Sure enough. Because, amidst their mortal babble, he
has seen the realissimum. Before him, clothed in glory, shim-
mers THE IDEA. Vengeance is mine. It is all a single piece now.
The truck will be his chariot. And he will storm the portals of
heaven. To bruise the Great Goon in His very citadel. It shall
be in the world even as it is in his mind.

Christopher studies the wrought iron of the balcony railing
outside his window. —She's supposed to come back. She said
she'd come back before . . .

—Ummm, don't put no money on it. That girl's like a goose. She wakes up in a new world every mornin'. You want to get between her and that sonofabitch's place.

—His place is upstairs.

—Here? You mean in this here building?

—That's it. Right over us. A nice clean kitchen. With a big table and all kinds of clean knives and stuff. Like a French restaurant.

—So you got to get somewhere between him and the way she's got to come.

—Why don't I stay here? And you can go downstairs.

Billy Bob grins. It is not a nice grin. It is a decidedly evil grin. —I got a job to do, he says evenly. —I got three hundred dollars. I'm supposed to kill somebody.

Christopher's eyes widen. Maybe Billy Bob is on that stuff of Mr Christian's too. —Kill . . .

Billy Bob throws his arms around Christopher's shoulders. —Boy, you just get where that damn girl can't slip by. You make believe there's a baby to be baptized, and you got to pour the water to save your ass, you hear? That's all you got to think about.

Christopher grins back. His expression matches Billy Bob's. Less professional, but with feeling. —I could save us the worry.

—No. You ain't a labor-savin' device. You're just a piss-poor priest with some funny kind of chance to do good. I want you to go do good.

—What if she won't. . . .

—You just hold on to her till I come back. It ain't anything else you got to do.

—You want me to hold her? You reckon I should deck her? She's got a head hard as a garfish.

—Ummm. That's so. But you could do it some other way. You ain't crippled above the ears. That's our kid you're lookin' out for, ain't it?

This time the smile is simultaneous and profound. They shake hands as Billy Bob moves toward the door.

Mr Christian has been watching the peasants from a great distance. They are tiny, and their troubles cause not the slightest ripple in the universe. But he has affection for them. For he is Everyman. About to do THE GREAT AND FORBIDDEN THING. For all of humankind. The universe is about to be disturbed. He raises his hand and gives blessing. —Youall do right. Youall bring things out right.

He follows Billy Bob to the door.

—Don't you want to stay around? Christopher asks him. Mr Christian's pupils are invisible, and he weaves in great circles as he walks.

—No. I got to take that truck where it goes. Everybody's waitin'. Whole world waitin'. Been waitin' long time now.

It is quiet now, and Christopher fumbles in his closet for a jacket. He will stand in the street, perhaps in front of the Borogrove Antique Shop across the way, and wait. Waiting smells like death, like hanging from a tree. But somebody has to do it. While Billy Bob and Mr Christian go their own peculiar ways. To murder? And create?

◦§ §◦

Dr. Aorta has been drinking wine and thinking of a small village in the Rhine Valley where, for a brief moment in the late thirties, he had found what most men call peace. Rest and rehabilitation after work in Spain. With the Condor Legion. He smiles slightly, remembering Guernica: a good job, a milestone. It had earned them vacation. They had dressed in mufti and traveled to Munich or Frankfort. Tourists. See Germany today. Tomorrow the world.

He sets his glass on the table and rubs his eyes. He is tired. The pressure, however banal, has begun to erode his energy. And, he thinks, there is no resource beyond energy.

There is a tapping at the door but Dr. Aorta continues staring into the darkness, fumbling with various memories, none valuable in itself, but each one curious, diverting—like a polished stone picked up at random in a grassy field, on the shore of a distant sea. It is smooth and round from erosion. Ages of geologic time have made it so. Or not. So it is with experience recalled. What is the use of turning each memory over, playing each reel in slow motion, searching for some word, the timbre of a lost voice; seeking a detail unnoticed before that reveals pattern in the maelstrom of action, the welter of life flowing backward and away. He recalls detail after detail, recites silently whole litanies of minutia. A long-stemmed champagne glass in which the form of a naked music-hall actress has been shaped by an anonymous artisan. Two swans in the Serpentine. Rain falling on a cable car above the peaks outside Innsbruck. The sound of jack boots monotonous and prophetic amidst the utter silence of a crowded Champs Elysées on a dull June morning. The woods at Compiègne a few days after: a *wagon-lits* car of archaic vintage, and the sun warm, the forest soft and breathless. Dr. Aorta seems for a moment to smell the larches, to feel the cushion of needles beneath his boots.

So. A meaning? Portentous and minute, he remembers masses of such things. But he cannot find a clue. Something has happened in the past few days. The dogged body of the red-headed girl. What had she said? *I love you.* Dr. Aorta rubs his eyes with clenched fists. He has begun to distrust phenomena. Suppose, beyond the hiss and roar, coarse and sweet, long and tight, hard and acrid, beyond all the counters of sense, there should be some rough beast toying with destinies, whose chief pleasure is to wait behind the shoddy sets. To assure the reign of madness, of things falling apart. Or together. Forever.

The knocking comes again. Dr. Aorta breaks from contemplation, shakes his head, and looks back on those volitionless fragments which already begin to fade. He shrugs. Madness is lurking. It is the priest: his possession is contagious. Perhaps if one could see Nieman's body, watch it turn to vapor in the hard knowable flames of a phenomenological furnace. It might be possible for Boundoch to tell him who and where. If he could watch the murder, add it to the collection of trivia flowing relentlessly through his mind.

A third time he hears the knock, crisp and insistent, at the door. He rises and opens it enough to see. An outsized young man with reddish hair and enormous shoulders stands. He looks as if he might work for a moving company.

—Power and light, Billy Bob Stoker smiles. —We been connecting some new lines. You had any trouble?

Dr. Aorta stares at him for a moment. Power and light?

—No, I have no trouble.

—Try yer light, would you?

Dr. Aorta snaps on the parlor light. He squints in the sudden and unwonted brightness. —Yes. It works.

—Good, Billy Bob smiles broadly, studying Dr. Aorta's face carefully. —That'll be just fine. Hope you like our service.

—Service, Dr. Aorta repeats. —Yes, good service. All right.

The door is shut again. The light is off. But Dr. Aorta is not comfortable. It is as if the furniture were plotting quietly. It is the heat. And the pressure. Almost fifteen years of demanding occasions. There is a limit. A man's power to resist is bound by finitude. Everything seeks its lowest energy level.

Dr. Aorta stalks back and forth, finds a shirt and forces his arms into it. He has heard nothing below. Boundoch will tell him who and where. He can see the job done. See again the certainty of phenomena being displaced. It is necessary to keep suspicion of noumena at bay. If transcendence creeps into one's assessment of the possible, something worse than boredom can result. He remembers his father, choking, stumbling under the burden of myths three thousand years old, made by a savage people to terrorize themselves.

Dr. Aorta glances at his watch. The girl is not due to arrive for another hour. There will be time.

Chapter Eleven

Marshall Fields gestures out of the alley. It is a sharp fast convincing imperious gesture, and Mrs. Mailer heeds it.

—What's eating you, you worthless burrhead? she snarls. It is nearly time to set aside her flower tray. Tonight an early meal at the tamale joint. And then talk with the man. Tonight Dr. Aorta will share.

—Save the compliments, Marshall Fields answers without rancor. —I got news for you people.

—What? Who needs news?

—Ain't nobody needs it. It just comes.

—All right. What?

—They found that girl.

—The one you . . .

—Naw. The one we thought we burned. They done drug her out of the lake. Know who she is. Know what carried her off, too.

—How could . . . ?

—Lissen. Just lissen. I ain't gettin' paid for this. Ain't nothin' but professional courtesy got me here talkin' to you. They got the word. They may got the word on that big doc, too. Man I know cleans toilets down to the station says he heard.

—Heard what?

—Shut up, woman. Heard a couple plainclothes jockies pissin' and talkin'. Somethin' about the man. Callin' him grade-A suspect of bein' some big-shot foreigner. One of them fellas they always lookin' for on account of the war. Some tie-up with all the cunt-cuttin' been goin' on. How you like that?

—I don't like it worth a shit. They got nothing. They're hitting in the dark.

—I seen 'em one way an' I seen 'em the other, but a hit in the dark is just as tough as a hit in broad daylight.

—He's too much for these tanktown bulls. They'll never lay a hand on him.

—Maybe. Hand ain't the worst thing they got to lay on a man.

—I got to go.

—Say? Marshall Fields asks Mrs. Mailer.

—Huh?

—What I heard. The rest of it.

—What? Mrs. Mailer asks. She is wondering how much news one woman can bear all in a bunch.

—He been doin' that kind of thing before, ain't he? I thought he knew it awful good for a beginner.

—The operations? Sure, he . . .

—Naw, I mean that burnin' in an oven.

—Oh, Mrs. Mailer answers in a small voice. —He never said.

—Don't need to, Marshall Fields says, fading into the alley's shadows. —Proof of the puddin' an' all.

✎§ ᠍᠍ᢞᢌ

They come and they go. They are always in there morning, noon and night as if He was afraid to be alone. Always somebody in there like He was a king with servants waiting for some dumb job to do, glad to do it because the King is pleased to have it done.

Mr Christian is parked in the Staff-o-Life truck just down the street from St. Louis Cathedral watching the front door. Old ladies and young girls with pieces of lace or handkerchiefs over their hair move in and out. A fat businessman or two. Even children and once a workman with a lunchbox and a newspaper under his arm. He don't like women's hair. Which shows what kind He is. Tourists and winos. All kinds. Two Negroes in blue shirts and khaki pants. He don't miss a trick. The fat and the lean, the strong and the weak. They all come around sooner or

later. Enough to choke an honest man. Going in to scuttle
around on their knees with Him laughing and doing whatever
pleases Him anyhow. No prayer to put Him off. No sob to turn
Him on. Finally bringing them all down with a shovelful of
dirt in their faces. Children with pox. Girls with bleeding groin.
Men with cancer or bullet holes or whatever. But all of them
coming down at last, the good and the wicked alike. And Him
yawning and sniggering as they beg for love and salvation.

Near mealtime they play out. A bologna sandwich beats the
wafer. There's hunger and hunger. Like bugs after a light. The
belly beats the soul. Only peter has a chance against belly. With
twilight, they drain out of the church and go to whoring, seeking out the fleshpots or some other way to turn their minds from
prayers that will never be answered.

So Mr Christian sits in the cab of his magic truck, high above
the flood of pigmies passing. He is waiting for dusk. He is shod
and armored. The Horse is as big as Behemoth. This time there
will be no mistake. The Celestial Curmudgeon will suffer.
This time only Direct Intervention, of which He is leery, can
stave off the Reckoning. Across Jackson Square, clouds hump;
there is a lurid pestilential glow beginning to rise over the Café
du Monde. If one tunes his ear, it is possible to hear the jaded
old Mississippi moaning a dirge as old as the continent. Time
cringes as the evening traffic mutters past, and every street lamp,
yet dark, is poised to illuminate the final and inevitable clash
of Christian with the Cosmic Crumbum. As the evening sky
curdles to the color of varicose veins, Mr Christian sits easy in
his cab, the faintest of superior smiles wreathing his dark face.
Awaiting the Great Encounter.

•⩊ ⩊•

Billy Bob is fumbling in his cardboard suitcase. Everything
is there, but he has to sort out the parts from amongst socks and
shorts, bowties and religious tracts. He finds the stock. It is no
more than seven or eight inches long. His father had carefully
cut it down so that it is no more than a sloped pistol grip. The
barrel is longer. Possibly fourteen inches, but sawed off so that
the barrel and the receiver, together with the shell tube below,

are a single compact unit. When he has put it together, the shotgun carries five twelve-gauge shells and one more in the chamber. It is short enough to hide up the sleeve of a coat. Like the raincoat Billy Bob has taken from Boundoch's room.

Now he is seeking out loose shells amidst clothing and brightly printed Sunday School lessons and assorted condoms in the bottom of his suitcase. As he finds one, Billy Bob inspects it carefully for stains indicating possible leakage of moisture into the powder chamber. These are not ordinary shells. The projectiles inside are wide and flat bits of lead with sharp edges. The plug at the forward end of the red casing is of lead, too. They have been thoughtfully designed and carefully hand-loaded. They are not suitable for doves or rabbits, for lion or bear or deer. They contain an absolute maximum load of powder, and the particles of lead are so shaped as not to wound or even kill, but to disintegrate a target. Billy Bob has seen his father and the sheriff each stand to one side of the door of a cabin in which a Negro killer had holed up. The first shot annihilated the oak door. When the man came running, firing a .38 pistol, his father and the sheriff had fired together. When the dust and smoke had cleared, nothing recognizable was left. Except for the .38

Billy Bob sits down on the bed's edge and loads his gun. He is smiling contentedly. As if beyond the room were a stand of autumn woods, and Jeremiah were yelping to be released. He feels whole and certain with a gun in his hands. Not because, generally, he wishes any of God's creatures harm. But in the divine economy, it seems that survival demands some of God's creatures must eat others. And, now and then, simply eradicate one another.

When he is done loading, he stands up, slips the raincoat over his shirt and jeans, then carefully fits the shotgun up the right sleeve. By cupping the muzzle in his hand, he can walk along unnoticed. It is invisible. Then he straightens his hand. The gun slides down smoothly. He catches it by the short wooden grip, snaps it straight before him at waist height. Perfect. The way his daddy had thrown down on that same sheriff one drunken rainy evening. Even now he can remember the sheriff's wide eyes: not scared. Simply frozen, noncommittal, waiting. And his daddy had laughed and clicked the trigger on the unloaded receiver. Afterward they had laughed together and drunk some more. It was a slick move. The kind of trick nobody would forget.

Outside the sun is low and creeping in and out of great purple and gray cloudbanks like something on the run. Billy Bob goes through his routine once more. It is flawless. As if he had practiced all his life. He hitches the raincoat up, twisting his shoulders. It is short and tight. But it will do. It will do just fine.

*§ §~

There are troubles and troubles, Mary Ann is thinking. There is the kind you can just turn away from, and the kind King Cole sings about: . . . *Walk it off*. But the kind she has is not for walking. It has to be faced. Or cut away. She shivers and shakes her head. No way out. It had not occurred to her that there are situations where every possibility is a bad one.

When she reaches the door of the apartment building, she thinks for a minute that the best thing would be to just go on up past Christopher's place. To that other apartment. To get on with it. Because if she just went on, it would all take care of itself. Nothing to decide. Like always. Just to float. Until somebody says, *Little girl*. Except this time not deciding is to decide. And maybe the little girl is riding in her belly.

—Hey, someone says behind her.

—Hey yourself, she tells Christopher, who is wearing some kind of crazy golf hat with its brim pulled down over his face. So that he looks like some uptown kid trying to play tough.

—Somebody's gonna tie a knot in your tail if you go around like that. Even a backslid priest ought to . . .

—Come on, Christopher tells her. —He's not in anyhow. He came out a few minutes ago. Walking fast. Come on.

—Where we goin'?

Christopher pauses as if he were standing on the edge of the Grand Canyon. He studies Mary Ann, who seems to have something like a smile just below the trouble that clouds her face.

How about, he is thinking, one last throw? That'll be the ball game. But how about one last cut at the ball? After all . . .

—Upstairs, he tells her, amazed at the coolness of his voice. Control has not been his long suit. It seems to be getting that way. Feels great.

Mary Ann is smiling, all right.

—All right. You got any of that beer left?

—Yes.

◄§ §►

The clouds are moving in again. More warm rain is certain, and Boundoch curses under his breath. Somebody has put the arm on his raincoat. People in the kitchen, people cleaning the rooms. All thieves. The old hog who plays wardrobe woman. She likes a good piece of fabric. Negroes all steal. Everybody says so. But then everybody who says so steals too.

Benny Boundoch is walking toward Dr. Aorta's apartment. Tucked under his arm is the unfinished script of *The Question*. It may be that he will have suggestions. Boundoch wants to talk to him while Dr. Aorta's gratitude is fresh.

A raindrop or two fall on the pavement in front of him. Traffic has begun to thin, and the narrow street, shadowed by closing clouds, is almost quiet. Benny walks faster. He does not know why, but it seems necessary. The rain, he thinks. Like who wants to get soaked?

A sudden isolated gust of wind raises dust from the pavement. Just behind it comes a curtain of heavy rain. Boundoch steps into a doorway, shielding his script from the wet. There is one passage, a Black Mass with terrible sexual acts and some other stuff in the Dom and Deg line. Maybe Dr. Aorta could fix it up. Too stagey. Too much what you'd expect. Too pat. It used to be easy getting an audience on the edge of its seat. You could send them running out of the house with a man in an ape suit. Now the whole business of shock is on another footing. The war has changed everything. Those goddamned newsreels. Ravensbrück, Auschwitz, Dachau, Belsen. How do you compete with a bulldozer pushing thousands of wide-eyed corpses into an open pit full of lime? Or the boxcars stuffed with bodies piled like cordwood? It takes excellent technical assistance. Somebody who knows.

The rain is past for a moment, at least. Boundoch starts walking again. As he reaches a corner, he glances down St. Louis Street. And sees Dr. Aorta walking rapidly back in the direction of Benny's place. Boundoch starts to call out. But he pauses. Someone else is walking behind. Somebody big and hunking. In a raincoat half a dozen sizes too small for him. Beside him there is some kind of weird-colored hound skulking along as if it were on stand.

Benny retraces his steps. They are headed for Bourbon Street. He can run a block down Royal, cut right, and intersect Dr. Aorta. He wonders suddenly whether Billy Bob is finished with whatever commission Dr. Aorta had for him. Will there be blood all over that raincoat? What you have to put up with to keep a star.

He is exhausted when he reaches Bourbon Street. The neon is already beginning to wink on. One or two Negroes in white shirts and matching aprons are rolling up awnings. In an hour or two New Orleans will become the Crescent City, America's Playground. Boundoch grins cynically: where you can buy two-bit beer for a dollar, watch forty-year-old gash take off cheap sequins, get rolled, propositioned by lovely girls who unfortunately are hampered with pricks, or buy tea for bar girls at inflated bourbon prices. Some playground. Nastier than New York. The grins are thinner. The laughs an inch or so closer to hysteria.

Benny leans against a wall, ignoring the dirt, trying to catch his breath. It is twilight now, and there is a haze in the air which diffuses the neon lights. It is hard to make out the edges of things: *Broadway Chili*, it says across the street. And

LOUNGE — TOOT 'N' TELL IT — LOUNGE.

One dump crammed in next to another. A Famous Absinthe House and an Original Absinthe House. Neither serving anything close to absinthe, since wormwood in a beverage is unlawful. A Bourbon Bar and a New Bourbon Bar. With yellow and

red and blue and purple flashing signs, bulbs going on in series and in tandem. Fingers pointing, neon girls winking.
Jukeboxes and broken-down phony Dixieland bands filling the
evening with worse sounds than ever came out of Greenwich
Village. Benny winces and squints down the street. There he
is. Is it? It is. His glasses catch and reflect the light so that even
a block away Boundoch can recognize him. Benny starts walking, lifts a hand to wave, wondering if Dr. Aorta can see that
far. And stops in his tracks.

Because, in a single continuum of motion, all beneath the
purple and gray clouds above, stained with the variegations of
countless neon signs, Benny sees the hulk in the midget raincoat draw abreast of Dr. Aorta, speak to him as the doctor
moves back in front of a gaily painted window, and then slowly
—so slowly that afterward Benny discovers himself counting beneath his hurried and uneven breath not simply seconds the
size of weekends, but divisions of seconds long enough to run a
newsreel both ways—he sees the hulk raise his right arm as if in
final and unappealable judgment. Sees that inexorable pointing
arm sprout from the raincoat sleeve, and suddenly explode
with a flat and ear-shattering roar that freezes Bourbon Street
from Canal to Rampart. Which is only the beginning, because, as if, indeed, someone were running a movie scene
backward and forward, the blast is repeated. And repeated
again until Boundoch, slipping down his wall, losing count
of the reports, his ears and eyes overloaded, not only cannot believe what he hears and sees, but wonders, as his hands
touch the wet pavement beneath him, as within one of those in-
terminable milliseconds he feels cold water well up from the
concrete below and warm water rush down to meet it, if this is
some kind of insane nightmare.

Because concurrent with the unbearable sound, Benny sees
Dr. Aorta literally lifted from the pavement and tossed like a
ragdoll against the window which dissolves behind him. Then
he falls forward just as the next blast strikes him. His arms at
first seem to be shielding his face as he falls alternately backward and forward to the shotgun's rhythm, but before the pan-
tomime ends, his arms are flung wide, uncontrolled, flapping

like the wings of some giant winged creature falling through space and time, struck by the absolute force of an invisible and unerring judgment.

Until at last the stasis is broken. Benny breathes again, blinks his eyes, and sees what appears to be a rumpled bundle of clothing lying beneath the shattered window. The executioner in his shrunken raincoat is staring down at his work while from somewhere that hound dog has turned up, and is worrying the torn pile of clothes, mouthing it and snarling.

His master turns away, beginning to walk rapidly now toward Benny. At which moment, seeing Billy Bob's untroubled face, Boundoch understands. If not motives and purposes, at least what he has seen. Not a thirty-second clip from a horror show run in slow motion. But the other. What is there, lurking behind words and gestures, coffee cups and fried eggs. *Reality*, he thinks, stunned beyond confusion or even simple terror. It's *real*. It's what happens. Brother.

He is trying without thought, the body operating unbidden, to shrink into that dirty brick wall. Could he dive gracefully through the sidewalk? Or climb into the low-hanging clouds?

Billy Bob Stoker has paused, stops, looks behind him where Jeremiah, so long away from the field, is not to be denied. He has one leg of Dr. Aorta's trousers between his teeth and is trying to drag away as much as he can. The lower part of Dr. Aorta's body, hanging to the upper trunk only by odd strings and tatters of flesh, muscle tissue and points of shattered spine, moves away from the rest, stretches and begins to give way entirely as Jeremiah tugs.

—Goddamnit, Billy Bob snarls back at Jeremiah. —That ain't nothin'. Leave it be. Just let it lay. We can't eat it.

The hound shakes his head and turns loose. He eyes the seething ruin, and then runs, tail down, to catch up with his master. Whoever heard of shooting what you can't eat? Why not take it along? Somebody would want it.

Billy Bob is trotting now. He sees Boundoch as he runs and pauses once more, the shotgun already receding back up his sleeve. Benny sees that the front of his raincoat is spattered with dark spots. There seem to be bits of something stuck to the coat. And to Billy Bob's expressionless face.

—Don't get shook, Billy Bob smiles wiping his face with the back of his huge hand. —I'm all out of shells.

And is trotting again before the first startled Negro appears at the door next to the shattered window where Dr. Aorta lies, takes one look, and howls, —Jee*esus*, lawd Jesus, take it away.

Is running by the time the next wave of rain sweeps down Bourbon Street, bringing Benny Boundoch to life again, pressing him into a dark doorway, his script held tightly against a skipping heart.

⋅⋅§ §⋅⋅

The rain brings Christopher around. He hears distant thunder; five peculiarly flat reports, one after the other, and just after it, the rain in sheets and spirals, falling out of the sky as if someone has pulled heaven's plug. Mary Ann is slipping her dress on over her head. Christopher watches her move amongst the room's shadows.

—Come here, he says.

—Huh?

He kisses her slowly, hands moving over her body like those of a blind man seeking to learn or to store in his tactile memory.

—You're a booger, Mary Ann says lazily. —You mean it. I'll say that for you. You're really all there.

—What kind of grade do you give for sincerity?

—Huh? Oh. A lot higher grade than for puttin' on like some people.

—Like who?

—Never mind. It don't make any difference.

—What do you want to do?

—I dunno. I'm too late for that operation. I was supposed to be there at five o'clock. You fixed that.

—Aw, Christopher answers depreciatingly. —You didn't want to go.

—No, Mary Ann says seriously, slipping into her shoes, squirming to adjust her brassiere. —I didn't. It made me sick to think about it. But I almost did. And I still don't know what to do about it.

—We could find us a justice of the peace. If you wanted.

Mary Ann smiles. She likes this boy, but he is not done with trouble. He has a long row left to hoe, and no way of knowing where it will take him. He is good as any and better than most. But Mary Ann knows how to pack for traveling, and a sometime wife and casual kid don't fit in the bag.

Even as she shakes her head, there is an indistinct yell rising from below. Christopher, his eyes still on her, moves to the balcony and stares over the side. Down there, in the gathering murk of Royal Street, he sees a figure clad in ill-fitting raincoat with a draggled hound leaning against the rain.

—Well, he hears from down there, —I done my part. How about you?

—She's right here. Okay. What happened . . . ?

—Come on down. We got to get movin'.

—What . . . ?

—Goddamnit, I ain't got all night. Youall come on down. We got to get movin'.

◄§ §►

Then they are walking, trying to talk with rain lashing their faces. Mary Ann has one of Christopher's jackets around her shoulders. Jeremiah is trotting the point as if he expected more game to turn up around each corner. He is ready now, in case some more of that big stuff shows.

—So that's it, Billy Bob finishes, the story of Dr. Aorta's judgment told and done with. —Wasn't nothin' to it. It's all square now.

—God Almighty, Mary Ann puts in, breathing hard from the fast walk. —I can't believe youall. One of you talkin' about blowin' a man all to pieces and the other one, supposed to be some kind of preacher, grinnin' all over hisself about it.

Which is true, very true. Christopher tries to straighten out his lips, but it is no use. They curl at the corners, his teeth show, and rain runs down from his crinkled eyes as if he were laughing and crying at once.

—Girl, you gonna die a fool. That sonofabitch paid me to kill Chris, and he'd just as soon killed you, and he wanted to kill my baby. . . .

Christopher's shoulders bunch. It is not the rain, though that has turned cool, and he is soaked through with it. He just knows what is coming.

—*Your* baby? You half-assed butt-snuffer. This is my baby. Just mine. You remember that.

—It ain't just yours unless you're the Virgin Mary come again.

—Mine, Mary Ann barks at him. —Not nobody else's. Mine.

—Some baby, Christopher mutters. —No telling what to expect.

They are in Jackson Park now, and Billy Bob is wiping off what looks like a long piece of gas pipe, handling it carefully with the skirt of his half-size raincoat. Then he tucks it in amongst some heavy foliage.

—Let 'em find it, he grins. —Ain't nobody gonna run ballistics on it.

—We could get some coffee, Christopher hazards. For some reason he feels lonely. As if they were gone and he is talking to himself.

Billy Bob still has hold of Mary Ann's hand. He is shaking his head. —I'm about as loose as anybody, he tells Christopher, —but I reckon we'll have to move on. Even these stooges can run things down if you wait around long enough.

They stand in silence, feeling the rain's quick pulse. It comes in scattered bursts now, and in between lies on the air like mist. It is hard to see the front of the cathedral across the street.

—Okay, Billy Bob says quietly, no longer trying to talk above the rain. —I got two tickets to Biloxi and money enough to keep goin'. I done purged the wrong and brought justice down amongst men. I took a life and saved two tonight, and that's square enough.

Mary Ann and Christopher look at him. Spectators at an impromptu street meeting. —I'm goin' home, he tells them. —I'm goin' back to Jesus.

Christopher shivers. This time it must be the rain.

—Will you come? Billy Bob asks Mary Ann, still holding tight to her hand.

—Come . . . ?

—To Mississippi. I swear to God by Christ and the Holy Ghost I'll do right, honey. That baby . . .

—My baby . . .

—Any sonofabitch's baby. I'll take care and raise it Christian, so help . . .

—Not too damned Christian, Mary Ann cuts in.

And Christopher shivers once more. The loneliness has arrived. Solid as ice and ten times as cold. It is night in Sussex and he is walking a dark road back from Eastbourne. To Emmaus? And the broken thing, the crucified thing, is in the air, along the road, before and behind him. He cannot tell if he is walking or running; whether away from or toward the thing. It keens in the darkness, a wail below hearing at first that mounts in pitch and volume, and all the world's agony is in it.

—There it goes, Billy Bob mutters. —Sirens. It took 'em long enough.

—We better move, Mary Ann says, to no one in particular. She reaches over and kisses Christopher. —I'm gonna try it, she tells him. —I'm gonna see if this bastard can play straight.

—Oh honey, Billy Bob bubbles, —I . . .

—Go shit in your hat, Mary Ann spits at him. —You done made promises enough to keep you busy till Judgment. Don't go overboard.

Billy has Christopher by the hand. —I'm gonna pray about you, he says. —It ain't nothin' prayer can't solve.

—Can it solve the wires out of an electric chair, Mary Ann asks, raising her voice against the sirens.

—Sure it can, Billy Bob answers strongly, dropping Christopher's hand, catching hers and heading out into the mist.

—Bye, Mary Ann calls back out of the gloom. —Bye, Chris. You be good.

—You too, Christopher answers her. But they are vanished in the evening gloom, and his voice sounds empty and small. The rain is barely a murmur now, and the sirens have paused in their shrieking. Christopher can hear drops of water falling from the trees around him. The grass is chill beneath his feet and in the distance there is a faint white glow where street lights should be. For all he can tell, the river port might be surrounded by mountains. Christopher feels as if he were down inside something, as if the whole town were Jonah's awful fish: a belly unaware of its contents, portending nothing. Somewhere he hears a truck start, hears the motor roar and fade, roar again. Christopher turns toward the cathedral, but it is not there. Only fog swirling, thick and dark enough to dissolve the world back into its constituents. Whatever they may be.

~§ §~

Mrs. Mailer looks like a chicken savaged by terriers. She is near hysteria by now. The rain slashes at her. She has dropped her flower tray off at Dr. Aorta's without even removing the precious contents beneath those wilted gardenias. Who sweats a few ounces when pounds are in prospect?

But she cannot find him. Cannot find anyone, cannot even pick up his trail. Now she is on Bourbon Street, caught amongst the crossing and flaring of neon. She is confused and knows it. He never comes to Bourbon Street, cannot stand the noise, the movement, the raucous hallucinatory aura of the place.

She thinks, later, when it is over and she has nothing to do but think, that the sirens had guided her. To this rainstrewn corner where Negroes, waiters, local characters, police, and newsmen are gathered in a semicircle around a blasted window and the remnants of an occasion sprawled beneath it. She is pushing through one layer after another of gawkers, follows a man with a camera and two others with a folded-up basket between them. Then she has reached the inner circle. She is there.

Before she looks down, she looks up. Above the pavement in tall broad neon letters it says

The Famous Door.

And then there is nowhere else to look. But down there.

Dr. Aorta lies supine a yard or two from the Famous Door. His body is nearly severed at the waist, ruined hands grasping at the dark liquid vacancy of his belly. Around him are gathered two city detectives, a reporter from the *Times-Picayune*, a coroner's photographer, a bewildered intern from Charity, the basket crew, two unsmiling young men in uncommonly well-pressed suits, and a truck driver from the sanitation department who had been parked down the street eating a hot pastrami sandwich in his garbage wagon.

Above Dr. Aorta's body are display signs showing Sherri Cleland in G-string and tassels, smiling, beckoning with bare navel and slightly outsized hips. Still higher, on the peeling marquee, neon tubes blink incessantly. Down below, Dr. Aorta's face, two streams of moisture coursing down his flaccid cheeks, changes color over and over again: red, dull yellow, nearly black. His eyes are open, squinted tightly as if still staring at something astounding, overpoweringly bright; something a long way off approaching with inconceivable velocity. From his mouth issues a frothy pink liquid which flows over his chin and vanishes in the folds of his thick neck.

One of the detectives turns to a uniformed patrolman in short sleeves who is talking into a hand microphone.

—Have you got anything?

The patrolman shakes his head. They listen to the hollow grumbling of the radio.

—They've got a guy, the patrolman calls out. —They found one on Perdido.

—What have they got on him?

—He's wearing a beard.

—Christ, the detective says.

—And he don't talk English very good.

—Hell, the *Picayune* reporter says, —that does it. Why waste
tax money on a trial?

One of the detectives is a young man. He has just changed
into plainclothes. Once he spent a semester at McNeese State
College and made a C– in philosophy. He wipes his nose on the
back of his hand and gazes down at the wreckage of Dr. Aorta
with infinite compassion.

—Christ, he says, —guy's walking along Bourbon Street with
his head full of nags or pussy. Maybe worrying what he owes on
a mortgage. Maybe his old lady's a bitch. But just an ordinary
fat guy walking along . . .

The other detective is older. He has worked at one time on
the Tulsa police force and is cynical even beyond his years. He
has been in the Army, too. A military policeman at Fort Ben-
ning for four years sees plenty. Horse's ass, witch's titty, we're
the boys from Phoenix City.

—Just walking along, and comes up with a gutful of buckshot. Bingo. No mortgage. So what if the old lady is a whore?
The nags and the bags don't bother you any more. You just lay
there. It ain't so bad. You'll have to give it a try.

—Hell, the younger detective says, his nose still giving him
trouble. —You can't even run an autopsy on him. Poor bastard.

—What's with you? the veteran detective sneers. —How do
you know? Maybe this guy was a slacker.

—He don't look like one of Roosevelt's sons to me, the reporter puts in.

The two unsmiling young men in their well-pressed suits
are squatting beside Dr. Aorta now. Each has a notebook and a
sharp pencil.

—I don't know, one says. —Just a fat man.

—Are there print records, photographs? the other asks.
—There's got to be something. Nobody can get rid of it all.
There's always something.

—Nothing, the first answers, lighting a small pipe and re-
positioning his shoulder holster as if he had just used his short-
barreled Colt.

—Pull back his shirt, the second young man says in a tone of soft but certain command. He writes something in his notebook about Caucasian male, stocky.

—In his armpit, the first young man asks. —You think . . . ?

—They all had it. Check.

The younger detective is still talking to his jaded partner, who pays no attention but stares at some signs just above the mess. One says SCHLITZ. The Beer. That Made. Milwaukee Famous. The other is wordless, but shows dark-skinned Sherri Cleland, legs parted, head thrown back, breasts dotted with circlets of cloth and hanging twists of gold tinsel, crotch shadowed by something that resembles a badger pelt with laces.

—None of us knows, the younger detective goes on. —We shave and dress and walk out on life's highway, and we meet giants and dark ladies. We cross our grandfather's tracks and blaze trails our kids will follow. Breakfast. Lunch. Dinner. Lying down and rising up. That's life. Never knowing . . .

The reporter tries to control his stomach. Carnage has no effect on it; barroom philosophy causes instant and massive nausea. He stares down at Dr. Aorta for relief.

—Something? the second well-pressed young man asks as his partner strips Dr. Aorta's upper body.

—I don't know. Maybe a shiny place. You sure there's no prints?

Mrs. Mailer shakes her head. All this is too much. She scuttles up beside Dr. Aorta's body and kneels on the messy pavement.

—Who are you? one of the young men asks, notebook and pencil poised.

—Uh . . . sister, Mrs. Mailer blurts. —His sister.

The police watch curiously as she cradles Dr. Aorta's head in her arms. The two well-pressed young men exchange significant glances. The second one takes a spotless handkerchief out of his jacket pocket and spreads it under his knee.

—Oh Georgie, Mrs. Mailer is sobbing, —Georgie, where is it? Tell me where it is. You don't want to die without . . .

—Ma'am, the younger detective calls to her. —It's not a bit of use. He's . . . gone.

—Tom, sugar, what have they done to you? Can't you make a sign? Just . . .

Meanwhile she is smoothly rifling not only his coat pockets, but even rummaging in his trousers. Finally, amidst the stewy debris, she dips into his watch pocket—where neither police nor neat young men have preceeded her.

—Al . . .

—Listen, lady, the older detective is saying, —you might just as well go talk to the city dump. It's no good. Look at him . . .

—Tom . . .

—Look at that, the younger detective smiles sadly. —A little old lady. Maybe not a dime in the world. See? She's trying to find out where Tom kept their little hoard . . .

—Al, the newspaperman corrects him, turning one shade greener.

—Georgie, the other detective says with finality. —She called him Georgie.

She has also found and removed a key from Dr. Aorta's sticky pocket. But the well-pressed young men are not fools. Exactly.

—Are you an American citizen? the first one asks. He has passed his pad and pencil to number two—who is primed to write.

—What do I look like? A nigger?

—I mean are you a citizen?

—Naw, I'm Shapirohito.

—This man—your brother. Where was he born?

—How do I know? It was a broken home. I don't know.

—He was a German national, the second young man says flatly.

—German? Maybe his daddy was a German. Mama wasn't careful.

The two young men rise and exchange that glance again. —You better come with us, lady, the second one says.

The younger detective frowns, turns to the reporter. —She don't know. She's confused. She never bothered. He took care of everything. Look. Life. It comes maybe in the back of a taxi.

And it goes out in front of The Famous Door. What are you gonna do?

—Kick your ass all the way to Westwego if you don't knock it off, the older detective snaps, his eyes on the well-pressed young men. One is politely removing the key from Mrs. Mailer's clawing hand.

—Hibernia National. God knows what name, the second one says.

—Georgie Tom Al, the first one laughs without smiling.

Not quite. Another name which they will not discover on the charred papers from South Africa filed neatly in the records section of *Schutzstaffel* headquarters in Berlin. And the box in Hibernia National contains only a document covered with neatly sketched streets, and a certain building marked. Just below the sketch are detailed instructions as to the location of numerous kilos of heroin. Written in German.

The newspaperman closes in. Despite his illness, he smells the blood of a story.

—This world, the next, and then the fireworks, the younger detective mutters as Mrs. Mailer is led away and the basket crew gingerly begins to lift Dr. Aorta onto their vehicle.

—Say, the man from sanitation says, moving up beside the elder detective. —I ain't got no sand. You reckon I better call in and get somebody over?

He rubs the toe of his high-topped shoe along the edge of Dr. Aorta's leavings.

—Why not? You call 'em.

—Somebody could slip down and kill theirselves.

—We don't want that, the younger detective says.

—No, not that. We'll be fillin' out reports all night as it is, his partner says, pushing into the disintegrating crowd.

Overhead, the insistent neon blinks on: red, dull yellow, nearly black. Below, on the fouled sheets of the basket, Dr. Aorta lies, his hands stuffed under him. His eyes, at last, are wide open, the pupils and irises flowed together in final and inextricable union. His face is no longer twisted, has eased into an open-mouthed expression of total and unutterable boredom. As if life's last gift were no more diverting than its first; as if, finally, the most extensive possibilities of the universe were as fearsomely banal as he had suspected all along.

৶ঌ ঌ৶

Christopher still sits on a bench at the edge of Jackson Park like a less than senseless thing. The mist is as thick as a fur muff, and he can bearly make out the cathedral opposite. It would be quiet except for some idiot down the street, invisible in the fog, who guns his engine and guns it again. He shrugs and rises at last. Maybe the apartment will be quiet. There are things to sort out. Tags and ends of this endless game of tag.

As he steps into Decatur Street, something seems to stay him at the curb: some ineluctable pressure like an invisible hand. Which is just quick enough, because he is hardly paused before a dark outsized bulk lurches past him like death's chariot, makes an absolutely impossible ninety-degree left turn and crashes through the closed doors of St. Louis Cathedral as if it were the vanguard of that shadowed host which, it is written, will once more challenge God's own angels on Armageddon's field.

The noise, surprisingly enough, is not so bad. Christopher's hands slowly come down from his ears. He is staring at the blasted doors when the second, louder sound of collision comes. This, he is thinking as his adrenalin recedes to a reasonable level, is fantastic. Is this the last day? Will Judgment come in fog with lunatics assaulting the outposts of deity? And then he is crossing the street, walking through the debris of the church door, trying to see beyond the inner darkness which so nearly matches that outside.

At first there is nothing to see but a lurid red glow around the base of the altar. Someone in a cassock is running around, howling about spilled gasoline, about candles and sanctuary curtains in a deep echoing alien voice. Christopher climbs over broken pews toward the shadowy bulk of the truck. Behind him other people have begun to flock to the cathedral. The scent of disaster seems to draw them, Christopher thinks mechanically, as if he is both clambering over shattered seats and simultaneously above it all, somewhere near the altar light which still swings crazily in long eccentric arcs above the shambles.

The hood of the truck is powdered white, covered with chunks and chips and dust from the broken marble altar. The golden tabernacle, its door crushed and swung open, lies beside one of the flattened tires. The cab of the truck is collapsed, with the panel body jammed forward, the windshield shattered, the steering wheel broken from its column. Christopher tries to pull the seat back from the smashed dashboard. He claws at unyielding metal, rips at cheap worn fabric, trying desperately to find the driver. When suddenly from below, he hears:

—Ain't no use trompin' on me. I can't use nobody trompin' on me.

Christopher nearly falls, turns quickly, casting about in darkness. Only the altar light and a rank of distant candles partially relieves the gloom.

—Where are you? Where . . .

—What you want to tromp on me for? The voice is soft and eerie, distant as the candles, low and uncertain as the light from the swinging sanctuary lamp. Christopher sneezes, his nose filling suddenly with the remembered odor of incense. Somewhere it is burning. Then his hands, searching along the littered marble floor, find Mr Christian Blackman.

—My God, Christopher chokes.

—Fo'get it, Mr Christian sighs. —How's it look?

—It's . . . The whole place. You've wrecked . . .

—Ah, Mr Christian says, his voice small and far away.

—The seats, the altar. Good Lord. Christopher pauses. —Even the tabernacle.

Christopher squints. Mr Christian lies half under the truck, the heavy frame resting on his chest. His dark face is covered with glistening darker blood. His hands fumble with his shirt, but something is wrong there, too. It seems his arms are broken. All around him, at his head, scattered near his body are tiny circles, glimmering white against the dark floor. At first Christopher thinks they are fragments of marble. But he leans closer.

—The Hosts, he mumbles. —You broke up the ciborium. The Hosts are all over the floor.

—Ah, Mr Christian groans. —What do you think of that?

—Think . . . ?

—Got to Him, huh? Can't ask for no more than that. Never could think up nothin' better than that.

—Listen, Christopher begins. Out behind, in the dark nave of the church, a crowd has gathered. There is a siren—or sirens—howling somewhere beyond. —Listen, I think you're . . .

—Ha, think, Mr Christian grins up at him. —Look.

Christopher follows Mr Christian's pointing finger down to a dark place torn out of his shirt. Squinting, leaning close, Christopher can see a hole at the base of Mr Christian's ribs. Big enough to jam the broken chalice into.

—Steerin' post went in. I tried to pull it out. But it wasn't no good. I ended up havin' to pull myself off it. The wind blew, and the shit flew. An' I'll be goin' in a minute, too.

Christopher wrings his hands. There is nothing to be done: no artery to press, no artificial respiration to be given. He is only a man, and there is nothing he can do.

—Listen, he says again weakly, licking his lips. —Sirens. They're coming . . .

—Shit, Mr Christian groans. —Comin' for what? To pick up meat. It's awful. I keep seein' that little old girl that doc had me drag all over creation. I bet I got to drag her on forever. Just like Him to put that on me.

Christopher sees police beginning to stumble over the wreckage at the back of the church. Someone in a fireman's hat, too, with a portable fire extinguisher.

—Gimme a cigarette, Mr Christian mumbles.

—I don't . . .

—Boy, you worse off than me. You ain't got nothin'.

—No . . .

—In my jacket. Down in the pocket. Easy. Easy . . . You want to pull me all the way apart?

Christopher feels something splintering inside himself. There are tears on his cheeks. —I'm sorry. I can't do anything right. Not the way I want to . . .

—Don't tell me, Mr Christian cuts him off. —Ain't I got enough troubles? On top of it all, my feet hurt. Can you reach off my shoes?

—No, the truck . . .

—Fo'get it.

Mr Christian is silent for a moment, drawing on his cigarette. There are police and firemen fumbling all over the sanctuary now. The old priest Christopher noticed earlier is running back and forth rescuing gold candlesticks. He has not come near the truck.

—Ha, Mr Christian laughs weakly. —I tore Him up all right, huh?

—Yes, you . . .

—Tore His place up good. Him layin' in there figurin' what to lay on ole Christian next. Then *wham*, little ole gold house knocked all over hell's half-acre. Surprise. Ole Christian done laid meat to Him. Next time around, maybe it'll be better. He done run out of meannesses. Used 'em all up on me this time.

—Forget it, Christopher says. —They'll have doctors here in a minute.

—Man, you dumb, Just country dumb. I couldn't make it to the sacristy.

Christopher turns and calls to a passing fireman. —Couldn't you help? This man is pinned . . . The fireman stares at him briefly and continues spraying the floor with some kind of foam.

—All right, Mr Christian says softly. —I'm ready.

—Ready?

—Yeah. It's all even. It's all right. I done thought it out whilst I was layin' here. You kin get me the holy communion.

—You want . . . the sacrament?

—Don't care what you call it. Just get me one. I ain't got all night.

Christopher stares at him, his own breath as short and fast as Mr Christian's.

—How . . . ?

—You can do it. You can't do much, but you ain't forgot how to put a little piece of bread on a man's tongue.

—Not me. I'm . . . no faculties. Your confession.

—Confession? Jee*zus*, Mr Christian moans, but not in pain, which he is well beyond. —Man, He knows. Look around you. Look at me. What you want me to say?

—Nothing. I just can't. I'll get the priest. He'll be back.

—Fuck that priest, Mr Christian barks. —I don't know him. Just 'cause he got on a robe.

—But . . .

—If you can't do it, who can?

Christopher closes his eyes. He almost topples backward. In the tympany darkness of his brain that mad cross of Grünewald's with its loathsome burden begins to sway and totter, starts to lurch forward, only to dissolve into bits of whiteness falling like snow, tiny crystalline beads. There seems to be the smell of olive trees and some perfume that might stir him another time, another place. Someone yells loudly to watch out for fire, and Christopher rights himself.

—They're all over the place, Mr Christian is saying, in a voice distant as summer thunder. —You said it yourself. Just pick one up and lemme have it.

Christopher leans like a broken robot, his tin fingers scratching at the scarred marble. At last he manages to lift one of the scattered Hosts. It is covered with dirt, spotted with some dark fluid. There is a print on it, as if from the sole of a shoe.

Okay, Mr Christian sighs. —The words. You reckon you can do right just this one time? Remember the words?

—*Corpus domine nostri Jesu Christi*, Christopher begins hesitantly, his fingers seeking Mr Christian's lips. —*Custodiat animam tuum. . . .*

Mr Christian's eyes rise beyond him, behind him. They are fixed on the slowly turning sanctuary light.

—Jesus, he says, almost below hearing, —wouldn't you know it? Tastes awful. You must of picked the worst . . . one. Last laugh. He jus' couldn't pass it up. Last laugh. . . . Jesus.

—*In vitam aeternam. Amen.*

Mr Christian's eyes are still focused on the revolving lamp, but they do not follow it. They have begun to glaze slightly, as if, somewhere in the dark ruined landscape behind and beyond them, snow has begun to fall.

&ea;&ea;

—Oh, the priest is saying, standing just behind Christopher. —The ambulance people are here.

—What for? Christopher chokes. —What for?

The priest leans down over Mr Christian, closes his eyes with swift fingers. —I'll get my kit. I'm sorry. I would have come over right away. But I thought . . .

The ambulance driver and his helper are waiting for two firemen to raise the side of the truck.

—What? Christopher asks desolately, his voice in fine control, but moisture flooding his eyes, blurring everything before him.

—When I saw you over here, I thought you were one of the priests. Your coat . . . it's dark. I thought . . . You were kneeling beside the Negro. I thought you were Father Tissot.

Christopher does not answer. He wonders vacantly whether he will make it to the side door before his spine ravels or eyes burst like squeezed grapes. He thinks again for an instant of that flayed beast on a cross somewhere in Sussex, and pushes as hard as he can. But the door is jammed. There is an overpowering odor. It is either gasoline or incense.

—Can I help . . . ? the priest calls after him.

Christopher does not answer. He takes hold of a doorpost. There is something between fog and fine rain filling the air outside. The crowd is held back by a few policemen. He can hear other sirens shrieking along Royal Street, going to another apocalypse. And when he falls down the steps, one of the policemen catches him neatly and lowers him to the ground as easily as if he were a child.

ANABASIS

". . . rose again from the dead . . ."

> *The Son of God died; it is by all means to be believed, because it is absurd. And he was buried and rose again; the fact is certain because it is impossible . . . I believe because it is absurd.*
>
> —TERTULLIAN
> *On the Flesh of Christ*

It is dark in the Quarter now. Fog still writhes around Christopher's ankles and whirls upward in converging spirals. Downward through it that same fine rain still falls. A few cars limp along the faint shimmering streets. Even as the air of Madrid can kill without shaking a candle flame, so the rain of New Orleans soaks through a coat before one knows it is falling.

Christopher is walking now, paying no attention to direction. And finds himself at last beside the river. The river itself is invisible. Only reflected light caught on its slow waves and shivered like bits of glass shows where the water is. Glowing out of darkness are the running lights of countless barges, massive darker shadows of tankers and freighters fumbling for haven or bound outward for the passes downriver that open into the Gulf. Above, Christopher can make out a single gull flying close by. It moves fitfully against windblown rain as if climbing invisible stairs or dodging some phantom steeple.

Beside the water, he finds an anonymous crate and lowers himself onto it heavily. He is not sad or apprehensive now. Not even lonely. Only emptied of everything. As if, at last, someone had found the bung, turned the spigot, drained away all the rare liquors of love and hatred, fear and guilt. Christopher frowns, watching the bobbing lights, hearing occasionally a ship's horn or the voice of one seaman calling through the darkness to another. It is as if this crate were a rocky promontory apart from seas which rise and fall, shaken by storms, one following on another. And cold, Lord, cold.

It is strange to be at peace. To feel all brain cells humming, sending Valentine messages to one another. Christopher wonders unconcernedly if he is in shock. If the circuits have been overloaded. Surely he is a child again. No. For the first time.

For the first time,
I'm falling in love . . .

No corpses of lambs or pale-handed spies or hardhearted rivals looming. Even beloved fairy godmother, source of life and anguish, has vanished. It is all gone with this soaking chilling wind. Like the papier-mâché fragments of a dream. Which fades as the sleeper stretches, yawns, rises again. Until within a few brief hours there remain only confused shadows of desire and horror, to be forgotten in the broil of a new day. And every day is as ten thousand years.

The brain at rest is a lovely thing to contemplate. An Inquisitor exhausted of questions. Tired enough to permit other functions previously crowded out. What is the answer? Oh indeed. What is the question? Didn't it rain, children? Oh indeed. And will again. So long as the sun rises and rivers run to the sea.

Overhead, a single street lamp, placed without apparent reason near the river's edge at the end of a block of dark warehouses, shines weakly down on Christopher. He glances up and sees the strange corona formed by rich delicate light falling through misty rain. There are insects seeking the bulb, trying madly to penetrate to the fire within. They flutter and creep an inch or so along the curve of its brightness, then fall away and vanish back into the darkness to be replaced at once by others. Or are they the same ones, moving toward the light, dazzled, terrified by it, flitting away only to be drawn back again as if each tiny midge were attached to the lamp by some tenuous and invisible pulley?

It seems to Christopher that the soft light falling through a swerve of tumbling raindrops is composed of three radiant circles: the cool diamond blue-white of an inner central arc, a warm red almost the color of precious ruby, or of blood. And a translucent third as muted violet as a Lenten vestment. But there is no definition, no clear edge between each circle, and the rain, the insects, a fitful wind beginning to rise along the river, blowing in toward the seething city—all of them merge and fuse into a fractured unity.

Somewhere in the deserted stretches of Christopher's memory the light recalls something. A hunger he cannot bring into focus. Those circles intertwined, merging with one another, then reaching out to permeate all the universe. Or is it the river, the rain? This sudden inexplicable peace? The light, the rain work some peculiar chemistry within the cunning passages and contrived corridors of time past. This tiny hunger, this faint need.

Then he remembers at least part of what he is trying to drag up from down there. Christopher rises from the crate, turns back into the city. Recalling with inordinate pleasure the Bethel Bar in St. Peter Street where he can find a quiet glass of ale. Ballentine on tap. Enough to cheer the living and the dead.

Telscombe, Sussex, 1963
Baton Rouge, 1966